The Black Opal
By

S.G.Norris

Hate and ignorance are not natural states of being. It is a choice we make to persuade ourselves we have no responsibility for the people and events around us.

Southern United States and Central America

Map Data © 2022 Google INEGI

Chapter 1

Nashville, Tennessee

The final chords trip off my guitar and close with a dance around the fret board, ending with a final memorable riff. I take a small bow as Roseanna absorbs her usual glory. Which is fine. They come to see her, not me.

Her voice rides a scale between deep double bass blues bouncing off the walls and the soft velvet of the heartbreaking melody. The unique blend is delivered with a husky edge that you'd expect from a well matured bourbon aged in Jamaican rum casks. She's just turned twenty-five, face of unblemished youth. Listening with my eyes closed, I'm in another century listening to the sound of the ancients.

The applause continues throughout the Nashville saloon bar and I lean over to wave a couple of CDs from the box at the front of the stage. A few cheers are loud, a sign of a good gig. Let's hope they've got pockets as deep as their cheers. A flicker of the eyes from Rose has a way to loosen even the tightest purse.

'No-one plays guitar like Donnie Knight. Take a bow Donnie. The best damn guitar player in whole of Tennessee or I'm Marilyn Monroe, ya hear me. Y'all.' I take the bow as instructed and the applause rises, but their attention is on Rose like bees dancing round pollen.

'Five dollar bills is all you need. We'll take cents if that's all you got. Damn, we'll take a hundred for all you rich cowboys showing off those new leather boots, loving the sound of Tennessee right here,' Roseanna says. 'I see y'all, with those fifty dollar hats from Henry's on the strip. Y'all be begging for the gear - all you need to end the day is the sound of Nashville right here. Country Rose, right here, y'all. High jiving, high flying.' People flock to her as she takes the dollar bills quickly and efficiently. The tattoos on her pale arms shimmer in the small spotlight

The show adrenaline slows in me and I hide a small yawn behind the back of my hand. Packing away my favoured classic Gibson guitar, I nod at Rose. She winks back. The bar is busy for a Thursday night and a few punters come and shake my hand. I find a cloth and wipe off the sweat before reaching out.

'Please take a CD,' I say, as dollar bills are handed over.

Roseanna gets her usual drinks from the bar as a few guys come to flirt with her. It's fun to watch her go into full rock and roll mode as she wows them with talk of her songs, and up close there are always questions on her extensive tattoos.

Time was I would be jealous, especially if there were some rich pretty boy lawyer types working on their cowboy fantasies, waving hundred dollar bills at her. Sometimes I want to shout across, 'she's not going to do you dudes!' but that wouldn't be great for sales. Let them believe.

I leave her to it and step out the back to have a smoke. A decent night's takings. I wonder if I need to go do the open mic later round on the strip. It'll get me an extra fifty but can I be bothered. Though Rose will bark at me for not getting enough together to go on tour. A proper RV so we can go properly on the road. So much for rock and roll, more like suburban housewife, I tell her.

But that's Rose, 1950's fashion icon and femme fatale, 1900s tattooed lady, 1920's Creole blues singer and 21st Century comfort freak. She's nothing if not a contrast. Nashville loves her. So do I. She's a wild spirit and not easily tamed. But why would I want to tame the fire that makes her what she is. I'm just a dude with a fancy guitar. She can burn down the house in two lines of a song.

The alley is quiet. I see a couple of chefs along the way doing the same as me, sneaking a cigarette break. It's a warm clear summer night which brings out the rotting smells of the back street garbage, but the smoke cuts through that as I get a minute to think.

The show's good. Living the dream, playing my tunes, and I'm happy for anyone to tell me I'm the best damn guitarist in the whole of Tennessee. Who doesn't want that? But Rose is right. It's good for now but we're better than that.

A gunshot followed by a cry. A woman.

Where did that come from?

I look down the alley but I can't see anyone and the two chefs are not there. I think the sound came from the south entrance so I run down looking from side to side into every yard entrance. Someone could appear from anywhere with a gun. I look again behind me. If they see me, they might not want any witnesses.

A scream for help this time, desperate, urging. Where's it coming from? I don't see any movement.

There's a turning further down a dead end alley. I try along there. The lamp on the corner is smashed. I slow down, focussing my eyes with the half-light from the streets around.

I see the shape of a woman sat up by the bins. She's holding her stomach.

'Hey, you ok?' I shout.

No movement around. Think she's alone. Don't want anyone leaping out and taking me by surprise.

'I'm shot?' she says weakly. Her English is laboured under her Spanish accent.

'What happened?' I ask as I reach for my cell phone from my pocket. I call 911 and start explaining where I'm.

'I don't know,' she says, 'I came down here to rest.' She points to her bag over the side. A rucksack and big Walmart carrier.

'You're homeless?' I ask. 'You didn't see who shot you?'

'No, no,' she says. She tries to move, to sit up more but she curses in pain.

'Stay still,' I say.

I kneel beside her and shine the torch on my cell phone over her so I can see her in the light. She's slim, actually quite skinny. Not surprising, if she's sleeping on the street. She's wearing a blue vest top and denim jeans. As I get closer she reaches out a bloodied hand and grabs mine. I wince a little but don't let go.

'Hold my hand, please. I don't want to die alone.'

'I called 911, they are coming.' I say. 'What's your name?'

'Daniela,' she says.

'Where are you from Daniela?' I ask. I keep looking round but don't see any activity. Just the two of us down an alley. I'm scared. I don't want her to die. But what can I do?

'From Honduras,' she replies. The effort to speak causes her to wince again.

'I'll go get help,' I say. I feel so helpless. This woman could die on me and I really don't know what to do. I wonder about my life choices. Being good at guitar never saved a life, did it?

'No, please, stay.' Daniela winces again and squeezes my hand. 'I don't know how long I last now and I can't be on my own. Not now.'

'Does it hurt?' I ask.

'Si, Si…yes,' she says, 'but the pain is fading, losing much blood.'

I take off my white shirt, then rip up it up to make a towel, pressing it on the wound. It's the best I can offer. We both push down but the shirt is full red in seconds.

'Please, my bag?' I lean over to the rucksack, returning my hand to the wound as soon as I can juggle my balance. 'Pocket, please.' I unzip the pocket and take out a photograph.

I can't see it well in the light.

'See the man, with me. Please go to him. Take the photograph. I came to see him. Need money for my daughter. The gangs take her. Los Sula Siete, Sula 7. We have nothing. Unless he give them what they want, she will be sold for puta or they kill her. I want her to live, come to US. He knows he's her father but he refuses to listen to me. He got the security to take me to the street. Please, I don't want my daughter to be same as me.'

She's crying but I can't think about that and instead try to keep the pressure on the wound, while holding the photograph in my hand.

'What's her name?'

'She is Opal. Please, put your hand in the pocket - there is a stone there.'

I reach in and pull out a small gumball sized stone. Shining the torch on it, I can make out different colour pigments in its mostly black form. It's smooth and heavy in my hand.

'It's a Black Opal. From Honduras. She is named from it. Just like her it is perfect. Her eyes have all the colours when you look at them. '

She whimpers as she speaks, words barely audible.

I study the stone again and then put it in my pocket.

'Promise me you'll help,' she says, 'promise. Find him.'

'Of course,' I say, not sure what I'm agreeing to but that doesn't matter at the moment. I just need to keep her alive.

'You are a good man, I feel it in you. You will see Opal someday. Please give the stone to her. She will know it's from me. She will know then that I never gave up on her.'

She squeezes my hand once more and I feel a tingling sensation through my fingers. On her lips is the inkling of a smile. A moment passes and the smile fades. She lets my hand go. Her head slumps to the left and I realise she's stopped breathing.

I hear a siren in the street and the noise of paramedics.

'Down here!' I shout. 'Now! She's dying.'

The ambulance crew are on her in seconds and I stand away. Shirtless and covered in her blood. I stagger back against the opposite wall.

'What's her name?'

'Daniela,' I reply. 'She's from Honduras. I reckon she has a daughter called Opal, like the stones.' I say the words but I feel them fading with Daniela's life.

The paramedics pound her chest and shout her name but I know she's gone. I can feel it. I turn away. The pain in my gut grows as I dare to glance at them as they work. I can't explain it, I only met Daniela seconds ago and yet I feel like I've known her all my life.

I fall to my knees, watching the paramedics work. Why do I feel so heartbroken?

Chapter 2

Time seems to be on pause. I stand in the street watching the comings and goings of the police and paramedics until eventually they push me away for more forensic examination. I feel tearful and weak as I return to the bar. The glory of the night's performance is washed away and all I feel is loss. I don't want to leave her. I'm letting her down. She only just came to me and now she's gone.

Uniform officers introduce me to the homicide detective.

'Detective Stephens,' she informs me. I don't shake hands given I'm still not cleaned up.

The detective is respectful to the extent that she appreciates I'm in shock but that doesn't mean she doesn't have a hundred questions for me. She's a small middle aged woman in a grey suit and black blouse. Her outfit looks uncomfortably tight on her. Her eyes are dark. Maybe the poor light in the bar doesn't show her at her best but when she smiles and her stare is less firm, I get the sense she's on my side.

By the time she's gone through the first barrage of questions, it's clear that I'm a witness, not a suspect.

I'm allowed to go to the wash room and clean up while she goes back to the crime scene. Bill behind the bar has a sweatshirt I can pullover and cover myself. I'm happy to get her blood off my hands and body. My shirt is lost to forensics but that's ok, I don't want to see it again. I feel so disgusting with the sticky drying mess of blood. Looking at the blood running off in the sink, I feel tainted, a victim. Am I marked now? She's left her stain on me and by default, I'm carrying the burden of her death. I don't want it. I scrub harder to rid myself of the horror.

The residual blood fades from view but I can't get rid of it all from under my nails and in the folds of my skin. It will have to wait until I'm home. I try to put out of mind that I'm still tinged with the scraps of her blood. It's stupid, but I can't shake Daniela out of my head. I feel the grip of her hand on mine, the moment she let go, the moment she passed from my grip to God's hand. I hope that for her.

And then the stone.

Putting my hand in my pocket, I find it, relieved it's still there. Taking it out, I can see more of it in the light. It's like a prism of reds, blue and greens frozen into this black/bluish shell. It's perfect, as she described. It must be worth a fortune. Why didn't she sell it to get the money for Opal? Surely that would have solved the problem, wouldn't it?

I put it back in my pocket. Definitely not giving this to the police or anyone. It feels important.

Roseanna hugs me as I come back to the empty bar. 'What were you doing out there? You could have been killed?'

'I wasn't doing anything.' I say. 'Just smoking. It was terrible, Rose. She bled out on me.'

'You should have come away. She was nothing to you.' Her tone cuts harsh but I don't want to fight. I'm too emotional for that.

'She was dying. I couldn't leave her.'

'If you'd seen her in the street any other time, you wouldn't even have stopped to look.'

She storms off to the ladies room, angry. Typical of her. Jealous and pissed when it's not about her. And yeah, I might not have looked at her any other time. But she was dying in my arms. I couldn't walk away. How could I abandon her in her last moments?

The detective comes back to the bar and finds me by the stage. A large bourbon is in my hand. No need to tell her it's not my first.

'Did you identify her?' I ask.

'I couldn't find anything in the bag. So we only know what you told me - her name was Daniela.' She pushes her loose brunette hair over her ear.

'There's something else,' I add, pulling out the photograph from my pocket. 'She gave me this. Said this man was the father of her daughter.'

The officer studies the photograph. 'Do you know who he is?'

'Me, no idea.' I shrug my shoulders. 'Should I know?'

She studies it again and a small smile breaks out.

'Not really,' she says, 'but in my line of work he's pretty well known.'

'So you know who it is?'

'Oh yes,' she says.

'And you can share the name?'

'Surely not, but given that you could easily see his face on the news tonight I doubt it would remain secret for long. This is District Attorney Ryan Carter.'

'Seriously. The DA. Wow.'

I sort of know what a DA is. I know there's one for Nashville, and I know they are in charge of prosecutions and are elected. But I never voted for any of them. Only time, I ever voted was for Trump cause the boys said he was going be good for us. Mom said the same. Though I don't give a shit about politics, the times I see him on TV he just looks like a deranged orange windbag. No-one I know speaks or looks like that. Who cares, anyway - I certainly didn't care about who was a prosecutor. Far as I see it, they all are rich guys in suits who look after themselves.

'Yeah, that's him, but let's keep that between ourselves for now, shall we?' She looks around and seems a little nervous. I guess she's thinking it might not have been a great move to share it with me.

'I need to take this,' she says.

Like I can stop her. I shrug to show my lack of resistance.

She puts the photograph in an evidence bag. I already stored the image in my cell so it's not an issue to let it go.

'Will you take that to Mr Carter?' I ask.

'Probably need to leave the investigating to me and my team.'

'But you will tell me won't you? I'd like to tell her family that I was with her when she passed.'

'You did say, she came from Honduras?'

'Reckon, that's what she said.'

She sighs and stands up. 'I'll let you know but if she's connected to Honduran street gangs, I'd advise you to keep away.'

I raise my hand in protest and then let go. What's the point in trying to find a family in Honduras? Probably impossible. I need to let it go.

'Oh, and do you own a firearm?' she asks.

'Like, yeah, but it's in the locker at home. I don't carry it with me.'

I've never been comfortable carrying a gun. My Dad insisted I went for training, and while loads of my bros carry them, I always felt it was inviting attention. Dad loved his guns more than us, and I wasn't going down any road he ever took. I never wanted to use it and never felt the need. And even tonight when I was shaking like a jelly in the street, it didn't even cross my mind. That's how much I needed it.

'I'll need to check it. I'll take you home and pick it up for forensics.'

Rose returns as Detective Stephens leaves. 'You take the van,' I say. 'I'll go back with the cops.'

She mutters, kisses me on the cheek and leaves.

I'm relieved when it's just me and Bill. He passes me another drink while he continues cleaning the bar.

I look at my hands and think of Daniela again. The tears on her thin face, the pain in her heart for her daughter. She knew it was the end, that she'd been defeated. But she was also calm. Was that because of me, because she'd asked me to commit to help her daughter? Was that why she gave me the precious stone? Did I promise her something? I've told the police, so what more can I practically do? Her blood still taints me though. I'm not sure it's enough to wipe clean the sense that she's now my responsibility and I owe her.

Poor girl.

She was looking for the father of her daughter. For money. Was she illegal, with no passport, no ID and no money? Maybe she was lying, as a ruse to blackmail this DA guy. But I watched her last moments. Daniela wasn't a liar; she seemed so pure. Talking about her daughter Opal, it was real.

But how did she get here? Was she one of them from the news storming the border? She came all this way and then was murdered in the street.

Did she deserve it?

She was here illegally. She had no rights. No reason to be here, so anything that happened was her own fault. Rose is right - any other time I'd walk right passed her, wouldn't have looked twice. But I didn't walk on by. I stopped to help her. She was real, a person, and I can't push her from my mind. A beautiful young mother, an orphaned child. Such a waste.

Why her? She was literally no-one. I replay the scene, the shot. The police must be putting it all together just as I am. There was no-one around, does that mean she was shot from a distance. She wasn't robbed. Does that mean she was shot dead deliberately? Targeted from the roof of a nearby building. It could be.

The detective might look at me like it's not important and I should move on. But I want to know. The least I owe her is to find out who shot her and why.

Chapter 3

Driving home in a police car, even a plain detective's unmarked car, makes me nervous. I get the back seat of her sedan. In the front seat I can see discarded chip wrappers and sodas from fast food joints. Reminds me of Mom's Uber. Though her Honda is more of a trash can.

We head out to the suburbs, my mind never far from the events earlier. I think of Daniela in the car beside me. What would she make of all this? What was it like where she came from? Odd, but I can imagine showing her around my neighbourhood, taking her home and grabbing a couple of steaks. Not because I want her - she's like ten years older than me - but I just want to treat her nice. Likely, no-one else ever did.

Pulling into my street, my musing is interrupted. Home already.

I put the key in the lock and Detective Stephens follows me in.

'You said your mother lives here?' she says.

'She'll be back soon. She'll be driving downtown somewhere. She does Uber.'

God knows what the detective will make of my mother. She has her own way.

I go to my room at the back of the house and to the drawer in my wardrobe. I take out my gun and pass it to her. She inspects it. It's obvious it's not been fired recently. It's not loaded. In fact, I've never used it, never felt the need.

'Ok, thanks.'

We're heading to the door when Mom walks in. Damn, I thought we'd get this done without involving her.

'Hello sweetheart,' she says, 'what's happening here?'

'Officer, this is my Mom, Venus.'

'Pleased to meet you, I'm. Venus by name, Venus by nature.'

Mom is like any woman you meet in the supermarket. She's all sweet and normal, asking you to reach for the grits off the top shelf. Once you pass them down to her, she starts her talking and ain't never gonna stop. She has no shame to pop out her scripture and start quoting it like she's in the chapel. There's no harm in her, but there are hours of my life I'll never get back. Judging by the comments on her Uber App rating, there's many a customer who would agree.

'Donnie what you been doin'? What's your sister going to make off of all this crime? Officer, this is a good home. House of God. You know my lovely baby Bernadette, blessed with one of his angels, is tucked up in bed right now. She is the most special child. Do you know she made me a heart cake earlier, with the best Mom ever written in the icing? Isn't she a doll?'

My sister Bernie is the best liar in the teenage world. She'll be in her room, but bed? No. She plays Mom like I play my guitar. She'll be on face-time with a guy, and there won't be much Christian about that conversation.

'Yes, sure,' the officer replies. The easy smile, nod and hands on hips do a good job of patronising her. Mom won't care either way - she'll read it like an invitation for another reading.

'Mom, cut it out,' I say. 'There was an incident downtown. I was a witness is all. No need to worry yourself.'

'Was it one of those crazies? Those drugs on the street are so bad these days. Illegals and aliens.' She turns to Detective Stephens. 'You should be cleaning those people out. God's blessed this city with beauty and we don't want those sort here. This isn't New York or Chicago.'

The officer makes for the door and I can't say I blame her.

I follow her out to the street. She opens her car door

'So what you gonna do?' I ask her.

'What do you mean?' There is a line of sweat on her brow which she wipes away. Oppressive humidity, even at night, this time of year.

'I mean are you gonna see the DA and ask him about Daniela.'

She looks into the car and then back to me. The patient smile from earlier is no longer on show.

'I'll file my report, same as I always do. After that, it's out of my hands.'

I wonder whether to push it but I'm not sure what to say. Will she investigate, or is this her washing her hands of Daniela? Reading her current demeanour, I decide to let it drop for now.

'You'll let me know what happens won't you?'

'Surely will,' she replies. She gets inside, slams the door shut before I can say anything more and drives off.

I go back inside ready for the inquisition.

Mom is in the kitchen.

'Where's Roseanna, is she not keeping an eye on you? Getting mixed up with trouble, Donnie. What is it with you? Told you, that weird music you mess with and working in bars… the devil isn't far behind,' she bellows from the kitchen.

'Roseanna's gone home for the night. We'll pick up tomorrow.' I ignore the devil stuff; I already wasted too much breath over it for years.

Mom returns with her usual choc milk shake. Her late night treat.

'I'm going to bed,' I say. I don't want to do the late night talk thing she likes to do. Her opinion isn't going to stop coming and I seriously do not want to hear it.

In my room, I put on my headphones. The guitar of Jonny Marr kicks in and I'm transported. Morrissey sings and I'm following along to 'There is a Light That Never Goes Out'. I've played this song so many times and wish Roseanna would let me perform one time outside the open mics. Wrong crowd, she says. This is Nashville, not flaming Manchester. They want misery with cowboy boots and divorce, not a bus and city no-one's ever been to or even wants to.

She's never understood my interest in 80's English music. My buddy Frank who runs a music store in downtown spun me a few discs years ago and I was hooked. It was the contrary tunes. Country music is full of storytelling, it's part of the fabric of this city and practically every Tennessee child is born with a twanging guitar in their hand and a favourite Dolly Parton song on their lips. When I heard the upbeat strumming of Jonny Marr and the hard moulded tone of Morrissey I was absorbed into the same story telling - not of my hometown, but in an opposite and frantic way. Rose just thinks it's a soundtrack to serial killing. Music to die to.

Plus Morrissey inspired me to be vegetarian. Always thought about it but he made it cool for me. Never touched meat since.

The song plays on.

To die by your side, is such a heavenly way to die.

A wonderful cry from lyrics only Morrissey could write.

Immediately, I'm drawn once more to Daniela. I open my Mac and type in Honduras in the maps App. I've heard of it but never thought about where it is, what it is. How far away it is. I wonder how she got to Nashville. Looking at the state of her when she died, she was not someone who came on a plane. I think about the news and all of those pictures of people marching through Mexico. The invading army as Trump talked about. He's so full of shit - they weren't exactly an invading army, but they were desperate to get into the US and would do it illegally. The boys talked like it was some kind of war. I laughed. It's a few hundred people – seriously, the army could deal with that before breakfast, just the usual Trump bullshit trying to make us angry. I bought all that before the election but now I'm over it. He bores me, like the shitty kid I remember at high school. Had to find a new way to curse every day just so we'd notice him. He comes on, or any of the bullshit politicians, I just turn it straight off. Got my music, got my girl.

But Daniela could have been one of them. She had to get here somehow. Looking across Mexico, drawing the line from here to Honduras. How do you walk that? Maybe a bus. It just looks so far. All I can imagine is, she must have been desperate. No-one does that unless they have to. She mentioned her daughter, Opal - it was all to get money for her. To free her from a gang. Something about Sula and 7. I google them. Los Sula Siete, a street gang. Linked to MS-13. Named after the street they come from in San Pedro Sula, 7th Street or Calle.

They have a viper or snake tongue as their emblem, most of their members are tattooed with it. I see images of many tattooed dark-skinned men with the tongue wrapped around the seven. Scary stuff.

Another thing politicians talk about like some invading army. I ain't never seen them. The images on google are threatening though. Shaved heads, ugly tattoos, guns and machetes.

I take out the stone she gave me and google Opal and Honduras. There it is. Black Opal. It's worth as much as a diamond. Why did she keep this? It could be worth thousands. Wouldn't that have paid for everything she needed?

Should I sell it? Rose would absolutely tell me to do it. That's our RV right here in my hand. Pausing for a second, studying the colour fragments cast hard into the stone, I wonder about its value, maybe its power. I hide it in a small box at the back of my drawer. It can wait until I decide what to do.

I move on to checking out Ryan Carter. His face is all over the net, just as Detective Stephens said. He looks just like a smug politician, telling us how he's here to do us a favour. Seriously, who believes this shit? The DA is a job, right, so why vote for it? It's the same as voting for the garbage man. His job it to take out the trash, I'm never going to ask whether he's qualified to do it or not. Like most of us, we only care when they fuck it up.

I flick through but I'm quickly bored. He's been around the Republicans. He made some money out of some mining business and he endorsed Trump. Mining business in Central America. Mining minerals and precious gems. That's the link right there. How he must have known Daniela. He was having a fling with her on his trips down there. I wonder what he promised her. Was the opal a payoff to keep her sweet? He's married, couple of girls at college. I can see Daniela turning up with her news wouldn't have gone down well. He'd sure have wanted her out of the way.

I wonder if that's the answer. Did he hire a killer? Daniela would have been a big inconvenience. Will Detective Stephens follow up? She just said she'd file a report but I saw the look in her eye when she checked the photo. She sure as hell took it all in.

The music moves on and I close the Mac. Nothing I can learn but I'll be asking the detective what she thinks tomorrow.

Chapter 4

I'm awake earlier than normal.

Even from the back of the house I can hear God rock playing and Mom singing along. Mental note to get some headphones for her. But then I would just get the singing and no music to drown it out. That would be a slow torture.

I don't know where I got my music gene from, but it wasn't from her and it wasn't from Dad. He couldn't navigate a tune if it was written on a whore's ass. Seems, these days, it's the only thing that keeps his attention longer than a bottle of beer.

My parents are like a gold star statement for everything wrong with this country. Too much fricking God and not enough decency. Everything is a fight, black and white, wrong and right. A few more people like my dad could do with jobs that stop them drinking and whoring, that might sort a few things. Too much time on his hands to get angry about everything. Blacks, Hispanics, democrats, liberals, hippies, gays, Bill Gates. They all took something from him. Everyone to blame except him.

Mom thinks God is behind it all. We are being punished. Like God gives a shit about us. I asked her what damn good thing God ever did for us one time after she was bellowing about his love for us after dad got busted another time. All I got back was a slap so hard my cheek was red for a week.

Oh and guns. Dad loved them. Paranoid, especially if a black kid came near. Frigging sad as it gets watching him rack up armour like he's the National Guard. Poisonous toxic mouth. I didn't want any of that shit in my head. At one point, he spent every dime he had buying every piece he could. Rifles, AR15.

I only ever see dead people when guns are around, and now, after Daniela, it just confirms it all over again. Now Dad's left home, I'm rid of them. Some of the boys love their weapons like they got an extra dick. Massaging and oiling them like they want to watch it come every time they use it. Damn show offs, they all are.

No message from Rose this morning, so I ping her a good morning hey, with a Rose emoji. Predictable but she loves it.

No reply; she's probably still sleeping.

It's nine. Too early to ring the police department? There will be someone there. But I decide to leave it. Even if Detective Stephens is on shift, nothing will have changed since yesterday.

The pain on Daniela's face comes to me again. The contortions and that easy smile when I held her hand. I was with her when she passed. That's got to mean something hasn't it?

Stupid crazy woman, why did she come here? It's all over Fox News, hundreds, thousands coming here. Stealing our jobs, so desperate they'll work for less than Americans. But Daniela was different, wasn't she? She didn't want a job, that's what she said. She wanted to get to her lover, to get money. That's what she told me. Why would she lie? She knew she was dying. No reason to lie.

Ah fuck, I'm beat. Just a sucker for a sad story.

I'll go eat some breakfast, play some tunes, and then go find Rose.

***

I park the van in the lot opposite 1st Street as usual.

Rose said she will meet me there for our usual 8:00 p.m. slot. Nothing out of the ordinary, but I'm shaking. I hear the gunshot like it was the first time. I've heard guns all my life, everyone has. But this is a sound I can't forget. Piercing, rapid. Personal? I suppose whoever's on the wrong end of a gunshot is going to say it's personal. But I hear that shot like it was coming for me.

I tried ringing the detective earlier, but she was out. Left a message for her to call me. She won't, not unless they're short of suspects and need an arrest to boost the numbers. Or a few white boys like me to balance the equality figures. It'll show it's not only people of colour who get a bad rap.

Not that I have a clean rap sheet. I suppose I know my way round the courthouse, picking Dad up from the slammer every time he beats another whore who won't give him it for free or takes a pop at some pimp. Dad is a cowboy in the Wild West as far as his delusions go, and can't work out why no-one gives a shit what he thinks.

Tragic for him. Even more tragic for me.

Why am I debating my dickbrain Dad?

Because I don't want to leave this van, is why. My hands are on the wheel, I'm in the same place as I witnessed a murder only a day ago.

Think about the music. Playing the strings, ramping it up loud. I can do it, I tell myself. Forget Daniela. I'm not a shivering wreck. Country Rose. That's us. I'm the best guitar player in Tennessee. That's me every night.

I pull the door handle on the door and get out the van nearly stumbling when my feet hit the ground. I steady myself and go to the back. I grab my guitar cases and cable bag. For a moment, I check out the bright logo pattern down the side of the black Chevrolet van and the pink rose emblem. It's me. It's what I'm about. My pride and joy. It's ten years old but with a glossed up the front grill, it looks mighty fine. Added side rails and embossed wheel arches. But inside is the real treat. Top half set aside with a mattress and fridge, in case we get a gig out of town. The rest is custom shelves for all the gear. It's not the RV that Rose dreams of but it does the job for now.

No time to think about that now. Need to keep moving. I head downstairs to the basement floor of the lot. In no time I'm on the strip, heading inside.

Get on stage, get playing. That's me. Best guitar in Tennessee.

Rose is waiting at the bar, chatting away, her usual Tequila cocktail in hand.

'Where the fuck you been?' Rose says. 'We didn't do sound, anything?'

'Hey, good to see you too flower. You look hot.'

She does look hot. She's gone full retro tonight - bright green dress with bold pink roses, like a fifties home girl. The same pattern scarf wrapped in her hair. The tattoos colouring her arms and neck crush the image of purity, like a flower fading in the fall; when the rot scars the delicate petals. I see her like the flame on a Sambuca cocktail - I want to taste it, but there's going be some serious burning in the mouth.

'Donnie, forget it. You've got more chance of a date with my dead gran than a kiss from me tonight. Ready to play or not?'

I lean forward to kiss her anyway. She turns a cheek so I settle for that.

We take to the stage. My heart is beating more than usual. I enjoy the adrenaline rush at the start of a night. A nervous energy pumping through my veins. Picking up the guitar, hearing the first twang of the strings. Practice means I know I'll get it right but I don't feel it until the first bars are done.

'Welcome y'all. We are Country Rose. This here is Donnie Knight. Yes sir, he is the knight of old England. And he plays the best damn guitar in whole of Tennessee. Don't believe me now, come see me at the end and y'all owe me ten dollars. Got it y'all?' She points to the people at the tables, flashing her eyes at the men. She knows her trade and that's why I love her.

'Go Donnie.'

I break into the first riff, loud and rich. The Gibson sounds perfect, the pure sound coming through the same in this bar as a ten thousand strong concert hall.

Rose kicks in with her harmonies and we are a go.

That's what we do.

I don't pay attention to the crowd too much. Apart from needing to concentrate on my playing, I get distracted. I see faces and yeah, sometimes pretty ones, and it doesn't help. I'm happy to let Rose do the flirting. The men are the big spenders and that's the cash we need. If we're going to make a go of this, dollars are king.

And at the end of the night, those flash cowboys flicking out the dollar bills as she chats away are not going home with her.

Doesn't matter how many bills go in the pocket, this ain't no strip club.

During a break, a suited guy sits close to the front. He has a glass of water and no food. A moustache that looks like one of his bushy eyebrows slipped. I wonder if he dyes his hair to hide the grey. Not that I care about these guys hanging around. All sorts follow Rose around waiting for a hint of attention. But then I see it's me he's looking at. Of course, he's a cop. Should have known earlier - no-one looks like this down 2nd Avenue.

I try not to let it get to me. I look the other way to Rose and to the crowd further towards the bar. Anything not to make eye contact, anything not to think of last night. I hear a bum note and Rose turns to me. Her eyes flicker with annoyance. No-one else will notice but she does.

I push it back. I hate dropping a chord. I do an extra riff as a fight back. Rose knows my cue and takes a break with a glass of water and just lets me solo for a while. After a few minutes we are back on it and she's singing again. That's one thing we have learnt from playing together for years, we know exactly what space to give each other.

The show ends and I let Rose do her thing. I think about going for a smoke but I daren't go out. I head to the bar instead. A few pats on the back as I pass the diners. The cop is waiting for me.

Janey, the tiny student behind the bar, hands me a beer.

'Is there a problem?' I ask the guy straight.

'No problem,' he says, 'you're good. Decent show.'

'Great thanks.' I take a sip of beer. 'There's CDs over there if you want.'

'Why the hell would I want a CD when I can go into every bar in this town and hear the same shit being played? I'll admit you can play guitar, but you are not going to trouble my checking account.'

'Ok, I reckon there is a problem?'

He stands a little straighter. I guess I'm going to learn what this is all about.

'I reckon you're right. Nashville PD.' He shows me his badge. I see his name is John Henry, Detective.

'And what can I do for you?'

'You called my colleague earlier.'

'I did.' I take another drink. Someone else pats me on the back from behind and looks towards me as if to chat. John Henry gives the guy a dirty look and he heads off. Charm itself.

'She's been reassigned. It's my case now.'

'Ah ok,' I say, 'then did you find anything about it? Who the girl is? Do you know what she was doing down town?'

'Look, Mr Knight. Call you Donnie perhaps?'

I nod.

'Donnie, when I say it's my case, I'm closing the case. She was no-one. An illegal. She got shot on the street. Could have been anyone. She goes whoring around like that, going to get in trouble.'

'But someone murdered her.'

'You know that? You got actual evidence?'

The stress on "actual" lingers so long in the air that I could link a chord to it. It's almost that he isn't from round here but wants to sound like he is. I don't respond, instead try to stare him out.

'If you got something to share with me, I'll be glad to hear it son.'

'Like that's it? She dies. Nothing happens?' I turn away, I fear I'm winding myself up more than him. He's as stubborn as a desert rock. He's not going move.

I can't believe this is a cop talking. She was murdered.

'Don't call the police department. Don't mention any names. Tell you what, son, I see you're not hearing me too well. Take some time to think about it. I suggest you play your music. Keep that girl of yours happy and the world's going to be good to you.'

'I reckon, you're surely covering it up? Because of the DA?'

He grabs my shirt and pulls me closer.

'I knew you weren't hearing me. I said, go back to your girl.'

He keeps picking a word in his sentences to lengthen, to make his point significant. This time "hearing". Instead of sounding important, it comes out at higher pitch, like a bum note in a decent tune. I want to laugh and imitate him but also don't want to waste another moment in his company.

'This is the last time we'll talk. One thing for you to consider when you're up there. Next time you think about asking a question like that; remember one thing. You're the only witness. Might just be you're the only suspect as well. Last person to see her alive.'

He stares at me but I don't compete this time. I look away, hiding my smirk. My is ego is a little bruised that he has the better of me, smug amusement is all I've got. But I also know that showing it isn't going to get me anywhere, so I hold my tongue. Time to suck it up.

He turns away and walks off. I finish my beer and Janey hands me another.

Rose comes over. 'Who's that?' she asks?

'Cop.'

'Seriously Donnie. We don't need this shit. What did he want?'

'He warned me off. Told me to stop asking questions. Daniela was illegal. Blah blah shit.'

'Yeah, he's right though. That dead bitch been eating you up. You even dropped a fucking note tonight. Let it go.'

'I know Rose, but it's just not that easy. She was murdered and I saw it. She's dead. I want to forget about it, but every time I close my eyes I see her face, I see the blood.'

'Jesus Donnie, go see a shrink if you have to. You witnessed nothing but an illegal getting plugged. If she'd stayed where she came from, she wouldn't be dead. 's all I got to say about it.'

I can't handle this and go to the bathroom. I take a moment to piss and then decide I don't want to face Rose right now, so go outside and smoke a cigarette.

The back alley is quiet, just as the night before. No noise, no gunshots. Some chit chat in the distance but none of the sirens and drama of this time yesterday. I should let it go. Daniela was nothing to me. I get it. She shouldn't have been here. They roll the dice coming here, shouldn't complain when it doesn't fall for them.

Then I see her face. Feel her cold hand in mine. That short smile she gave me and I can't deny her. Whatever happened, Daniela was a good person and deserves more than being written off. Or am I just a fool?

Chapter 5

It's midnight by the time we head back.

We both decided against another session. I plan to drop her home before going back to mine.

I ramp up the music in the van. 'Heaven Knows I'm Miserable Now' clicks in. Jangling Johnny Marr guitar and Morrissey's funny lyrics.

'You fucking with me, Donnie?' Rose asks. 'Seriously, man you got some issues.'

'It's cool,' I say.

She presses the next track and This Charming Man starts.

'Damn, I hate this song.' She switches to radio and usual Middle of the Road Nashville sound fills the car. I let it go. No point arguing.

The cell phone rings, conveniently lancing the worsening mood.

It's Mom.

'Hey Venus,' Rose says, 'how y'all doing?'

'Hello Roseanna, you beautiful creature. Hope my boy's treating you well.'

'Course I am Mom, no need to ask,' I say.

'If he treated me like he treated his guitar, there would be no need to ask,' Rose adds.

'Ahh so blessed my darlin',' Mom says, 'I just got message from Uber saying my account's been suspended. I got a complaint. Bad one. Won't tell me but says I'm suspended pending an investigation. Lord help me, what did I do?'

Mom's pitch raises as she speaks. I look at Rose. She shrugs.

'Mom, it's cool. I'll be home soon. We'll talk then.'

In the rear view mirror I see blue flashing lights. The siren sounds as it approaches behind and I assume it wants us to stop.

'We got some company,' I say to Rose. 'Mom, cops are stopping me. I'll call you back.'

'Ok, be careful. Some strange thing's happening.'

A few seconds later, an officer approaches the driver side window. I wind it down.

'Problem officer?'

In the poor light I can't see the face well. It's a tallish black officer.

'License and registration.' He asks.

I reach to the shelf behind the wheel and hand him it.

'Step out the car,' he says.

'What's going on,' I ask, opening the door.

'Got a report you were drinking earlier, Mr Knight. I observed you driving down the street like you lost a bit of control. This fancy van of yours stands out like a stripper at a bachelor party, you know what I mean?'

'Like I had a beer hours ago. This is bullshit.'

I start to shake. I've never faced up to a cop like this, especially when I didn't do anything. Beginning to see why Black folk get so angry if this sort of crap happens when you done nothing.

'Smell it on your breath, smells to me like you consumed a whole lot of liquor. Turn around. Face the vehicle. Arms spread. You carrying?'

'No, I'm not.'

He searches me. I stay quiet thinking, this is crap. He knows I've not been drinking. If anything I smell of smoke. Those two beers I had earlier are long out of my system.

Once finished he turns me around to face him again.

Another officer appears at the passenger side.

'You too, ma'am. Step out please.'

Rose appears round the van. The uniform officer follows her. It's a fatter white guy. Seems younger than the one who spoke to me. Rose is standing with her arms folded.

'Ain't she a pretty one?' The fat one says. He pushes her closer to me.

'Want to tell me what's going on?' I ask.

'Told you, got reports you been drinking.'

'Then test me.' I say, 'prove it.'

The black officer pushes me and I slam into the van.

'We don't need to prove anything. If I say you've been drinking, then you've been drinking and you won't say shit back to me. Got it? If I say you are carrying an unlicensed weapon and I find one in that van of yours, then I'm going to be right.'

'There's no weapon in the van.'

'That's what you say. Should I check? We can do that?'

'Reckon you already heard him,' Rose says, 'there's nothing in the van except our kit.'

'Oh yes, you're the singer right. Less like a Rose, more like a thorn. Or just a whiny rattlesnake with sting in her tail? Does she talk dirty when you're fucking her? Does she curse you? Turn you on, that kind of thing? Hard face bitch need a slap before you get her going?'

I move towards the cop and Rose pulls me back. 'He's not worth it, Donnie. Leave it.'

'She talks some sense.' He pushes me back on the van.

He turns to the other officer. 'We done here?'

'Think so. These two are beginning to irritate me. We might end up turning this van over and finding all kinds of weapons and stolen goods. That would be terrible.'

The officer laughs as they walk back to the car.

'Fuck was that about.' I say to Rose.

'That was about you,' she says, pushing me. She walks back round to the passenger side and I get in and drive off.

'What do you mean, it's about me?'

'Take me home. I'm done with this bullshit today.'

I turn to her, sick of her sniping.

'Tell me. What's eating you?'

'Think about it Donnie,' she shouts. 'Do I have to spell it out? Since last night your world turned to shit. Even your Mom got turned over. Tell the cops what they want to hear because this shit is going to get worse if you don't ditch that Latino bitch.'

'Jesus, Rose, I only asked a fucking question. They didn't need to turn this on me.'

'Go and un-ask the question. Tell that cop in the bar earlier you don't give a shit about that woman. She deserved to die and all that shit.'

'Can't do that.'
She slams her hand on the dashboard.
'Damn you can.'
I don't respond. My mind is still racing. I'll not let this go. Cheating bastards don't want the truth to be told. I can feel it now. They're all fucking lying to me. Don't know what I'm going to do, but I'm not walking away - never mind what Rose says.

Chapter 6

The next morning Mom has her license back. No explanation given other than the complaint was withdrawn or wasn't proven.

'Donnie, will you get the groceries?' she asks, 'I need to make up some hours on the road.'

'If you give me a list.'

Normally I would say no, but I could do with the distraction today. Any normal day I would go see Rose, we would rehearse, hang out, chat. But she's not replying much so I decide to leave her to stew. She's one of a type, Rose. It's why I love her but she's the flip side of a coin, heads or tails. One day the best person in the world, the next the moodiest cow. Got to take the rough with the smooth.

We're playing again tonight so I'm hoping we can get square before then.

I take the van to the out of town Walmart, trying to put last night out of mind. The threats, the harassment. It's connected - but why so aggressive? I only asked a question. But then these politician types don't want to be anywhere near trouble. Mom's always got Fox News on, in between the damn pastors on the Christian networks. There are political scandals every minute of the day. Who knows which are fake news and which are true. All goes over my head. I used to think if you heard it on TV then it must be true, but fake news confuses everything. It's why I stick to my music. If people are fine with me, I'll be fine with them.

Does Ryan Carter have something to hide? If it wasn't true and it came out in the media he would just do the fake news line, like Trump. Works for him. Once he denies, no-one believes. Of course the democrats and New Yorkers are desperate for Trump to be guilty. Lennie was telling me in Casey's bar, that's what they fucking expect. Trump is never going stand there and say he did it. Fucking Dems are stupid and gullible if they think he is going to own up. No guy ever owns up until he's in front of the judge, and even then they plead the fifth. Ryan Carter could do the same.

The fact that he didn't help Daniela, or maybe even worse, it was him that had her killed, makes me think he is not to be trusted. I imagine she scared the horses in the DA's office if she came in there shooting her mouth off.

I arrive at the store and park up. A Honda pulls up beside me. I step out the van once she's stopped and start towards the store.

'Donnie.'

A voice shouts from the car. I look back and see it's Detective Stephens. She's in joggers and T-shirt standing by the car.

'Get in.'

I walk round to the car door, check around the park for anyone watching before getting in.

'Sorry for the mess,' she says. The same coffee cups from the other night are on the car seat and tissues stuffed in the door pockets.

'No biggie,' I say, 'remember I said about Mom's car. She virtually lives in it. Diet Coke sticks to everything.'

'Look, I don't normally sneak up on people like this,' she says. 'In fact, I never do. You can see I'm surely not in work clothes.'

'I suppose not.' I'm not sure what to think. I suppose this tells me at least she cares.

'Two things I want to tell you,' she says. 'I figured you deserved to know given you were there when she died. First, there isn't going to be an investigation.'

'Why?'

'She's a Jane Doe as far as they are concerned. No family, no-one to pursue the case. No political will for scarce budget money. It'll get left in the tray for a while as an open case but no-one's going to be looking. She's just not important enough.'

I sigh. This is crazy. 'It's a cover up right? Because of the photo?'

'Which brings me to my next point. I heard you got a visit from John Henry.'

'Not as friendly as you,' I say, half smiling.

'Yeah, ain't that right. Trust me, I have my moments as well, especially when witnesses start messing me about. You should stay away from this. That photograph. Touched some nerves, a lot of nerves. I can't say more but there's a lot of people looking at that photograph and thinking it's a grenade going to blow up in their faces. You got me?'

'All the more reason for doing it by the book isn't it? Surely that's what they do on the TV. Follow the book, no-one's going to criticise you.'

She shakes her head.

'I see you've never been on the inside of a police department.'

'So what about you? You came out here, reckon you think there's something dodgy about it. What you going to do?'

'Me? Absolutely nothing. I asked the question to the chief, for the whole of the next day he sent me out to the meat processing plant checking for illegals. Punishment. He knows I'm vegetarian and hate those places. The smell, the animals. I was sick all last night.'

'Me too, I'm veggie as well,' I say, feeling sick at the thought of it. 'That's bad.'

'See that's a small thing, but the point was made. No-one wants to die on this hill, least of all me.'

'Ok,' I say.

'I get you liked her. I'm sure she was a nice lady and it's tragic she died the way she did. But there isn't a cop in this city going to pick that case up if they want to keep their job and pension.'

'You can't just ignore it.' I feel tension growing. I can't breathe. The hypocrisy. 'How can you say you care about her and tell me you're not going to do anything? You're as bad as the rest of them.'

'I'll pretend I didn't hear that. I came to you as a courtesy. If you don't want to talk properly then go do Mommy's shopping and go home. You're not a choirboy, so grow up. This is a police precinct. Crime and politics stack up like shit in a horse stable. It's got to be picked up but most of the time, cases like this, no-one wants to smell it or touch it. Any excuse to put something to the back of the queue, they are going to take it. But that doesn't mean I'm not looking or not finding out what I can. But you had a warning last night and another will come. If I go back in to the chief and ask another question, Lord knows where I'll end up. I don't like dead girls in the street any more than you do. But I can't rock the boat or we'll both be on the outside. You got to know, Donnie, there's little good going to come of this, and the chances of finding a proper suspect or any decent evidence are zero to nothing. As John Henry said, go home, do your music, live your life. If I find anything I'll tell you.'

I shake my head. It's a good speech but I'm not buying it.

'All I hear is you saying the same as those bastards. She ain't worth it. It's not good enough and you know it.'

'It's all you're going to get, Donnie.'

I get out of the car and slam the door. Immediately she pulls away. I light up a cigarette and watch her drive away. Fucking no-one wants to know. She was a person, someone murdered her. Does no-one care at all?

Chapter 7

I decide to do some proper reading on Ryan Carter.

Lots of searches on my MacBook, quite a few articles, mostly supportive. Though there are few scandals from his time in business.

He's not what I expected. I thought of him as just another smart ass Republican who got his job because he had a rich daddy and a Yale education. Perhaps college would have made him too much of a liberal.

Carter owned and ran the mining corporation I read about before. He started in a working class family, found his way into management. He worked on mining projects all over South and Central America, speaks fluent Spanish. His profile talks of a love of Central American culture and history. But his politics are hard right wing, libertarian. Big on energy, climate denial, anti-immigration. Seems a bit weird, how he can claim to love Latino people and then deny them immigration. He talks about illegal trafficking and drugs. People being exploited by evil communist gangs.

The scandals go back to some mining accidents where his corporation was to blame, or they didn't pay compensation to the families of dead or ill workers. Usual corporate bullshit

He came to Nashville due to a friend in the Republican Party. Loved the region and settled there. Better climate and loves country music. Considers himself an honorary Tennessee native. Lifelong Republican, big on law and order. Been the District Attorney for the last three years.

I've never bothered checking on a politician or businessman like that. Never needed to, I suppose. Surprising how much information there is to dig through. At least I can see why he was in Honduras. He owned and ran the mine and I guess had his fling with Daniela. She must have been some local girl he took up with. Wonder how many years ago that was.

My cell vibrates and it's Gary, Roseanna's brother.

'Hanging out at Casey's. Y'all coming down?'

Casey's is a sports bar down at the Top End of 4th Avenue. It's a regular meetup. I could do with the distraction so get in the van and drive over.

The bar is quiet. Nothing much doing on a midweek afternoon. Like all sports bars, it's open plan, pool tables spread around and TV on every corner.

Gary is at one of the pool tables with Hugh and Frank. Gary is older than me and Rose by a few years. He's tall and rough, black hair which is messy and needs cutting, as well as a thick goatee beard. Truck driver like his Dad. When Rose and I first dated I thought he was going to kill me. Looked me up and down like I was a load to be put in the back of his truck. But he cooled. He loved the music we played and since then has taken it as his mission to turn me into a man's man and not just a boy with a fancy guitar. Of all my ambitions in life, being like Gary is not one of them.

Hugh slaps his hand hard in mine, the steroids he's been taking, pack his biceps like he's wrapped them in tow rope. He used to play the drums for me, but he liked his beer too much and we ended up replacing him with a beat box. Hugh turned his addiction elsewhere. Only two places I ever see him now is here or the gym. He does some work at an auto repair shop but it seems earning money is definitely third on his list of preferences.

And then Frank is the opposite. Quiet, married with two kids before any of us was even at drinking age. Old school friend, got no grudges, no edges. Works at the music store in town and always happiest when we can share tunes.

I order a soda and pick up a pool cue. The TV screens scattered around are showing a baseball game.

'You off the beer?' Gary says.

I take a first hit at the balls. A stripe rolls in the pocket. I take aim once more at the cue ball.

'No, got pulled by the cops last night. Reckon, I need to stay clean.'

'Oh yeah, reckon you do. Rose was bitching bad about that. Cops took a real shine to you, didn't they?' He scratches his dyed black goatee beard and ruffles his hair.

I pot another ball and ignore him. Should have known a ribbing was coming.

'What about this Latina? She eating your dick or something?'

Gary's jet-black hair coupled with his sick fuck obsession with everything cruel reminds me of oil out of car engine or boot polish that blackens and smears everything it touches. Scrape it off for a week in the bath and still it stains. Rarely got something good to say worth hearing.

'No she ain't,' I reply. 'Will you just lay off with your bullshit mouth? She just got shot. I was there. Nothing else.' I miss the next ball holding the cue too tight. I stand back from the table resisting the urge to smash it over Gary's head. He would love that.

Hugh takes his cue and continues the game. 'What's the story? She a whore or something?'

'No, don't you start now. What is it with you guys? She was looking for someone. I just thought it was sad.'

The balls roll in and no-one speaks for a moment. I don't know how to explain and get the impression the more I say about her the more I'm making myself a target for them to fuck with me. I also don't want to cheapen who she is or what she was doing by discussing her like this. Seems to me she was a better person than that.

Frank and Gary strike up at the next table.

'What did Rose make of her?' Hugh asks. 'She won't have been doing any of those social niceties, I bet she's cookin' up a real storm.' He laughs at his joke and we all join in because his booming voice is like a pedal kicking hard on bass drum. It resonates through the floor, and we all feel it, whether we like it or not.

'Rose thinks she deserves all she got, being here illegal and all that,' I reply.

'And what do you think?' Gary asks from the other table. He sounds as though he just scraped his tongue on a rat's ass and wants to lick the tiny drops of shit off of it. He hisses and spits his words like a pot of stew that's been boiled dry on the stove for a week.

I take a moment before replying. The conversation doesn't seem to be dying like I hoped.

'She has a point, but someone still shot her right. I mean, that's murder isn't it. She wasn't hurting no-one was she?'

'Vermin,' Gary says. He ruffles his hair again. Why does he do that? Some kind of nervous tick with him. 'She's a parasite. On her own, she don't harm anyone. Get a whole bunch of them and then they spread plagues, diseases, you name it. A whole heap of problems. Way I see it, whoever shot her did a good thing.'

That foul disgusting mouth again. Make's me want to puke.

'Fuck Gary, that's no way to talk,' Frank says.

'Yeah, lay off it,' Hugh adds, his voice booming through the room. 'We don't know the first thing about her. Didn't need to call her vermin.'

'Just putting it out there. Some people going to think that. Probably the cops do as well. One less bit of trash to clean up.'

Too much, I turn quickly on Gary, cue in my hand. He turns back to me and we square up.

We stare each other out for a few seconds. I look into his eyes, shadowed by his dark fringe, looking for something to level with in there. Nothing but dark stones stare back. Whatever joy or love there once was has left this shell. I turn away. The last thing I need is a brawl. I play another shot and take a drink of soda. I avoid looking back.

'Told you he was soft on her,' Gary says. He checks the wall mirror and redoes his hair. How can someone look so rough but then constantly check his look.

I shake my head, ignoring him. Don't rise to the bait.

'Home run!' I hear a shout from the bar and all attention is turned to the TV. 'Smokie's strike.'

I carry on with the game. Black remaining. I line it up and enjoy the satisfaction of it striking the pocket and the firm sound as it rattles down the rails under the table.

'Good take,' Hugh says. He turns back to the sport and then back to the table. He puts fifty cents in the machine and racks up a new set of balls.

Frank comes over. 'Seriously, you ok, Donnie, with all this shit?'

'It's sweet,' I say, 'it'll go away. How's the shop doing?'

'Got a whole lot of new vinyl coming in, but it's a slow burn.'

Hugh is on a roll and the balls keep falling for him.

'Tourists will be back around in the summer – reckon you'll shift a few then.'

'Hope so,' he says.

'Still best business in town,' I say. 'Like who don't want to own a music store in Nashville?'

'Yeah right. The only people who don't want to own a music store here are those that have to make a dime from it.'

Hugh cleans up in one visit. I high five him while I go to rack up again.

Just normal. Thank God they are not talking about me anymore.

Chapter 8

After tonight's show, I decide to do the Open Mic.

I feel the need to indulge in my own music. Rose sits it out at the bar while I get to play some of my new arrangements.

I go with a short set of This Charming Man, Ten Storey Love Song and my new indulgence, a solo version of Fools Gold. I use the beat box to add a bassline. The good thing is that apart from a few Brits hanging around, most people haven't got a clue about the origins of these songs from thirty years ago, so I can play around a bit without offending any geeks of the original.

After the show I get a few people coming up, which is always a good sign. I feel better for expressing myself. Letting the guitar drift with the mood and singing. I'm not the best singer but can handle the harmonies. I try to keep the vocals level and avoid extreme ranges, as I know I'll drift out of tune.

Eventually I join Rose at the bar.

'Happy?' she asks.

I kiss her on the cheek.

'Sweet,' I reply.

'That's good,' she says, staring down at her beer, 'because you've been whining like a kid with his dick in a vice.'

'Seriously.' I grab a Coke and take a large drink. I decide not to respond as I don't see the point in antagonising her further. If she's simmering like a pot on the stove, it's best not to turn up the heat.

'How much we take tonight?' she asks.

'Reckon, two hundred, not bad.'

'That's shit, Donnie. How we going to make anything with that kind of return.'

'It's midweek, always quieter. What's eating you Rose, you're never like this.'

She drinks some more before turning on me.

'What you going to do Don? We need to double that cash, treble it to get anywhere. We need a plan and I don't see one, do you?'

I think about the black opal, but don't react.

'I reckon, I keep talking to new bars, bigger venues, but you know the scene round here. There's hundreds of bands chasing the same dream. It's cool though, You'll see. I'll go back on the website, do some more promo, chase the email addresses of the subscribers.'

'Yeah you do that, you'll get us fifty cents from some suckers.'

'We could do a live video thing. Request spot. We tried it before, we could plug it a bit wider, make a YouTube channel. There's lots of options. Stop being so negative.'

'You remember last time we did the live video. How many sad fucks asked me to flash my tits? Sick fuckers.'

'Yeah I know.' I sigh. She's not wrong, but this negativity is so unlike her.

She empties the beer glass. 'Take me home.' She walks out without looking at me. I finish my drink and follow her. Oh the joys.

***

I lie on the bed and watch her return from the bathroom. Rose stays most days of the week, except when she's in a mood or wants to reclaim her own space. Mom adores Rose, plus she's scared of her. Won't have a bad word said about her, least when she's around. Maybe because Rose flatters Mom just enough to keep her sweet and stop her complaining about her staying. Who knows?

Rose unzips the dress and it drops to the floor revealing her open back. She unclips her black bra and a full black angel tattoo is revealed across her shoulders. The blood red edging scattered over the core of the tattoo enhances the power of the image. The fallen, innocence tainted. She climbs into bed without looking at me and turns her back. She doesn't speak before she falls sleep.

I flick through my cell and review the mentions. The usual positive comments, everybody loves the show, loves what we do. But as Rose says, it isn't bringing in any money.

Watching her sleep, her anger distilled in her steady breathing I wonder what's happening. She's always the fire. She always talked of me providing the fuel and her the flames. Listening to her tonight I get the feeling that it's petering out. What's the plan? I really don't know.

***

I wake to the sound of an SMS.

Six thirty. Who the fuck is messaging at this time. Rose doesn't stir so I don't have to suffer any grumpiness from her.

'Got something for you. Coffee at corner of Lafayette and 7th. Will be here for an hour. DS.'

Detective Stephens.

Wow, it's early. But I'm not going to miss the opportunity either. Rubbing my eyes I get out of bed quietly not to disturb Rose. I slip on last night's clothes and sneak out the door. Mom will look after Rose when she wakes up.

Thirty minutes later I'm at the coffee house. I order coffee and bagels and join the detective at her table at the back. She's back in work clothes today, the similar tight fitting business suit that fights with her curves. I shouldn't judge her. I mean she works hard, I've no doubt, she's a decent enough person. It's just that if I see these things, she must too. What do I know?

'You made it then?' she says.

'Do you always start this early?'

'Surely do. It's a working life, you should try it sometime.'

I shrug and take a bite of the bagel.

'What's the news?'

She passes me an A4 sheet. I'm surprised by the emotion as I take a look at the large photograph of Daniela. Daniela Seles, to be precise. Born 1987 in San Pedro Sula, Honduras, thirty two when she died. I read a little further.

It's not clear how she got into US but probably a gang operation on the Texas border wall. There are a few details of her injuries.

'That's it?'

'What else do you want?'

'Suspects? Court dates.'

She laughs. 'Even if I had those, I would hardly be sharing them with you. What I told you the other day holds true. This is going nowhere.'

I look at the sheet again. 'So what are you telling me?'

She pauses, perhaps choosing her words.

'Like I told you, I surely don't like this any more than you do. I don't care who she is or where she came from. That's not my concern. But she was murdered on the streets of this city and I don't like to see that. Look, stay out of it. We have procedures. Don't get involved. I'm not going to rock the boat to see this over the line. I'll do what I can because I would like to do the right thing. But it is likely to be left in a growing pile of unsolved murders.'

I nod along and eat while she talks.

'I know you are angry and I guess I am too. I didn't become a cop to dodge situations like this.' Her tone becomes softer and I assume I'm being patronised. 'You've got to also know, I'm not stupid enough to get myself fired, because I see which cases are given priority and this isn't one of them. I suggest we satisfy ourselves with knowing who she is. Perhaps you can say a little prayer or something. It will give you some closure. Write one of your songs about her, who knows. But let it go now.'

'Not sure I can. I was with her when she died.'

'I have to let it go every day of the week, when people walk out of jail on technicalities or fancy lawyers. If I didn't let it go then I would go insane. But I can't let it go while you're calling me or playing the amateur detective.'

'All I did was ask a few questions. I'm hardly interfering. I just thought the cops of this town would defend an innocent woman murdered on the streets.'

'I'm sorry to be a disappointment to you. But that's the reality. If I find anything more, I'll let you know. At least, be pleased that I came to you. Most cops would slap you in cuffs for even asking. Surely you know that.'

'I do. Reckon, I met a couple the other night.'

I squeeze my hand, anger still burning with the balls of those cops. Harassing me and Rose like that.

'We done? No more calls, Donnie. You're a nice kid. Go back to your girlfriend and leave it.'

'Have a nice day,' I say.

I get up to leave. Part angry, part sad, part disappointed. Overall I feel empty, useless. I know what she's saying, but I can't turn Daniela off in my head so easily.

As I approach the door, a small Hispanic guy with a hoody barges past. I turn to complain until I see he has a gun. He goes to the counter.

'Empty the till,' he shouts at the girl who served us moments earlier. He waves the gun around randomly, pausing to point at selected customers cowering behind the seats.

'Put the gun down,' I shout, from the cover of the door.

'Donnie, get outside,' I hear Detective Stephens shout, 'don't be stupid.'

I step out of the immediate view of the doorway. The hooded man is now face to face with Detective Stephens, her gun pointed at him.

'Put it down,' she says, 'I'm a police officer, you don't want to shoot anybody. Drop your gun.'

Without warning, he shoots at her. She fires back instantly. He falls to the floor and I run to the detective. She's bleeding out on the floor. The receptionist calls 911. I look to the hooded man but he's not moving. I grab the gun off him and shove it away. I then tend to the detective. Only days later and I'm holding another woman dying in my arms. I'm desperate that she won't end the same way.

I stare at the man on the floor and wonder if this was a random raid or he came here deliberately to kill. He didn't hesitate to shoot and that makes me very suspicious.

Chapter 9

John Henry turns up and I'm not surprised.

Detective Stephens has gone in the ambulance. I've been questioned by two different cops and then comes John Henry.

'We meet again,' he says.

I look at my watch. I've been here hours. It was supposed to be a quick trip out. Rose messaged and asked where I was. I haven't replied, knowing it will be a conversation that isn't going to go well.

'She invited me here, in case you reckon it's me who wants to get involved.'

'You're still here though, aren't you?'

'I'm not committing a crime. Don't see the problem.'

'There's a dead man over there. Seems a problem to me.'

'You don't think it's a coincidence either?'

'Don't get smart with me,' he says. 'Seems to me you are starting to attract trouble. Like shit and flies. Smelling bad to me.'

His accent continues to irritate me more. I'm a southerner and I know I sound like I just got out of bed, but this guy can stretch a word like "bad" out for a week and still not be finished.

'You're the cop - isn't that your job to solve the crime? As I just said, not sure I've done anything wrong.'

'Just saying it like it is.'

Like it is is is. The preaching echo in his superior man tone is the opposite of Gary's greasy snake but wind me up the same way. No fucking joy and I'm done with it.

'I can go right? Because you really haven't got anything on me, otherwise I'd already be cuffed and in the cells.'

'Look kid, I know every cop in this city. I got one in there fighting for her life. She doesn't make it, I'm holding you responsible. I can turn this into a thing right now. Any time my Captain asks me if I got a suspect for this shooting. You're my first choice. Think about that next time you sniff around my officers, just because they're decent people and try to do you a favour.'

John Henry holds his arm out to show me the door. I don't hesitate, slamming the café door hard. I want to turn round and go back and ball at him. The absolute bastard. How can he accuse me? What the fuck have I done except ask a question?

Outside in the street, I light a cigarette and walk towards the van.

There is a news crew opposite. A young black reporter catches my eye and sprints over to me, microphone in hand. A camera is close behind.

'Amy Ryder, Nashville News Network,' she says. 'Were you just inside the building? I hear a cop was shot, can you tell our viewers what happened?'

The words tumble out fast like a rehearsed line. I push her away and the camera man stumbles.

'Get away from me,' I shout.

'Hey, hey, I'm just asking questions.'

I turn sharply towards her, blowing smoke in her direction.

'You and me both,' I reply. My tone is sharp and I immediately regret it. I sound like a complete pig. 'Sorry, I didn't mean to be rude.'

The reporter wafts the smoke to avoid breathing it in and takes her opportunity to point the microphone at me again. I take a step back and feel the building's wall behind me. 'Err, I don't think I should say anything?' I look around. There are people watching all around the coffee shop. I'm not sure what to do. Should I say something? Bastard John Henry would deserve it if blurted it out. He hates me anyway.

Amy Ryder isn't keen on letting me go. As I edge away, she edges with me.

'Did you see the shooting?' She asks, the same rapid fire approach.

'I did,' I say. 'A Latino guy I reckon, something like that, came in. He had a gun, he shot the detective. Didn't flinch when she asked him to drop his weapon.'

I suck on the cigarette again and then throw it away. This time I blow the smoke away from her face.

'And did she get a shot out?'

'I think he's dead, I don't know. Paramedics took over.'

'Why did he shoot? What was he there for?' Her eyes flicker quickly as she speaks. She's young, keen, pretty. No malice. Should I be answering more? 'Do you know why he was there? Did he say anything? Was it gang related?'

'I dunno. I was leaving. I don't think he said anything.'

I've probably said enough. I move forward to get back to the sanctuary of my van. She follows me, giving me a little space.

'Look, what's your name? Why were you there?' she asks. 'It's just questions. People will want to know what's going on. Cops won't say anything about it. Just the usual bland statement. Give me something I can take back.'

I stop. I look back at her. Again the wide eyes, the enthusiastic smile.

'My name is Donnie Knight,' I say. I feel my hand shake a little and grab the cuff of my jacket to stop it. 'I came here to see the detective who was shot. We had a meeting about a case. That's all, then the shooter came in.'

'Do you think the case was connected to the shooting?'

'No, otherwise he would have come after me, wouldn't he? Look, I should be going.'

She pauses for a second and I wonder if I can escape while she get the next question ready. I move but she grabs my arm.

'Quit with the camera,' she says to her colleague. He drops it and she switches the microphone off. She steps closer to me, the cameraman turns the other way.

'Look, I can tell you know more than you're saying. I understand, it's a lot of pressure.'

'Like, err, yes,' I say, because I'm not sure what else to add.

'Camera's off, no recording. Tell me what's on your mind and I can do some digging. Maybe it'll be useful.'

I look around. The cameraman is hanging around but his back is turned. People hanging around are watching the action at the coffee shop. No-one is looking at me.

I take out my cell phone and find the photo of Daniela with Ryan Carter. I show it her.

'This woman was shot three days ago downtown. The detective was looking into it. She's an illegal, Daniela Seles from Honduras. That's...'

'I know who that is,' she says. 'Can I have this photograph?'

'Give me your number?'

She shows me her card. My hand is fully shaking as I type in the number. I shouldn't be doing this. As Mom would say, I'm inviting the fires of hell onto me. I can see John Henry cursing before sending a car for me, but I've gone too far to go back. Daniela deserves this. I press send and rush away before she even has chance to say thanks.

Chapter 10

Driving back, my heart is beating fast. I bang my hand on the wheel, annoyed at what I just did.

The news is on the radio, and while they are talking about the shooting, nothing I said has made it to the bulletin yet. It will soon enough.

My gut wrenches, cringing with the fuck up I've just made. I thought I was so clever hanging one of John Henry and all I've done is punch myself square in my face. So hard on the nose I should be bleeding out all over the van. Cops going to hate me, Rose is going to dump me, Hughie and Gary going to laugh so hard I won't be able to show my face anywhere round town.

Amy Ryder got herself a scoop, and I can see her flashing that photo round every source she's got. What will they do? Arrest me? But I didn't commit any crime. Not that this will stop them busting my ass.

I shared a photograph which was given to me. It wasn't a secret. I'm not a suspect or anything... well, yet. It's all true, but whoever in the DA's office is protecting Ryan Carter will blow up as soon as the photograph hits the screens. His wife, family. There will be a panic.

I arrive back home.

Mom is sat in front of Fox news with a bottle of Coke. 'Where you been Donnie? Rose is real cranky about you.'

'Went to meet someone,' I say.

'You don't have to tell me,' she says, 'Lord will judge you either way, he will. But Rose, she's got more fire than a volcano and she's erupting uncontrolled today. You better put the lid on her fast or she going to explode for good.'

'I'll call her soon,' not quite sure what peace I can make. I grab some juice from the fridge. My cell is vibrating on the kitchen unit.

It's Rose. Whatever I have to say no longer matters. As Mom just said, the volcano is ready to blow. Deep breath.

'What the hell you done?' she screams down the cell phone.

'What are you talking about?' I say, 'I just went to get some coffee.'

'Turn the fucking TV on, dick brain. Your photo and that cop you went to see are all over the news.'

I pick up the remote.

'Hey,' Mom complains as I change the channel to local news. My face is there, telling the world all about the shooting. A younger photo of Detective Stephens in her police uniform is shown with the caption 'cop fighting for her life.'

Amy Ryder does a piece to camera explaining what I said to her, and then the killer line. The witness told me there might be a connection with the shooting of this immigrant woman. Daniela Seles's picture appears and then seconds later the photograph I shared.

'The detective was looking into the shooting of this woman, and how she's connected to Ryan Carter, Nashville District Attorney. So far the police department have denied any connection exists or that they're aware of the photograph. District Attorney's office have so far not commented.'

'What the hell, Donnie Knight?' Mom says. 'What Devil's mess you been mixing yourself with?'

'We're through,' Rose shouts down the cell phone.

'What you talking about?' I say. 'All I did was tell the truth.'

'I told you not to go soft over that girl. Then you did. You wet your pants like a love sick boy. She's dead, Donnie, don't you see. Ain't nothing you gonna do will bring her back. You know that.'

'I know that,' I say, ignoring Mom's ranting in the background. 'But this doesn't change anything. I just told them where to look, is all.'

My gut goes through the same spin cycle forcing me to lean forward to stop me wanting to throw up. Of course, they are right but what do I do now? What's done is done.

'Donnie, you're a sweet boy,' Rose says, 'but you think like a child. You think cops are going to take any notice of you. Remember the other night when they turned us over? That's every night now. We're screwed. They'll get you back for this, they will get us back for it... even worse.'

She ends the call and I'm left with Mom staring at me. I turn and head to my room, immediately feeling ten years younger after being scolded, shouting "It's not fair!" out loud.

But much as I know they are all correct in what they are saying, I'm also clinging on with my fingertips to the feeling that I am the good guy and I'm not ready to let go.

Still got no idea what I'm going to do next as the door slams behind me.

*****

It doesn't take long to decide.

I lie on the bed trying to shut it out but my cell vibrates constantly. I pick it up to answer and as I hear the first voice I realise it will be the media with more questions. I turn it off and switch on the TV in my room. My face is now the story. I daren't check social media as I can imagine that my quotes will be cut and chopped. Shit, what have I done?

'Donnie, there are cars outside,' Mom shouts from the hall.

I get up and go to the front window. There are TV crews outside. How the fuck did they find me? Stupid question, I suppose. Just infuriating.

'Sorry Mom,' I said. 'I'll get them away from here.' I don't know quite where to go but decide I need to get them away from the house. Put some distance between them and home.

I go to the back, grab a bag and some clothes. I pick up one of my guitars, hug Mom.

'Where you goin'?' she asks.

'Reckon, I'll head out for a while,' I say. 'They'll leave you alone then.'

I realise I've forgotten something and go back to my room. I reach for the box at the back of the drawer and drop it in my bag. I'm not leaving that in case someone turns this place over. Who knows?

She stands looking at me as I return from my room, eyes watering. I wish I could say something.

'I won't be too far,' I say, not sure what that means. 'I'll call Rose, she'll look out for you.'

I go through the garage and flip it open, rushing to the van before the crowd forms. Cameras point at me as I reverse slowly, trying to avoid the crowd. Once into the street, I put my foot down and race away.

I check the rear view mirror. Nothing behind.

I was right to do it, wasn't I? I just told the truth. But I also knew what I was doing when I spoke to Amy Ryder. Time to admit that rather than pretend I was some kind of victim. She knew what she was doing as well though. She knew how wound up I was after the shooting and laid it on thick about doing my duty. I was also angry at the police for making out I was the problem.

Now I'm the focus of everything and everyone. That wasn't how this was supposed to go? How long before the police come knocking? Detective John Henry will be shouting my name into every squad car. I should lie low somewhere. Take the sting away from Mom and Rose.

Where should I go? Maybe Frank or Hugh will let me crash if they are not laughing at me.

A few minutes later I'm at the junction for the highway. I pause, deciding which way to turn. My thoughts bounce like a hard struck eight ball round a pool table. A car behind me sounds a horn. I can't delay any longer.

I go with my instinct, my first guess and turn left, southwest towards Memphis.

Heading across the junction to the on ramp, out of nowhere, a pickup cuts across me and slams into my front fender as I swerve. I grab the wheel hard and manage to keep control as the pickup hits the sidewalk. I pull over to the side of the road out of the way of the traffic and jump down from the van. The pickup is rammed into a lamp post. The driver jumps down. He comes over to me.

'Sorry man,' he says, 'I didn't see you.'

He's a rough looking Hispanic, darker skinned in a blue
overall. Tattoo up the side of his neck with a skull and cross
bones. His eyebrows are studded.

'You nearly killed me,' I say, blood pumping through my
veins. I am already on edge, though my internal rage isn't ready
to take up a suicidal physical battle with a guy who I'm guessing
might have a knife.

Not a knife but worse.

He pulls a gun.

The second time today I'm facing an armed attacker.

'Get in the van,' he says. I look around, shaking, desperate to
see someone else looking this way. Anyone I can appeal to help
for.

No-one is watching. There's nowhere to run. No-one's going
to stop this happening. No-one who knows where I am or
where he is likely to take me.

I step backwards, taking it gently, my eyes fixed on the gun. I
daren't turn my back. I open the driver's door and he follows
round to the side and gets in.

'Drive,' he says.

I carry on up the freeway past Belle Vue, losing more of the
city tracks. The van drives ok, though I can hear the front fender
rattling. I decide to keep the speed down in case the whole
thing drops off.

'What do you want?' I ask.

'Your face is all over the news. Pretty boy like you.'

'What's it to you?'

I hold the wheel firmly, my eyes shifting to the right every
few seconds. The gun is pointing directly at my gut. I want to
study the shape of the gun, the barrel, the trigger and follow his
tattoos all the away along his bare arm. But I must watch the
road. I want to know more about this man who is ready to kill
me, whether one false move really will mean he will pull the
trigger.

There are scars over his cheek bone. This skin is dirty and
tainted. Either he doesn't wash often, or personal hygiene is an
unnecessary luxury. Not that any of this matters. He is scary.

'You created a problem, you gringo asshole. You blabbed to the TV and cops.'

'What you talking about?' I know what he's talking about but I don't understand why he's concerned. I glance at the gun, checking it's still pointing at me.

'Daniela Seles was here to pay a debt. We sent her to get money from Ryan Carter. She fucked up- though she can live or die, who gives a shit, money or not. Carter though, he's the one. He owes a lot of people in Honduras. One day we'll get him. Now you've made a mess. Fucking cops are all over him like horseshit. We can't move. Situation is, you gotta get the money and pay. The debt is now yours.'

'What! I can't do that? Why me?' Shit. How much is this guy talking about. The wheel moves in my hand as I keep looking to the right.

'Because of you. You made getting the money harder. So now it's on you. $50,000 in twenty-four hours. If you don't have it then, debt goes up ten thousands a day. Once the debt gets to $100,000, you can't pay it, I understand. So we decide then what you're worth. We'll take you to one of our hideouts. Put you up for ransom.' He laughs with a childlike cackle. 'If we don't think you're worth much we will just torch your shitty van with you in it. Neat eh?'

'I haven't got $50,000 dollars.'

'Sure you have. Man of your means. Ten thousand for this fancy van for a start. Keep looking.'

'And what do I get for my $50,000, what debt am I paying for?'

'Oh you can have the daughter. Some teenage pussy. What do think? Fancy that?' The same laugh again. 'You have to go to San Pedro Sula for her, because if you don't... well you work it out. Google what they do to young girls in The Sula 7, how they break them in. You want to save her, you better go get her.'

I stare ahead on the road. Scared for what to do. My mind is racing. How, why me? This isn't my world.

'Come off here,' he says.

'But it's nowhere.'

He points the gun more firmly, so I indicate to the right. As I come down the off ramp, there's a sign for McCrory lane. I don't know round here at all, but there is a gas station. I pull over to the side, getting a few frustrated horn blasts from behind. I don't care. I'm glad to get him out.

'Don't forget. 24 hours. I'll be looking for you.'

'You got a name?'

'You want my address as well?' he laughs. 'Call me Crazy Cruz. Don't bother checking it; it's bullshit. You'll know it's me.'

I turn left and under the highway and down the lane to the side. The road is lined by trees to the left and open verge to the right. After a few hundred metres I see an entrance to a deserted Baptist Church. I pull into the empty car park and get out. I walk around trying to process what happened.

I'm shaking. Walking up and down. Scared and panicked. He was gonna kill me. They still might. Fucking Hondurans. I can't even think about that. Then, $50,000. It's crazy.

How am I going to get that? Should I go to the cops? He didn't look like the type of person who took much notice of cops. Cops going to have nothing good to say to me either. Fucked if I know what to do.

Chapter 11

I pull up outside Hugh's auto repair place, assuming that he's actually there and not down the gym. I walk through the door and pleased to see Hugh tapping away on the computer. He's wearing the company t-shirt with his biceps stretching the short sleeves to the limit. His hands and arms are littered with black grime obscuring his tattoos.

'Hey Donnie,' he says. 'What you doing here?'

'Got a problem with the van. Reckon someone took my front fender off.'

He steps out from the desk and follows me out the door. He walks round each side of the van.

'Will book it in, but gonna cost a few bucks.' After inspecting the car he walks over to me. 'What's going on Donnie? You get turned over by the cops, you saw that girl shot, you made the news. And now this. Some shit going down with you.'

Hugh's deep voice gives him a sense of authority that draws me in. Though he's as flawed as all of us, whenever he comes with his caring Uncle voice, I'm ready to get in the confessional and let it all go.

'Tell me about it,' I say, unsure where to start.

'In my memory, you ain't never got pulled for parking in a marked bay. You ain't done shit. You the equivalent of Saint Theresa when it comes to crime, and now it's like you're top of the cops' hit list.'

'It's about right,' I say. 'Look Hughie, you got a car I can take for a few days? Need to lie low for a bit, you know. Can't hide out much with Country Rose all over the side of the van.'

He thinks for a minute.

'Let me make a call. Johnny outta town has a few wreckers. Still work alright but no-one wants 'em.'

He goes back inside and picks up his cell. I stay outside, thinking about what to do next.

Hugh returns with car keys. 'I'll drop you down there. He's got a couple of old station wagons might do you.'

We climb into his pickup and drive off to Johnny's wrecker's yard.

I decide now's the time to tell Hugh what happened.

'This morning, the guy who hit me, was part of some kind of Latino gang. Called himself Crazy Cruz, like some kind of nickname. Told me I got to give him fifty grand by tomorrow otherwise they're going start either racking up the debt or killing me or god knows what other shit they capable of.'

'Shit man, this is bad. How come he's onto you?'

'Because I got my face on the TV and reckon I'm an easier target than Ryan Carter. He's got the money but he's also got the security. I got neither.'

'Fuck,' he says. 'What you going to do? Go to the cops.'

'The cops? You're kidding me, right. Like they're going to do anything. Assume they even believe me, what they gonna do? Plus soon as these gangs smell police anything could happen, none of it good. I'm scared Hugh, seriously shitting it.'

Hugh doesn't say anything for a moment. He's watching the traffic and I see him checking the rear view.

'Now you're getting paranoid as me.'

'Yeah, was just a thought? What you going to do with the car?'

'I don't know, to be honest. I reckon I should quit town for a few days, maybe they'll get bored of looking for me.'

'Zero chance of that, man. These people don't forget. And what about the kid. You said this is a ransom for her. What you gonna do about that?'

'Seriously, I don't know. I mean how can I help a kid in the fucking murder capital of the world? I didn't sign up for that. San Pedro Sula. You heard about that place? Makes the south side of Chicago look like a kindergarten. I searched the net and you got to see the stories there. Guys like you and me would be pulled from school and doing drug trafficking, the lot. We'd have no chance.'

'Strikes me, you involved whether you like it or not. I don't know what to tell you Donnie, but doing nothing ain't going to get you out of this. They get their claws into you, then they are not letting go until that debt is paid.'

We continue in silence though Hugh's words echo in my mind. Seems I'm involved whether I like it or not. My heart is beating fast and I can feel my eyes watering. I didn't sign up for this. All I did was ask a few questions about a girl who got shot. Now I'm on the wrong end of a vendetta. How the fuck I'm going to pay them that kind of money. How am I going to get them off my back?'

Chapter 12

Johnny wants a hundred dollars for the car and I hand it over. Nothing I can do right now so it seems the easiest thing to do. He shows me round to a blue Volvo. I look inside. Old leather torn seats. Smells like someone pissed in it. Must be twenty years old. Carpets worn through to the rust metal underneath.

I place my guitar and the backpack from the van into the trunk. Not a lot, but it's all I've got.

I get inside and start it up. He hands me the registration document. It's supposed to be going for trashing but he's not got round to it.

The engine turns over and then dies.

I try again, give it some gas and it seems to be happier. I step out again and let it run for a while. Checking the back of the car I can see black smoke. Round the other side is a hole in the bottom of the door that I could put my foot through.

'No-one said you wanted environmentally friendly,' Johnny says, splitting his words into several additional and unnecessary syllables. His laughter echoes as he walks back to his cabin, reckon he's happy he just got a hundred bucks for nothing at all.

'You take care, Donnie,' Hugh says, shaking my hand.

'I will,' I say, not really sure quite how I'm going to do that.

I return to the car and drive back out to the road. The rattles and complaints chime with my mood. Nashville downtown signs ahead of me. One last roll of the dice. Ryan Carter. Maybe he wants this problem to go away as much as I do.

***

I think about calling in advance and seeing if I can get an appointment. Carter might not even be there and in which case,

I'm likely wasting my time. But if he already knows who I am, reckon he's hardly likely to hold the door open. I'll have a welcome party of Nashville's finest. I'm best to take my chances. Surprise might be the best approach I have. After all, if he's not expecting me, he has no time to prepare or deflect.

Driving down through Belmont district I check all the big houses and the gates hiding away the rich owners. I've never looked too close, never been the jealous type. I'm happy with my guitar and Rose and taking the cash where it comes. Never too complicated. Never asked anyone for anything. Except today. I want to knock on those doors and ask for that cash. They wouldn't notice. It's just a blip on their radar, but chances of them handing even a dollar out is zero. I think about Daniela and how much she would have had to beg for a dollar only to be spat at.

Never once have I felt of myself as in need. Definitely not desperate. Now I feel sick. My stomach is in turmoil; there's a jackhammer in my head and I'm in a constant state of paranoia. This Volvo is as noisy as an empty refuse truck and smells pretty much the same. I'm seconds from pulling over and emptying my guts in the street. One thing I need to do before I go further in this is get the interior hosed down.

I pull into Washington Square and find a space. Heads turn as I get out the car. Obviously a noisy rust bucket like this is not normally seen this end of town. I walk towards the DA's office flapping my shirt to try and get rid of the smell. If they get too close and smell that car on me, they'll think I'm trailer trash or some hobo, hillbilly type.

There is a security check as I enter the building. I put my cell and keys in the tray and step through the metal detector. The reception desk is off to the right.

A young black woman smiles at me as I sit at the desk opposite her.

'I'd like to see Ryan Carter.' I ask.

'I'm afraid that won't be possible. He's busy in meetings all day.'

I'm not sure how she knows that as she doesn't check. However she holds her smile for me, assuming that will complete the transaction.

'Look, can you call up to the office and tell him I'm Donnie Knight. It's urgent and I think he might want to see me.' Her pose remains frozen while she appears to process my information.

After a few seconds, she turns and speaks to an older suited male colleague behind her. He is wearing a headset, no doubt with a direct line to security. She turns to him and whispers. He nods and I assume that means she can call upstairs.

'Please wait a moment.' She proceeds to a back office.

I look around to see if I'm getting the attention from the security guards, but no-one looks my way.

The receptionist returns.

'You can go up to the office. Fifth floor. They'll be expecting you there.'

She hands me a form to complete and a lanyard. Relieved, I head to the elevator and press five on the panel.

At the top there is another reception with a more traditional desk and a large Stars and Stripes flag displayed behind the desk. There is also a photograph with Ryan Carter stood beside Donald Trump, both smiling, thumbs up.

'Take a seat,' the lady behind the desk says, pointing towards the leather sofa. I sit down as instructed. 'Mr Carter will let us know when he is free.'

I sit back, studying the panelled walls, noting people coming and going from the desk. Time ticks along, and I realise it's been several minutes with no sign of him coming out.

My mouth is dry. Maybe it's the nerves. There's a water cooler by the door so I pour myself a cup. At least my shaking calms a bit. Sitting here for a few minutes has given me chance to get my thoughts together, rehearse what I'm going to say.

A few minutes later the office door opens and Ryan Carter steps out. He is jacketless in a striped pink shirt and blue trousers. He is smaller than I imagined and has grown a beard.

Even so the blue eyes remain prominent and busy as he checks me out.

'Donnie Knight?' he asks, reaching out to shake my hand.

'Yes,' I reply, standing up. 'Thanks for seeing me.' I'm not sure why I'm being so polite given the situation, but I assume these are the rules of entry. A standing fight in the corridor would not be helpful.

'Seems you've become famous overnight. You came alone?' he asks.

'Absolutely,' I reply.

He shows me to his office and I step inside. I resist the temptation to look out of the window and follow him to his large desk instead. Turning to me, his smile is fixed. I reckon that's the same smile he offers to any folk coming through this door he deems not worthy of his time.

'Let's cut to the chase,' he says, 'I saw you on the news and I've got to say, I have no idea who that woman is.

I stay quiet, not sure whether to debate him. I wonder if he's forgotten her or not. I find it hard to believe he would forget someone as striking as Daniela, but who knows how many similar women have passed his way.

'I can't tell you one way or another,' I say, adding as much care as I can to my words. I figure he will twist and turn anything I say like most politicians and lawyer types. 'She gave me the photograph. It was the police who told me who you were, otherwise, I reckon wouldn't be here in front of you. The detective explained you were a public figure. Until she said your name, I wouldn't have known you.'

He nods, exaggerating his movement, but giving nothing away.

'Look, whatever you seem to think happened, she didn't come to me. Honestly, I've no idea. I decided to see you now so I can assure you that this is a non-story, and perhaps we can both agree to move on. Let it go, you know what I mean?'

'I wish I could, Mr Carter,' I decide to keep the respectful approach, 'but it's not as simple as that.' My voice wavers as I speak. I feel like a child explaining this to him. It's not that I think he's innocent or above me, more that I get the sense that any minute this is going to turn ugly and I'm going to end up dumped in the street.

'I got threatened by a gang today. Latino gang, The Sula 7s or something. Some kind of gangbanger called Crazy Cruz wrecked my van on the highway. He wanted money.'

His eyebrows rise as I mention money.

'How much? What exactly did they threaten you with?'

I explain what happened. I got nothing to hide with this guy, so don't feel I need to be careful. I need the money first - my pride can have a day off.

'He was very clear that you were the target, and that they felt you owed them something back in Honduras.'

He stands up very deliberately, walks around the desk. I never met anyone properly in a suit like this. Never been my thing. Seen it on the movies and the TV news. I can't work it out but as he circles his desk, scratches his beard and even just the way he hangs his arms, gives him power. I feel smaller and he gets bigger. This is how these folk get away with shit.

'I'm beginning to feel that this is blackmail.'

'Not from me,' I shiver and stutter before speaking. 'I'm just telling you what they said. I just want them dealt with.'

'Have you reported this to police?' he asks.

'No, I came to you.'

'You think I'll give you fifty thousand to make this gang go away, just like that.'

'I thought it might be in both our interests.'

'Sounding like a threat again.' Inevitable he would start to blame me for this, just like everyone else.

'It's not a threat. I'm scared, Mr Carter. These people threatened to kill me. And still perhaps they'll come to you for more money, regardless of what I do. I honestly don't have any money. What would you do in my shoes?'

He pauses. Has he realised that this is real?

'Plus, she has a daughter, Opal - she told me about her. Did you know about the kid?'

'You really need to stop now.'

'She's named after the stone. From the mine you owned? You must know all of this.'

'Enough,' he says, his voice firm. He's used to getting his way I reckon. 'You do realise how many people try to find something to blackmail me with. Make up some kinda crap to get me to free them or do something. But none of them succeeded. You know why? Because I don't have anything to hide. Do your worst if you think you've got leverage over me. Otherwise get out.'

'I'm not blackmailing you. They threatened me.'

'Then I suggest you stay away from these people. You really don't know what you are dealing with.'

'And you do?'

He is red in the face and I realise I'm not going to get anything else from him.

'The police need to get involved in this. I'll call the chief and you can speak to him and make a statement.'

'Mr Carter, if I go to the police, there's a good chance they will murder me. You must know that.' I can't believe I'm actually saying these words. I saw that guy's face. Forgiveness was not his thing.

'The police will protect you.'

'Will they?'

He sits back down, looking at his laptop. My time is over.

'I can't get involved with this. I'm sorry. I don't even know this woman, you have to leave. I'll ask my assistant to take you to Police Chief. Don't come here again.'

He looks fully to his work and blanks me. After his show of not knowing, the last few minutes have convinced me he's lying about Daniela. The talk of the gang panicked him. I reckon he knows what I said is right but he daren't admit it to me or himself. 'The police will protect you,' he says as he closes the door.

I don't hesitate walking out the door. If he's calling the police chief, I don't want to get caught up. The cops will use me and I'll lose control of everything. I'm better on my own.

Chapter 13

Back in the Volvo, I decide to go back to Hugh's auto repair shop. Not sure I have anywhere else to go and I need to get the smell out of this car. It's like driving a washroom.

Luckily, even though it's late afternoon, he's still there. Must have caught him on the only day in the year he actually works. He puts the car on the rack and asks one of the guys to clean it.

I tell him about Ryan Carter. I've got to get it off my chest. I'm a kiddie swimming in an alligator pool, unsure whether I'm going to drown or be eaten. Either way, I don't see myself getting out.

Hughie is his normal straight-talking self. Refreshing and frequently intimidating with the voice that resonates like a double base. Not in Gary's sinister style, more that I'm about quarter his size. His chest is like that of a bull.

'Hey dude, you one brave son of a bitch going there. That's like the dragon's lair right there. Surprised he didn't arrest your ass for even asking the question.'

He hands me a soda from the fridge. I'm grateful for the refreshment.

'Honestly, I was so damn nervous. But he's in on it. Definitely, guilty as sin. Could see it in his eyes.'

Hugh leans on the counter and I wonder if it's going to break under his weight.

'He isn't ever going to admit it,' Hugh replies.

'Or give me $50,000.'

'Hell no, but you did ask. Credit to you for asking.'

'Got me nowhere.'

Hugh nods and looks over to the car lot.

'How much money you actually got?'

Been asking myself the same question.

'I reckon, I could get ten thousand from the bank. Me and Rose saved up for a new RV to go on the road. She'd kill me before the gang did if I took that. Could get some from Mom but don't think she's got that kind of money.'

But then I've got the black opal. That must be worth a bit. Maybe that's the answer.

Hugh stands straight with the mention of mom.

'Venus is a clever lady, Donnie. You don't know your Mom. With your dad's history likely she's been stashing cash for years. But that ain't the point. These gangbangers shouldn't be bankrupting you and her.'

'You sweet on my Mom?' I ask.

Hugh laughs. 'No man, I just got respect for her. How she coped, is all. Don't give me any fancy bullshit. Anyway, you carrying?'

'Got a 45,' I say. 'Though, actually, cops have it. I had to hand it over for forensics.'

'Fuck man, you just going to tickle someone with that. You need somethin' proper. I've got something that will make them pay attention. Will put it in the back of your wagon.'

'Reckon, I'm not good with guns, Hugh.'

Even talking about them makes me shudder. The last thing I can see myself doing is spraying bullets, gangbangers or not. I'd drop the thing before I shoot it.

'Donnie man, someone threatened your life and those you love. You gotta be armed. What the fuck. Kill or be killed.'

I drink the soda and wonder if that's the answer. Kill or be killed. I never thought about killing anyone. But then no-one ever threatened me before. With what happened to Daniela, I know these people are dangerous. It's not a debate or a possibility. It's guaranteed.

'When you going to meet this guy?'

'Says he'll find me. Which means I need to stay local, I think. If I run and he can't find me then there could be consequences, right?'

'What if we ambush him? Me and Gary could be waiting. Between us we can do some serious damage.'

'I don't know if I should bring you guys in on it. They will have back up. People gonna get hurt, you know.'

'We're friends, aren't we? In it together. Besides, don't want these illegals ruining our city. Strikes me that it's the right thing to do. I'll call Gary, he'll be on it right off. Especially if someone threatens his sister.'

He's right. I can't argue. But I'm more scared than ever now. With Gary and Hugh in play there's going to be blood spilled, and I won't be in control.

'Let me call him. Actually starting to enjoy this. Don't worry Donnie - this is going to be a lot of fun.'

Fun is the last thing on my mind.

***

I've lost count of how many beers I've drank at Casey's. Rose arrives and I can't lift my head up to say hi.

'Donnie, you look like you in one of those songs from that miserable music you listen to. How's it go, you know? God knows I'm miserable now.'

I barely have the ability to grunt in response.

Rose sits opposite me her arms folded.

'Gonna speak?'

'Don't know what to say.' I reply. I'm speaking words but not sure if they are right or not.

'Where's the van?' She asks.

'At Hugh's, getting cleaned up.'

'Hugh, when can I get the van back?' She shouts to him at the pool table.

'Couple of days,' he booms back, 'will be fine. Need a couple of Ks to cover it though.'

'You know we're good for it,' she replies. 'Just make sure you give the keys to me, not Donnie.'

I want to object but there's no point. I don't have room or ability to argue.

'What you going to do? Venus was asking after you. Have you called her?'

'Figured it best I keep some distance from y'all, you know. These people seem pretty scary.'

She looks at me, her eyes cold. I know I've upset her. It wasn't what I intended.

'Tell you what's scary, Donnie. You don't fix this thing now, we're through. I'm not being cleared out for a damned illegal. Fucking stupid, let some girl you don't even know fuck your life up like this, and then my life. What the fuck's wrong with you?'

'Nothing's wrong with me. Reckon, I just tried to do the right thing.'

'The right thing? You reckon? Every time I seen you this week you dig the hole deeper. Donnie, stop digging. We got a show to do. If you ain't going to come back, I'll go to Cliff over at Frenchies, and I can start again on my own.'

'Don't do that,' I say. I can't look at her.

'What you expect me to do? Seriously Donnie. I got to earn a living. You got to earn a living, and as far as I can see all you got is a fucking guitar, and without me, no-one ain't going to listen to your whining. So either sort your shit out or... well, I said it.'

'Gary and Hugh going to get these people off my back. I promise, then it's over and I'll be back to normal.'

'Gary and Hugh, going to clean up your shit.' She shakes her head. 'I'm off. Hugh can sort himself out but if my stupid-ass brother gets arrested then it's on you, remember that.'

She turns to leave and I return to my beer. I down the rest in one, then rush to the restroom and puke my guts up into the sink. I try to rinse my mouth and wash my face, feeling more crap than I ever did in my life. Once I'm sure I can walk back to the table, I shout for another beer. I don't feel like stopping drinking just yet.

Chapter 14

My cell rings. Slowly I rub my eyes, move slightly, feeling stiffness in my back I realise I'm in the back of the Volvo, stretched out on the folded rear seats. I lift myself up slowly and feel the pain in my back. Light streams through the windows. How did I get in here?

The windows are steamed up so I reach to wipe them and realise I'm in Casey's car park. Guess someone dumped me here.

I pick up my cell phone which has since rung off. I don't recognise the number but see whoever called has tried five times already. I open the door, manoeuvre my body out and stretch.

My head is banging and feel like I've just unfolded myself from the inside of a suitcase.

I straighten my clothes and walk over to Casey's to see if I can use the washroom. I need to wash my face if nothing else.

The cell rings again and I pick up.

'Oh so you're answering now?'

It's Cruz. I should have guessed.

'You got the money yet?'

'I'm working on it,' I say.

'Your business not mine. Twelve at the interstate where you dropped me yesterday.'

His accent is light, less obviously Spanish, like he's been in the US for a long time. But the tone is sharp, carrying the threat in every line, just in case I might mistake this for friendly business.

'Ok,' I say. Not sure what else you say to a blackmailer. Pleading doesn't feel like a great negotiating tactic or enquiring after the health of his family.

'Oh and just you. None of your redneck friends or cops. You got it? Hang a left like you did yesterday. I'll see you before you see me.'

'Yes, sure.'

'You got it? Because if you not listening to me now, things going to happen. Got it?'

The call ends and I'm shaking again. I put the cell in my pocket and try the door. No sound.

I feel the weakness in my groin and inevitably can't hold it in and run round the back of bar trying not to wet myself even when I'm shaking like a jelly. I relieve myself in the corner.

Back in the car, I pull out into the street. Where do I go? Can't go back home in case the media are still camped out.

I call Hugh.

'Surprised you're still alive this morning,' he says. 'You took a lot of laying down last night. Like putting a screaming alligator to bed – you're as slippery as fat carp when you get wasted. Don't get stopped by the cops, will ya - bet if I sniff, I can smell your breath from here.'

'Got to meet Cruz at 12,' I say, ignoring his attitude.

'I'll get the crew together.'

'No, no. Look I need to freshen up. Can I come to your place?'

'Come to the gym, I'm down there. Will let you in.'

Five minutes down the road and I'm at the boxing gym. It's the kind of place that makes me feel nervous. All these guys are busting every weight to look bigger and harder than the next guy. There is a serious amount of self-love in there. I also think there is a serious amount of self-love shared between them in the shower after, and I don't want any of those guys coming on to me. Hugh opens the fire door and lets me in. Sweat and body odour permeate the air and I want to retch. The bathroom is worse. I run the water and wash my face but I daren't breathe. I won't even look in the stall. I don't know if anyone ever cleans this place but I pity the one that has to.

Back out in the hall I look into the gym room. There are three or four men lifting bars. Heavy Metal music blasts out the speakers with no-one seeming to pay attention to it or working to any beat as they converse as if in the street. Muscles seem to bulge at random angles on the men and look freaky. I really don't get it. But then they don't get a guitar-playing snowflake either.

'Here's the plan,' Hugh says, appearing from the small office. He's wearing a loose shirt and tight shorts. I have to look away, as not much is missing from view.

'No plan, Hugh. Told me I can't have anyone there with me.'

'Course they'll say that.'

'It's the interstate ramp. Going to be hard not to be seen.'

'Think we care about that? You go in. We'll be close behind in the pickup. Take him out on a drive-by. He won't even see us coming.'

Hugh makes it sound so easy. 'I don't think this guy's stupid.'

'Oh, they always stupid. The reason they work for these gangs. If they had any brains they'd got clean away by now. They're too stupid to realise that they're just as much the victim as them they murder. Whoever runs this gang won't give a fuck about what happens to him and he knows it. Only requirement is to get the money - if he winds up dead, then they'll just shrug shoulders and move on.'

'But they'll still come looking for the money, even if you pop them.'

'Yeah they might. But they'll see they ain't dealing with a toilet bowl licker like you. No offence Donnie, but you're not exactly fronting up fear in them.'

'None taken.'

'That piece I put in the back of your car? Still got it?'

'Sure.'

'Good, keep it by you in the front. Armed and ready. No safety.'

'Ok,' I say. I look around the room at the men in here. I shake my head. This isn't my world. I'm supposed to be playing, singing, making music. Is that what they think of me? Fit only for dousing my face in the toilet. I want to be sick, I really do.

'Meet us at Casey's, 11:30. We'll be ready.'

Chapter 15

I decide to waste some time at the mall, wishing I'd gone earlier instead of the sweat shop gym. I could shower for a week and never get that stench off me. The stale smell in the car is actually an improvement. Though with the valet, it's not as bad as it was. Still think Rose won't go anyway near it.

At the mall I pick up some fresh pants and a shirt. Fresh clothes put me in a better mood. I shouldn't be spending cash given the current situation, but I'm not intending to pay anything to this gang if I can get away with it. Though I'm nervous as hell and completely reliant on Hugh and Gary to come through.

Stepping outside the store, my cell rings again.

'Hi Rose,' I say.

'Y'all good?' she asks.

'Not really.' I pause, looking up and down the mall, looking for words that won't antagonise her. 'Sorry Rose, I don't know what to say. I didn't mean to get into this mess.'

'Just deal with it Donnie, don't bring it home. I need you back, you hear me?'

'I hear you.' She's right. I get it. It's not my world, it's not my battle. I shouldn't be doing this.

'Stay safe.'

The call ends and I return to the car, rubbing my eyes. The call rocked me. Rose doesn't say a lot but when she does it counts. I felt the words like a blade through my flesh. It hurt. In a good way as well as bad. Good that she needs me, but the harsh part is the consequence of not coming back. She's hurting too. I bang my hand on the steering wheel, annoyed I even got into this.

Daniela isn't my problem and despite the cloak of guilt she passed onto me, there is nothing I can do. Opal, her daughter, is no doubt suffering, but I can hardly go to Honduras myself and rescue her. Last time I checked I don't own any superhero pants. What the hell was I thinking? Maybe I can write to some charities in the region and ask them to look out for her. That's something positive isn't it? Or maybe once the cops get over all the noise of this case, I can go back to Ryan Carter and plead with him to do something. He must have contacts in the country given his old business there. Surely he could do something if he wanted to.

First, I have to deal with today. I'll go see Crazy Cruz, let Hugh and Gary do the business and then try getting on with my life, hoping they just leave me alone. Would I care if they kill Cruz? Yeah, probably, but I'm starting to see this as him or me. I'm too scared for it to be me.

I drive over to Casey's and Gary is there. Two other leather clad, bearded guys are alongside him. Both of them holding AR-15 rifles or something like that. Both look like they belong in a warzone. I wonder if they wear this get up for their Call of Duty sessions. I figure Nashville never needed guns, but this is like something out of a terrorist boot-camp.

'Hear you got some trouble,' Gary says.

'Grateful to you backing me up,' I say. I'm grateful but also terrified. The puke creeping up from my gut reminds me why I hate guns. I'm still expecting to be the one who is going to end up dead.

'Ken, Jackie,' he says pointing at the two men. 'This is Donnie, my sister's guy.'

They both nod at me and I nod back. Gary's words linger on 'guy'. He knows what he meant by it.

Hugh pulls up and there are handshakes and grunts between them.

I get in the car and drive off towards the Memphis highway. The rifle is by my side on the front seat, ready to fire as soon as needed. I'm more likely to drive the Volvo into a tree than I am to fire that thing. But I do as instructed. If I fuck it up I'm going to end up dead, or Gary might come finish me off.

In the rear view mirror I can see the four of them. Gary is driving, Hugh beside him. Ken and Jackie are in the back, no doubt looking forward to the shooting party. I get the impression that they've saved all their gun money for a moment like this. Like they been waiting for Santa and now he's has given them a proper reason to shoot a foreigner.

Holding the wheel tight I stick in the slow lane. No attention seeking, no fancy driving - feels like this journey can take as long as it needs to. Like water in the pan on a hot stove, doesn't matter how low the heat - eventually it's going to boil.

I indicate right and pull down the off-ramp at McCrory Lane again. As I approach the junction, I slow down expecting Cruz to be visible.

I don't see him. No sign of a car.

There are no trees, nowhere to hide. Nothing to see.

I turn left as instructed and head down the road. In the rear view mirror, the boys in the pickup turn to the right, I assume they are trying to be discreet and don't want to look like they're following me. Checking behind, there's nothing there, so I carry on. The trees are thick to the left so no way anyone can come from there. I see the entrance to the deserted Baptist Church again and pull in to the parking lot to turn around. I swing the wheel of the Volvo, which feels like pulling the weight of a truck. The car slowly makes the turn and I head back towards the road looking for another car or a sign of life.

Back towards the junction, Crazy Cruz is standing in the middle of the road.

He's pointing a rifle directly at me.

I stop the car and put my hands up. He flicks the rifle in the direction of the road which I assume means to get out. I edge out the car, looking to the passenger seat at my rifle. Could I grab it quickly and shoot him before he shot me. Not a chance. I can't reach it. No time. I regret not thinking this through more as I step slowly out.

Where are the boys? How far have they gone in the other direction?

Both feet now on the ground, hands in the air, I move tentatively round the car door but leave it open in case I have to rush back. I walk forward, knees like jelly, barely able to put one foot in front of the other. All the time the gun is pointing firmly at me.

'Got the money?'

'No,' I say, voice wavering, 'reckon you know I don't have that kind of money. Look at me, look at my car.'

'Think I care about that? You needed to come back with fifty.' He raises the gun a little more to emphasise his irritation.

'I went to Ryan Carter, he wouldn't give me a cent.'

He laughs.

'Did you ask nicely?'

I realise he's mocking me.

He points the gun down a bit.

'If I shoot you in the balls, you going ask him nicely again. Maybe try asking not so nicely.'

'I will, I will -'

'Only, you need double now. One hundred thousand.'

'It's impossible.' I say.

Just as I speak a gunshot sounds, and Cruz turns behind him. I hadn't seen or heard the pickup - they must have parked further down and followed on foot. Another shot and he falls to the floor. He is holding his hip, trying to reach round. He gets some rounds off but there is no sound of pain or squealing. I see Gary and Hugh appearing from the cover of the field. While Cruz is distracted, I run back to the car and grab the rifle. In seconds I'm standing over Cruz pointing the gun at him.

The gun feels heavy in my hand. Cruz turns to me, struggling to point his rifle. His face is creased no doubt from the pain of the wound. I'm shaking again.

'Pussy,' Cruz says.

I still can't fire.

He lines up the rifle and I'm as much a target as he is. I have to shoot now. Me or him. I squeeze my finger. I have to do this. Now.

His head explodes and I drop the rifle. Unfired.

Gary and Hugh come over, high fiving. Jackie and Ken appear from the other side.

They stand over Cruz inspecting their trophy.

'Got him with a beauty,' Ken say, caressing his gun like a proud parent.

I'm shaking and can't stop. The puke comes without warning and I run to the roadside and empty the contents of my stomach into the ditch.

Hugh comes over, pats me on the back. 'It's done now.'

They grab the body and push it into the deep ditch by the side of the road and roll him over so he is out of view. The body rolls over and stops with a splash from the stagnant pool at the bottom. The wild green weeds cover him easily. He won't be found for a while.

I can't help but stare as they work. Efficient, cold. I'm stood still. The horror of the kill is overwhelming. Looking down at my hands and clothes, blood is splattered everywhere. Touching my hair, it feels sticky. Horrible.

I should do something but I've no idea what. I know he would have killed me, shot me dead, cold and unrepentant, but I'm watching them hide what's left of his body and I feel some sadness for him. I want to check he's alright. Crazy Cruz, or whatever his name actually was, is dead. He's not alright and no amount of me checking him is going to change that or make him feel better. Only me.

Just like when Daniela died, I feel something for the victim. Though you can hardly call Cruz a victim, he was still a person. Like it wasn't all his fault. Is something wrong with me?

'Here,' Hugh chucks a towel over to me and a bottle of water. 'There's shorts and t-shirt in the back. Get changed. When you get home, shower straight away then burn these clothes. You hear me? Burn them. Not a trace left. Got it?'

'Yeah,' I say, slipping out of the pants I only bought an hour earlier. Should have thought of this, I guess. I watch the others do the same.

'They'll be back, Hugh,' I say, returning to the car. 'They won't let this go.'

'Told you,' Gary says. He tussles his hair and then wipes his gun, never once looking to the ditch. 'This is the only language they understand. They'll think twice before coming for us again. Go back to Rose, get back to playing. You'll be fine.'

I get in the car. Place my hands on the steering wheel, I slowly turn the ignition. The weight of responsibility hasn't moved. I shift into gear and leave them to their chat. I'm sure inside thirty minutes they'll be in Casey's sharing a lot of beer. They'll organise alibis and forget all about Crazy Cruz, denying his existence, especially if the cops come knocking. How do they do it so easy?

For all Hugh's reassurance I know this is not going to be like that. My surety this morning that I could go back to normal has been blasted. Witnessing Cruz's head blow apart isn't an image I can discard. It will haunt me. Not just that, but the image of me standing over Cruz, unable to kill him myself. What did that say about me? I can't close that circle quickly.

Gangs don't do walking away. They find Cruz isn't coming back, they'll look for payback. I don't believe they care a fig about Cruz himself or any others of the brothers, but killing one of their gang has to be paid for by someone. And that someone could still be me or Ryan Carter. I don't know. Someone still has to pay.

I drive slowly back towards the highway, my mind not letting go. Blood and brains appear in front of my eyes. The moment his head bursts in slow motion. Do I see the shock on his face the millisecond before he explodes? The moment a life is expunged. Just like Daniela. Three times, if I count the coffee shop yesterday, witnessing someone die. Is it all because of me? I see John Henry's face; that what's he's thinking.

My pulse is racing. My hands hard on the wheel but I'm hardly moving forward. Sweat pouring down my face, desperate to break the spell of faces judging me, I shake my head. The car hits the verge and stops dead.

I get out and walk around, gulping air. Is this what a panic attack feels like? I pull a bottle of water out the well of the car and drink it in one, wiping my face and mouth. The t-shirt is drenched and too big anyway. Definitely for burning. I take a cigarette from my pocket and light up. The smoke calms me as I hoped.

Looking back down the road I see, I've hardly driven two hundred yards. I can even see the pickup and the boys standing around.

'Don't move.'

I drop the cigarette. I replay the instruction but can't work out which direction it came from. A young voice but who?

'Hey,' I say, staring into the bushes. There is a path to the left through the hedgerow.

'Don't move.' It's a cry now. A child. Desperate perhaps. My eyes strain to see. A movement. Twigs snap, brushing branches. A shot rings out, piercing the silence. Then a squeal of pain.

I rush into the undergrowth, diving for cover. At the other side of a bush, I see a young girl lying on the ground. She must be in her teens, maybe a little younger. She's wearing a red vest top and white shorts. There is a small rucksack on her back, pink denim. I wonder if it holds all her favourite things.

The dust from the ground stains her clothes and darkened skin. A pistol is on the floor in front of her. She is watching for me. I move closer but she hears me, gets up, runs further away.

I grab the gun and chase after her.

She falls, trips and in a moment I catch up with her.

'It's ok,' I say. She tries to kick me and pull away as I grab at her.

I decide to leave her be and step back. 'I'm not going to hurt you,' I say. 'What you doing here? Where did you get the gun?'

'You killed Papá,' she says, tears in her eyes.

The weight of the words hit me like a punch. I fall to my knees. In the distance, through the bush, I can see a pick-up truck hidden away. He must have left the car here with his daughter in while he went to deal with me. She will have seen everything.

'What's your name?'

'Mia.'

'Nice to meet you Mia,' I say, trying to keep her calm.

'Did you kill him? I saw you.' Her tone is bitter mixed with tragic grief.

It must be horrible for her. I don't know what to say. How do you explain to a kid that her dad was a bad man and got killed doing a bad thing?

'Where's your Mom?' I ask.

'She's dead. Papá has a girlfriend.' Mia dips down suddenly. I turn and see it's Gary and Hugh coming through the same path I just did. They must have heard the wild shot before she dropped the gun.

'What you doing?' Hugh says. 'Thought you was going to leave it to us.'

'I found her,' I say, not feeling the need to explain anymore. Mia stands boldly, pretending to be tough, but her arms are shaking, her eyes wide open with fear. She looks around but knows there is nowhere to run. She looks back at me as if I'm now her saviour.

'This is a problem,' Gary says.

'Who is she?' Hugh says.

'You shot Papá,' Mia shouts, pointing at the rifle in Gary's hands.

'So what if I did little girl? What you going to do about it?' The cruel flat tone of Gary's words mocking the child, chill me. What a cold bastard. Mia bursts into tears and drops to the floor. I go to her and try to hold her. She takes my comfort and buries her head into my shoulder.

I look at Gary and Hugh who share a glance.

'Don't even think about it,' I say.

'She's a witness,' Gary says. 'It's a kid, but she's a rat. Got to be cruel to be kind. Few years' time she'll doing tricks behind 2nd Avenue. I know it and so do you. Maybe she'll do your old man if he can still get it up by then.'

'You're a piece of work,' Hugh says.

'Someone gotta make the hard yards here. Suggest you step aside, Donnie, and let us finish the job.'

'The fuck I'm going to do that. She's a kid. She's done nothing.' I'm not letting go. I know who she is, who her Dad was, but that doesn't make killing a kid alright. I'm not going to do it.

'Get her the fuck away from here,' Hugh says. He's angry at me, but I can see he's not big on killing kids either or he would let Gary finish her off, and maybe me along with it. 'Seriously Donnie, if you want to go soft on her, get her away from here. No-one can find her. I must be fucking out of my mind. Gary's right. She's a witness. Moment those Latinos get her story we've all of us got targets on our backs.'

'I already have one.' I say. Pulling Mia to her feet. 'But I'm not going to let you kill her. I'll take her to cops.'

'Are you fucking crazy?' Gary points the gun at me now. 'The same thing going to happen. Think they are going to look after her? Think they are not going to ask the same questions as the vermin gangs do? Think she's going to keep her dirty rat mouth shut?'

'I'm not a snitch,' Mia shouts.

'See, the vermin blood is running strong and true, Donnie,' Gary says. 'She's one of them alright.'

I grab her hand and pull her away with me. She comes with me but is nervous, looking around at every moment. Her other hand holds her rucksack tight to her shoulder. What she thinks of me matters less when the alternative is Gary.

'Pussy,' Gary shouts. He fires his gun in the air and instinctively we both run. Back at the Volvo, I put her in the nearside and jump in. I drive off quickly towards the highway junction. All thoughts of what happened are gone. Now I just need to get away.

Beside me, Mia is staring ahead. She's in a trance-like state. I guess shock is taking over. I take the turn towards Memphis for no good reason other than going back into Nashville feels like inviting more terror. Seriously, what do I do with the kid?

Once they find this guy is dead and I have the kid, what hell would that unleash? But if I take her back or take her to the police, Gary's right - chief witness is sitting right beside me. They'll find a way to make her talk if it takes all the ice cream and candy in Nashville. I can see the look on John Henry's face now as he invites one of his cops to slap the cuffs on. Easiest arrest of his career. Then Gary and Hugh all going down for murder. And me, accessory or otherwise.

But then, am I about to abduct a child? Who even knows she exists - Cruz's girlfriend?

My cell rings. It's Rose. I don't know what to say. I shake my head and beat the steering wheel. Mia breaks from her trance and I look at the tears in her eyes. There are tears in mine as well. In the last hour, I've just torn my life apart, and I've no idea what for. I don't know what to do except keep driving. I can't go back to Nashville.

The cell rings again. This time I answer it.

'Rose, I'm sorry,' I say before she can speak. 'It's ok but I need to quit town for a few days. The gangbanger is dead and when the cops find out, I'll be in the frame.'

'Donnie,' she shouts, 'come home.'

'I can't. Not yet. I'll be back in a few days when the dust settles. I promise. I love you.'

I wind down the window and throw the phone out onto the tarmac, unable to listen for the reply. It's hard to think anything but my life being screwed over. I hope Rose will forgive me, but then I haven't got my head around what a mess I'm in, so how could she? Still, I got to run. I shiver with fear, wiping the tears from my eyes. I don't have a choice.

There's no going back now.

Chapter 16

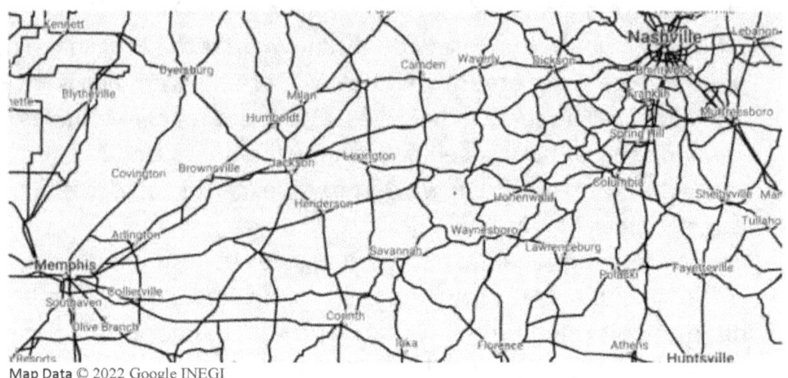

Map Data © 2022 Google INEGI

Nashville to Memphis

We sit in silence, both numb. Time suspended. The car rages with resistance as I try to maintain even a moderate speed. The noise deafens constructive thought as I try to imagine a way out of this. A way back. And what to do with his newly orphaned kid sat beside me.

My heart hasn't slowed. I'm holding the wheel like a resistance bar and my knuckles are stretching the skin on my hand.

She's cried and then stopped. Barely looked at me. Staring intently ahead. I can't imagine what's in her head. I don't want to either. I've got enough of my shit to deal with.

'Let me out now,' she screams.

'Mia, I can't,' I reply, 'we're on the highway.'

'Don't say anything. Don't speak to me. Bastard, gringo, killer. Let me go.'

She reaches for the door arm and I lean to pull her back. The Volvo swerves, with my hands loose on the wheel, like a super tanker hit by a tidal wave. The whole motion of the car shifts as I try to wrestle it back in line. The car overcompensates and drifts to the left hand lane. A horn blares from a saloon car racing past. Holding my breath, I manage to hold the wheel straight and settle back into a straight line.

'Don't touch me, pedo! Where you taking me?'

She curls into a ball, hunched up on the seat. Maybe she scared herself. This car is not made for jerky fast movements. The next swerve like that might see me turn it over.

'I can't let you go now. It's dangerous on the road. We're in the middle of nowhere. Look, I don't know where we are going but I'm not going to harm you. I promise you that.'

'This car is shit,' she mutters.

'You should try driving it,' I reply. The shared joke seems to dampen the tension for a moment. I take a deep breath, relax my hands and keep going forward. She's right to ask where I'm taking her though. I'm asking the same damn question as well.

There's a truck stop just over the Tennessee River and I decide to take a break. Another hour has passed and there's hasn't been much in the way of words. I could do with some food and probably Mia could too.

I pull into the car park, park up at the far corner and consider how to play this?

'You want something to eat?'

Mia nods.

'Burger, fries? Coke?'

Again a nod. OK that was easy.

'Are you going to run if I leave you to go inside?'

This time, no reaction.

'Where you going to run to? We're hours from anywhere, you got no money. Anything could happen to you.'

Silence.

'Look if you run, you'd be doing me a big favour. You know, I don't know what to do with you, but if you're gone then I can go ahead, do what I like. You get that don't you? But if it's you you're worried about, I'd stay in the car. Looking all these big fellas here and those trucks. What they going to think of a young kid like you.'

'I'm not scared of you or anybody.' She spits the words out to make her point. But she is scared, and I decide not to labour the point.

'Look, I'm going to get some food. I don't know what I can say to persuade you to stay except, like I already told you, I'm not going to let anyone hurt you. If you run away, I can't do that. Deal?'

Mia doesn't look at me, just stares through the windshield. Finally she nods.

I get out the car, lock the door and don't look back as I head into the restaurant. I put a cap on and pull it down over my eyes to avoid people's glances or any cameras. I try to look as normal as possible as I walk inside. I've locked the door but she can wind down the window and escape the second I turn my back. And maybe she'd be doing me a favour. Standing in the queue for the takeaway, I glance across. Why is it that I don't want her to run? Could this be the worst decision of my life, taking a kid like this? But what's the alternative? I can't take her home, can I?

With my arms full of takeout I walk back to the car. I flip a dime in my head. Heads or Tails will she still be there. Heads yes, Tails, no.

Stepping closer I go to the passenger door. Immediately I can see the window down. Tails it is then. Getting closer I realise my fears are misplaced. She's sat there, dead still.

I pass her the food and walk to the other side. I get inside and open a pack for myself taking a bite of the veggie burger and forcing a collection of fries into my mouth. I didn't realise I was so hungry.

'You did go then?' I ask after a few moments. 'Why did you come back?'

She doesn't reply and continues to eat.

'Where you going to take me?' She asks.

I don't reply as I haven't got an answer. I chomp on more of the veggie burger and then turn the question back on her.

'You said your dad had a girlfriend? Do you like her? Want to go see her?'

She eats her burger. I'm pleased that she is hungry and taking food from me. I could do with a little less tension in the car - currently it's worse than Rose on a bad day. She packs some real red hot vibes when she's pissed with me. Though I don't see much changing soon. There's a lot of questions but not a heap of answers coming.

'No,' she says after taking a swig of Coke. She burps after speaking.

I laugh and so does she.

A moment of silliness breaks the ice for a second, but then silence again.

'Is she a bad person?' I ask.

'She doesn't care about me. Only Papá. She's fucking him so he gives her money. She hates when I'm there.'

'Hey where you learn to speak like that,' I say. I give a half laugh but realise it's not the time for ribbing her.

'I'm not stupid, I'm thirteen you know. I've seen them doing it. Disgusting.'

'Thirteen?' I say out loud. What an age. Her whole life ahead of her. What was I doing when I was thirteen? Middle school, guitar lessons, touch-football games.

'You go to school?'

'I did, but it was scary. The boys from other gangs hanging around outside. They were looking for me, watching me. One day they grabbed me. They grabbed my hair and pulled me into a car. I kicked and screamed and a teacher saw it. I got away. Since then Papá won't let me go. Mom used to read to me but Nicole, Papá's girlfriend, didn't care.'

Mia speaks quickly, her accent a cross between Nashville and Hispanic. Seems when she's explaining she takes on the typical Tennessee drawl in her words, but then as she gets stressed her words shorten and I can hear the Spanish influence.

'And your dad?'

'He couldn't read, he couldn't teach me. He showed me how to use a gun. A knife. He once got me to stab an injured street dog to show me I could do it. It was horrible. I cried.'

I sigh. This is horrible. What do I do with her? I can't take her
back to these people. Anything could happen - but then if I'm
caught with her, who knows what will happen?

The food is over and I gather up the trash and take it to the
dumpster.

'Why did you kill him?' she asks once I'm back in the car.
'What did he want from you that you had to kill him?'

I open the window and light a cigarette, trying to blow the
smoke outside.

'That's disgusting,' she says, opening her own window.

'Sorry,' I say opening the door a little as well to let the air
out. I need to smoke. I hate all these questions that I can't
answer without sounding like… well anything other than me.
Donnie Knight, a nobody from Nashville, involved in multiple
murders and cover ups.

'You know the business he was in right?'

'You doing drugs, is that it? Owe him money? It's ok, I've
seen hundreds of junkies.'

I shake my head. Take another draw on the cigarette and
chuck it out. I close the door and put it in gear.

'He said I owed him money - I messed up his operation to
get money out of someone important.'

'How did you do that?' she asks.

I take the ramp onto the highway, mindful of cops and other
law enforcement, but don't see any around.

'Honestly, I don't know. I was a witness, told the media.
Made it more difficult for his gang? What do you think?' My
answer is sharp, more than I expected. These questions. I
haven't really got a clue how I ended up on the wrong end of
this and everyone assumes it is part of some grand plan.

She sits quiet for a moment, staring out the highway? Is it
the end of the conversation?

'He would have killed you, right?'

'Yeah, I think so.'

'But he didn't?'

'I'm here, aren't I?

She shakes her head. 'He should have killed you.'

The words cut, threw me. I look at her and back to the road. Did she just say that?

'Did your Papá kill many others? You seen him kill before?' I feel I have to ask. She can't see I'm not the bad guy. I guess to her I am.

'If he didn't kill them, they'd kill him. Simple as,' she says, her tone flat.

I keep glancing at her but she won't look at me. She stares straight ahead.

'And me? Did I deserve to get killed just like the others?'

'Not my business,' she says. 'I just know my Papá's dead and now I got no-one.'

My mind drifts back to Daniela and her daughter. Feels so familiar. The same thing could happen to Mia. There must be a ton of orphan kids around Tennessee born to gang members. It scares me thinking about the consequences for them.

'Do you have grandparents? Family anywhere else?'

'I never met them. Apparently I have some in Honduras, where Papá comes from. But I don't know who they are, he never told me where they were. Papá talked about Abela, his mother. She looked after him but he got recruited in the gang when he was older. He never saw her after that.'

'What was your Dad's name?'

'Cruz,' she says. 'He always was Crazy Cruz to the others.'

So it was his real name.

'Would you like to go to Honduras, to your family?' I ask, like it's a drive down the road to the mall.

She nods but doesn't look over. I wish I knew what to do with her. There's a lot of pain in the seat next to me and I don't figure that's going to turn into love for saving her from Gary anytime soon.

Honduras. That country, those people all over again. Same as Daniela. All roads lead to Honduras. Except it's impossible. What the hell am I doing? Definitely not driving thousands of miles to a country I've never been to. I've seen the news, I've seen what goes on there. Not a place for a wimp like me. My wimp credentials are well and truly proven in the last hours.

Though some might argue I just saved a child's life, that's definitely not what Mia thinks. And all I got to feel is that I trashed my own.

Perhaps I could put her on a plane there. Yeah, but no passport, no ID. Unaccompanied. With what money?

We carry on driving. The direction is Memphis but that's not the destination.

That's a mystery I'll have to solve. Pretty much like the rest of my life.

Chapter 17

Reaching Memphis, I pull into a mall and park the car.

'What you gonna do?' Mia asks.

'I reckon I'll look for an ATM,' I reply.

'What the fuck? You reckon?' You wanna stick an advert on the TV whilst you there. You know cops gonna be looking for exactly that.'

I look at her. She stares back, her head at an angle, forehead creased, questioning me.

'We need cash.' I say. 'We can't manage on fresh air.'

She reaches into the foot well and retrieves her pink rucksack. Rustling around for a moment, she pulls out a roll of dollars. 'I took it from Papá's car. When he was shot, knew I would need money and wanted to make sure I got it before the cops did.'

I take a deep breath.

'How much is there?'

'Dunno, maybe ten thousand - lots of fifties and hundreds.'

'OK,' I take a pause, thinking about the cash Crazy Cruz was coming to get from me. That cash is extortion, drug money. I wonder who was expecting it back. If Crazy Cruz doesn't return that kind of cash, dead or not, it's going to be missed. Whoever it is, is going to be very pissed off and... I don't need to think more about the 'and'. A reminder that going back to Nashville is not a good idea.

'We're going to need some fresh clothes and some stuff for rough sleeping. You ok to get something for yourself?' I ask.

She nods with a short smile. I wonder if she's ever gone to a mall and shopped on her own.

Should I follow her around? Make sure she doesn't run? What's the point - she's smart enough to give me the slip in the mall and it's better we are not seen together.

'You go get what you want. Don't get too much - you can see the car's not that big in the back. Just enough to be comfortable, right?'

She looks in the back and I guess what she's thinking.

'You got any better ideas?' I ask. 'I'll sleep here in the front. You can have the back. Back here in one hour, right?'

Mia opens the door and heads for the entrance. I'll go a few moments later. Time for a cigarette first.

I watch her stroll, swagger almost. The confidence of a teen. By rights she should be scared, nervous or something like that. A dusty brown patch on her shorts reminds me of the scrabbling on the floor with Gary. She needs fresh clothes. Her darker skin and dirty clothes will attract the wrong kind of attention. To look in her face, it's easy to see an innocent kid, kind of cute as all kids look but slightly buck teeth on her upper jaw which a more attentive parent might have felt necessary to fix with a brace. The real clue to her upbringing comes from her eyes, dark slightly bloodshot but often fixed in stare of wonderment. What am I, a psychologist now? But for me she smacks of a kid who never had a happy day in her life. Maybe only since her mom died. Shit life and now me. Poor kid.

I think about the bloody clothes in the back, plus I need to get rid of those I'm wearing. I could dump them in the trash can but too many cameras here. Burning them is best, just as Hugh said. I wonder where they are now. What will Rose be thinking? Gary will have told her. She will be going crazy without me calling. This is bad. Once I'm safe, I'll call her. No point beforehand, as it won't do her or me any favours.

Finishing the smoke, I put on a cap and dark glasses to go into the mall so I can be more discreet. Still feel self-conscious, though. People stare, but more likely looking at me as a guy who can't afford a proper car. In the mall foyer there is a big screen with the local news network playing. Yesterday's news on Ryan Carter has gone. It's moved on to a Trump rally somewhere, everyone getting messed up over another Twitter message. Seems I'm already old news. Doubt John Henry will see it that way, but he's not here in front of me and for now that's good news.

I wonder about the ATM. I've got two hundred dollars in my wallet but that's not even close to enough. Mia's right, the moment I go to the ATM, I'll leave a record and give myself away. But I can't rely on her cash supply, especially if she isn't planning on hanging around. She would disappear before I even realised she'd gone.

Would I keep running then? Where am I going anyway? The answers don't come other than putting some distance between Nashville and wherever I am. Whichever of cops and gangs are looking for me, feels like distance is the only asset I've got. Lie low, keep cool and hopefully the storm blows over. Hopefully finding something else to keep them busy other than me.

I decide to get some clothes and food supplies, then see how it goes. There's a few days to get through yet. Not that a few days of perpetual driving fills me with any pleasure. But again, alternate choices are something I don't have.

In the camping store, I find a small stove and a gas bottle. At least I can make a hot drink. I grab a sleeping bag and pillow as well. I'm glad it's summer. It would be freezing if it was winter.

∗

I'm standing by the car looking at my watch. It's already gone past the hour and getting dark when Mia appears. She's changed into jeans and a fresh yellow top with a sweatshirt in her hand. She's also bought some Canvas shoes. I get the impression she enjoyed her hour.

'Were you getting worried?' she asks. I sense a smile for the first time as she teases me. It won't last and should not delude myself. Reckon, I allow her the moment and open the door for her like some kind a chauffeur.

'Got you something. She hands over a basic cell phone and a sim card. 'Burner,' she says. 'Figured we might need something.''

I nod. Yep, she's right, and clearly better than me at this game.

We get into the car and head over to the drive thru, picking up more burgers and fries. I've got to find some better food options in the next few days - this is all just shit.

Driving out of town again, I take a back road out to the forest. I find a dirt road and head off for a hidden parking spot. It's pitch black as we pull up. But it's fine, there's no intention to go anywhere and at least up here, we aren't going to be disturbed.

As soon as I park up, I pull a beer from the box in the back. I catch Mia looking at the beer and guess that she might have had one or two before, despite her age. I hand her one. Doesn't seem much point in pretending I'm any kind of parent.

I set up the camping stove and make a drink. Meanwhile I grab the bloody clothes from the back and start a small fire. I'm happy to light a cigarette and take a moment's relief, though I prefer to watch the flames burn deflecting my mind from reflecting on the day. To say I've fucked up would be the understatement of the century.

I don't say anything to Mia about the burning clothes. Not sure I want to explain how I'm destroying evidence of her dad's murder.

She joins me outside after a few mins.

'You were talking before about being a witness? What was it?'

At least her tone is more civil. Inquisitive instead of nasty.

'A woman, Honduran woman got shot. I saw it happen. It was downtown.'

'Was it Papá who shot her?'

'I don't know,' I reply. 'When I say, I saw it happen, reckon that's not strictly right. I heard it and then found her in the alley. Do you know anything about it? Was a few days ago?'

'Dunno,' she says, 'could have been. But did you see him or something? Is that why you killed him?'

'Let's be clear, I didn't kill your Papá. And no, I didn't see him. I didn't see anyone.'

The fire crackles away and the nervous silence returns.

'Who was the woman?' she asks. 'Why was she killed? Was she a whore?'

'I don't think she was. Her name was Daniela Seles.' I realise throwing my cell phone away I don't have the photo of her. Instead, I pick up the burner cell and search the news sites where the photo was shared. I show her the photo. 'She was from San Pedro Sula, do you know it? She has a daughter, your age I think - Opal. She wanted money from the father, but someone shot her.'

'I think that's where Papá came from. He said something about it once. I dunno, can't remember... didn't take much notice.'

She sits quiet again and I don't elaborate further. In the dark I can't see her face, which is good as I don't really want to know too much of what she's thinking, struggling enough with my own issues. Let her ask her questions. I don't feel I have anything to hide.

'Did you know Daniela?' I ask. 'Was she part of your Papá's gang? Sula 7?'

'Los Sula Siete. No she wasn't part of the gang. I never saw her.'

Sitting out in the pitch black takes me back to teenage days, hitching a ride with Gary in his pickup, drinking and smoking till late. Mom would kill me when I came back reeking of it. Innocent days compared with this, but the smell of the wood smoke, the sound of the trees moving in the breeze, all feel so familiar.

'You really serious about doing this?' Mia asks, taking a sip of beer. She burps quickly afterwards.

'How do you mean?'

'Running away with me?'

I think for a moment. Is that what I'm doing?

'What do think I should do?' I ask.

'Is that what you always say when someone asks you a question you can't answer?'

I laugh. She's a smart one.

'Ok so how far we going to drive? Another state? Texas, Mexico. Going to get me out the country? You got a passport with you?'

'In my bag.' But then, she hasn't. 'Reckon, I haven't thought that far ahead. We just need to get away. Think it over?'

'You reckon a lot,' she says, dragging out reckon to be a long note and I cringe at my own voice being repeated back to me. 'Definitely no mistaking you come from Nashville.'

What else to do except smile and feel my stomach turn over as a teenager mocks me.

'You going to smuggle me out and then get me into Mexico?'

'Seriously, why you keep talking about Mexico? I don't know where we are heading.' She's obviously thought further ahead than I have. I haven't got past what happened this morning. It already feels like a life in a day.

'I'm not going to grass on you. You can drop me off at the mall in the morning. I'll manage.'

'Reck...' feel myself saying the word and stop myself, 'I can't do that. Anything could happen to you, Mia.'

'Chances are Dad was going to get killed anyway, he was crap at doing stuff. Too soft. That's what she used to say, that puta girlfriend of his. He wasn't tough enough. Let people go. He got shot. He was bound to get killed at some point. So whatever was going to happen would happen right. I've run drugs before. I can survive.'

'No, no,' I say. 'You know what else they make you do, don't you?'

'Course. I'm not stupid. It's why I'm not going back. Not to them, not to the puta.'

'Where will you go then if you don't go back?'

She shrugs again.

'I'm not going to let anything happen to you,' I say with a bravado I'm sure she knows is delusional. We both know I can't possibly honour a promise like that.

'I'll survive,' she says. 'I'll hitch a ride to some place I can get work. Wash pots in a café, do something like that and get a bed. You got any better offers? I'm not your problem and you don't want me around.'

I don't know what to say. It would be a relief to get rid of her. The guilt of her dead dad is something I could do without. Plus, how can I look after a kid?

'There must be somewhere I can take you that's safe. Like a refuge or something for orphan kids. You don't have to tell them you came from Nashville. Does anyone even know you are missing? Or care?'

'No-one cares. And you're not taking to me one of those places, full of weirdo pedos. Drop me there and I'll run as fast as I can to get away.'

'They can't be all be like that.'

'I know someone.'

I look up, surprised. Relieved. 'Who, where?'

'Maybe we can go there tomorrow. Albuquerque. She'll know what to do.'

'That's New Mexico. It's hundreds of miles or more. How come she's going to be able to help you?'

'She's a lawyer and definitely ain't no pussy like you, if that's what you're thinking. And you got a better idea?'

My words thrown back at me. Kid doesn't miss a thing.

'Does she know you? Is she ok? What will she do?' It sounds crazy, driving so far, but a minute ago we were talking about Mexico.

'She knows me for sure, knew Papá and all the others. She's a lawyer - they're in the same game of dodging cops, right? Dunno if she'll know what to do but it's better than living in a field right here.'

I shrug again. I need to think about this. She's right but feels like driving to other side of the world only to get stuck with another gang problem. The Volvo will fall apart before then.

'You play that?' She's nods towards my guitar in the trunk.

'The best in all Tennessee,' I reply.

'Play me something,' she says.

I sit on the lip of the trunk and stretch my legs out. I put the guitar on my knee, just about managing to angle it so can play comfortably. I pluck away at the strings randomly playing. I drift into a set of chords and find myself singing The King of Rock and Roll, another favourite of mine from an eighties English band, Prefab Sprout. The line about bragging to the children in the street seemed appropriate but then the silliness of the chorus, 'Hot Dog, Jumping Frog, Albuquerque.'

'Albuquerque. You just made that up?' She laughs.

I end the chorus with a final strum. The last note I drag out as deep as I can go.

'Albuqueerrrrquueeeeeeeeeee.' I sound like a punctured airbag.

'That's so not a song,' she laughs.

'It's absolutely a song. Eighties. Reckon, well before your time. Just came to mind like it was written for now.'

'You need some new songs,' she says, 'that was terrible.'

I put the guitar down and drop the back seat so I can make a bed. I then wander out to the bush to take a moment. Listening to the sounds of the forest, I pause before going back. I can hear squeals and buzzing of insects. Even in the dead of night there is no silence.

I climb back into the car and see that Mia has already curled up in the front seat. I stretch out in the back of the car, feeling the hard floor under me. But I'm exhausted. I pull the sleeping bag over me. Doesn't feel like sleep is going to come any time soon.

Chapter 18

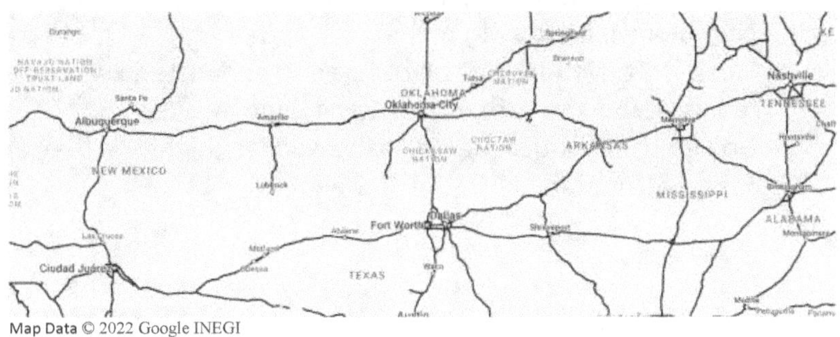

Map Data © 2022 Google INEGI

Memphis to Albuquerque

I wake up to a loud squeal, and lift my head but see nothing. I move my body, trying to get comfortable so I can see. It's black out. The window has steamed up so I wind it down. The night sky is lit up with stars. Beautiful, but cool. I don't want to move to go outside despite feeling broken from the hard floor.

Thinking I either dreamt it or it was an animal, I close the window and try to move to a decent position on my side. I must have been sleeping on my right side as that hip seems particularly sore, so I switch to my left.

Closing my eyes, I try to drift off. I see Cruz's face again. I feel my horror, the shock over again. Then I think of what would have happened if he'd shot me. The blood on my clothes would have been mine. A hole in me. Would I have felt it? Did Cruz feel the pain before he died? It was so quick. Should I have died then? I was so slow to act. If Gary's friend hadn't have fired that would have been me. Mia was right, I should have been killed.

But I wasn't. I survived. To what end? To be in a worse mess? Why didn't I stay out of it when I could? Why did I talk to the press? Why did I call the station all those times?

Because of Daniela. She deserved to have justice. Her daughter does as well. Does that mean Mia deserves the same?

Maybe being around these violent men has hardened her more. Death and violence are routine. Sad way for a thirteen year old to end up. What chance has she got?

At the moment that chance is me. Hardly a resounding success being landed with me.

Sleep isn't coming. Last night I was so exhausted I was out like a light. Now I'm sore, bruised and wide awake.

Do I go to Albuquerque? Like she said last night, neither of us has a better plan.

***

After a trip to the gas station to freshen up, we drive east on the I40 towards Little Rock on the long road to New Mexico. I haven't come up with a better idea since the morning. Sleep must have come to me at some point, but it took a while. My eyes feel like dried up waterholes and my back like a broken bridge.

The Volvo moans in complaint as it maintains top gear. After three days with this car I'm beginning to get used to the feel of it and how to keep it moving. I miss my van - this is like manoeuvring a sofa towing a train. I feel like I'm dragging it along by leaning forward in my seat, encouraging another two clicks on the speed. The noise is irritating, sounding more like the engine's in the seat beside me than under the hood. Not even a working radio to drown it out. This thing could die any minute on us and we would be seriously screwed.

Still, it's a car, and the only means we've got to get anywhere. All I ask is that it keeps going forward.

'Tell me more about the Albuquerque woman,' I ask Mia.

'She's a lawyer, worked for my Papá. When Mom got killed Papá was arrested and she got him off.'

'Oh ok,' I reply. 'So why exactly do you have such a good relationship with her that she won't just take you to the local gang trailer park and then invite them to take turns in busting my balls?'

'Because that's what Sophia said to me. Sophia is her name. If I ever needed anything, I could go to her.'

I think about what she's saying. I'm missing something.

'Sorry, I don't buy it. Why is she in Albuquerque and not Nashville?'

'You know we weren't a normal family. Sophia worked for the gang. I don't know what she did; she was there along with a few other faces in suits. Rich kids, but it was us making them rich. I was told we paid them to keep us out of jail and that's all I needed to know. None of us saw fancy money like that. We sleep in a trailer whilst they go back to nice houses paid for by Mommy and Daddy. She was one of them, but she was different. Talked to me like she wasn't scared. I can't explain, except she made me feel safe. No-one is ever safe, but she gave some confidence. But then she got in too deep. Papá's girlfriend did something. I don't know what. She drugged her or something. She had an OD. I told you, Nicole's a real bitch. Jealous cow. Sophia was too friendly with Papá and me. Nicole didn't like it.'

'So Sophia ran away before Nicole killed or drugged her again?'

'You don't run away from the Sula 7. She got moved out. Albuquerque. She called me to check I was ok a few times.'

'And you think she's still there?'

'Dunno. We can't exactly call ahead.'

'And you are sure she won't just call the Sula 7?'

'I just know. She won't.'

I keep checking her face to see if this is some kind of con, but I can't see any of the malice of yesterday. The more she talks about Sophia, the more she seems positive. Not that I'm totally convinced, just that I'm finding less reasons to not go. More answers are needed.

'Why did Sophia work for the gang?'

'I don't know. Most people don't get a choice. Sula 7 come knocking, then you either do what they say or if you don't... If you go to the cops, it's worse. They find a weakness, like a kid or family member, threaten to kill them. They usually do it anyway once it's over. They find a way to get control of people.'

'You're quite the expert.'

'Yeah, I am. Just remember, it's in my blood.'

I turn quickly to the right. She's staring straight ahead. Was that a threat or just a throwaway line? I'm the one driving the car but I think Mia is far more in control than I am.

***

The drive continues through the day, but we are barely past Oklahoma and my eyes are struggling to see the distant horizon. It's time to stop. The long straight highways are boring, and whilst the landscape is flatter and less green, I can't tell where we are. It's late afternoon, and so time for food and rest. I check the cell phone for the distance from Memphis. Five hundred miles. No wonder I'm cooked. Especially in this heap. Feels like I walked not drove.

'Are you ok staying in the car or should we go to a motel?' I ask.

'I can handle it,' Mia says.

'Sure?' I was secretly hoping she would scream for a bed and I would concede, trying to get the motel owner to take cash only.

'Well if you're going to hand over your credit card to the owner, then every cop in the state is going to come knocking on the door by five a.m.. Sure - this shitty little car will do just fine.'

Why is it I'm letting a thirteen year old dictate the odds?

'It's not my fault Crazy Cruz trashed my van. There would have been a whole heap of room in there.'

'Make yourself useful and go to the liquor store. The least you can do for abducting me is let me get drunk.'

'It's an offence to give alcohol to a minor,' I say. At least the mood is lighter. The tension of last night has gone.

'And it's an even bigger offence to abduct a kid. Even a nobody like me will get you a full life term in the slammer.'

I laugh. 'But you came by your own choice.'

'If the cops catch us, then I'll be screaming that you raped me and tied me up.'

'What the fuck, Mia? You can't say that.'

'Serious, Donnie. I got to protect myself. If they take me back to Nashville, I'm going to have to play it smart. I'm going to be victim all along the way until they go soft on me. I'll need them crying. Papá did the same with me when he got arrested. Trained me to cry real well and plead bail or whatever so he could look after me. Once they're not looking at me, I'll run.'

'You'd get me arrested though? I'd be in the slammer.'

'Best you be good to me then. I like Bud, if you're asking.'

I shake my head. I'm so dumb, being played like this. I pull off the highway and into another mall complex. Time for another cigarette as she goes ahead as usual.

Once the cigarette is done, I wander slowly to the washroom. What am I doing? She's right that I don't know who I'm dealing with and I'm completely out of my depth. The further I go from Nashville the less I feel I can go back. More than twenty-four hours since I spoke to Rose. Feels like forever.

I enter the mall and pull my cap once more over my head.

Even keeping going is not a good option. I'm walking a tightrope between two mountains and the rope is fraying as I get further towards the middle. At some point the rope will break and I guess I'll be clinging on for dear life. Even if the rope doesn't snap, I don't what's waiting on the other side. Cops? Another gang? Or maybe some other random mess that I haven't considered.

Perhaps Mia is right. At least a few drinks from the liquor store will blot out all the fear.

It's an hour later when I see a sign for Dead Woman's Crossing. Seems as good as spot as any to explore and there are no buildings or properties in sight. I find a bridge over a river but not much else. A place to park and stop with no-one around. Inconsequential place for a significant name. The evening light soon fades to dark. I work my way through a stack of Burger Kings and a case of Bud.

Whilst I'm outside smoking, Mia is googling the place on the burner cell phone.

'Dead Woman's Crossing is named after a murder of a local woman. She was decapitated and they never found her murderer. She haunts the bridge. Love a good horror story. Do you think we'll see her tonight?'

'Reckon, the only thing I intend on seeing is the back of my eyelids. You hear me?'

'Don't be boring. She was trying to run away with a baby. Got divorced. Husband must have been evil. 1905. Bet he beat her or was horrible to her. Must have been him who murdered her. Come on. Why didn't he get hung for it?'

'Most likely, Mia, he was white and rich and that pretty much got you off most things in those days. Saying the same now, I'd imagine. You got enough money in these parts you can murder the Pope and they'll let you walk.'

'Especially if he is an immigrant, right? Or gay.'

'Exactly that,' I say.

And with that we get the car organised for sleep again. The prospect of the hard floor of the trunk does not fill me with joy.

Crawling into my sleeping bag I think about home. I miss Rose. I hadn't thought too much about her in the craziness of the last forty eight hours, but she should be here. She would have cursed and complained about the car the journey the food, even the beer. Even with all the complaints, I would love to be curling up with her, making all the pain go away.

Chapter 19

I wake up with my head clouded with thoughts of Rose. If it wasn't for the awkwardness of moving in this hard metal box, I might have gone for the burner cell and dialled her number. I will at some point... I'll have to. Only when I'm safe or I think she is. The police must be monitoring her cell - or am I being too paranoid? I really hope she's safe. Gary and Hugh won't allow anything to happen to her. Same with Mom I expect. As long as they aren't on the hook for killing Cruz. Given that Mia and I are the only witnesses, it's hard to imagine how the cops would know it's them.

I can't worry about that at the moment. The point of me running away was to make it safe for Rose, Mom and Bernadette. Contacting her won't help.

We met at a gig. Surprise, surprise. I was in a teenage band, going anywhere from Fleetwood Mac cover to the inevitable crap original song to a rocked up version of a Dolly Parton classic. Rose was in the crowd, though crowd was not really the right word - it was a few friends and family. Maybe a few hangers on. She was hanging out with a few girlfriends who came along. It was probably the last time I saw Rose with girlfriends. She has never been a girl power type. Nor has she ever been a man's woman or some shit like that. Rose was just her own thing. Set her own likes and dislikes and no man or woman was going to tell her what to do. Her looks were a little tamer in those days. Less tattoos, and her hair in a pink beehive. That's what caught my eye that day. She stood out like stripper in a churchyard and whilst we were the ones on stage, the show was all her in my eyes. I bummed a few notes that night, which is why I try not to look at audience's faces these days - it distracts me too much.

Rose hung around after the show. 'What a bunch of losers,' she said. 'You trying to show off to me with that shit? You got more chance of making a girl sterile than impressing her any.'

She spoke and I was done. Her voice like crushed sugar on a bass drum. I didn't know that this is what I'd been waiting for all my life. Close up, her light green eyes against her pale white skin were faded pebbles on a baking hot beach. Despite her acid tongue, no-one else comes close to that combination of beauty, character and fire. She was made for music; anger, passion, energy, and balls to say anything and do anything she wanted.

I replied with some trash talk but she didn't pay no mind to that. Her next line was the line I remember to this day.

'See you up there on stage. You can be the fire or you can be the wood, burning away until you're nothing but ashes. You can't be both. You wanna guess what I'm?'

'The fire,' I feebly said.

'And what about you?'

That's where it started and now's where it likely ends. I might not be ashes yet but I'm burning badly without her.

I look at Mia. Youthful innocence lost in a dark stare. A face fixed forward because looking to the side, maybe there are too many things to see, thing she doesn't have. Heap of reasons to not look back at all. She has something of Rose in her. A spark that fires when needed. I guess you don't live her life without quickly learning what's needed to survive. Trailer parks, murder, drugs and God knows what else. Did Daniela have that same instinct? I never had to face that kind of shit... until now, I suppose. I'm finding no instinct for survival. I'm happy to keep running but come some point I have to turn back around and face whatever troubles come. Damned if I'm going to handle it on my own. I'm as likely to be on my knees praying to God or pleading for mercy before I get a bullet in my head. Would Mia be like that? Look how she was when faced with Gary and Hugh with AR15 rifles pointing at her. She didn't squeal or cry.

Dead Woman's Crossing. Ain't that a thing? Woman disposed of for some guy's convenience. Hope she haunted him to his grave 'till he was shitting his pants every night. Did she know her destiny before it happened? Daniela was brave until the end. Another woman killed for someone's convenience. She knew she was dying. Coming all the way to the States was dangerous but still she did what she had to. Strikes me the women in these stories are making all the hard yards.

What about her daughter Opal? I picture her in some kind of camp with other girls, ugly brutal men all around. How does she keep safe? What's the future for her? For Mia? For me?

Somewhere in Albuquerque, is my next guess. We get an early start. With a decent drive and the car holding out, I'm hoping to be there sometime in the afternoon. The landscape changes to a more arid landscape but still with the wide prairie-like vistas.

Mostly it's boring. We don't talk. There's not much to say.

I'm sick of the car, sick of the noise the engine makes, the boring road. If Mia does have this good relationship with this lawyer woman, do I leave her there? Is it far enough away to be safe for me? And then what do I do?

All these questions. I dread the next minute, the next hour, the next day as each will bring me closer to a bad outcome. But I can't turn back.

The distance markers count down to less than a hundred miles and I feel like we're getting closer.

Time for some planning. I turn to Mia.

'How do I know I can trust Sophia?'

'Not sure you can trust her. But I can,' she replies.

'So as long as you're alright, then I'll be.'

'Lift your head out your ass. How did you ever get laid? You're a pussy.'

'Seriously. Is this where we are now?'

'Yeah, what do you think?'

'So smart girl, what should I be doing? Maybe I just dump you on the fucking highway.' She turns away. 'Sorry,' I say, regretting raising my voice. It's one thing to let a kid wind you up, but I'm also arguing with myself. At this point, she's just an extension of my alter ego telling me I'm better off turning round and going home.

Mia doesn't engage with my apology, instead she stares out towards the prairie. After a few minutes of silence she responds.

'What do you exactly want to happen?'

I look at the road ahead. The wagons, the trucks and the endless road to nowhere.

'Plan A,' I say, 'We get to this place. Sophia's a nice lady. She puts on the news and I find out all the bad guys got arrested. I can go home and you can stay with her. Everything goes back to normal.'

'You just dump me?'

'Would you rather stick with me? You would be better with her wouldn't you?'

She shrugs. That wasn't quite what I expected, but then maybe she has no idea what's going to happen either. Perhaps I'm giving her too much respect for her streetwise experience.

'What about Opal?' she says. 'You going to let her suffer in Honduras? You given up on her?'

'What can I do for her?' I ask. 'Look at me, you just said I'm a pussy with no plan. How do I get even close to getting her away from a gang and then what do I do? How do I get a foreigner into the US? I'm nobody. Nothing. All I'll end up doing is getting her killed and probably me and maybe you too. Like I said before, I'll call a local charity - that's about the best I can do.'

'Pussy.'

'Whatever.'

'Now who's the child?'

I feel guilty for abandoning Opal, but what do I do? It was never my fight in the first place. If I hadn't been in that alley, I wouldn't even have known she existed. Except now I do.

'Plan B then? Especially as Plan A is shit.'

'You don't have a sweet kid setting, do you?'

'Where I come from, we don't have the luxury. It's shit and if you tell me otherwise, you're lying.'

'Ok, I don't know,' I say. 'I was going to take it as it comes. I was hoping your lawyer friend could advise us, help us. I don't know.'

'We got how long?'

'One, maybe two hours.'

'Better get thinking then, Donnie. Because something you going to learn about Sophia: she don't take no prisoners either. You get the wrong side of her and she'll be calling Nashville up and they'll be smashing your sorry ass before you can find the keys to this shit tip Volvo.'

'Thanks for that,' I say. 'I feel so much better.'

***

Outside Albuquerque, we pull into a mall.

Mia takes out the burner cell phone. She slowly types the number from her own cell. I open the window and light up a smoke.

Mia looks at me, her face screwed up, unimpressed once again with the smell of smoke. I hold my hand out the window to pacify her.

'You ready with what she's going to say?' I ask.

'I am.' She pauses though. Her finger hovers over the call button. We've spent two days preparing for this.

She calls, the ringtone coming through loud on the speaker. It rings for some time.

'Hello?'

'Sophia, it's Mia,' she says, her hands shaking.

'Don't come to the house.' Sophia says quickly. A squeal follows and the call is cut.

'Shit, they must be there,' I say.

I feel sick. We look at each other. This wasn't a possibility we discussed. Surely it was obvious. They would know Mia was missing and this might be where she would come.

'What do we do?' Mia asks.

'You know the address right?'

'Have it written down in my cell, always had it.'

108

'They must have guessed you would come here. Where else would you go?'

'We have to help her,' Mia says, 'especially as she just warned us off.'

I think about the gun in the back. My heart is beating, bile rising in my throat. I've never considered using it, even at the cross roads two days ago, I was more aware of Gary or Hugh shooting than me. Now I'm the protector.

'I can call the cops,' Mia says.

'Once they hear the sirens, they'll kill her and run.'

'But if I'm there, I can be the distraction. They'll come out the house for me and that might give us chance to get her away.'

'You are not bait, Mia. It's too dangerous. I'll go in, you wait outside. I'll reason with them.' I'm saying the words but even I don't believe them. I stop speaking before I confirm my own idiocy. I look around the parking garage, checking every angle. I've been running for two whole days and never once been as paranoid as I'm now. Perhaps I should have been checking.

'My idea is a better one,' she says.

'I think we should just call the cops and leave you out of it. If we warn the cops to take them by surprise, no sirens, they might have a better chance.'

'How you going to convince the cops to do that? They not going to even believe you, some loser fugitive from Tennessee. They'll come for you before they even think about Sophia.'

'I could lie,' I say.

'And they still won't believe you. Cops are stupid but they definitely don't take instructions from idiots calling them up.'

'Ok.'

I pull the car back onto the road, driving slowly and tentatively. I'm not rushing to get there.

After twenty minutes we arrive in Fair Heights, a residential district in the east of the city. I head down the wide avenues, the houses not that different from my home suburb, except the yards are dry dust bowls rather than green and lush. The street's deserted - no-one outside in the heat of the day.

'It's further along the street, pull over here.'

'I can't believe you're going to do this.'

'Like my Papá used to say: always do what they least expect.'

'Reckon, that turned out well,' I say without thinking.

'Shut the fuck up.'

'Take this.' I hand her a handgun that Hugh gave me that's been under my seat. She needs something to defend herself and I'm no good.

'Remember, the minute you see me running. You come. Come fast.'

'I know, I know.'

She runs along the path towards the house until she's out of view in front of the house. I decide to get out the car so I can get a better view. I feel such a coward, but I know I would be unable to manufacture the same response as her.

Then I hear the screams. And she can scream loud.

'Rape!' she shouts.

Running into the centre of the street.

'They raped me!'

She screams loudly again, louder, more fire with each lungful. I see a car pull over. People coming out the houses. They must be hearing her on the other side of the city.

'Call the cops!' I hear a voice from a house.

There's a crowd gathering now and a few start to head closer towards Mia. I see guns out, the men of the street ready for trouble. This might not end well. If the neighbours start shooting, anything can happen.

I see a dark thin figure come into the street. He grabs Mia. Other figures approach her but the man pulls a gun. She screams again, more fierce and harsh. I think there is some genuine fear in those screams. I jog closer.

'Let her go!'

One of the neighbours shouts, his arms stretched out with his weapon cocked and ready. It's a stand-off.

A shot is fired from the house. Everyone turns and Mia takes her chance, shoving the dark man and escaping his grip. She runs out of sight while the stand-off continues with guns pointing. The darker man backs up towards the house and I hear a siren. I return to the Volvo, thinking I better be ready for Mia if she comes back.

More shots and I'm scared now. I start the car and drive closer. If Mia is going to get away, I need to be on point. The neighbours gather around the house, hands switching between cell phones and weapons.

The sirens are closer and the cops appear in the street from behind me. I pull to the side to let them pass. The cops are out the car, more shooters pointed. The neighbours disperse in response. The cops engage fire immediately. I don't hear any screams but I fear what I've started. What if one of the neighbours is killed and I caused this.

The shoot-out continues. The police approach the house and I'm sure whatever happens, it's all over now. Cops will raid the house, they'll find Mia, and then it won't be long before they find me. I may as well as hand myself in. I see a movement to my left and see Mia and a tall brunette woman behind her. They run across to the car opening the door. They jump in the back as I turn the car round. It's so big I can't turn in one go and I hear a shout from the cops.

'Go, go,' Mia shouts and I ram the gas pedal down and screech out of the street.

'Are you alright?'

'We're fine. Drive!' the woman I assume is Sophia shouts. I look in the mirror and I can she is bleeding from a head wound.

More sirens but I'm not stopping. I pull round another corner on the estate and force the gas pedal down. The engine complains and misfires but I ignore it and keep moving. The worst getaway car ever. Ahead, I can see the up ramp for the freeway. It's heading east but I don't care. I need to get away. Again I put my foot on the gas back the way we came this morning. Looking in my mirror, there is no-one following, but I assume they can track me on the highway here so I turn off the next ramp and head off into the scrubland to the south.

We pull onto a hidden dust road and as soon as I'm out of sight of the road, I stop. We all get out and take a breath. I grab some water from the back and hand it to the woman.

'Sophia?'

'That's me. You must be Donnie Knight.'

She's tall, slim and dark. Older than me but not sure by how much. She's wearing jeans and grey t-shirt which is torn at the top.

I pass her some towels from the back.

'Sorry about all this.' I say.

'We got her out. We did.' Mia is hyper and excited jumping around.

'She's some kid,' Sophia says. Her accent is Spanish but her English is good.

'How did you get her out?' I ask.

'There were only two of them. Once she was screaming outside, one had to go see. As soon as they came to the door the other guy panicked and started shouting. That was my chance. I found Mia by the side fence.'

'And the cut?'

'That was a gun butt after the call. It hurt like hell but it's nothing.'

'What do we now?' I ask.

'Get the fuck out of here.'

'Where to? What about your house?'

She shrugs.

'You want to go back there? It's a house. I rent it. Fuck 'em. Cops will be all over it now. I can't go back there.'

'Where do we go then?'

'South, Mexico. We need to get as far away from here as possible.'

'But we haven't got passport or ID,' Mia says. 'It's why we came to you.'

'Good then that I know someone who can help. But it's going to be expensive. First let's get away from here. It'll be dark in an hour. Got a beer?'

I hand her one from the case in the back. She downs it in one long drag.

She wipes her mouth and then goes to the car mirror to check her appearance. She wipes the blood from her forehead and from her hair. She walks off into the bush and I don't ask why. Mia is sat on the hood.

'I knew she would make things better,' she says.

'Better?'

I get in the car. I suppose it's good to have someone who has more experience of dealing with these people but I in no way think things are better than before. I say nothing though - what's the point? I don't want to doubt her confidence in Sophia - in fact it is best all round if they both are happy to get along. As for our situation, whether I think the cops are my enemies or The Sula 7, both them are going to be more pissed at me than ever before. Reflecting now on what happened back in Nashville, a good lawyer would have fixed the whole thing with Cruz, whatever Mia told them. I shouldn't have panicked. But that ship has sailed. Technically I still don't think I did anything wrong, but there isn't a soul in the land who's going to believe a word that comes out of my mouth.

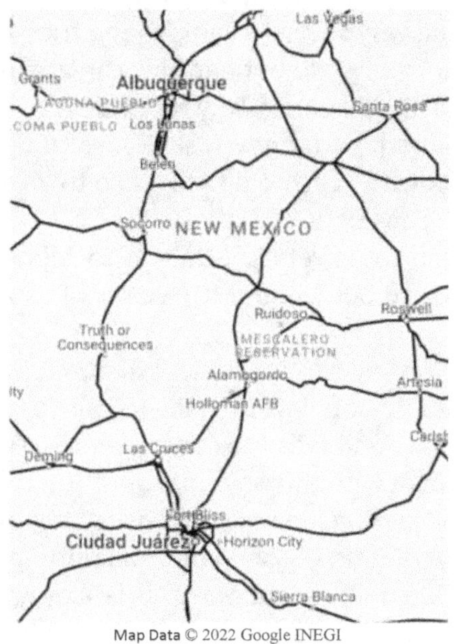

Chapter 20

Map Data © 2022 Google INEGI

Truth or Consequences, New Mexico

Another night, another fast food joint.

Now there's three of us debating our situation over burgers, veggie tacos, fries and more bottles of beer. A definite theme. It's a clear desert night and we still need to decide where we can stay.

Who knew there's a town called Truth or Consequences approaching the Mexican border? I don't claim to be clever or insightful but whoever named this place knew what they were doing. Though the less interesting revelation from Sophia is that this was a deal done for hosting a game show. Its real name was Little Springs, but Truth or Consequences feels exactly the right place to be having this conversation

'We need new transport,' Sophia says. 'It can't be long before they find us. Plus this shitty vehicle will result in one of us killing the other before any Sula 7 find us.

I smile at the way she says vehicle. She tries to say it the way southerners do, ve-h-ic-le but her Mexican accent makes it sound as if she's talking up a new rap chorus.

'That would require money,' I say. 'Just for the record, with gas and fast food, my cash is down. If I go to an ATM, that's a gimme for the cops right?'

'You said you could get ID,' Mia says to Sophia. 'We're fifty miles from Mexico but without ID, we might as well be back in Nashville.'

'I'm all for Nashville,' I say. I thought about it more and more since we picked up Sophia. I'm going to call Rose soon as I get done. Head home and face the consequences. Gangs or no gangs, I can't deal with this anymore.

'It was your fucking idea to come here,' Mia snaps back. 'Fucking pussy. All that bullshit about not letting any harm come to me. You only care about your fancy gringo ass. You brought me here because you thought I would snitch on you to the Feds. Admit it.'

'Tell me again what the fuck you got me into,' Sophia asks.

I give her a rundown of the last week.

'And this Honduran kid? What you doing about that?'

I shrug my shoulders. 'Nothing I can do, right? As Mia says, I'm a gringo pussy who can't wipe my own ass without a perfumed napkin. What do I know?'

'She's right about that. And Mia, you thinking I'm going to play Mom or something?'

Mia stares hard at Sophia.

'Mia, you're a smart kid but I'm no fucking mother. I can barely sort my own shit.'

'I don't need a mother, I need some where to live. I never asked you for a thing. Nothing, nada.'

This conversation is spiralling like piss spraying round the can and it won't be long before it turns to serious shit. Though I'm in no mood to rescue it either. Come to think of it, suits me that we all get angry and walk out of here, three separate ways and never look back. Guilt or no guilt. I'm not a hero.

'And where were you both going to go if I wasn't here? Set up house in a tent in the desert? Busk for money on the highway. The Guitar Pussy and Niña Puta, you can call it.' She flicks her hair back mid-rant and eyes wide, arms in the air, pretending to laugh at her crap joke, before banging her hands on the table. 'Oh that's right, you were going to fucking Honduras, find some family of Mia's who she doesn't even know. Like hell you are. Oh, then find the gang who's holding this Opal niña, steal her away from the locals, get her out of the country. Then even more crazy, getting her into the US. And then you were suddenly expecting the DA of Nashville to drop everything, pay you $50,000 dollars, take the girl into his happy family, pay off the gang and everyone living happily fucking after. You couldn't make up this shit. Wasting my time. I heard better stories from my mama when she's telling me about poor people starving because I don't wanna eat a smelly disgusting pig's intestine.'

I'm silent. I've nothing to say. I take a drink of beer, resisting the urge to smash it on the table. I look to the door. Is this the moment to go? The Volvo will just about get me back to Tennessee. I need a smoke, if nothing else, give myself a minute to think away from these two bitching at me.

'We're fucked aren't we?' Mia says.

'You think?' Sophia says. 'And thanks very much, but you've fucked me along the way.'

'I'm done,' I say, standing up.

'Sit the fuck down,' Sophia says, standing up to me. I'm just about taller than her but she's as scary as Rose on a bad day. Her face is rock solid fury and I think she's going to flatten me if I move a muscle. 'You don't get to walk away from this.'

I take my seat slowly without taking my eyes off her.

'What do you think I'm going do, Sophia?' You already laid it out fair and square. Make me out to be the fool all you want, but it don't change anything. I should go.'

She shakes her head at me and then at Mia. Her face blushing bright red.

I think being here is a major mistake. She's off her head.

'You bring me hell, get me kicked out my house. Lose my job, my money, everything I worked for. Yes I'm loco, crazy woman. I see the look in your eyes. You thought I was going to save your asses but now you wanna run away. No fucking way. You are in this with me. Got it?'

We both nod silently. Even my mother never got this angry.

She bangs the table.

'Got it?' She shouts, leaning forward, her eyes seeking out a response from us. We lean back, her ferocity uncomfortable, scary. I look round the diner. Only two tables with folk at them, all of them staring at us. Sophia isn't concerned.

'Say it,' she demands.

'Yeah,' I say.

'It's cool,' Mia says.

'Either of you run away… I'm coming after you and I'll kill you.'

I believe her. I thought I was running away from one burning house fire and now it strikes me Sophia could set the whole state ablaze, talk about dragon fire. Good work, Donnie.

'As for the girl in Honduras,' she says, pointing to me. 'You can't ignore her. That woman went through everything to protect her daughter and if someone doesn't get her out of there then she's going end up turning tricks or drugs. Or just dead. That might be the better of her options.'

'I can't go there,' I say. 'It's too far, and I wouldn't know what to do. Her father should be dealing with it.'

'It's your conscience, kid,' she says, 'but one day you might grow a pair and do something good with your life.'

'Says you, protecting murderers, drug dealers and rapists,' I reply. My anger at being lectured to is not going to fade quickly.

'Fuck you,' she replies, 'you don't know anything about me.' She returns to eating her food.

For the moment, the talking seems to be done and the food is consumed in silence. I can't wait to get out of here.

'I need some sleep,' I say as we return to the car. 'We can drive to somewhere quiet and rest. You and Mia can sleep in the back. I'll push the seat back and sleep. Seriously, I can't drive another mile.'

There are no objections so I pull back out of the car park. As we drive to the outskirts of the city, I hear sirens.

'Is that for us?' I ask Sophia.

'Let's assume it is. Give me the wheel. No more townie driving from you – we're going down to the lakeside. Rio Grande, the reservoir not the river. It's not far out of town. We can rough camp there. It's kinda quiet save for a few townies looking for a bit of car sex.' She looks in the back and back at me. 'Though looking at us, I damn hope no-one thinks that's what we're going to be doing.'

'Gross,' Mia says.

I pull over, shaking that thought from my head. Not even worthy of a response. With my eyelids feeling like they are carrying fishing weights and eyes dry as the grit sand outside, I'm too tired to argue about driving. She's free to take the wheel.

She jumps into the driver's seat and revs the engine. In a squeal of tyres we race away. Three days, I've been in this heap and I never got it to move like that. We hit the intersection at the edge of town and go directly across. The roads are empty and we go down the canyon road. Though it is pitch black it's not hilly enough to hide the car lights from the highway.

'We're close to the reservoir. I'm going to kill the headlamps and navigate with my eyes. That way, no-one will know we are out here.'

We slow down and for a moment I can't see anything of the terrain ahead. The moon is close to full and the lights of El Paso in the distance provide a shimmering amber glow.

After a few hundred metres of crawling we pull up.

'This'll do,' Sophia says, 'Bit of bush to hide the car from the road.

I get out. I can hear waves breaking lightly on the shore off the lake. I keep walking to the edge and find myself stripping off and walk on into the water.

I need to clean, refresh myself. It's very shallow at the bank so I don't succeed well but I'm grateful at least being able to sit down in the water. I take a few minutes and then head back to car. Neither Sophia nor Mia pay any attention to me. I take a towel and dry myself off.

Sophia is sat on the tailgate drinking more beer. I open one too and light a cigarette.

'I've got an idea,' she says. 'It's all or nothing, though. I mean seriously dangerous, high risk and probably stupid. But if we don't do it, we'll be fucked anyway. Like Mia already said.'

'What's the plan?' It's a relief that it's calm Sophia now, not the raging bull from the diner. At least she's thinking ahead.

'Leave it until the morning. I need to think it through. I might decide it's too stupid anyway.'

'A clue?'

'You learn a lot of stuff working for a gang, not least where they hide their gear and ways of working. In fact, I invented a few schemes. Money laundering is an intricate business. If you are going to do it well, you need clever people like me.

I nod along and think I've heard enough. If she's thinking of messing with the gangs, well I already know how that ends. I ask a question instead.

'How did they get to you?'

'What do you mean, "get to you"?'

'I mean working for gangbangers, rapists, drug smugglers, pimps. It's hardly top class work, they must pay you well.'

She laughs.

'You ever been in a courthouse?'

'Yeah, my Dad was a regular - he has a thing for cheap whores.'

'And looking across at them in the dock. Did you ever see one in a suit? Smart dress? Wife, parents and family from church looking on with their gold plated bibles?'

'Course not.'

'Unless you working for the big city firms with them white collar clients with suitcases of cash, this is your brief. Pimps, gangbangers, murderers. They don't come with families and bibles.'

I look up. Stars fill the night sky. The full moon is glorious. Moments like this, I wish I took the time to know something of the stars. But I was bored at school, learnt guitar instead and this is where I ended up. In a desert in New Mexico with a crazy lawyer who seems capable of anything, including self-destruction. I take an extra drag on the cigarette, enjoying the sensation of smoke filling my lungs.

'But the gangs,' I say, 'that's a different league, isn't it?'

'I'm Mexican. I speak Spanish and English well, so I'm already useful.'

'There is no shortage of lawyers who speak Spanish.'

I feel my attempt a being smart is about to get shot down as her faces opens up, her eyes wide in a very definite 'what the actual fuck' response.

'Correct, smart boy. Round of applause. You really got me. Listen, Donnie Dick - is that your stage name? This is never about me taking dirty money or Spanish or your moral bullshit. Who the fuck hauls your Papa's ass out of jail every time? Someone's got to do it or you would know visiting times at the Nashville penitentiary better than the cocaine dealers. Yeah I get paid for doing what's needed, that's the job. But working for these people is not like any job. It comes with a commitment which is not optional. It's not enough to just be a lawyer, you have to be on the inside. That means you have to be compromised? Understand? That way I go the extra mile in any cases. That way, I'm prepared to break laws, use equally compromised private dicks who will snoop and find information. That takes a certain determination of purpose based on the price of failure.'

'So that means you're compromised, is that it?'

'They gave me a heroin addiction.'

'How did the hell they do that?'

'It didn't start there, dick boy. I didn't come into the office one day with my arm outstretched with a sharpie arrow telling them which vein to inject.'

I ignore the insults. Reckon, it's something I'm going to have to get used to with her around.

'They target lawyers like me. College fees to pay, student loans. They know we are looking out for the big law firms; rich kid jobs and we don't have the right connections. They offer some freelance work, through a low-level practice, bonuses off the record. Of course, the practice is in on the take as well, but I don't know that until I am already too well involved. They made me think I was the smart one, playing the system. I do well, I get more work. Doing well means get them off charges, staying out of jail. Taking pleas is fine as long as they got cash, they pay the fines all good. Even if they got to serve a few years, also fine as they are protected well with other members on the inside and compromised jailors. And they can run drugs on the inside same as they can on the outside. Lawyers like me are there to limit the damage, especially for those at the top.'

'Anyway, I get close. Knowing people, they draw me in. Look, I don't need to justify myself. I see the look on your face.'

Absolutely not sure she can see the look on my face in the dark but I've already learnt that being a smart mouth isn't going to win me any favours.

'I got invited in with the gang bosses. I know, don't need to tell me anything. I should have seen it coming. There was product everywhere and I took a few lines. Tequila, whisky on top. Extra bucks were everywhere, and I thought I was doing well because all those slimy bastards want to fuck the lawyer in a suit. I thought I could read them all, men they all the same with a pretty girl in a skirt and pantyhose.'

'I overplayed my hand.' She pauses for a moment, sipping from her bottle and I guess we are getting to the crux of the story. 'They wanted sex they could get girls anywhere anyhow. Not one of them ever cared about dating or serious seduction. They wanted women they took 'em. I was there for one reason only and that was for recruitment. Got trashed one night too many and that was it. Tied me down, injected me, raped me as well. They did what they always do … made me a victim, made me their plaything to abuse as they needed. Once they had me on that shit, I was theirs.

'Afterwards they clean me up, give me new clothes, place to live, fancy car and feed me regular gear as long as I do the job. No way back and no way out.'

'You could have gone to the cops.' I realise as soon as I say it, that's not an option and never would be.

'You get it now?' She asks. 'I would be dead if I spoke to a cop. Plus, you ever know a cop do a favour for a lawyer?'

She tips her head at me as I shrug.

'I know where this leads. I know one day I'm going to be lay in a gutter somewhere and no fucker is going to stop and help me. I'll die there. But every day I'm still alive and surviving is one day I can use to get back what I want... which is my life...my future. If I didn't fight for myself, I'd just inject it uncut and pure. Wave adios and go out with the best hit of my life.'

I sigh. Throwing the last of the cigarette. How do I respond to that?

'Have you got a fix now?'

'No.'

This explains some of her moods. Addiction never made anyone easy to be with.

'How long before you go before you need another fix?'

'Not long enough,' she replies.

Chapter 21

I sleep ok but I'm not sure how much. I wake up several times. Exhaustion is like a heavy blanket over my head while discomfort means I toss if off frequently as I seek a position which doesn't involve some part of the car sticking into me.

The lecture from Sophia didn't help either. I'm so conflicted. Last night I convinced myself I had to go home and now she's telling me that I got to help her out and then fix the Opal problem in Honduras. Both seem so alien as well as scare the pants off me. It's been four days since I left Nashville. it's already feeling like a lifetime. I resolve to handle one day at a time. Nothing else I can do at the moment. Any grand plans will have to wait.

The lake provides a source of replenishment for all of us as dawn comes. Truth or Consequences might not be the safest place for us and we needed to decide on an action plan even to get some fresh coffee.

Sophia looks pale, her brunette hair curly and straggly after wading in the river. I could blame the circumstances but I think another few hours without a fix is adding to the pressure.

We gather round the back of the car, drinking the last of the water.

'What's the plan?' I ask.

Sophia wipes her mouth and rubs her face hard.

'You ok?' Mia asks.

'No, I'm fucking not,' she shouts back, raising a hand. 'Sorry Mia, I didn't mean that. Just tired is all. You know? Todo está bien.'

'Puta!' Mia replies.

'Ladies, please.'

They both turn to me with hard stares. Now I'm the target.

'Can we get back to the plan, Sophie?'

'Sophia, is my name. I'm not your fucking girlfriend.'

'Sure, Sure, Sophia. Just play nice y'all.' What did I do?

'Nothing as usual,' she responds looking me in the eye. She also imitates my voice with an extra few flat notes on the last syllable of 'usual'. Getting used to it now.

'Look, we need cash and a lot of it. Priority number one. Part of my supposed day job is working out where to shift drug money, legal and safe. Always better to use out of town joints no-one gives a hoot about.' She pauses, kicking the fender.' Actually two priorities. Dump this junk and get something better. Then do some raids. How much you got in cash?'

'Five thousand,' Mia says. 'Stole it from Papá's truck. Might be a bit less as we spent some on food and gas and some of the bedding.'

'Ok, give it to me - my face is not the one all over the TV. Mia, you wait here. Donnie, drive me to a car lot. Drop me and I'll see you back here. We can then switch over and go do the next job. Figure we'll get a van with some space in the back for sleeping. We might not be sleeping in a bed for a good while.'

'And then?'

'We gotta go back north and fire east a bit, place called Vaughn. There is a ranch out there with a thousand beasts... only he's shifting more meat than McDonalds, if you read the books. There's a whole complex, café, bar, got barely ten customers a day but read the till roll and you'd think they was selling cookies in the centre of New York. It's what it's about.'

'And how do we get the cash?' I ask.

'We're going to take it from right under their nose. These scammers don't take any notice of security. They rarely need it. One look at their faces and no-one comes near. The tattoos, the guns, the threat of the Sula 7. No-one will go near them.

'And why would it be ok for us?' I ask.

'First of all, we're already fucked. They already going to slay us once they find us. In theory we got nothing to lose any more. Can't kill us twice. But second and most important: these gang boys are not smart. They don't get an education like you home boys. All they got is guns and a dick for a brain. Ask Mia, she knows. It's easy to screw with them. They don't piss without getting it down their pants.'

'She's right. They look mean, but they're very stupid.'

'So that's alright then,' I say. 'All sounds so easy. And then once we have the money, assuming we aren't hanging from a meat hook by the end of the morning? What next?'

'We need passport and ID. I know some people in El Paso. But it's going to be expensive - hence we need that money.'

'Where we going?' I ask. 'I don't recall us deciding on any destination.' I'm all for a plan, but Sophia's priorities don't feel like mine.

'You tell me, lover boy,' she replies. 'If you're asking me, I want to put some distance between these crazy people who want to slice me and you open. Figure you want the same. Reckon that means getting over to Mexico until we get far enough away and enough money to get ourselves a new life. Honduras is kind of good this time of year. Nice beaches. Fancy that?'

'Sounds to me like running from a lynching, then falling in a bear pit. Either way, I see my life expectancy somewhere around this time tomorrow... if I get lucky.'

'You got a better plan Donnie Dick, I'm all ears, you know.'

'Don't call me that.'

'Sorry pretty boy, couldn't resist...reckon you know what I mean?' She drawls her words, mocking me again.

I shake my head and get in the Volvo. I really don't need this shit.

'Wait here,' Sophia says to Mia.

I stare back at a disgruntled Mia sat by the roadside as I fight to turn the Volvo. Getting new wheels feels the only positive for the morning.

***

An hour later, Sophia returns in white Ford E van. She has a new NY branded cap, sunglasses, fresh jeans and black T-shirt. I take a moment to look inside, pleased she got something

125

decent. It has a bench seat at the back that folds down to make a kind of bed, plus a 2nd row seat that Mia can at least lay horizontal. Enough room for us to bed down in it as well for a road trip.

We empty the Volvo and push it down to the lakeside out of view of the road. It will be found eventually but hopefully long after whatever this is, is over. My guitar and the overnight bag I carried from Nashville are placed in the back of the van. I check on the opal, hidden in the pocket in the lining of my bag. I roll it around in my hand, conscious of its beauty, mesmerised by the colours. It feels solid and pure. I put it back before I note its value. Thousands of dollars' worth but it doesn't feel like mine to give away or sell. That would be wrong, wouldn't it?

We drive out the valley using the back roads. It's slow, but once again I'm not in any rush to get to the destination. I'm not a veggie for nothing and the prospect of a meat factory as a destination is as chilling as it comes. I've avoided the conversation, no-one taking much notice of my choices at the fast-food places. Not that it's priority as a topic of conversation.

We arrive at a large yard beside the road. A café lies deserted at the back of the car park and a warehouse over in the distance. I guess that's the place to avoid.

Then it hits me.

I freeze. My guts churn inside. I can see out to the fields at the back and the smell of shit and the farm operation is strong in the air. I can't see the steers but I don't need to. I think about the blade, the slaughterman and the...

My stomach empties before I get to the drain outside the café. I wrench two or free times before I'm able to stand up again.

'You done?' Sophia asks.

I wipe myself down and ignore her. I follow towards the café door but she can't resist another jibe.

'You really got no stomach for this work, Donnie. Reckon you and your guitar need to get back to your peace camp, singing songs around the camp fire with your girlfriend. What do you think Mia?'

To her benefit Mia says nothing. I don't think she's quite on side with Sophia and her attitude yet. It's a blessing.

'What now?' I ask as we take a seat. I wipe my mouth with the serviette in the holder on the table.

'We get coffee,' she says, 'and wait. They will come with daily cash rounds. There's the auction mart at the back as you already saw. They go there first, check the takings before the meat trucks go to town. Make sure there is enough cash to balance the till. Then they come here.'

'How much will they take? Don't most people pay on account these days?' I try to make this conversation sound normal but my stomach isn't on board. It's turning like a laundry drum.

'Yeah, that's the legit business. That's why there's a shop for the average walk-in. To wash money you need a cash business to rinse it. So they bring the drug cash, drop it in. Later, in the day, it goes in the security vans to the bank. Clean as a whistle. Job done.'

'But there is literally no-one here. How do they get away with it?'

Sophia laughs. 'You're so fucking naïve. Think about it, Donnie. That money pays for lawyers like me if the Feds ever catch up with them. Local cops earn but a dime for a shit job. Not a cop in this state who can't be bribed, blackmailed for the right price. It's the way it is. Everyone just looks the other way. And if anyone does decide to pay attention, then that's a big risk to them, their families. You know what I mean. Look at you back in Nashville with Crazy Cruz. Sorry Mia, talking about your Papá this way, but he'd have no problem with slicing you up like a joint of meat in that slaughterhouse over there. It's the way it is.'

'Quit with the meat stuff, will you.'

'Okaaayyy.' She fakes a smile but ignore it.

'Shouldn't we leave Mia in the van, if The Sula 7 are coming here? Keep her safe, with all these shooters around?'

'What do you think, Mia?' Sophia asks.

'She needs me,' she says. 'I'm the distraction. One thing they're crap at dealing with is a mouthy kid. See what I did yesterday.'

I can't argue with that.

The table is close to the door, under the air con. A small relief as I'm struggling to breathe in the heat of the day. My armpits are probably growing disease spores, I feel so sweaty.

The diner is empty. Like Sophia says, if they're pushing thousands of accounts through the till, any one coming here for a tax audit would know in seconds this place is dodgy. The owner is a large man sitting behind the counter. His gut struggles against a white coat. Greasy hair under a catering hat which I imagine under close inspection reveals dandruff and bad skin. Some tattoo markings cover his skin. He looks like he's been in the slammer at some point - but then so many folk from small town America look just as rough and are proud of it. No-one going to tell them smarten up or get healthy otherwise you might find a rifle up your butt.

A young girl, barely older than Mia, serves us. I wonder if she's family or not. Pity her, if that's her parent. I thank the Lord for my God obsessed Mom and even my crappy Dad for a better offering than this kid has.

'Be ready?' Sophia says.

'I am, trust me.' I'm ready like I've got a brush shoved up my ass. I feel like I've been nothing but ready for everything to go wrong for the last week. Bring it on.

A pick-up arrives in the car park.

'They're here.'

'What do we do?'

'Shock and awe is what we do. Just be ready to run.'

Mia leads the way out of the diner. Sophia goes next and I follow closely behind acting like we are a family, hoping nobody noticing anything different.

The two gang members step from the pickup. One is completed bald with tattoos covering every spare bit of skin. I check out the snake tongue shape on the top of his head. A bolt earring stretches his earlobe to the extreme. The other wears a cowboy hat and large moustache. They are both wearing dark denim and look like they haven't washed in a month. Two large rifles are across their backs, knives strapped visibly to their shins.

Mia runs towards the men. They watch her with curiosity but no obvious concern. The bald headed one mutters some insult in Spanish and moves towards Mia to push her away. In a rapid movement she pulls a knife from her sleeve and stabs the moustached guy in the thigh. He screams and tries to grab her but she dodges quickly out of the way. The bald man, pulls his rifle and moves to point it at us but Sophia is well ahead, pulling the gun I had in the Volvo. She launches herself full force at him and he is pushed to the floor. I follow up behind, grabbing the rifle from the back of the moustache man. He goes for his shin knife but Mia kicks his hand, grabbing the knife as well. She stands on his hand as I point the rifle at them both.

The bald man squeals as Mia stamps hard on his foot. They were not expecting this.

Sophia points the other gun as the disarmed men recover on the floor. 'Mia, get the bag.'

Mia climbs in the pickup truck and retrieves a rucksack. She plunges the knife into the tyre so they can't follow us.

The fat diner owner appears with a rifle and moves to point it at me. Sophia turns and fires a round into his leg. He falls to the floor before he has chance to get a shot out.

'Run,' she screams.

I go to the diner owner and kick his gun away. Trying to point my gun equally at the two on the ground setting to get up again. Sophia is already at the wheel of the Ford and starts the engine. The side door is open as I dive inside and close it. We race away as shots are fired. The metal frame of the van is pounded but Sophia has her foot to the floor and we are away in the distance. Luckily they don't hit the tyres and we get away fast. Thank God we dumped the Volvo.

The desert roads are mostly straight so there is little sense of losing someone until we are miles in the distance. They will be looking for us. We already had targets on our backs, they just got bigger. Like the mad woman in the front says, they can't kill us twice, though at the moment, I figure they might want to bury us, dig us up again, just to work off all their anger.

'That was something,' I say. I'm dying for a smoke and my heart is still beating out of my chest.

'It's the way this has to be. These people will not hesitate for one second to kill us. The only way to handle this is to beat them at their own game. Be fast and efficient.'

'But we didn't kill anyone.'

'No, but maybe we should.'

'I'm not sure I'm cut out to be a murderer.' I say.

'Time to rethink that position, Donnie. And maybe your vegetarian sensitivities. Going to be a lot of blood spilling and you don't want it to yours. And if you don't, I might kill you myself for slowing me down. Even Mia's contributing. You see how she just stabbed that *cabron*. That's guts and training that is.' She turns to look at me in the back with a pretend smile. 'I might be the one with the addiction, but I'm not planning on checking out early.'

Sophia's addiction comes to mind. She's sweating, which is not unusual in this kind of heat, but her blouse is just full on wet. I'm still working out with her what's normal and erratic but her moods are seriously high voltage and she is constantly hyper. Other habits are itching and rubbing her hands on her legs and body as if she's trying to shun something out of her. I guess that all makes sense.

I stare out the window across the desert rocks, shunning thoughts of Sophia injecting shit into her veins, instead recalling the image of Crazy Cruz's head exploding in front of me. And then Daniela bleeding out in my hands. Oh for the peaceful days of Nashville. I still am no murderer, no matter how much talking Sophia does.

Chapter 22

New Mexico to El Paso, Texas

We head back South across country avoiding the highway. Sophia is behind the wheel while Mia and I count the money. It takes for ever as the money is not bundled, some of the bills are well used and dirty. After counting it, the total is nineteen thousand dollars.

'Is this all drug money?' I ask. 'Any other crimes I should be aware of?'

'Extortion, weapons changing hands, protection rackets, kidnappings. Select one or all of the above.'

'This is a serious amount of cash.'

'Welcome to the world of crime, my friend. There's a reason people do it.'

'Honestly, I heard of money laundering and I suppose I knew it was about making money from crime into legal bills - but seeing it like this? There's a clever process behind it.'

'That's the just the basics, Donnie. But it doesn't end there. When it comes to a tax audit, that little café is going to have a problem explaining how much profit it's making and that fat slob is no more going to want to pay his taxes than anyone. So now it's washed clean, and he can't pay himself a bonus as that is also going to attract a tax hit as well. Plus Marcos, my ex-boss, if you going to call him anything, wants that cash in his greasy pocket to pay for his whores and his security and all the other rewards of being rich. He is not going to pay the fat man at the diner any more than he has to. So here comes the secondary business operation which is where people like me add a bit of creativity.'

Watching her explain amuses me. The enthusiasm for the topic, shows she takes pride her in being able to be able to dodge law enforcement. Not sure it's something to be telling the grandkids.

'I set up fake businesses on the internet with overseas addresses and accounts. We process hundreds of fake expense transactions creating a legitimate service. For example, the diner there could pay for a consulting service or an interior designer as a way of building an expense for the money to be legally spent. The consultancy money then passes through offshore accounts into the gang leader's bank account or typically into Panama or other low tax countries. That cash appears as income against fake property assets like holiday lets in the Caribbean that no-one ever checks up on, as most of the time the Feds don't have the manpower.'

'That's complicated. I thought it was all supposed to be simple.'

'Simple is how you get caught. The world of banking has changed radically in the last twenty years. It's no longer about suitcases of cash. Cash is more easily traced than banking transactions nowadays, especially with CSIs all over it. Offshore banks are far more useful for hiding money.'

'Just so I get it – there's $19,000 dollars in this bag. It will be all run through the tills, but to avoid the idea that the diner is sitting on masses of cash, it's then used to procure invisible services. That way tax is dodged, the gangs create more income streams offshore. No wonder the country is going down the drain.'

'To be clear, this isn't just what criminal gangs are doing. Every other business that's cash rich is shifting money through similar schemes to dodge tax. Welcome to the modern world of private planes and islands.'

I make a noise to demonstrate being wowed. I am wowed. Should have paid attention at high school. Back home in Nashville, all I wanted to do was play guitar and dreamed of making an easy living. But I should have gone to banking school instead. Could still be playing my music but I would be a hell of a lot richer for it. No need for an RV if I got my own plane.

'So we didn't make $20k?' Sophia asks.

'No,' I reply.

'It's going to be tight then.'

'What for?' I ask.

'Paying for IDs etc. Need a decent whack for that.'

Shit. All the violence for nothing. 'Does that mean we need to do another joint?'

'No way,' Sophia says, 'we burnt that bridge for now. They'll be ready for us if we go anywhere near one of their drops.'

'Will Marcos work out where we are heading?'

'Your guess, is as good as mine, no? Let's imagine they're expecting us to try and get out of the country, then perhaps there is a risk they will follow us south.

'But they also don't know what we are planning. We could be heading to hide out in the US somewhere. Maybe in the north where it's safer.

'Who knows? They'll wait for the right moment. They have bigger chips to burn with the cops hanging around Albuquerque right now. Just be aware, they won't forget about us. In fact, don't be surprised if they haven't gone round visiting your place in Nashville. They don't play nice or fair.'

I feel sick. I hadn't figured they would go back with me gone. Hearing Sophia, my complacency was stupid. I've not even called to check; too obsessed with my own situation. Even now, I can't stop to call – there's too much at risk. Once we get to Mexico, I'll send a message. Just get through the day and then I can check they are ok.

We arrive at El Paso. Coming into the southern city, it feels a world away from Albuquerque, a universe away from Nashville. Albuquerque was an unremarkable dirt town, just a stopping post on the way to somewhere else. El Paso has a different feel. Busier, bustling. Surrounded by the hills the scenery is more dramatic. And the real highlight of the city, is that a few miles down the road is the Bridge to Mexico. And whilst for some Mexico may seem more dangerous, for us it offers some short term freedom from US cops and local gangs.

Entering the city outskirts off the highway, we drive into a back street and into a yard with a few garage businesses. One advertises itself as a printer.

The car park is empty and I'm relieved to step out and stretch my legs. It's still baking hot outside but the car is getting a little claustrophobic, especially given that harmony shows no sign of breaking out between us.

The streets are deserted. No sign of any customers or other activity.

Sophia leads the way.

We enter a small reception area and a small man, skinny, heavy moustache, in his fifties, appears.

'Miss Aldrez,' he says, 'long time no custom.'

'Lionel, you have no shortage of business in this town, not just me.'

'Got to be careful these days, you know. I do less and less. Someday I need to retire and get away from this.' He looks at each of us in term, starting intently. It makes me nervous and wonder if I should stare back or look away. Perhaps that's his job with ID forgery, studying us for risks or threats. I'm glad I'm not a vulnerable woman or I would be calling him a creep.

'You know and I know, Lionel. Retiring is not so easy.'

He mutters to himself and then asks. 'What do you need? You know I'm not keen on walk-ins.'

'An urgent one. Kind of personal. Three passports today.' She waves her hands to me and Mia and then to herself.

'You running? What's going on? I don't like surprises. You're checking out? If they find out I've given you a passport that could be it for me, my wife... my kids.'

He closes his book and packs his glasses away.

'How they going to know? I'm certainly not going to tell them. Other forgers exist.'

'Don't use that word. I'm a printer and an artist.'

'Yeah whatever. Can you do it?'

He looks at each of us again. Creepy. He opens his glasses case again.

'What ages?'

'Thirteen,' Sophia says, pointing towards Mia.

'Fourteen.' Mia says, 'I had my birthday yesterday.'

'Fourteen,' Sophia says with a sigh.

'Happy Birthday,' I say to Mia.

'Donnie. How old? Keep the focus.'

'Twenty-seven.'

'And forty-one.'

'US? $10,000 each. Let me see what I got.

'Five thousand. That's the usual per book.'

'I should charge treble just for you Miss Aldrez. You're going to get me killed. Hablo Espanol?'

'Si,' she replies.

'I can do Mexican for you and her. US for the boy. $18,000 take it or fuck off.'

He gets up from his chair and goes to the back room.

'That's going to clean us out.' I say.

'I'm doing the business here. Shut your slack yellow mouth. This is not a guitar shop where you pick a cheaper wank handle. Quality matters. This is serious.'

I shrug resisting the urge to say something. But keep quiet. It's not worth it.

Lionel returns with a camera.

'Up against the wall,' he says.

After taking each of our photographs he returns to the chair.

'Tomorrow morning.'

'We need them today. We can't hang around until tomorrow.' Her voice is raised and her eyes crossed. She looks to the street. I feel the same tension. We can't wait another day.

'You want them right, you wait until tomorrow,' he says, defensive.

'Come on Lionel, it's not like you're waiting for the ink to dry. I'm paying good money. Your daughter's school fees are right here.'

'Yeah, it'll pay for my fucking funeral when they find the bits of my body. Five o'clock. Not a minute earlier.'

We walk back out to the car. I'm wondering how we manage getting back into the US with Mexican papers, but I daren't ask another question. It's for Sophia to handle her own crap.
Maybe she doesn't intend to come back.

Chapter 23

We are back. It's five in the afternoon and I'm relieved we can get on the move again.

As a group we are barely communicating. Perhaps we all have too much to reflect on. I do. Mia and Sophia have taken to talking in Spanish when words are actually shared and I've giving up trying to guess what's going on between them. I'm assuming that the switch to Spanish is talk about me rather than to me but I'm not going to get paranoid about it. It matters little in the current situation as we need to stick together.

El Paso isn't very interesting but it's a hundred times better than Albuquerque, which was definitely some kind of elephant's graveyard. I miss the vibe of Nashville. It's not as high octane as New York or Chicago - it has a laidback feel. People are generally easy going. Life happens in a roundabout way. The music is always to the same beat. Here, there's the same slow element and there are many more Spanish voices in the streets and the bars. But it's dull, boring. Can't wait to get out of here.

We park up as before at the print shop and once again it's quiet. We enter, dutifully in line and wait for Lionel to show his face.

He enters with three envelopes.

'Check the names and date of births in here. This is now you. Be aware that at some point these may be tracked as fakes. I buy up a stock at a time of fake names and IDs I can use. I can never tell if the electronics are still valid, you'll only know when you get caught. Could be a year, could be tomorrow... could be never. Oh and you may find you've aged a little. I'm not caring about your sensibilities.'

'Ok thanks,' Sophia says.

'Don't thank me, just fuck off out. And Sophia, we are done. Take your business elsewhere.'

I open mine and see my new name. Blake Harrison. 1988. Jesus, I'm already 30.

As we walk out the door, still perusing our documents, none of us are paying much attention.

I look up and two pickup trucks are waiting outside.

'Shit.'

They must have turned up whilst we were inside. Both of them full of heavily tattooed men clad in black denim with AR15 rifles pointing directly at us.

I hear the shutters closing behind. 'Fucking Lionel,' Sophia says.

The three of us stand like statues. We have no moves to make, lined up like a firing squad. I begin to shake. I never signed up for this. I never went to war, I never fought anyone, even my gun has never been fired and here I am. All because I cared about a woman being murdered.

A door opens in the first pickup.

A tall fat man appears wearing a cowboy hat, a moustache that trails down into his chin mixing with the neck tattoos.

'Perdedores… desgraciados… ladrones… coños,' he says, each insult stressed for maximum effect.

'Buenas tardes, Marcos,' Sophia says.

I'm not sure of the precise translation but I recall something about losers and bastards. I think conos is something like pussy I recall from teenage years spent looking up slang words for stuff. I get the point.

Sophia stares calmly back, arms folded as if this is normal. Mia hides behind her slightly. Sophia has some balls, that's for sure, though I bet inside she's as scared as I am.

Marcos, clearly the leader or boss or whatever they call him, swaggers towards her. I recall her mentioning him this morning when she referred to the gang leader. He grabs Sophia by the neck with his large hand and pulls her forward. She scowls at him as he sniffs her. Odd to watch.

He curses in Spanish and I miss what he says. He pulls a knife and jams it into her stomach. Sophia cries out and fights to push the blade away as she falls to the floor. Mia screams and rushes to help her. Marcos grabs Mia and slaps her so hard she falls to the floor. He directs some of the gang members to grab her. It's not hard to envisage what they want to do with her.

I rush towards Sophia but Marcos pulls a pistol on me.

'Stay where you are,' he says, reverting to English.

Sophia is on the floor bleeding. She crawls to the doorway to try and get safe. I don't know what to do. I can't watch her die like this. Like Daniela. Behind the pickup Mia screams.

'I can fucking kill you all now. Easy. Bullet. Knife. No questions. Dead before you know it.'

He comes closer to me, gun in my face. Menace in the dark eyes, sweat on his brow running over his aged face. I want to collapse, I cling on to fresh air. Is he going to kill me? Is this it? I can't move.

He turns to Sophia on the floor. I breathe a moment.

'That doesn't get me my money back or pay the debt.'

Back at me now.

'Your debt is now five hundred thousand dollars.'

Another scream and then a shout from one of the men. Mia scrambles out from behind the car with another gang member trying to grab her leg. She is kicking at him, her face bleeding and top ripped. Another man appears clutching his crotch. He pulls a gun on her and she spits at him, cursing back at him.

'Leave her,' Marcos shouts.

He walks over to Sophia spits on her. 'Puta. Take your Mexican whore. If she isn't dead, she knows what to do. $500,000 dollars. Clean, washed, in my hands. No cops, no dirty money. One week. Seven days. No money, no life. I kill your family. Then I come and find you wherever you are. Mexico, America. I find you. You can take the kid and the whore with you, I don't want them.' He pauses, pointing to Sophia. 'I want to kill her now, stick the knife in and twist it hard inside and pull her guts out. I want her and you to know not to fuck with me. I still might do it. Seriously, you got to work hard and get my money. Otherwise I do her, you watch me, then the kid, then you.'

He kicks her one last time and walks back to the pickup. The others follow and they depart. I run to Sophia and then bang on Lionel's door to open up. He might have some bandages, something to stop the bleeding. But there is no response.

'Come on, let's get you to an ER.'

She stands, leaning on me and holding her stomach. Mia gets in the back with her. 'You ok,' I ask.

Mia says nothing and looks away, clinging to her torn strap, holding it in place. Her eyes are damp with tears. Not difficult to guess what those men were attempting to do or even what they did in the short time she was there. What a mess.

Ten minutes later, I park up and walk with her to entrance of the Emergency Room. Mia takes over and walks her in. 'Remember, it's a domestic, you don't want the police involved.'

I stay outside and wait. I see a payphone in the corner. I can't resist any longer so I pick it up and dial the number written into my memory.

'Rose,' I say.

'Donnie, where the fuck are you?'

'I can't say, Rose. I can't come back. Not yet. It's too dangerous for you. Stay safe. Stay home. Please.'

'Donnie, what happened, where are you? The police… they've been looking for you.'

'Can't say, don't ask. I love you.'

I put the cell down and slide down the wall crying.

Chapter 24

After an hour and two coffees I feel stronger. It's late evening now and we still need to get going. I want to get into Mexico tonight. Even if it's just to get over the border. It feels one step away from the police finding me. Then, I can breathe and we can make a new plan.

Sophia and Mia appear. Sophia walks slowly, holding her side, but seems ok.

'You ok?' I ask.

'I was lucky. It didn't go deep and missed the important stuff. If Marcos wanted me dead, he would have used a lot more force and probably gone for the heart or the throat. He made sure it hurt and that it was punishment. Marcos isn't stupid. With me dead, all he could expect would be more killing because there is no chance of you raising any sort of amount that would keep you alive or make it worth his while. That's why I am still walking and talking. Incidentally, also why you are not dead.'

I ignore the dig. I haven't grasped how utterly out of my depth I am yet, but Sophia is here to remind me in case I ever need to know.

'What did they say to you in there?'

'ER nurse stitched me up and told me to rest. She wanted to refer me to a ward but told them her, I had no credit card and no insurance; my husband had stolen it from me when he beat me. She had no choice. Handed me a check for drugs and hasta la vista.'

'What now?'

'To the border?'

'Just go.'

'Are you going to be ok to travel. What if the wound doesn't hold in Mexico?'

'Quit with the stupid questions. Just drive. I'll be ok. Fuck, you're not my nurse or carer or God forbid, my boyfriend. Jesus Christ. I am ok. I got painkillers and if not and I die. Then you won't have me chewing your butt off every five minutes and I won't have to hear your whining Nashville drawl.

'Pity the nurse didn't stitch up your mouth.' I slow my voice down to cause maximum irritation and take a tiny satisfaction when she returns an ugly stare.

A smirk from Mia, quiet in the back shows me my counter landed well.

I head towards the Highway. The sign for Juarez and Mexico is ahead of us. It might just read freedom in glowing lights. So close to being able to breathe.

'Turn off quick,' Sophia says. 'We got to dump those guns in the back. Border guards might check and we would be arrested.'

I turn the wheel at the last minute, getting a blast of the horn from the car behind. Round the next district is a mall with a rear access road. Further along are some garbage bins. I stop, pull my hood low over my head. I give the handles a rub with the towel first and then dump everything in the trash.

Minutes later we are back at the intersection and head south towards the Bridge of the Americas. The bridge famously crossing the Rio Grande, though other than the immigration posts, the traffic jams could be for any city interstate.

Looking over towards the Mexico to USA route on the opposite bridge, the traffic is spread for miles. We seem to be in the minority in leaving the country. The US border guards walk alongside the car but don't stop us. We move along in turn to the Mexico Immigration posts. We are waved down as expected. I wind down the window but Sophia leans over to speak.

'Hola,' she says.

'Passports?' he asks.

Sophia and Mia flash their new passports as I do mine. The border guard takes a quick glance and then back at us. He smiles and waves us through.

With a big sigh of relief we drive on. As soon as we hit the freeway through Juarez I find the first exit and pull into the city. Now we are in Mexico, away from American cops, for the first time in days, I can sleep in a bed. Juarez and Mexico are not the final answers to what to do next but at least I can breathe.

It doesn't take long to find a hotel, park up. I carry our bags and Mia helps Sophia to reception.

She looks shocking, hair tied back, face swollen and eyes that are sinking low with her energy levels. God knows what they think of us. But it hardly matters. She hands over cash and we rent a family room. The girls share the big bed, I take the other. None of has have much to say before the lights go off.

I lie back and close my eyes, trying not to let my mind drift far. I'm in Mexico, exhausted, scared for my life, owing a drug gang half a million dollars and I don't know what's going to happen tomorrow.

Exhaustion takes over and I'm asleep before I know it.

Chapter 25

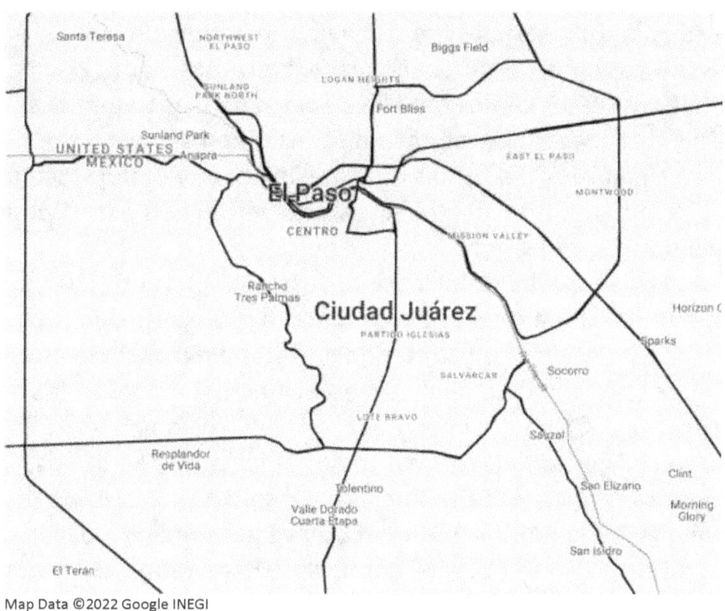

Ciudad Juarez, Chihuahua, Mexico

I wake up. Another day and this time another country.

Last night, I could hardly keep my eyes open to consider the state of the hotel room. Now as daylight fights its way through the thin curtains, I can see it is clinging onto life. It probably looked good the year I was born but now the wall colour is indeterminate from nicotine staining. The lamps and furniture are full of dust and insects.

Across the room, Mia is asleep, but there's no sign of Sophia. I get up and walk to the window. There is a café downstairs with chairs outside but she's not there. It's only just past nine so she can't have gone far.

I wonder if I should go get coffee and leave Mia to sleep, but I decide it's best not to leave her. We need to stick together, for better or worse.

I decide to negotiate the shower. The bathroom is small with the shower barely a cupboard space. I push the door closed and turn it on. Water comes out like a spurt and dies to barely a trickle. I squeeze the wall soap dispenser and some indeterminate liquid comes out smelling barely of floral scent. It will have to do, though I think yesterday's dip in the lake would have made me cleaner.

As I try to wash, I think back to yesterday. Twenty-four hours but almost a lifetime. Robbing a diner, a shootout, fake passports, another confrontation and stabbing, a trip to an Emergency Room and finally an escape across a border. It's a life in one day and I'm not sure if today will be any better. We've still got to decide what to do. At least I spoke to Rose. Her deep rasping voice so familiar and so delicious. How's the saying go? You don't know what you've got until you lose it.

I swear to myself that I'll get back to her as soon as I can. We will fix this and get back to normal.

Stepping out the shower, barely aware even if I'm clean, I catch the mirror. My eyes are faded, tired and bloodshot. Modelling an eighties goth look, not that different to Sophia yesterday before we took her to ER in El Paso. I look closer at my face, rubbing my eyes to cleanse them some more.

I think about what Sophia said yesterday and the other night. Am I a coward?

I'm still here, aren't I? I didn't run. The question is, what would a brave man do? Go back to Nashville, see my family and face the police? Sophia thinks that's the coward's way out, but it feels like the hardest route to me. Running further away is the action of a coward, isn't it? Regardless of whether I think I can run some fanciful rescue mission. The mirror offers no answer to the question, so I get dressed with a fresh T-shirt and pants.

Returning to the bedroom, Mia is still asleep. The door swings open and a flustered Sophia comes in carrying two bags, one full of boxes. She dumps them on the bed, grabs a clutch bag and runs to the bathroom. I hear the shower start up and assume she's going to be some time.

Given she's going to be a while, I decide to search through the boxes to see what she's been doing. Inside is a laptop, three cell phones. A couple of other bags.

'Been shopping?'

Mia sits up on the bed.

'Sophia has. How are you doing?' I ask. The bruise on her face has gone down. She's wearing a fresh T-shirt and sweatpants we picked up last night.

'I'm alright,' she says.

Judging how she dismisses the topic so easily I suspect she's not. But no point in pushing it at the moment.

'Mia.'

Sophia pops her head of the bathroom door.

'Si?' Mia says.

Sophia asks her something in Spanish. Mia gets up and searches in the other bag, retrieves some clothes and passes them to her. Sophia closes the door again.

A few minutes later she returns a different person. Clean, hair loose and damp, instead of tied back. She's wearing jeans and white branded t-shirt, some Spanish label I'm not familiar with. I suspect she's taken something as she reaches tentatively for the bed and lies back for a moment. She then curls up in a ball, her hand on her wound. I wonder how long she's going to be.

Whilst she's resting, I grab one of the cell phones and the sim card. After ripping it open I load it up, activate the SIM and start surfing for news.

Not much to report. Whatever news it was, the agenda has moved on. I check my watch getting impatient to get going.

I return to the bags again but stop when Sophia stirs. She gets up from the bed and takes them from me.

'All ok? I ask, but my question is ignored. 'Will someone please just speak, say something, say how they are feeling. It's like being in a school detention, where no kid dare speak in case teacher hits us with another punishment.'

'You weren't the one being molested by those pedo cabrones. If they did that to you, you would be crying all the way back to your girlfriend. Don't ask me to speak about it. You really want to know where they touched me, what they said?'

'Sorry,' I say. 'I was just asking is all.'

'Well don't,' she replies. 'If I want to tell you something, you're going to know about it right away.'

'Got it.' Wish I'd kept my mouth shut.

'You're not used to sharing with women, are you?' Sophia asks with a smile. First one, I've seen ever from her.

'I'm used to women,' I say, 'got a mother and sister and a girlfriend. They are crazy sometimes but got to be honest here, they are like easiest women you ever going to meet compared with the two of you.'

Sophia isn't listening as she unwraps an oblong gadget from one of the boxes. Holding her stomach for a moment, I notice the hesitancy and the wincing on her face. The pain is still there and will be for some time, I guess.

'Come on, we have work to do,' she says.

Very happy on this occasion for the subject to be changed. Sophia has this wide smile, her eyes wide. Humming a song even. This is weird.

'What work do we need to do?' I ask. 'Finding $500,000, you mean?'

No reply as she adds some batteries from the bag.

'What's that?' Mia says, sitting up in the bed.

'It's a card reader,' Sophia says.

'So how are you going to get the money? Marcos said you would know what to do.'

'Listen to me children,' she says, her tone higher, superior. 'It was a challenge from Marcos. He says it like it's one thing. Go out and steal an amount of money from one place when he knows that's impossible. If it was that easy, we'd do it every day and we all would be living on an island. He knows how to get that kind of money together, usually, drugs, prostitutes etc, but he's throwing it over to me to see if I'll resort to those methods. He wants to see how low I'll go to survive. He loves that kind of thing. It's a loyalty test he gives to his generals or the politicians he pays off. Impress me, scare me. It's like he gets off on the power trip it gives him. So now he wants me to find all this money. If I do... and we will somehow, it will actually impress him. But that's not why we're going do it. We're doing it because if we don't, then he can't be seen to be weak in front of his generals. He will kill us if we don't. But we're not going to deal in drugs or prostitutes, we haven't got time or set up for that. We are going to have to take some different risks.'

'Life or death risks?' I ask.

'Yes, life or death, with an extra chance of death. Dead if we do or dead if we don't. What do you choose?' She says it so matter of fact, reckon though when she sounds 'death' it sounds like 'debt' and I get awful confused. Her English normally is pretty good except she speaks so quickly. it can be easy to miss what she is saying. Fortunately, her mood provides sufficient context for all I need to know.

'Are we going to steal it like yesterday?'

'Donnie, do you think it's going to come off a tree?'

'Steal from who?'

'Anyone we can. Get creative, do something. Why am I the one with all the ideas? Do what you know how to do. Write a song on your guitar and sell a million copies or get some YouTube channel where all your girly fans can chat to you.' She's laughing hysterically now. Mia and I look at each other. 'Oh I forgot, your music is shit, so Mia tells me. Maybe that's why you only play to losers in a two-bit bar in Tennessee.'

I try not to react. She's crazy, this woman.

'She's high,' Mia whispers to me. 'Ignore her.'

I nod. I suppose I should have guessed. Sophia carries on with her stupid laughing.

'Here's an idea, smash that guitar for firewood, there's ten dollars in an instant. See how easy it is.'

She takes a deep breath and pauses. She goes back to fiddling with the card reader. Maybe she realises she's all over the place. Honestly, not sure if desperate Sophia is better than this irritating schoolgirl act.

'Get ready to go. You too Mia. We got to go.'

'Can I at least get a coffee?'

'Yes, that's going to be our first stop. They can be our first targets.' She turns to Mia. 'Fifteen minutes. Go go go.'

Mia slowly gets up from the bed and goes to the bathroom. Sophia opens the laptop.

'I got to get online. We need some bank accounts to store the money.'

I wonder if this drugged woman is safe with this online complexity, but she shows no sign of doubting herself as she carries on humming.

***

I get my coffee but I'm far from relaxed. Today was supposed to feel different than yesterday, and it does in that the border feels like it's protecting us from something. Yet, here we are in Mexico, setting up our own private crime wave.

Sophia is something else, and wish I could be like her - not a druggie, but assertive and confident. She is so alive and focussed. Her moods are the same as Rose's, petulant and nasty at times, but Sophia is a doer. Hands on. Rose is about getting other people to do her bidding so she can just be herself. Sophia is self-sufficient; Rose wants a man like me to worship and honour her demands. Not that I'm complaining. It's all good. Sophia is a survivor that's for sure and I suppose whilst she's surviving, I am too.

How much of Sophia is messed up drug energy? The fix in the morning has brought a better mood but still erratic behaviour. I daren't ask where she got the drugs from and I don't really want to know. She touches her wound from time to time but it doesn't appear to hinder her. Her focus is back now though, constantly watching, checking and thinking. It's exhausting to watch, but probably what I need. If it was down to me, on my own, who knows where I'd be. The coward thing again. But also, I've never been in a situation like this. There is no user manual or a practice book for gun fights. Though you could same about performing on stage. Performance is in the moment, rehearsals help get the technique right but it doesn't cover the energy of a crowd. It always demands more each time and if I can't give it that extra every time I play then I might as well go back to playing tunes in my bedroom. That's my bravery.

The feel of Juárez is different than El Paso. It's separated from the US by a bridge over the Rio Grande but the sounds, the atmosphere are all Mexican. The café and the street are interchangeable with any American high street, perhaps a bit smaller, and the street is busier. The curved red banner crowning the concrete structure above gives a more Latino feel and the coffee is definitely a few degrees stronger. The walls of buildings are full of graffiti, making the street look rougher. People scurry quicker and the dirt in the streets has more in common with the back alleys of Nashville than the glossy, shinier main strips. It's supposed to be violent and tense here but mid-morning is not going to be prime-time crime-time. And I don't plan to hang around to test the nightlife.

Mia is drinking a milkshake and I have my usual coffee. Sophia is on double expresso with extra sugar.

'Now we are in Mexico, what do I need to know?'

'They speak Spanish here,' Mia says. Her giggle goes on a little longer than I'm comfortable with.

Sophia high fives her.

'Do you want to practice your Spanish, Donnie?' Sophia asks.

'Hey, I only asked. I'm not the comedy act.'

'Come on, let's practice,' she says. 'Say, "Hola", then "¿Cómo estás?"'

Mia giggles again.

'Haha. You are all so funny. Tell me something properly about Mexico. I admit I know nothing.' I place my hands in the air conceding that whilst I want to know something useful this is going to be an exercise in making me look a fool.

'Alright, I'll behave,' Sophia says. 'What can I say to an American? Mexico has a far more interesting history than your country. It is not quite as big, not quite as many people, but it has one of the oldest civilisations in world history, the Mayans. It has multiple ethnicities, and should really be one of the richest countries in the world, what with the natural resources and populations.'

'So why isn't it?'

'Probably something to do with being ruled and raided by other countries forever. More recently the record of corrupt presidents and the effects of drug trafficking. It's ruined communities and affected international relations. Not enough investment in infrastructure. I could go on but it's not interesting.'

'Why do people come to the USA then? We're constantly told they want to steal our jobs and rape our women. Why did you come?'

'Whoa, where did you get off the privilege bus? Seriously Donnie, you been watching too much Fox News.'

I put my hand through my hair. A bit of embarrassment. I didn't mean it like that but I can see how it came out.

'Sorry. Though, you're right - I do see a lot of this shit on Fox news, Mom has it on constantly.'

'People come for all sorts of reasons. But as you are going to see whilst we are here no-one runs to the USA and risks their life doing it for nothing. You told me about that Honduran woman. Was she stealing your guitar and playing your songs? Was she hell. She was looking for a man to pay his dues. People run from gangs, guns, threats, poverty. You don't even know the half of it. But also, as for stealing your jobs? Someone coming from Mexico, English their second language, qualifications like mine from a Mexican college, has to apply for a green card and still gets a job ahead of you, then what does that say about your education system? People in America are just pissed because we work harder and do more than you fat lazy privileged rednecks.'

'Whoa, now who's sitting in the judgement seat? You really need to get over yourself.' That comment cut harsh. I'm no fucking redneck.

'Works both ways, Donnie. We're people too. 120 million people in this country, yet your president likes to say we are all one thing and builds a wall to keep us out. Like we're some kind of enemy army. You want some anger, some argument, let's have it.'

'I'm no Trump fan.'

'You literally just quoted him.'

I push my hair back wish I hadn't started this. 'Let's change the subject.'

'Good idea.'

Mia giggles again, enjoying my embarrassment. I look round the café and wonder what we are supposed to do here, dreading stepping into more crime.

'What do I have to do here?' I ask.

'Spill the drink, complain a bit,' Sophia replies. 'I'm going to the ladies room. As soon as I get out of sight, start. I need five minutes to check out the back room set up.'

I look at the woman behind the counter, large and robust, probably family run.

'Do we really want to rob from these people? I don't think they have much anyhow.'

'Donnie, you don't get it. Feel sorry for them if you want. But then we get to the next place, do you want to cry for them as well. Maybe the son's ill, mothers pregnant, father's blind… you feel sorry for all of them. So who we going to rob or cheat?'

'I dunno. I just see people trying to making a living. Speech you just gave me about loving Mexicans and yet you want me to rob them. Maybe it was the way Mom brought me up but I seriously don't feel comfortable doing this.'

'Look, that's different. That was about judging people, not about this situation. I told you back yesterday. What goes through the till in these places has little to do with selling coffee.'

'You mean a gang like the Sula 7 could be running a place like this.'

She laughs.

'They don't run the café, they just abuse it for their purposes,' she says.

'OK I get it.' I don't need any more lectures but seems to me the nice people who own this will be the victims as well. But I get it. 'Let's get on with it. Explain to me what you are going to do.'

'There are three options. First, these people are terrible at security. Laptop will be open with bank screen or logon details written down next to computer. It's family run so everyone can log on with same details. So ideal world, I can log on to the bank directly. Second, I can take snap shot of password and bank details or I can download their hard drive onto mine. But that can take too long. Third I can just run a credit card in a handbag or in a wallet pocket through my reader.' She pats the bag in her hand. 'It's all there.'

'And you're a lawyer?'

'I've seen it all kid - every court room is like a university of crime. You get cops, experts explain exactly how money changed hands. It's only by knowing every technicality of these procedures that I know how to get people off. You get it? I'm also good at it. You ready to watch?'

I look at Mia. She nods.

Sophia gets up, taking a small bag with her.

She walks passed the bar and is out of sight. Immediately Mia pushes her glass on the floor.

'You stupid bitch, you made a mess. It's all over the place.' I swing my hand round to pretend to hit her and knock the table over with my leftover coffee. The woman behind the bar comes out complaining in Spanish. Mia complains to her pointing at me. I pick up the odd word but I see she is making it out to be my fault. I decide to make more of it to manage the time.

'You lying bitch always complaining. Come here.' I try to grab her again and she screams like a banshee. In my opinion, she's getting too good at this screaming thing. It creates a genuine fear in everyone around. The large woman tears into me and pushes me out the way. She goes to the corner and comes back with a brush and cloth.

Mia continues the argument.

'You're a bad parent. You always hitting me, making me feel shit. You're ugly, and you can't play music for shit.'

She's enjoying this a bit too much. I grab at her again.

'Don't you touch me.'

She runs behind the woman who is now on her knees cleaning the floor. The mop is waved at me feebly so Mia grabs it and does it more forcefully.

'Hey, hey,' the woman grabs the mop back.

A few minutes have passed and Sophia hasn't appeared yet. I need a bit more time. I see a glass fridge with some cakes in. Should I fall into it or smash it?

I need to show more anger. I reach to another table first and grab a pot. I smash it hard on the floor. The woman now comes at me with the mop. No longer the peacemaker, she has rightly decided I'm the bad guy. She pushes me towards the street, cursing in Spanish. I don't need a translator.

I open the door as she follows me out.

Sophia appears from the same door. She shoves some bills at the woman and drags me out. Mia follows behind.

We walk quickly away. I look back and the café woman is watching, probably confused with what that was all about. Round the next corner we slow down.

'Did you get anything?'

'20,000 pesos on the credit card, plus the bank account details. There are some numbers on a sticker, so I'll try them once we get back to the hotel.'

'You're good.' I wonder how I can feel so jubilant about stealing like this - but as I keep being reminded, it's this or nothing.

'We got an hour. I suggest you get all you need and we get out of the city. Once she realises she's been robbed, they will be looking for us.'

A few minutes later we are packed, Mia and I waiting for Sophia, who's busy with the laptop.

Sophia calls me over.

'See,' she says.

I stand over her and look down at the screen.

'There 100,000 pesas sitting in the account. See all these small transactions, payments? How many people you saw in the café?'

'No-one, just us.'

'Exactly. See what I mean. That's gang cash washing its way through the system. All I'm going to do is redirect to our little account.'

'But won't the bank block it, or try to contact you to take it back?'

She shakes her head.

'It's part of a network of accounts I use. Sure they can dig but by the time they track one account, the money has moved to another. Once it's in offshore account, they run out of jurisdiction. They can't get the money.'

'And the café, what happens to them?'

'I could care less but unlikely,' she says closing the laptop and pushing it into her new rucksack.

'I care. If they're now going get beat up by the gang or worse because they lost the money, all we're doing is shifting our problem onto someone else. We're cowards, getting other people killed instead of us.'

'Works for me,' she says.

I look at Mia and she shrugs her shoulders.

'I can't do this,' I say. 'It's heartless, selfish, mean.'

'Yeah and I didn't ask you to come to my house and bring your problems to me. But you did and now, unless you got any better ideas that meet with your superior morality.'

'No.'

'Then this is what we do. Time to get moving. You might think you're safe in your cosy world with your fancy girlfriend and your guitar, but you're in my world now. You're only ever one street away, one unlucky day away from getting bust up badly. Ask Mia. She knows. Her Papá was in the mix every day. He knew one day he'd be on the wrong end of a bullet or a knife. He didn't moan, he just did what he had to do, including raising Mia. It's a sorry life, kill or be killed with these people. Sooner you get used to it, sooner we all will be happier.'

I shake my head. I'm not even sure where I'm supposed to be going.

Chapter 26

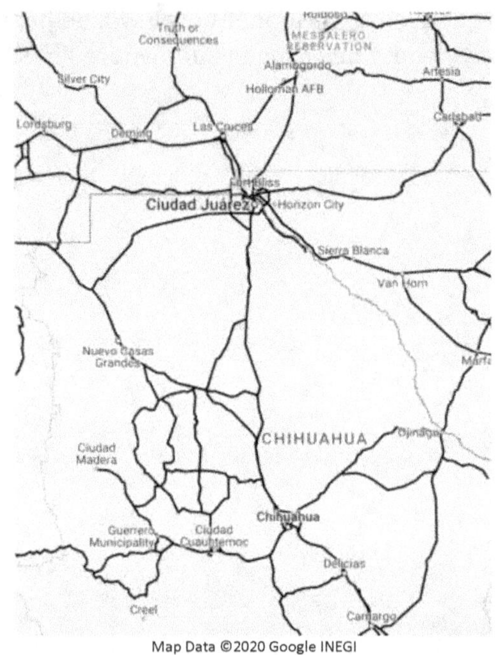

Map Data ©2020 Google INEGI

Ciudad Juarez to Chihuahua

We leave Juarez and start on the highway south, reckoning half a day's driving will get us through Chihuahua.

The road is barren and empty. Apart from the odd shrine by the side of the road or a gas station there is little or nothing to see. Welcome to Mexico, the land of not very much at all.

'Reckon we stop in Chihuahua?'

'Reckon we don't. I say we get there do a bit of business and keep driving. I'll drive tonight. You can sleep. We'll get down to Durango by the morning.'

'Seriously, where are we going?'

'We need to put some distance between us and Marcos. I need time to solve this and you need to help me.'

I stare at the endless road. It feels more and more like a road to nowhere. The same idea as yesterday - running away from something, not towards it.

'How can I help you? You don't think that much of me, you already made that clear.'

'Grow up, will you. We're not here for likes and appreciation.'

She spits her words out. When she's direct her Mexican accent is sharper, her words staccato and expressive. The high from this morning has diminished. I'm not going to engage with this, it's pointless. Not for the first time, the urge to stop the car, hand her the keys and take a bus back to the USA is tempting.

'I've got some friends in Honduras.'

'Honduras?' That place again. Daniela, Opal. Ryan Carter. All roads seem to lead there.

'Reckon, if you've grown a pair in the last few days, then you can do your heroic business. I can get us out of this mess with the money.'

I turn my head to the side. She's looking out the window to the west, talking normal again, like the anger of two minutes ago was never there.

'It's miles away, hundreds of miles. It would take us a week.' I looked it up last week. I never really thought about the distance of places but I'm now.

'If we keep going we'll make it in three days, switching the driving. If we can get through Durango by tomorrow, next day Mexico City. Maybe one more day we're in Guatemala.'

She lists these places and yeah I've heard of them - but I've no idea about the distances, or even if they're safe for us. I think about a reply. If I say what I'm thinking she'll call me a coward. My stomach churns and I feel my hands getting sweaty on the wheel. Honduras feels like a black hole. No longer driving away from but toward danger.

'You're crazy. It's dangerous, seriously dangerous. Gangs everywhere. They see someone like me, I'll be dead in seconds.'

'Honduras is a country of millions of people, many just like you and me who go to work, feed their families, have fun and get on with their lives.'

I shake my head. I'm not having this bullshit.

'If it's so damn beautiful, why is half the country trying to get into the US? You smoking some shit if you can convince me otherwise.'

'Of course, there are a lot of people affected by gangs. Hundreds, thousands... but not millions, Donnie. Millions is just people surviving. The economy is screwed, the government corrupt but people survive, do stuff, adapt.'

'Will your friend or friends know how to find Opal? Are they connected to Sula 7 or other MS13 type gangs?'

She sighs. I watch her reach into her bag and retrieve some pills, then she washes them down with a slug of water. With whatever shit she's stuck in her this morning her body is processing some serious cocktail of drugs. No wonder she's moody. But then she got a knife in the gut just a day ago, I might be seeking pain relief in whatever form it comes, if that was me.

'Everyone from there is affected in some way,' she says. 'So yes. My friends are good people. I helped them out with some stuff when they came in to the US. They got deported but at least I got them cash to return home. It's what I do.'

'Ok.'

'I can't promise they can help with Opal, but feels like a safe place to go to. And if I'm honest, I'm all for trying to help girls like Opal and Mia. They need all the help they can get because if not... you know what I mean?'

'I think so.'

'Come on Donnie,' she nudges my arm. 'Live life, this is it. You tell me what you think this is about. When you talked about that woman dying in the street, I could've wept right there. You cared Donnie. You cared, so don't pretend to me that after all the shit of the last few days, you don't want to do the one thing to make all this worth it. Pull that girl out the fire, Donnie. Sure as hell if you don't, if *we* don't, that girl's going to be dead by the time she's twenty. Either raped, drugged, trafficked or just good old fashioned murdered. If you can live with that then maybe you're no-better than that politician you were bitching about.'

'I'm not like him,' I shout. 'I didn't ask for any of this. Ryan Carter, he let Daniela down. He even knows about her and still didn't lift a finger.'

'Wow, some anger.'

'Don't mock me.'

I'm not taking lectures from this crazy woman. I hear the engine raw and realise I've sped up, holding tighter on the wheel.

'I'm not mocking you, Donnie. I want you angry. You should be fucking angry. These people, they are the worst; terrible, vicious, the devil's scum. You going to do something about it or just let them win?'

'He going to wet his pants,' Mia says from the back.

'Nobody asked you,' I shout back. Shaking my head, I sigh. This is too much.

'Ryan Carter owned an Opal mine in Honduras,' I explain. 'He mined precious stones. Must have made millions of dollars. This money to him must be like a bad night at the casino. It won't touch him.'

'Black opals from Honduras. That's some serious gems. You ever seen one?'

I shake my head. I don't want to say what's on the tip of my tongue. If she thinks I've got that stone in my bag, she's going to be all over it. I can't. No matter what freedom it buys me, I don't want to lose that stone.

'All the mines got blown up. Gangs took over once the government was corrupted. Better to blow them up than leave drugs gangs mining that shit. Can you imagine if those commies got hold of that kind of revenue? It's bad enough already. I bet you right now that DA creep has a stash of those gemstones somewhere. Keeping it hidden until he needs it.'

'I wonder if - ' I say.

'What?'

'Daniela didn't tell me much. Just that she had come to get money off him. But it's a long way to come to buy freedom just for Opal. Anything could have gone wrong on her own. Perhaps the price of freedom was some of those jewels. The price of her daughter's... his daughter's life was the key to whatever vault he's stashed them in.'

'That's a lot of wondering,' Sophia says.

'Yeah I'm making it up. Just seems high risk, to come all the way to the USA to get money from the father, whoever he was. Place like that, those people will have known if she was involved with the mine owner.'

'Could be right. All the more reason to find out. What do you think?'

I keep my head straight, glaring into the distance. I'm not giving her the satisfaction of being right. Not today, not ever. Though I'm starting to do much more thinking about Daniela and her relationship with Carter. There is definitely more to it than I considered.

Chapter 27

We drive on with nothing much to say. The mood calms as the sense of direction and time kicks in. The destination is south and there's a lot of miles to cover.

Ryan Carter. I can't get him out of my head now. Is he really sitting on Honduran jewels or am I in some adventure book, imagining diamond mines like gold mines of the Wild West? It's possible Daniela did exactly as she said, came to the US for the money from him. But it's also equally feasible she was sent. The Sula 7 or whichever gang in Honduras had paid for her trafficking got her all the way to Nashville. And then what? Did he silence her or did the gang kill her when she failed in her mission? Was it just bad luck?

My visit must have unsettled him. He could make me out publicly to be some crank, easily dismissed, but he'll know that his situation is dangerous. The politics is the easy bit, easier than being the target of gangs.

According to scroll feed on my cell, the news cycle seemed to die down when I disappeared. The Trump visit to Nashville for a rally has given the local media some grits to fill up the long hours of cable of TV. I'm relieved they have moved onto whatever bullshit he is pedalling this week. Good for me and probably good for Ryan Carter that there are other stories to run. If anyone does ask about my video, the police department will give the no comment angle, pursuing enquiries nonsense. No doubt he will tell his family it's some Democrat trap being laid for him. They all just carry on as normal.

How's his conscience work? How's he get up every day knowing his daughter is in serious danger and just carry on like the sun just came up and the flowers are smelling sweet? He's got some serious balls to do that. Kisses his wife and kids. It's sick. One day, I mutter to myself. One day he will pay. I'll see to it. If I ever get back from Honduras, that is.

I flick through the radio for music but it's all the same, Spanish guitar, dance stuff. I can't get with it.

It's late in the day, my stomach's groaning and I'm bored of driving.

'We need to eat,' I say.

'There's a place coming up.' Sophia checks her watch and seems agitated. Every few seconds, she shifts in the seat, scratching her head and checking her cell.

'Is it just food or business as well?' I know the answer as soon as I say the words.

'Business, though I doubt it's going to trouble our total much. It's too small.'

Again she is acting nervously as she shifts around. I think I know the signs now. It's only this morning she got a fix. Maybe it wasn't much. Who knows?

'Ok. I can see how we need to keep getting money but we need far more restaurants like that in Juarez to get five hundred thousand bucks together. We can't do that. Not all the places we are going will be that careless will they?'

'You're right. We can get cash but not enough. We're going to need to do something different. As I said before, take some risks.'

'Dare I ask what a different looks like? We're not robbing a bank are we?'

She shakes her head.

'Not too far off,' she says, 'but not in the old fashioned away. Can you imagine the three of us turning up for a robbery? They would be on the floor laughing as they kicked us out the building on our asses.'

'You can hack a bank?' I ask.

'Not hack. I'm not sure either, it's crazy anyway. Messing about with these people is asking to be murdered. You saw already the nastiness in Marcos. He is not the diplomatic negotiator. In Spanish we have a saying... tiene al diablo metido. He has the devil inside.'

'Ah right,' I say. 'He might be the devil but he wants his dollars. As you said before, he can kill us only once. He isn't that stupid is he, or like you said yesterday, reckon he would have finished us off in El Paso?'

Sophia stares back at me. Her curiosity drawn on her forehead, eyes wide with scepticism. Am I missing something as usual?

'Once is a little too many for me, Donnie,' she says.

'We're still here though - that's something?'

I wonder. What if money is power in this situation? The more we have, they less they have. I try to put it in words, though, I worry I'm once again going to look like a naïve kid.

'This is mad, I know. But you already have access to their banks. You move money around for them. Are you the only one with access? What if you stole their money? That way you would have the power?'

'That way I would be dead. Followed by you, then Mia.' She shakes her head, then shifts some more in the seat. A bead of sweat is visible on her forehead.

'But if you had the money and they didn't have access to it? It's all about money, the bigger the number the better the lifestyle of these drug gangs. They would need you alive more than dead otherwise they are stuck, can't pay security and can't hide their money.'

'Sorry, Donnie. You better run to Alaska or Outback Canada or Antarctica or some desert somewhere, because with ideas like that they go far to find you. You will need to be so remote that the only audience you'll have for your guitar will be polar bears.'

'But you said already, these small time take downs are not going to give us the money we need. We're fucked either way.'

'Quit with the mad stuff. I said we needed to be brave and take risks, not be fricking stupid.'

'Yet here we are running to Honduras. That seems stupid and crazy to me.'

'We got to do what we got to do, right? Until we get a plan for Mia and a plan for you, then we have to keep safe. I'm serious about helping those girls who've been kidnapped. I can't let it go, even if you can. Plus to run, you've got to have somewhere to run to.

'I reckoned I was the snowflake in this car.'

'I did already have a conscience - otherwise why do you think Mia came to me? Because, I looked out for her, and for others like her, before I got shifted out for getting too close. I'm not going to dump her just like that. The same reason you didn't dump her as well. You care just as much as I do.'

'Yeah, I get it.'

I relax a little, wishing I understood this better. It's all a bit crazy and I get that, starting on this road, it's not possible to turn back. But for all my ideas, Sophia's the only one with real answers, and I have to believe her otherwise we have no chance. And maybe the people she knows in Honduras can help us. Though that feels less possible and scarier the closer we get. And yet here we are. Racing to the desert sunset.

Chapter 28

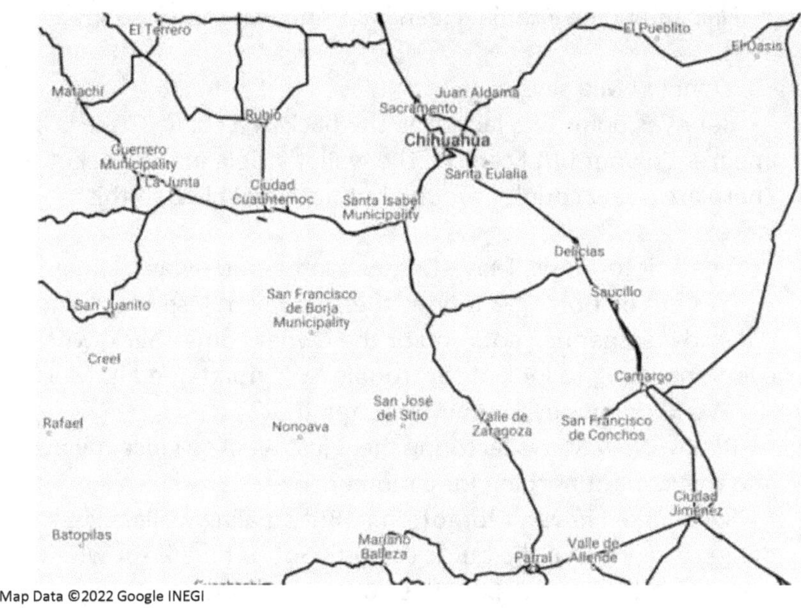

Map Data ©2022 Google INEGI

Chihuahua to Parral

The light fades on the day and I'm beat. A town called Parral is signposted so we pull off. It's rough looking and there's minimal light, but there are a couple of small places to eat. I can't wait to stop and walk around a while. A bistro type place called Josephine's with pink walls looks friendly enough. I'm past caring as long as I can eat something.

At least the food is getting more interesting. Gone are the fast-food joints and burgers, and we are now into the land of tacos, beans and salsa. I can fill up on this all day long.

Sophia looks tired, her hair, straggly from the heat, now tied back, and her skin pale. Nothing much left of the fresh Sophia from the morning. I watch her head straight for the ladies room, wondering what's going through her mind. She didn't mention the wound in a while and when I enquire, she shrugs it off. With the pills she popped earlier, I wonder if she feels anything much.

Mia and I take a table. I lean back and want to close my eyes.

'Donnie,' Mia says.

Her eyes point to a jacket on the back of a chair. There is no apparent owner but I can see the wallet visible in the pocket. There are a few couples around but nothing linked to this jacket.

'Leave it for now,' I say. 'Owner can't be far away.'

'Yes but if I don't get it now, then we might lose the chance.'

'And if someone spots you or the owner comes back, who's everyone going to look at for trouble? We don't need it, Mia.'

'We need money, or you forgotten that?'

Really. Now Mia is lecturing me. I just want to close my eyes and think about nothing for a moment.

'Of course I haven't forgotten it. But stealing wallets is dangerous. What if the guy is armed? Got to time it for when we are ready to leave. Sophia's not here either. You know we got to get going as soon as you're done.'

'I'm going looking for her. But she'll agree with me. We gotta take what we can.'

I look around the room. My leg kicks the seat underneath me, showing my nerves. I put my hand on my thigh to stop it.

'OK, go check the bathroom and then we can decide.'

It's dark outside and I can't see much. Not that there is much to see. The road goes from open barren landscapes to barren hills and mountains. Always the same dull colour of brown sand and rock. I never thought I would miss the green lands of Tennessee.

I order two beers and a Coke. The owner brings back a menu but doesn't speak.

Mia comes running back into the room.

'Donnie, she's gone,' she says.

'What?'

'I can't see her. Bathroom is empty.'

I run to the door and see the Ford has gone. Has she run?

'Where's she gone?' Mia asks.

'I don't know. But she'll be back,' I say. Hoping more than believing it. 'Remember what she said earlier - she cares about you.'

We return to the table. 'I'll call her. She'll have the burner cell with her.'

'She said only in emergency,' Mia says.

'This is an emergency.'

'Let's get something to eat. If she still isn't back, then we call her.'

I nod but I'm not comfortable. It doesn't feel right.

***

I eat some cheese and bread with salsa. I need to fill up on carbs to give me energy for the next few days. I grab some tacos and bean dips as well, passing the time.

'Why are you a veggie?' Mia asks, staring rigidly at my food choices as if it was dog crap I was messing with.

'Why do you eat meat?'

It's a rehearsed reply because everyone assumes I'm a weirdo. Mia is working her way through a beef taco. I can see the grease and oil dripping from the sides. I used to turn away from it but now it doesn't bother me.

'I eat meat, 'cause I got to eat something, right. I never got to choose.'

'Fair enough. Up to you. I got a choice.'

'Where I come from, you would have been...'

'I get it,' I reply. 'But tell me. Why do people think that I'm a weak person just because I don't eat animals. Some people, eat veg, some fish, Jews don't like pork. Some are allergic to all kinds of shit. Yet I'm the freak. I don't tell you, you're a freak for eating the flesh of sentient animals, which is far freakier from where I'm sitting.'

'Not saying that.'

'You are, it's there in your eyes. Judging me.'

'Just saying, I didn't get a choice. I ate what was there or I starved.'

'Got a choice now. Plate of salsa here, rice, beans. Eat it.'

If I have seen a face shrink quicker in disgust, I can't remember. The grimace is a work of art.

'No thanks, got mine.'

'So, it's a choice then.'

She scowls back. I ignore her and continue eating.

In between mouthfuls of food, I'm checking the cell to see if there was a message and I missed it. There isn't.

An hour has passed since we arrived and no sign of Sophia.

'What do we do?'

'About the wallet?'

It's still hanging in the jacket - no-one came in to claim it. Perhaps the owner left it. 'No, about Sophia. We said we'd call.'

'A few minutes. I think we take the jacket. You should wear it like it's yours. No-one will notice.'

'Let's check on Sophia first. Then we decide.'

The restaurant door swings opens and Sophia appears. She looks stressed and anxious, her hair stringing, damp patches under her arm. She falls into the seat on the table.

'Where you been?' I ask.

'I needed to score,' she says. 'Had to go exploring in the pueblo.'

I shake my head in weary resignation that this is my world now. Theft, drugs and coming soon, kidnapping.

Sophia grabs Mia's drink and downs it in one. Mia is about to complain but resists.

'Are we done? Can we go?' Sophia asks.

'You haven't eaten?'

'I don't need food, we need to go.' She passes me the keys. 'Donnie, can you drive some more, I need to... well, you know.' She looks down to her arm.

I'm exhausted and don't want to. But also I'm not going to say no. If she's just taken more shit than I'm happier if she sleeps it off.

'I'll drive for one or two hours after that I'll need a break. I can't keep going.'

'It's fine. I'll be good by then.'

'Finishing up? Come on.'

'You might want to starve but I need to eat. Best meal I've had in days.'

I'm not rushing after we've been stressing about where she's been for the last hour.

'Donnie was telling me why he's a veggie,' Mia says. 'Says he's not weird.'

Sophia laughs.

'Donnie is what is commonly known as middle class, Mia. He gets to be whatever he wants to be.'

I ignore them both as I use the bread to wipe the last of salsa.

'You not vegan? That's on full trend these days?

'Nope, veggie. Don't like meat, don't want to eat it, so I don't. What's so difficult to follow?'

'You're the one missing out,' Sophia replies. 'Never bothered me eating nice juicy steak, running with blood.'

'Quit now.'

They both laugh.

'You know it fits you so well, Donnie. Musician, nice guy, doesn't like guns, veggie. It's all there. You probably wrote poems for your girlfriend. Sensitive.'

I glare back trying not to give them the benefit of winding me up.

'Whether I eat meat or not, what the fuck difference does that make? Doesn't me any lesser. Least I'm not pumping my body full of chemicals. Look at you. Eyes like flying saucers, veins running with poison, yet you dig me because I got food choices.'

She curses something in Spanish, but I don't care.

'It's ok for you to give me shit, but if I call you out, then I'm the bad guy.'

She avoids my eye.

'We done or what?'

I push my plate away and wipe my mouth. I'm done.

'Donnie,' Mia says.

Her eyes shift to the jacket.

I look at it. There is only two other people at the tables. It doesn't belong to them. What about the owner? Must be them it belongs to.

'You go first,' I say. 'I'll follow.'

'What's this about?' Sophia asks. Mia points to the jacket.

'Move quickly. Do it,' she says, not needing any debate on the risks involved. 'Don't run, act natural.'

We throw some bills onto the table and I go to the bathroom. Mia and Sophia head to the door. When I return to restaurant, the jacket is still there. I take one last look around, march through and pick up the jacket, placing it over my shoulder. I don't look back as I reach the door.

Outside, I breathe again, unaware I'd been holding my breath since I picked up the jacket. I see the white Ford is waiting with the door open, the engine running ready for me to jump in. I start to run. I've done it. Adrenaline kicks in as I reach the car.

A noise and a shout comes from behind as I climb inside. I don't stop to look, ram the gear into drive and race away before anyone can stop us. We speed along the dark road with my foot hard to the floor. Mia takes the jacket beside me and starts checking the cards and the cash. In the mirror I see Sophia spread across the back seat. There are no lights in the rear view mirror, so at least that problem isn't following us.

It's so dark now and I try to settle in for the next stretch. I could be anywhere, driving anywhere, because out here just seems to be nothingness. The sign for Mexico City comes up. 800km. Not even close.

Chapter 29

Parral to Mexico City

For the next twenty four hours we only stop for gas and
food. Sophia is on better form today - clearly the drugs having
the desired effect. I don't want to think too much about the
consequences of her addiction or how she's going to get
beyond it. That's a fight for another day, and one that likely I
can't win on her behalf. She'll have to do that all by herself.

We are now on the road to Guatemala. South of Mexico City, the scenery has changed from desert to city and now to forest. The landscape is green as we head first to Veracruz and the switch over the hills to Oaxaca and Chiapas before the border for Guatemala.

Driving through the night proved uneventful, but I get the feeling that was more luck. Sophia is confident she can talk or pay her way out of any situation, but as we get closer to southern states I feel less and less safe. Guatemala and Honduras are legendary in terms of crime, carjacking or just good old murder. I can only imagine Mexico this side of the border will be the same.

In the last two days, I've driven nearly a thousand miles through Mexico, and I'm not sure I've learnt anything about the country other than it feels like it goes on forever, even more than home. But then the road is never going to be the best place to see what goes on. In another life, we would hang out in bars and night clubs, eating all the wonderful food. Instead we just drive and drive.

Reaching La Tinaja, we find a motel. I crawl off the highway with all perception of distance and speed blurring. I can barely focus on the lights from the entrance. I grab the bags and my guitar and take it inside. Arriving in the room, I'm so glad to lie flat on a bed and it's only the desperate need to eat that stops me falling asleep on the spot. The motel is rough but I'm done caring about what or who was here before me.

The last few days I've hardly considered playing my guitar. It used to relax me, easy therapy. Instead, I just want to curl on the bed and sleep. But I need a shower first, as do Sophia and Mia.

After each of us freshens up, testing the barely working water flow to the limit we go down to restaurant next door. More rice, beans and tacos. But I'm not complaining. Sophia brings the laptop down with her.

All through dinner, she is quiet, tapping away on the machine, occasionally cursing in Spanish. Mia is playing games on the cell phone, hardly looking up even to eat more fries or slurp her Pepsi.

'What's the plan?' I ask.

'To get rich and run away,' Sophia says, her focus not shifting from the machine, the tequila and lemon barely touched beside her.

'You keep saying that, but we don't have any more ideas than yesterday.'

'I've been thinking whilst we were driving. You were right yesterday.'

'Me right?' Wow - slap my face with a baseball bat, those are words I never expected to come from Sophia's mouth.

'For once, yes. We do need the upper hand and the only way to do that is to make Marcos need us alive more than dead. And that means taking his money from the accounts. It's the only way this gives us control.'

'Carry on.' I know I suggested this a day ago but I was blustering. The logic is straightforward, the consequences stark.

'So I already explained some of the money laundering stuff. Few more things to learn about the world of money in modern times. Firstly, it's all online. The serious stuff is. The paper stuff is useful because it's anonymous and easily moved from person to person, but not in large quantities. Online you can add as many zeros as you like. The money exists only as lines of code. It can be moved and exchanged quickly, internationally, different currencies and also to places where those amounts cannot be seen by authorities or tax regulatory jurisdictions.'

'Is that like bitcoin?' Mia asks.

'Sort of, but that's a different concept. That's a currency in itself, though equally good at hiding money from being traced, because its source code is spread throughout the internet.'

'Ok,' she says and goes back to her game.

I open another beer and take a sip.

'I reckon, I get the overseas banking bit,' I say. 'But how do you get at it. It's all passwords and security. You're not a super hacker.'

'Like I said before. I have passwords for The Sula 7 and remember - I got some for those accounts we stole from. I have dummy accounts already set up in various countries and I did find a useful back room geek in Hong Kong who wrote me some code which moves money from one account to another quickly. It's amazing to see it work. The money is so far from where it started it's impossible to get back. The geek also gave me a way to hack email accounts. Gives me a short window to find account emails and if someone is stupid enough to store a password in their email account, I can find it.'

'Where do you find geeks like that? In Hong Kong? How is that they don't just rob you themselves?'

'They could, but robbing the people paying your wages is not sustainable. This is a side line from ransomware and other internet scams. Plus you steal from the wrong people one day they going to find you. I found him, like you do with all this internet stuff. Dark web. I know the only thing you ever looked up was porn, Donnie, but honestly, just think about the darkest, wildest thought you ever had and there will be a forum for it with a discussion group of likeminded nerds ready to tell you in some stupid teenage code-speak what you need to. Duh! Like it's obvious, dude, everyone's doing it. They are all keyboard trash monkeys who are seriously retarded, but they do know stuff. These geeks advertise on these forums to get likes. I checked this Hong Kong dude out and used him a few times on schemes I've done before. The good thing - out of Marcus's gang, I'm the only one who deals with him or even knows he exists. The other gangbangers, apart from the accountant and the fake ID people, are too stupid for this kind of intelligence. Whores and guns are all they think about.'

'Cool. So that's the hacker. But how do we keep Marcos and the Sula 7 from killing us when he finds out we stole his money?'

'Because I'll make it clear that killing me will mean I move all the money into various kids' charities round the world. He will never see it again.'

'Wow, that's big.'

'Yeah, this is dancing with the devil. High stakes poker. All I have to do is convince him we're serious.'

'But isn't the point that you have to give them the money back to stop him killing us? Once you give it back reckon then we've no longer got any leverage?'

'I'll operate like a bank. They can come to me, ask for money and I'll give it. As long as I'm not dead - and you, of course.'

'How long can you keep that up?'

'Until we come up with a better plan. I'll give them some incentive, bit of interest. I'm just the linchpin.'

'This is mad,' I say.

'If you've got a better plan, I'm all ears.'

'They are bad enough to tear us limb for limb out of spite, regardless of the money.'

'I can't legislate for stupid. But Marcos isn't stupid. And if he doesn't get that money back he's going to be just as dead as me. He has to deal.'

I drink my beer again and leave her to her work. I wish I had her confidence. I still think one of these days someone's going to cut my throat in my bed.

The restaurant door bangs open and my expectation of throat cutting seems to have been brought forward. Three brutish men walk in, slamming the door, and stand like they are contestants in the world's worst version of WWF. Sophia immediately shuts down the laptop, leaves the table and heads for the washroom.

'Hey, senorita,' he shouts instructions in Spanish. Sophia ignores him and runs to the stairs. She cannot afford to lose that laptop and she needs to get it out of sight.

One of the men follows her. The other two come over to our table. They both look rough, heavily tattooed with words and symbols I don't understand but suspect don't represent their charity work.

'Americano?' he asks? 'Tu auto?'

'Si,' I nod.

'Hey, él no habla español,' Mia says.

He turns his attention to Mia, speaking quickly and aggressively.

'He wants to know why we're in Mexico,' Mia says.

'And what should we tell him,' I ask her.

Mia speaks to him in Spanish. The man other plan replies and laughs.

'I told him you're taking me to visit my aunt who's dying.'

'And what did he laugh at?' I ask.

'He wants to know if you're fucking me or not? He wants to know if you're a pedo.' She says the words but I can hear the disgust in her voice. She's used to these people but the hate for them is written across Mia's face.

The first man speaks again.

'He wants the car keys,' she says.

'But it's our car, I can't give that to him. What will we do?'

'Give them to him.'

It's Sophia, screaming in pain. She's being dragged back into the restaurant by her hair. She doesn't have the laptop so I hope she got it somewhere safe. She is dumped into her seat.

Sophia grabs the keys and throws it at the gang. I get up to protest but a rapid hand movement smacks me back down. I don't care about the car, I just care about being stuck in the middle of nowhere with no means of getting away.

One of the men heads to see the café owner who's watching from behind the counter. It's clear that he knows the gang. Cash is handed over from the till with no questions asked. Protection money, cartel money, who knows. But it's paid without question.

Business completed they congratulate each other and head outside. We watch silently as one of them gets into the Ford, revs it up hard for effect and then drives off. The owner comes back with fresh drinks as if to pacify us. I'm still shaking as I watch the guy drive the Ford round the car park, revving and screeching the tyres. After a few turns he turns it back towards the restaurant and races back towards us. He jumps from the car just before it hits the bollard, smashing the front.

The gang man gets up from the floor laughing and joins his friends back in their Pick-up. They drive off again. I'm sick. They didn't want the car. It wasn't even about money. It was just hard faced cruelty.

I go outside to inspect the damage. The engine is still running and I try to back it off the bollard. The front fender is smashed and lights broken. But I'm able to reverse it. The transmission seems ok but it's not safe to drive. I park it up at the back of the car park. Sophia has returned with the laptop and is speaking to the owner.

I shake my head at her.

'He says we can get a car in the next town. He'll drive us there in the morning.'

Not much to be said. We go up to the room, irritated and tired. What was the point of all that? Because they can, is the answer. Because they can. As I fall asleep, Sophia is typing away on the laptop. I wonder if that was bad luck meeting those three or a sign of things to come.

Chapter 30

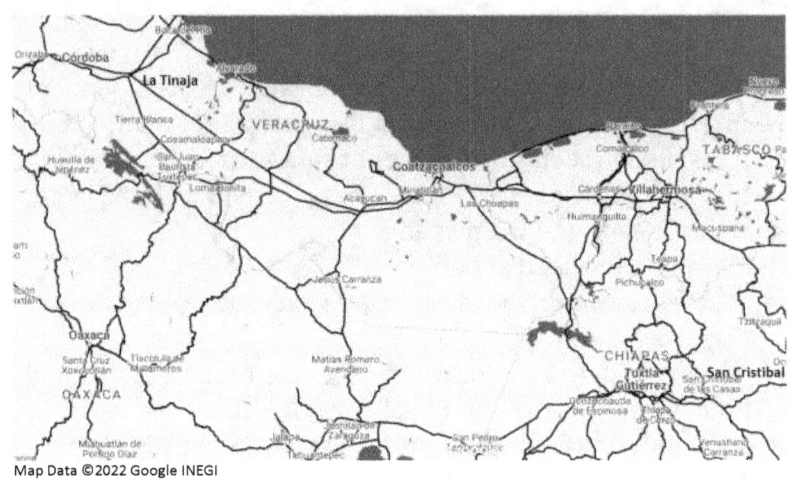

Map Data ©2022 Google INEGI

La Tinaja to San Cristobal de las Casas

La Tinaja is a step back into another rust belt town in the US, only it feels sadder and poorer. I don't want to call it a dump. It seems mean, as people here are just trying to make a living out of what they got around. Far as I can see that isn't that much at all. The streets smell of burning rubber and the air is thick with humidity.

I see these places, same as the US. They grew up out of some crossroads or staging post. They may be farming grain or animals and provide jobs, but as the years go on no-one wants those jobs anymore. The kids run to the city for a better life and the town seems to die out in plain sight. Any one round here who has money is hiding behind a big wall and a lot of guns. Just like those thugs who turned us over last night, there's no-one to stop them.

The café owner drops me at a car lot at the end of the high street. He parks the car and comes in to help with the purchase. Picking up a car is a relatively easy transaction. A few thousand pesos handed over and a large ten year old white pickup truck in return. With Mexican plates, at least we blend in a little better. My guess is the owner added a major wedge on the price for a gringo like me but cash has become less about the amount these days and just about having what we need to keep moving. He's probably doubling up on tequila rounds as soon as we are out of town.

I drive back to the motel and pick Mia and Sophia up. Inside an hour we are back driving. Only another seven hundred miles to Guatemala. Nothing at all.

The distances on the road signs hardly seem to go down. But keep going we must. We can't turn back as that just seems even further away. At least I kind of know where I'm going. I'm not happy about it but it feels like a purpose. A problem to own, which may or not be successful.

In a day and a half we should get there.

The radio is playing a local channel and I've switched off from trying to guess the Spanish. The music for the most part passes me by now. The mood over Latin music seems to perpetual about dancing and romance. I don't hear the story telling in the lyrics or the mood like you would in country or the indie rock bands that I like. But then if I knew Spanish better that might be a different feeling.

'Oh shit, it gets worse,' Sophia says

She turns up the news on the radio.

'Hurricane off the Caribbean is heading our way. Could be making landfall in two days' time. It will skirt down the coast of Belize and then Honduras. We are literally driving into the fucking storm. Oh Jesus, why the fuck are we doing this?'

'Shit.' I've never been in a hurricane. I've seen tornadoes – they're common in the Midwest. Whenever any of the big hurricanes hit the east coast they've usually gone down a few notches when they cross Tennessee.

'Are we gonna be safe?' Mia asks.

'How the fuck do I know? Going back, standing still, going there. We've got shit coming. As I said about a hundred times on this journey, any of you got a better idea, I'm all ears.'

'Ok, calm down, reckon she was only asking.'

Sweet happy Sophia seems to be on a break.

'The next person asking is getting out this car and can fucking walk there.'

'And who put you as the boss of me?' I say. She is a piece of work this Sophia - a mouth like a sewer drain and a mood like a punched rhino.

'Hey, you can walk too. Y'all started all this shit. You came looking for me. You can both fuck off here and I'll deal with my own business. Far easier than dealing with you amateurs. You should be fucking grateful right here. I put my ass on the line, screwed my job, my home. Hell I'm even getting you the money. Even better, here we go. Drop me the next town. Keep the fucking car, I'll get my own. Do your own thing, see how far you get the both of you.'

'Sophia, stop it,' Mia says.

Sophia bursts into tears in the front seat. I go quiet and keep on driving. Out of nowhere, she rams her hand hard into the dash multiple times, cursing with each strike. Mixing despairing cries with yelps of pain. She grabs at a water bottle from her bag, then a bottle of tequila, then back to the water. Some pills follow the mixture, and I'm wondering whether I'm witnessing an overdose.

Throwing her head back against the headrest she then holds still. Perhaps all that cocktail of shit is processing in her system. A few minutes of silence, she stretches out and the tension goes.

'Is she ok?' Mia asks.

'Sorry, babe,' she replies to Mia. 'Just so fucking tired of this nightmare.'

She sniffles and searches in a bag. This time only a napkin is retrieved and I'm hellish relieved. Fucking Walmart pharmacy and liquor store all on one sack.

'Sorry,' I say, reaching out a hand to her shoulder. 'You're right, we'd be dead without you. I don't even know what would've happened.'

She says nothing and we carry on. Another one hundred miles gone and still hundreds to go.

Deep breath and carry on. Both of them are quiet. Maybe we've all said enough for today. Leave them to it. Though with Sophia, it's only a matter of time before she rages again.

****

I need a comfort break and we park up at a lot. Returning to the car, Sophia is back at the laptop, using her cell as a hotspot

'How's the money going?'

'Nearly there,' she says. 'I rehearsed with a few thousand dollars. That's like pizza money to Marcos and his bosses - he's spends more on cigars than that. I got it through three countries with manual moves last night. Once I get the bot working we can do a lot more.'

'Tell me,' I say, 'I reckon if this is so easy to do - I mean, hack accounts, launder it and steal it, run it to offshore accounts - why isn't it happening all the time? I mean, you could have done this years ago and run away. Anyone of these hacks could do it anytime. It would be chaos.'

'Same reason you don't rob a bank on the high street every day. Sooner or later you going to get caught. You've got to run fast and hard because you steal from these people, they will kill you.'

'That doesn't make sense. How would they even know it was you or anyone who did it? The internet, you said yourself, you can hide easily. You can be in Outer Mongolia and in the middle of the pacific and still do the same thing. How would they find you?'

'Those nerds aren't brave enough to do anything on their own. They shit their pants if anyone serious came for them. All talk, mostly boys who can't talk to women, bragging about being the hardest weirdest fuck. That's their world, let them have it. In the real world, people who understand this and can

182

do it, is a small club. These gang leaders like Marcos got noses like dogs. Criminals, gangs, rich fools. They can sniff out the disloyal ones, the ones taking their own cut, the grasses. They got a major talent for it. It's what got them to the top of these organisations, you know. They find traitors and cut out their hearts so everyone can see what the price of treason is.'

'I get that.' Horrible, but after getting close up and personal with a few of these Sula 7 in the last few days, I've seen all I want to of their methods.

'So they know it's you that has the money. You already said you would hold it to ransom. I still don't really get how they won't just line you up and me and Mia and shoot us.'

'Power, Donnie. While we have the money, we will have the power. Like I said before, I'm open to a better plan. Maybe you can ask your guy with the opals to let us into his mine or his vault, pay it off that way. My plan isn't perfect and you're right, they could murder all three of us. Fuck the money and all that. But my instincts say they'll play ball. Losing that much money would destroy the gang. Without hard cash, the wheels of gangs like Sula 7 would fall off. No money to pay members, no money for bribes, got to pay up front for coke and heroin in thousands of dollars. Killing us would satisfy their revenge but would be suicidal. When a gang like Sula 7 falls apart there is blood everywhere.'

I can see it clearly. If debts aren't paid, then they will come after the leaders or those that owe the money. Rival gangs will pick up the pieces. Carnage. Maybe this plan does have some merit. But each time we talk about it I want to be sick. The fear in my stomach and dread that for all the horror we've seen already. This is only the start of it.

Chapter 31

Once again the day rattles on slowly as we progress into the mountains in Southern Mexico. The roads narrow and it becomes a battle to get past wagons heading the same way. Occasionally there is a passing spot with an extra lane and there is a swift competition to race in front of a wagon before the lane disappears, relaxing for a few minutes until the next wagon or farm truck appears. It's relentlessly boring. The landscape changes little from rolling green forests and mountain views. A lot of land but not a lot to fill it.

The journey is exhausting. I can imagine some hippy cool folk thinking about the pleasure of driving these roads and exploring a country like this. It's a crap way to see a country. The view from the driver seat is the wrong end of a truck and even the times when the view opens up, my eyes are focussed on dodging passing cars and bikes. The food is mostly sugar and carbs and my gut is like a tank of liquid swishing with soda and beer. It's not a surprise that conversations in the car are mostly impatient and argumentative when we are all pumped with shit. Sophia is taking on a double load with the poison in her veins. I try not to think too much about it. There is enough to worry about in the coming days.

We hit mid-afternoon at San Cristobal de la Casas, a mountain town. I already like this place as we drive through the suburbs. The colour, the feel, is much more European. There are people around gazing at the buildings. So different from the metropolis or dirt towns we've passed in the last few days.

We park on a street close to the centre. Lacking the energy to go find anywhere else we enter the nearest place. It's a kind of artisan bistro that offers tacos, enchiladas, fish and veggies, nothing unusual. But this is fresh, well cooked. It smells amazing, what I dreamt Mexican food in Mexico would smell like. Sour and spicy, chilli tingling my taste buds, cooled by a fresh salsa and sour cream. I devour a plateful. Sophia and Mia are less interested in the food, but then they've have a far better choice than my veggie limitations. Another plate of bland beans and rice is not something that troubles them.

The woman serving us has a more ethnic Central American look, rounder facial features, a shorter, bulkier body. It has been a noticeable trait in the people we passed in the street. Another sign that we are further from home. She doesn't speak English at all, so Sophia does the usual convenient translations. I've become too lazy to try to guess recognisable words.

Mia is curled up in her chair, half dozing. I want to drape the animal skin covering the chair around her. What must have gone through her mind in the last week? Dad murdered, she's stabbed someone in the leg, run away from home with strangers and no idea what comes next. Then again, I could say the same for myself as well. I'm no more equipped to handle this than Mia.

A young waiter, Mia's age, possibly the woman's son, serves the food. He keeps returning back and I notice he has his eye on Mia. Each time, he tries to engage with her. He's good looking, with a bit of dark fluff growing round his chin. Not old enough to shave but old enough to be flirting. At first, she doesn't reply, but then after a visit to the bathroom, I see her chatting to him at the bar. Good she's found a friend I suppose.

I'm yawning already. Sophia shouts Mia to come.

Across the road is a guest house and we check in. Whilst I could do with the sleep, I decide to take an hour to myself to wander around. A cigarette post dinner contrasting with the semi-decent mountain air. Walking towards the centre, the town seems relaxed and carefree. People as in any place heading home from work. There are squares with restaurants and bars with people sat outside. Music playing. Spanish guitar inevitably and I feel a yearning to string up mine and set up and play. Though I might struggle to attract an audience with rockabilly out here.

In the centre, I stumble upon the main cathedral. I think of Mom and how delighted she would be to see this. The vibrant yellow colour on the front wall, the humble structure, magnificent in its simplicity. The subtle lighting almost candle like, gives it the welcoming aura of a small chapel rather than the imposing buttress of a cathedral. I take a walk to the opposite side of the square where a few tourists are lining up the large cross in the square against the cathedral. I try the same shot and realise it's a visual camera trick to make it appear as if the cross is forged into the cathedral wall. Mom has dragged me round many a church but never something as interesting or colourful as this place. It could bring about a few conversions just by its welcome feel.

I wonder what Mom's doing now. I want to call her but not yet. Soon. Once I get to somewhere safe and I can reassure her it's going to be alright.

I move on, enjoying the refreshing time to myself. I try not to think too much about my plight as I might sit on the floor and cry and never get up again. At least the chance to walk around and have a normal experience this far from home is a blessing.

Realising I need to get back, I head back towards the guest house. The street slopes down from the centre opening up a vista of the mountains. With the fading evening light it creates a magnificent end of the day. I make a promise to return here and see it through the lens of a proper tourist rather than a passer-by.

I smoke a last cigarette before going back inside. Sophia is sat in the bar with an espresso and a tequila. Which one is the drug and which is the pleasure?

'Mia in the room?'

'She went to sleep. I wish I could do the same.'

I pull up a chair.

'Cerveza,' I say to the lady behind the bar. 'So how do we get across the border?' I ask.

'We rock up in the car, show our passport and drive on through,' Sophia says.

'That easy?'

'Not really. Though it could be,' she says. 'We'll go to La Mesilla, as it's a small border town. Checked the map and it's just a one road town with a border down the middle. Likely if the border guards are awkward they can be easier paid off.

Down in Cuidad Hidalgo there is too much attention. It's the main Southern Highway and full of refugees heading for the US. We're best avoiding that.'

'Yeah – reckon they're all running away from the places we're running to.'

'You said it.'

She orders another tequila and heads off to the toilet again.

It's some time before she comes back and I wonder if she's taken something again. My glass is empty by the time she returns. She looks no different so I don't know if she did or she didn't shoot up. I've given up trying to guess what's going on with her mental state.

'These girls like Opal?' I ask. 'What really happens to them?'

'What do you mean?' She asks knocking back the drink in one gulp. The lady returns and tops it up.

'I admit my view of the world is limited to suburban streets, but all I can imagine is some kind of children's home. I get that they're not social workers running the place and that there will be abuse and neglect. But what do they gain from doing this? It's like - abusing kids is for the weirdos and pedos. Most men wouldn't want to do it - or am I being stupid and naïve?'

'Well, sort of. I'm not an expert either. Here's what I heard, and what I saw with girls like Mia. She was lucky that her dad protected her from a lot. It's not even that the other women look out for the young girls. Half the time they're high or themselves being abused. They are in no position to act as care givers or parents.

'Like all these gangs, it's all about fear and bravado. You survive by being meaner than the next guy. You got to scare people into submission. Compassion is weakness. Like you say, they'll have buildings or dormitories where they keep them. If they're lucky there will be water or they get fed. But yeah abuse, neglect. Think as well that these girls might be coming up to puberty. They need proper support and care. The only thing they got for a carer is sweaty men who need somewhere to stick their dicks every night. It's sick really. The parents go crazy. Their sons are already gone, recruited under threat of death. What these girls go through before they are even sixteen is heart-breaking. Unreal, unimaginable, to us, but nothing but real to them. They survive, or at least some do, but what do they become as people. Fucked up world. Think of it - their brothers might be the ones who kidnapped their sisters, or be guarding them. The girls become currency and leverage for more money.'

I'm shocked. I turn away, not able to look Sophia in the eye. It's stories, anecdotes but I also know it's truer than a lie. It's like charity adverts we see on the TV. They know how to play a crowd, squeeze the last bit of empathy out of an audience to get donations. We turn away because the message is rammed down our throat. We ignore it in the end, made up shit, another sympathy case wanting hard-earned bucks. We're immune to what's behind it because it's not us. We can't imagine it because if we did imagine or it understand we would do everything in our power to stop it, wouldn't we? We'd donate, we'd complain, we'd fight. But we turn over the channel or the ad break is over and we are back to the TV show. We know what we are doing when we ignore it and turn the other way. Horror is for other people.

So it carries on. These gangs can do what they want and their only fear is not that they get arrested for any of their crimes but that another gang with bigger weaponry steals their pitch.

'Death seems like a relief from all that.'

'You'd be surprised, Donnie. Most people are not that keen on dying as a choice. They still got to feed themselves, parents, and other kids. Others will try to escape. Hence why you get all those people walking to the USA. The ones Trump calls the migrant army, coming to steal your job and rob your house.'

I hang my head a little. I listened to that crap from Trump and believed it. Did I believe it? Or did I just think it sounded a convenient reason to shut them out? In reality they're just people trying to survive, fleeing from these evil bastards killing and raping their kids. It's sick.

'I still don't know how we're going to be able to help them,' I say.

She sighs.

'Donnie, at this point, I don't know either. I want to try, though. Everything else is so fucked, including me. I want to do something. If I get one kid out and free then that's a good thing isn't it.'

'I know. I'm with you. But what does free look like?'

'I don't know that either. But it's enough for me. I need to sleep now.'

She leaves the bar and I drink the last of my beer.

I take a moment to think about what's going on back home. I daren't check. I know if I call or check Facebook or anything I'll want to go back. That's impossible at the moment. In fact I can't imagine how I can go back without getting killed or someone else killed. Keep going forward. Tell myself Rose will be fine. Gary will look after her, so will Hugh. They know I'll be back. Just wish I did.

Though does Rose want me back now. I've run out on her, lied to her, gone against everything she wanted me to do. But then she was speaking so badly of Daniella and Opal, like they somehow deserved it. My stomach churns as I think about. Did I just voice something to myself that I'd never considered for a second before?

Sophia returns to the bar disrupting whatever conclusion I was coming to. Her eyes are wide, her face pale.

Something's wrong.

'Mia's gone,' she says.

'Where? How?' I ask.

'She's not in the room, the bathroom, anywhere. Shit.'

We check the foyer and the washroom and then out into the street. It's dark and street lights are poor. The pickup is there still but I've drank too much to drive.

'Try the cell,' I say. 'This is an emergency, isn't it?'

'Just ring it.' I've never seen her looked panicked before. Normally when she's stressed, beyond the mean words and quick anger, she's carries a concentrated look. An energy driving her. Tonight, her eyes are moving rapidly from right to left, she appears unsteady, feeble. Fear removes her power. She's angry but lost.

No reply. I shrug my shoulders.

We look at each other. She steady's herself on the chair. My heart is racing, her panic is affecting me. What do we do?

'She can't have gone far,' I say.

'Mia doesn't know anyone here, where the hell could she go?'

Looking out the window, we both speak at the same time.

'The bistro.'

'The dude she was talking to before. She's gone somewhere with him.'

Seconds later, we bang on the door and the lady who served us returns.

'Mia?' she asks,' ¿Está tu hijo en casa?'

'No,' she replies. They exchange some more words. She goes inside and returns with a cell phone.

'He's gone out with friends,' Sophia informs me.

The lady ends the call and chats to Sophia who then drags me along the street. 'He's in the centre - she gave me the name of the place they hang out.'

We rush along. I'm exhausted but can't afford to stop now. We can't lose Mia. Because... I hadn't even thought about what the consequences were of losing her like this. Because, she's one of us now. Part of us. We can't lose her.

I replay in my mind, every fight, every moment since I found her. Since we came together in this adventure. What is she to me? Goofy, awkward, cute kid with a smart mouth. Nothing on the surface, but underneath everything. The first time I've felt any responsibility in my life. I don't want to care about Mia, but I do. Brave, wild, but wise and strong. She'll grow up to be one hell of a woman. If she makes it that far.

Ten minutes of fast walking and we are back close to the square I was at earlier.

'Here,' she says.

A group of boys are on the street corner.

'She's not here though.'

I see the boy from the bistro. He's leaning on the corner, his tongue working its way into the throat of a girl. Too old for Mia. If she's not here, then where?

Sophia storms into the group. The guys collect around her. Chests proud, fingers pointing.

I stay back.

A stream of Spanish spews from her mouth. Sophia doesn't take the gentle enquiring approach.

Sophia shoves one guy hard and the rest get closer, pushing back. She stumbles backwards but balances herself. Typical Sophia, she isn't going to be bullied and is back leaning into the face of one guy. I've seen the biggest of guys in high school gangs threaten and bully, but none could create the ferocity of an angry Sophia.

The boys aren't for holding back and continue the pushing. Tension is rising.

The bistro dude's girlfriend storms into the crowd, grabs Sophia by the hair and slaps her hard. Sophia is on the floor and I can't leave it any longer. She's going to get hurt. I run towards her and grab Sophia as she scrambles to her feet.

The boys are laughing as the girl hurls abuse after abuse in frantic Spanish.

Sophia goes for her but I drag her back and run away back to the square.

'What the fuck was that all about?'

'Fucking cabrones, smart mouthed. They need a lesson in life, cabrones.'

'Calm down, Sophia.'

She pushes at me but the fire is dying.

'She's gone off with one of them on his scooter. He took her for a ride out of the city.'

'So why the excitement?'

'Because one cabrones thought it was funny to tell me, he was going to break her in. I want to kill him.'

I see it now. I feel it. Bastards.

'If he harms her, Donnie, I'll kill him,' she says.

'I get it. I'm certainly not here to stop you. But let's keep a cool head. We need to find her.'

'Any ideas?' She asks.

'Do we know where they went?'

'They wouldn't tell me. I tried pushing them to tell me.'

'I saw that,' I reply. 'I take it they didn't cooperate. Let's get the car, go look around.' I'm exhausted, neither of us fit to drive, but we can't leave her.

Sophia decides to drive. I'm not going to argue with her in this mood. The engine roars as we race away. We go street to street looking for a scooter. No sign of it or Mia.

'She will be out of town. Somewhere quiet if he's planning something.'

On the outer city road, she spies a track up towards a small hill.

'There,' she shouts.

A vista sign advertises some beauty spot. Perfect lover's location.

The backend of the pickup slides to the left with the understeer as Sophia races up the hill. The dust from the stony surface kills any visibility in the night. Sophia isn't going to slow down so there's no point suggesting it.

Reaching the top of the track, there's an open space with a few cars and pickup trucks scattered around. No sign of a scooter. We park the car and walk round peering through the undergrowth for any sign of people. Sophia goes up to the first Pickup and bangs on the door. Again she's isn't one for discretion and pushes the car until someone steps out.

A guy, naked above the waist, pulling up his trousers, swears at her.

'She's not here,' I say, dragging her away again, there is no point pissing off more people.

The naked guy returns to his truck. I hear other cars fire up and begin to leave. No-one here wants to be seen.

We return to our pickup. She's muttering to herself as she races past the cars leaving.

'Where now?' I ask.

'I don't know,' she screams, 'stop asking me. Think for your damn self. And don't say fucking cops.'

'I'm not that stupid, Sophia.'

One day, I'll turn on her and the words I want to say won't stop. But I bite my lip, because one thing I learnt about Sophia is the more you bite back, she comes back a hundred times worse. It's like pouring oil on a bush fire.

'Let's go back to the Bistro,' I say. 'Maybe the owner's got some ideas of the favourite meeting spots.

Once again we are banging on the door. The woman returns. This time there are no smiles and no polite social exchanges.

I witness a full throttle outbreak of Spanish debate. I turn away; this is getting us nowhere.

Looking back towards the hotel a scooter pulls up and Mia steps off the back, handing her helmet back to the owner.

'Mia,' I shout, running over.

Sophia is past me before I reach her and levels a firm right hand at the scooter rider. Taken by surprise he falls off, the scooter tumbling with him. Sophia isn't stopping there as she launches a series of punches and kicks.

'Stop! Sophia, no!' Mia screams, pulling at Sophia. I join in and pull Sophia off. She wriggles and elbows me as she breaks lose. She goes back for more.

'He didn't do anything,' Mia screams. 'Leave him alone.'

'Where the fuck did you go?' I demand to know.

'For a ride, nothing else. Fuck you all,' she screams back. Tears in her eyes as she beats at Sophia.

'Ok, reckon y'all calm down.'.

The guy gets back on his scooter, the helmet hiding any expression as he looks back at us. He must think we're mad. He races away. Sophia sits on the sidewalk, her head bowed in her hands.

I leave her alone, unable to control the anger and fire burning in her body. I wonder if she needs more than help for her addiction. That's not just drugs but a lifetime of frustration exploding.

'She's loca.'

I look to Mia. She seems fine, confused but not the face of a girl who's been assaulted or abused.

'Seriously, Mia, you should have told us you were going out.'

'Yeah and what would you have said. You ain't my parents. You got no right to tell me anything so I went. Big deal. He was nice. I enjoyed it.'

'And he didn't harm you?'

'Fuck you Donnie, who the hell are you? Don't pretend you care.'

'Of course, I care,' I say but she doesn't acknowledge me. 'I do care,' I whisper, just loud enough to hear the words myself.

Mia is no longer interested in me. Instead she stares at Sophia, still sat on the sidewalk.

'Loca,' Mia mutters as she turns back and walks into the hotel.

Drama over. I leave Sophia to her misery and follow Mia inside.

Chapter 32

San Cristobal de las Casas to Guatemala to Frontera La Mesilla. Guatemala Border

The next day the morning is slow, the mood one where words are not desirable. The first person to speak is likely to invoke the wrath of one or the other and therefore no-one does. And as such there is no rush to get organised and start the car. It seems destiny can wait a few more hours.

Even whirlwind Sophia has spent much of it asleep. I'm grateful as well not to behind the wheel yet. It's too much to contemplate and if I can delay it another few hours then it's all good to me. Sophia was talking yesterday about a hurricane coming. I checked the news on the TV in the hotel and there is most definitely one heading to the Caribbean coast of Yucatan and down along the Central American Coastline.

If we delay a few days we might miss it, but then where will we go in the meantime? This place feels safe and we can get online to do all that Sophia has planned. But it's also not what we said we would do. The more we delay the more we might just fall apart.

It's well into the afternoon before we are all together in the hotel reception. I feel a hundred percent better for taking the time out. Even Sophia looks less stressed.

Her skin has more colour, her hair less greasy and her eyes clear and relaxed. Mia is texting on her cell, no prizes for guessing who with. Perhaps she needs to be a kid for a while.

'Can I use the laptop?' I ask. 'I can send an email to my family. Let them know I'm ok.'

She pauses for a moment.

'Ok, but nothing about where we are or where we are going? No funny business.'

'I'm not a child.'

It's annoying feeling like I'm being judged but I can ignore it. I pray it won't be for too much longer and this situation sorts itself out.

'Talking of which, Mia don't tell your boyfriend where we're going.'

'He's not my boyfriend,' she replies. 'And I'm not a kid either.'

She pauses. I can see from the way she's looking at Sophia that more is going to be said.

'Don't go there, Mia,' I say.

She's not going to listen to me as she stands up, finger pointing.

'I don't care who you are or why we are here. Do that to me again, you'll never see me again. Humiliating. Even Papa never did that to me.'

'Get over yourself, Mia,' Sophia replies. It seems for once Sophia isn't interested in a fight and instead passes me the laptop. She gets up to go to the bathroom. Perhaps, there are greater priorities.

I log on and quickly scan for news in Nashville. Nothing much except Trump. I see a by-line for Amy Ryder on a link and click on it. Nothing important, but it reminds me I have a contact card for her in my bag. Might come in useful some time. Nothing on the website about me or Detective Stephens. I haven't even called the hospital to see how she is, though she's probably ok. If she had died there would have been some kind of follow up on her.

I log into my mail and send something short and sweet to Rose. Something like, I'm ok, will be in touch in a few days. Getting closer to the end. What more can I say? She will be angry at me either way for not coming home but whatever happens I'll have to make it up to her. We've never been apart like this and reckon, I don't even know if I have a relationship to go back to. What will be left after all this?

I've not even picked the guitar up in a week, trashed everything to run like this. Not even sure I understand why.

I've gone from witnessing a murder to racing away across America through Mexico chasing hundreds of thousands of dollars, a kidnapped teenager and potentially precious stones. I quickly google the value of black opals. I get lots of images coming up of the stones, just like the one I have. The line I pick out the most is where it states 'can be worth as much as diamonds'. The word 'can' seems to be doing a lot of work in that sentence. I click on the link but there is no more information except an explanation of how stones values are governed by supply and demand and black opal being rare and difficult to mine creates a higher value. The problem with supplies of stones from Honduras is that many of the mines have been closed due to corruption and cartels. Is that why Carter got out of the game? There is no set valuation on the link so I can't guess what it is worth. I would have to take it to a dealer and they would try to convince me it was worthless and pay me nothing for it. Another thing I should have paid more attention to at school: how to con a conman.

'Time to get going,' Sophia says, returning from the bathroom. 'We need to be at the border before it closes. Too much time wasted already today.'

I close the browser and shut it down. Nothing much to know or learn.

A few minutes later I'm back behind the wheel and driving south from the city.

The road continues as yesterday. Slow progress through mountain passes and small towns. Wagons and local buses block the way, plus the odd farm vehicle. Painfully tedious but we have to keep going. We are offered stunning views in the gaps between the trees. It's easy to feel guilty for not spending more time in these places. Everything is a means to an end yet I'm missing out on so much. I've never visited anywhere like this, content to think of home as the only place I need to be. Even when we talked about going on tour it was always round the US, maybe California, West Coast stuff. Seeing San Cristobal has changed my mind a little. Its culture and simple charms were welcoming rather than scary. Though I don't need the drama of last night to return.

Even the language factor could be got round here with a phrase book or a tourist guide. Maybe I should learn Spanish.

Where would I ideally like to go? The Caribbean always looks pretty and scenic but is also expensive. The money Rose and I have won't get us far. Beaches in Costa Rica and Mexico are the same. I never thought of going there. Maybe I should. It's a thought for the future. When we're done saving and got what we need, we can take a holiday. Do something other than music for a week.

When all this is over. When we have enough money. When she is speaking to me again. A lot of when and even more ifs. I sigh, deep breath. Keep driving Donnie. Future's coming at you fast...as is Guatemala.

The countdown markers for the miles to the border dwindle to single figures and we are almost there. The sun is lower in the sky and it won't be long before it disappears over the mountain ridges. It goes dark pretty quickly afterwards.

Approaching the town of La Mesilla, it's hard to know we are leaving one country and entering the next. It is a single street lined with hotels and typical shops with a border post at the end of it in the middle of dense forest. Not that I'm sure what I expected in a remote place such as this. But it feels a little underwhelming after the Bridge of America in El Paso.

After days of driving another country creeps up on us from nowhere. Guatemala.

We progress slowly down the road checking out the street markets and stalls at the side. Colourful buildings and people, making a living from the border trade. We drive up to the border post, Sophia at the wheel. The guard approaches and I get nervous again. Clammy hands and shaking legs are the outer signs but my fast beating heart is the worst. I must have the worst poker face. It's good that the light is fading and they can't see what I look like properly.

The guard checks the pickup and reads the papers. I already feel better that it's a Mexican plate and not US.

He returns to the driver's side and he and Sophia have an exchange in Spanish. I watch her reach into the pocket of the car door and retrieve her purse. She shows him some paper wrapped around some bills. Of course, this is the way it works.

He takes the paper and steps away. The gate opens and we drive on through.

'What was that about?' Mia asks.

'Told me had a choice. Pay 1000 Pesos and no inspection necessary or an inspection of the car would take a few hours, might be ready tomorrow, might be more charges to pay.'

'So you paid.'

'Paid double just to be sure. Either way, we would have paid. At least this way we keep moving.'

'Ok, cool.'

The town seems little different from where we've just been in Mexico, same people same colours. But a different country. Noisier, with more motorbikes and red Tuk-Tuks. Never seen those before. Thought they only had them in India.

'Hotel and sleep,' Sophia says. 'We can't drive in the night here. Too many risks, too dangerous. Tomorrow we start at dawn. One day to go, people.'
    'Welcome to Guatemala,' I say.

Chapter 33

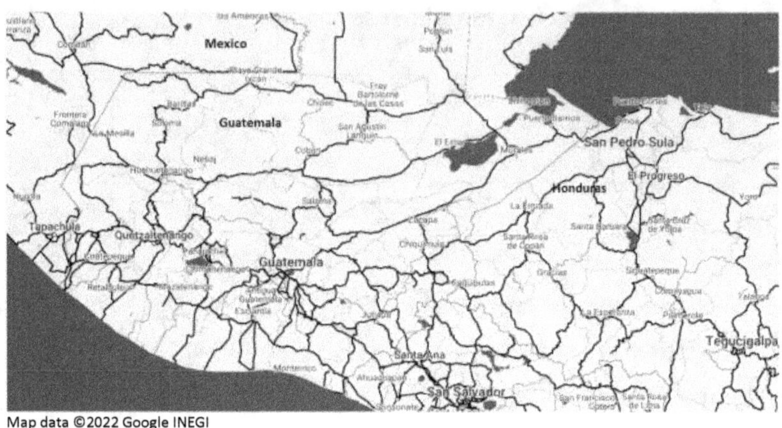

Map data ©2022 Google INEGI

La Mesilla, Guatemala to Honduras border

I didn't sleep well last night, despite the exhaustion of the drive and the ongoing nightmare of my current existence. Crossing the border feels like a step closer to the dragon. My mind is an empty tin can with an annoying stone rattling round in it. It won't settle in one place. I'm expecting bandits to hijack us, the car wheels to fall off in the middle of the mountain roads, even to come across some long lost indigenous tribe who will force us into some ancient rituals with sacrificed animals. The stuff of my worst nightmares.

None of this is true though. Driving through Guatemala, weaving our way through the slow mountain roads is no worse or better an experience than the last days of Mexico. The views are dramatic and the roads poor in places but life goes on pretty much the same as everywhere we've just been. The Tuk-Tuks are a pain but outside the towns and cities there aren't many.

Things happen I'm sure, not that we intend to stop anywhere today. I have to remind myself for all the talk of dangers we're going to, the worst thing that happened was the death of Daniela in a place I never thought as dangerous. So it's all relative.

One of the striking features along the high roads is the many logging companies and mining corporations, a few with recognisable American brands or at least non-Spanish names, which is sure sign of where the money and ownership comes from. It all comes back to Ryan Carter. The reason for all this. He came to these countries, made his money, and left to pursue a life of luxury back home. Whether Carter ever knew he left behind an unwanted legacy that he still seeks to deny is another matter. Though, I'm sure he does know all about Opal and Daniela. It doesn't add up otherwise. Opal is in her teens. He didn't leave Honduras until early 2010's. They lived locally, so when he went back home, he left Daniela and Opal behind. He can deny it all he likes but that truth can't be hidden for long. Was he sending money to them? She had that big opal stone. Was that a payment from the mine, a payoff so he could go back to the US with a clear conscience?

If there is one thing I want to achieve from this, despite finding Opal, is to make him pay and admit what he did. The more I think about it the more I reckon he was involved in Daniela's murder and he wants all this to go away. It's too convenient for it not to have been him.

There are two practical routes into Honduras, one a mountain pass and the other low down by the coast. The coastal crossing point is further but also closer to San Pedro Sula. Given that there are supposed to be even poorer roads in Honduras we decide to head further through Guatemala. Getting delayed another night en-route doesn't feel like a good choice. Especially as news of this hurricane hasn't gone away. We have a chance of being in the city by midnight. That feels like an achievement.

After miles of slow mountain roads we are eventually heading downhill now and approaching Lake Izabel. There are a lot of tourist signs for the lake along the road so I check it out on my cell phone. It's a tourist spot in the centre of the country with waterfalls and mountain trails, wildlife and birds. There are a few backpacker websites linking to it and I guess that fits. Driving through these slow roads doesn't fill with me with any wish to go near it.

Despite my earlier thoughts about nice holidays in exotic places, I think of lakes as poor substitutes for a beach and more insects to bite me, especially in these rain forest areas. The ones in the US near us are full of all sorts of critters, plus folk with guns wanting to fire at anything that moves. Macho bullshit.

But some people like them, in which case they're welcome.

'Look at those clouds,' Sophia says.

As we come over a mountain pass down towards the lake, there is a good view of the terrain ahead. The skies are darkening. In the distance, the horizon is dominated by a dark wall. It looks menacing, apocalyptic, and we are driving towards it.

'Are we going to make it in time?' I ask.

'I think we got an hour to get into Honduras,' she says, 'assuming they'll let us in. They might close the border to tourists - you never know these places when bad weather is coming. They completely shut down. Who can blame them?'

'They can't send us back though,' I say. 'We would be stuck completely.'

'I know, but what do they care,' she says.

'Hopefully a donation to their favourite charity will help the decision making.'

She shrugs beside me. 'That's a default now.'

Chapter 34

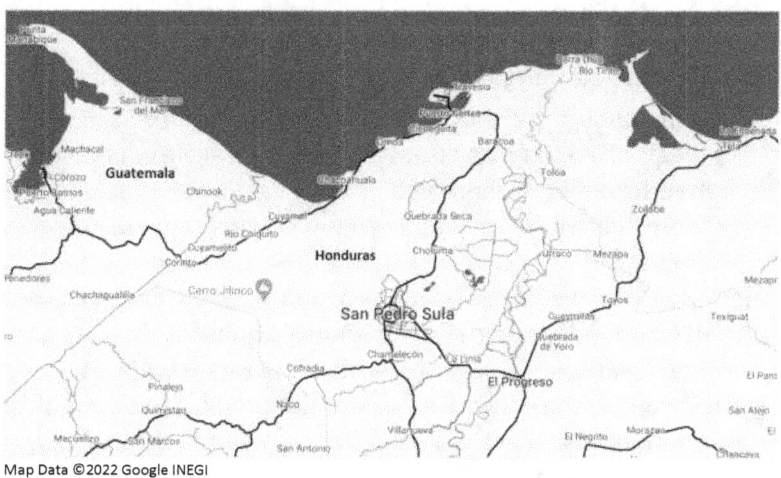

Map Data ©2022 Google INEGI

Puerto Cortes to San Pedro Sula, Honduras

If I thought the approach to the Guatemala border was a bit of an inconsequential place, coming into Honduras is like going down a farm road. The road surface itself is deteriorating, perhaps something to do with the enormous cattle wagons we are passing. I don't want to think where they are going to end up. Fortunately, Sophia and Mia are too focussed on other matters to see an opportunity to wind me up about my sensitivities.

We stop at a gas station before we reach the border, a mile down the road, and replenish supplies. Who knows how long it will be before we can stock up again. Mia picks a stack of candies whereas Sophia goes for the cooked chicken. Either of those will make me puke if I smell them, so I stick with chips and tacos to boost my carbs. Best I can get.

Sophia takes the wheel again as the better Spanish bribe negotiator, and I play the dumb American fool in the passenger seat. Seems a role I'm good at. The pot holes are big now and the road cut up. It's hard to figure there's a border down here but that's what the map says.

Eventually we are greeted by a sign ahead.

Feliz Viaje. Bienvenidos a Honduras.

'We're here,' I say out loud.

'I'm not sure we should be celebrating,' Sophia says.

'Feels like a long way but we made it, is all I'm thinking.'

'We haven't got there yet.'

'So this is where my Papá came from. It's some dirthole,' Mia says.

'Hey, girl, we're not going back home, so best you get used to it. Don't judge too quickly. Alright?' Sophia says.

The Guatemalan border guards lift the gate without checking. On the other side we are directed off to the right by the Hondurans. There is a small car park in a far better condition than the one we just passed, so no complaints there. A white concrete shack awaits us.

'I think this is going to be expensive,' Sophia says.

We get out of the car, passports in hand and approach the border agent standing unimpressed by the door.

Sophia speaks to him in Spanish.

'He wants to know why we're here. Told him we are visiting family.' She looks towards Mia.

They exchange some more words and she turns back to me. His eyes look me up and down as well.

'Wants to know if you're fucking me and what I'm doing with a toy boy gringo.'

'Did he actually say that?'

'Kind of. Apparently it's not a good time to come to Honduras.'

'And what did you reply.'

'It's a fucking long way back.'

'How much does he want?'

I'm fed up with being made a show and return towards the car. One of the agents block the way. This is tenser than I expected.

Sophia peels off some bills. He takes the money roughly from her hand and then leans closer to her.

'Enough for you only,' he says in loud English for me to hear. 'Costs double for Grencho Americano. Extra insurance costs, unless you want to pay another way.' He smiles at his creepy joke.

Sophia locks eyes with him and snarls. I can see her temper rising. She's not ready to give in yet.

'Just pay him and let's get out of here.'

She pauses and then hands over a few more bills. He laughs in her face and she turns away without reacting. He invites us in to stamp the passports with no more words. We both walk towards the car feeling sullied. Dirty creepy bastards.

Once in the car we are allowed to proceed. We've made it now. We are in Honduras. A big sigh of relief and a sense we are close. It's not just the storm brewing off the coast that's making me nervous but a feeling that fate is playing a part. It's coming to us and what will be will be.

It's four in the afternoon. An hour along the coast and then a drive uphill to the city.

The drive to the coast is pleasant. Light fading but only a few kilometres and we are at the beach front. We are offered the best view yet of the coming storm over the Caribbean Sea as the swirling black clouds approach. I've seen storm clouds many times over Tennessee but these seem to belong to movie scene, like some battle of the Gods.

The beach front is deserted. Probably all the locals have fled to shelter. Any other day, I would have considered this a hidden beach paradise, but today menace fills the air for all sorts of reasons and shelter in the mountains looks like the best place to be.

We pull into a roadside space and take in the view. The smell of the salt is rich in the air alongside the same humidity of the last few days. The temptation to run over the road and onto the beach is strong but I hold back. I smoke a cigarette instead.

We can't hang around here.

Sophia is staring the other way, towards an old colonial style building with land around. The place is boarded up. In its heyday it would have been a magnificent house. Verandas and balconies, landscaped gardens and wonderful sea views.

'Wonder what the story is behind that place,' I say.

'You mean when it was built or why it's abandoned?' Sophia asks.

'Both I suppose. Seems a tragedy to have such a beautiful building lying empty.'

She shrugs.

'If you go back far enough, you'll find that it was built by locals in slave like conditions and as far as what happened to abandon it, it's probably to do with drugs, corruption and the wiping out of a family. It won't be a good story.'

'I reckon not.'

'And yes, it is a wonderful place and shouldn't be empty. Remember not to think about the building but the people involved. That is the tragedy.'

I can't argue with the sentiment so finish my smoke and get back in the car.

For a few moments whilst the others settle in, I take in the view. I like this place. I never expected to come here and feel even remotely comfortable, but I do. Maybe it's the coastline and the idea of a holiday on spectacular beaches, imagining Rose in her bikini, all eyes on her, relaxed, none of the worries of the day to think about.

Rose would hate it though. I'm not sure why and I imagine she wouldn't know why but she would find something to complain about. Food, flies, heat. I never really thought about that too much. I know Mia and Sophia probably think I'm a bit constrained in my ways, too much of privilege and all that crap. But Rose is a whole other dimension. Her blood runs so deep with the red of the South there ain't nothing going open her mind or change her ways. She don't want educating and anyone who tries will get a shoulder colder than Alaska.

Something for me to mull on. Maybe my eyes are open to a new world that I ain't seen before and scared as I am about what it has to offer, it's kind of interesting and exciting. In the last week I've seen more places than I ever been in my whole life and I swear that one day I will come back and do it again at a time when all the devil's horses are not chasing my ass.

The sky continues with it's fine impression of gathering horses, big black and noisy, ready to stampede. The horizon is full of foreboding weather in one direction and the ruined building in the other, the fantasy is gone. Time to get moving.

The road to San Pedro Sula awaits before the storm gets any closer.

Once we pass Puerto Cortes on the small peninsula the road turns uphill again. We are joined by masses of other cars leaving the town. It is a slow and stuttering drive despite there being two lanes. Everyone is heading the same way. There are people walking along the roadside with backpacks and takeout bags. It's an exodus.

The road surface is noisy but given the circumstances I begin to question why anyone says this is a worse place than Guatemala. Looks to be an improvement in many ways.

The road winds up through small towns and eventually, as darkness falls, we enter San Pedro Sula. Journey's end.

It's over a week since I left Nashville and I feel I've stepped into another world. This is the murder capital of the world but at the moment just feels like every other postcolonial Spanish town with its churches and colourful buildings. More important is a hotel and refuge for the night. No more driving. A hurricane is coming and who knows where to start with finding these gangs. Probably they'll find us knowing our current record.

I'm more than happy to dump the pickup on the street and walk in to first place we find. There are big city chains and probably a decent bed but that feels too public. So we settle for a small place on 8th Street. La Plata. We are lucky they've still got beds and as before we are back in a family room, huddled together. The windows are boarded like all the other places in the street. It feels scary and ominous. But lying on the bed with a beer in hand, I'm just happy to be here. Tomorrow is another day. But of course, it won't be any other day. I have no idea what will happen. It could quite possibly be the worst day of my life. Knowing that potential exists it's hard to know any other way of approaching it other than drinking as much alcohol as I can get into my body so that I can pretend it isn't going to happen.

'Do you need anything?' I ask, almost asleep on the bed without even touching much of the drink.

'Get me some powder. I'm going to need it - I need to get this business done before the Wifi is gone.'

'You're not serious? I just drove like a thousand miles, there's a damn hurricane coming and you want me to go finding drugs for your dirty habit in a place I've never been where I don't speak the language? Get your own shit.'

'Hell, Donnie. If you're wetting your pants over going to see some drug dealers, how the hell you going to negotiate your girl's release? You're going to be talking to some people who negotiate in the number of fingers or toes they take off before they come to an arrangement. Honestly how you ever survived a day in your life I really don't know. Did the kids at school pull your jockey shorts down once too often. Veggie Donnie, must have been like Saturday night live for your school buddies.'

Arrgh, my brain is exploding. This woman. Let me out of here. I take a deep breath before responding.

'Reckon nobody is going to be out now. It's pointless.'

'Jesus, Donnie, have you not learnt anything? Drug dealers don't work social hours with paid holidays. They're working, they got targets to meet. Trust me. Go find one.' She turns to Mia, 'Take her as well, make her useful instead of deadweight. She can translate. It will do you good to explore and see what's happening.'

'Fuck you,' Mia says, not moving from the bed.

'I've got to run this bank job tonight. Listen, both of you. You're crying like babies. Think about it. We are here because when this job runs, we are going to be sitting on millions of dollars, and every drug cartel between here and New York is going to want to kill us. We need to be safe. Number one priority. Get supplies, and if you want me not to want to murder both of you in your beds tonight, I need to make this pain in my head go away. You got me?'

'You scare the shit out of me. Does anything good ever come out of your mouth? I mean, cool it dude.'

'No and I don't give a fuck for your sensitivities. You know what? It scares the shit out of me too. But we are in this so fucking deep. Day after tomorrow is the day we are supposed to be back in El Paso handing over five hundred, and we're not going to be there. So, I need to do the business tonight and start the ball rolling. Otherwise, your mama's going to be sent back to you in pieces.'

Her ranting is going so far over my head now. I don't hear it anymore. Maybe going out into the firehose like beginning of a hurricane is preferable to this.

'Have you checked the account passwords still work?'

'Like a treat. Checked it every hour. His accountant is in and out of there like a kid at the candy stall. He hasn't got a clue when I'm logging in and out. It's so easy to steal from these people. It's the reason they've got guns - they never had the brains to run this operation.'

'Will leave you to it. What do I ask for? Coke, heroin? Is there some local word to use? Or maybe I ask for something that will put you to sleep for a week, maybe then we all get some peace round here.'

'Funny Donnie, y'all be dead without me and you know it.' She makes extra play of the y'all just to twist the knife a little more. She never misses. It must be exhausting being her.

'Mia will know,' she continues, 'Get what you can tonight, coke, pills, any of them. I might need all of it to get me through next few days.'

I finish the drink and grab a jacket. It's already getting cool. From being half asleep I'm now stepping out into a minefield. Why do I continue to listen to this mad woman? I suppose because I have to. Like she says, without her I'm screwed. I really am.

Mia follows me out.

***

The street outside is quiet as I light up a cigarette.

'Where do we look for a dealer?' I ask.

'Where do you think? Bars, kids on the street. They're everywhere.'

'But there is no-one around, how do I spot one?'

'Walk downtown, they'll appear.'

I zip my fleece up. The air is cooling and there is a strong breeze swirling in the air. It's a pitch-black sky and tension is growing. Or maybe I'm imagining my own fears. But a storm coming always creates weird atmospherics.

We walk on past houses and bars boarded up. Railings hard locked, garbage bins pushed to the side.

'How are you feeling about being here? You've been quiet.'

'I don't know,' Mia says. 'This is nowhere but then I can't go home ever, now. I have no home, do I?'

'I'm sorry.'

'You should be, this is all your fault.'

'Don't start with that again, I didn't ask for this to happen. I'm sorry your Papá got killed.'

She says nothing for a moment. 'It's ok. Would have happened sooner or later. He was never going to grow old working for Sula 7. I think I know that now.'

After a few hundred metres there is a café with a group of men outside.

'These guys?'

'Si, they will know.'

'You need to ask them in Spanish, they won't understand me.'

'Too fucking easy for you gringos. No hablo Español.'

We approach the guys.

'Hey, ustedes, tienen cocaine, algo mas?' She asks, straight out with it.

'Hey, cabrona.' Then they say something I don't understand.

211

A few sentences are exchanged and one of them points down the street. Mia turns to me and we walk on.

'Did he just call you a bitch?'

'Yeah, so I called him a pendejo, a pedo. It's all good. Dealer down the road. We need to knock on red door. US dollars only.'

We carry on walking. A cop car comes round the corner and slows. The driver looks towards us but then speeds up and carries on. Past the next block there is an apartment block with a red door to the basement.

'Is this it?' I ask.

'Looks like it.'

She knocks. After a few seconds it opens marginally. I can't see the face just a woman's hand reaching out. A package is exchanged with a few bills. The door slams shut quickly and the deal is done.

Ten minutes later we are back in the hotel. Time enough for another smoke.

'Congratulations, your first drug deal.'

'Actually Mia did the work,' I say, returning to my beer.

'Course she did. What did you get?'

'A selection,' she says, 'I don't know what you take. Some coke as well.'

'Good work, Mia. You were trained well. I'm sending you out again.'

I can't listen to this shit. I've spent my life dodging drugs. Of course, not everyone sees it that way, and the streets are full of kids who got hooked into it by mistake and I pity them, but this is not my world.

'How's it going?' I ask.

'I've spent last few minutes getting ready to send this money. But I daren't press send. Once I do this, it's all over.'

She pauses and takes a deep breath.

'If I press send, here's what happens,' she says, stuttering.

'I know, we talked about it.'

'Yeah we did but we are going to talk about it again because every detail is important and we have to get this right,' she talks rapidly, like she's prepared a speech in her mind. 'I press send and the ten million dollars goes from Marcos' account to an account in the Cayman Islands. From there it will go to Panama, then to Gibraltar and back to Panama again. After that the bot takes over for a few hours moving it between dummy accounts multiple times until it lands back in my nice new account in Belize only one hundred kilometres from here by the time the morning comes. By then, the accountant will have sounded the alarm and every gang member will be brought in, interrogated for leaks and blood will be spilt. All the time, Marcos will know it's not one of them as they don't have the brains to shit on their own. That will deal with his anger but all the while he will be working through every enemy he has.'

She pauses for breath.

'Do I save him the trouble and call him now and tell him what I've done? We won't have a cell phone line tomorrow and he could cause mayhem if he doesn't know who it is.'

'Call him now. May as well be now. He doesn't know where we are and he can't get to us. Once he knows we have the money, he'll have to deal with us right? He won't go killing my girlfriend, my family?'

'Not if we do this right. She returns to the laptop and looks up at me. 'Any better ideas? Last chance.'

I try to think but I can't. I'm here in San Pedro Sula trying to rescue a kid from a local gang who will have no idea who I am, plus find enough money to settle a debt with a gang for a murder I didn't commit, all so the gang won't murder my family. Plus get the Nashville District Attorney to pay for his daughter to have a new life in America. I'm not sure I understand how I got into this, never mind get out of it. I'm about screwed either way. If I go home and go to the police, then the Nashville gang will be all over my family and I'll probably be murdered in my cell. If I run away, they'll find me. If I stay here they'll find me eventually and I'll be easy prey to anything, probably kidnapped and ransomed back home. Who's going to pay for my sorry ass to be released?

'Do it,' I say.

She taps away for a moment.

'Done.' She eyes up the cell phone in her hand. 'Better make that call.'

Sophia holds the cell in her hand and dials but doesn't call. She walks up and down the room. I'm shivering and I'm going to puke up in a moment.

'Dial the number,' Mia says.

She has it on speaker, as we listen to the dial tone. It goes for some time before Marcos answers.

'Hola.'

'Hola, Marcos. It's Sophia.'

'Ah Sophia who owes me a lot of money. I take it you've been busy finding it and you are not going to beg me for more time.'

'About that. Maybe you want to call your accountant. I suppose I now owe you a lot more money. You can have your money back. All of it in fact, maybe with interest. But it is on my terms, you understand?'

A blast of wind causes a crash of noise outside.

'Where are you Sophia? Kind of noisy where you are?'

'Doesn't matter where I am. Time enough when you work out your problem.'

'Sophia? Are you crazy? You know what this means. We were so good together, you and I. Then you do something stupid like this, and I have to kill you.'

'No you don't. Think about it, Marcos. I have your money, and if you want it, I need to be very much alive and well. Plus my friends and their families. Anything happens to them or me, then the money will end up in charities helping victims of drug gangs and traffickers.'

'*Maldita perra.*'

'Marcos, don't be like that. I'll let it pass for now while you go check the money.'

The call cuts before any more conversation can happen.

'No signal. Wifi has gone.'

'You did it,' I say.

She grabs the open bottle tequila and takes a drink as she shuts the laptop. She's the one shaking now. Mia goes up to her and gives her a hug. I decide to do the same. As I put my arms around them both, it's the first time I feel that we are all in this together.

Another crash outside shakes us from our embrace.

Sophia opens the package from the dealer. She fiddles with a wrap and then goes into the bathroom.

I open a bottle of tequila from the stock on the side and take a big gulp. There is another crash and bang from the street. A howl of wind follows like an engine racing in the wrong gear. Rain is beating on the roof. The sense of uselessness is overwhelming.

Sophia returns. She staggers into the door, drunk like. She grabs the bottle again and then collapses on the bed.

I return to the bed with my bottle. I'm hoping the alcohol will kick in and wipe me out. Shut out the horror of the noise outside, the worry in my head about what we just did. For a fight back against the gang, it feels like the scariest and riskiest thing I've ever done. But it is done now. We have no choice and whatever the world leaves after this brush with destruction, I'll have to face it. Too much running away. Too much fear. I take another swig as the howl winds up another level.

It's going to be a long night.

Chapter 35

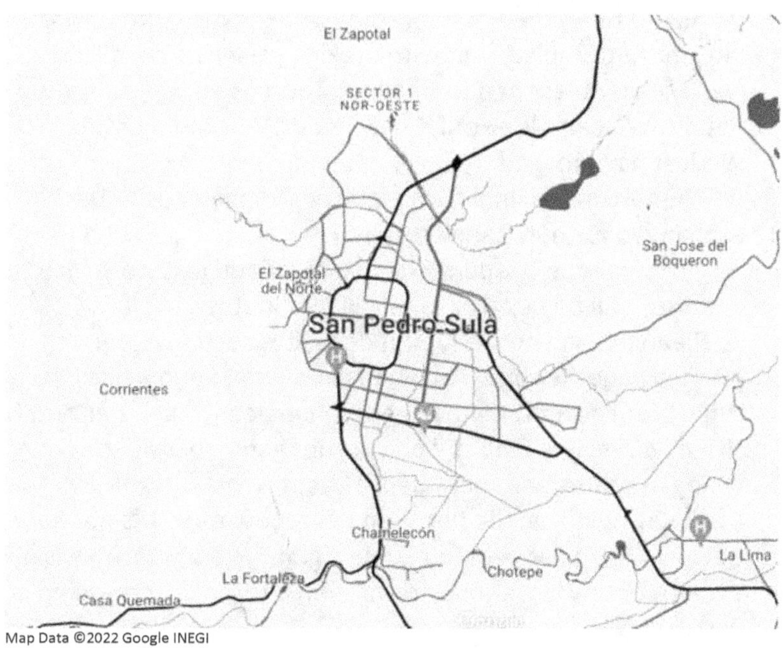

Map Data ©2022 Google INEGI

San Pedro Sula, Honduras

The escalating noise defies further explanation. The howls and roaring that began earlier in the night just get worse in scale. Constant battering like a drum machine ramped up to full, on a fast beat and I can't find the off switch. It eats into my head like a worm seeking out new crevices to terrorise. A hammer drill breaking into my skull. It feels like the hotel is being battered and blown around like a football kicked against the wall.

I compose more superlatives in my head as I try to define the noise.

Putting my head against one of my large Marshall amps at a gig and letting the vibrations flood through my body. Maybe, a jet engine outside with the plane window removed so I get the full noise experience.

All the time, there's a constant whining high pitch noise intermittently splattered with braking glass, a scream and a crash of an object or a tree falling. There is no way to know details. We can't look out. There is no TV or radio or internet. We just have to wait.

The torture technique of waterboarding needs to be exchanged for hurricane therapy.

Get someone to spend the night trapped in a storm like this and they will be begging to tell all in minutes.

Sleep doesn't come. Or if it does, it is seconds, then I'm jolted by another blast. Maybe I need what Sophia has. Whatever cocktail she took earlier has clean wiped her out. Mia sits shivering in a ball, still playing her game, barely speaking, crying in spates and then silence again. What a night.

I know wind can be fierce and overpowering. It's not hard to envisage for most people getting caught in a storm. This is not even remotely close to a storm. Even a tornado comes and goes in seconds.

This is a jail cell with no windows

Part of me is desperate to know what's out there, but the other part is wrapping myself in a ball, desperate to shut it out. Make it go away.

We have a cell phone light to see each other, but that has become pointless. There is nothing to see except us all, equally fearful. We can survive in this concrete shell, far enough from the coast to be out of the immediate line of fire, but still we know that when we open that door what's left of this city will be apocalyptic. I pray that people are safe, but I know just from what I can hear many won't be.

I think about those people walking along the roadside. The beachside communities we only drove past hours ago will be wiped out completely. Did they all make it to where they were going? Did they make it to safety?

Every question has no answer. We will have to wait until tomorrow and while our trauma still feels real and alive, I'm glad there is no cell phone and no power. It means no-one can find us and tell us if it has worked. We are in complete limbo and I'm happy to put off the realisation of failure for another day.

Sitting here in this madness I'm resolved that whatever is happening in San Pedro Sula tonight will change us forever. Regardless of what The Sula 7 can or cannot do to us, they are not immune to this storm and our horrific battle feels irrelevant while everyone has to fight for their lives.

***

It's well into the morning when the noise stops. We can hear people outside and all agree it's time to open the door.

Going through the downstairs of the hotel we can see dirty water running over the floor. The hotel staff are cleaning and picking up debris. The glass reception doors are smashed to pieces as is the board that was supposed to protect them. Maybe we were lucky the board held on our street window. Being a smaller space, it was probably stronger.

'Hay algo que podamos hacer?' Sophia asks.

'Nada,' the guy says in response and then he switches to English for my ears as I look out the door.

'Please don't go outside it's not safe, we will get food and water when we can. But don't go out.'

I stare through the open space and can see water flowing over the pavement, carrying debris and mud. It's not deep but it's fast flowing. Some people are outside but are drenched and looking desperate. We look at each other.

'I don't really want to go back to the room,' I say. 'Is there anything we can do to help?'

Sophia speaks to the guy again.

'Come this way,' he says.

He takes us through the back and I can see that the water has got through the kitchens and the back office rooms. The basement looks a complete pool of sewage. That will need completely draining, but only once the street is cleared as it will just fill up again.

He hands us a mop and gloves and the tasks become obvious. Dump anything that's garbage outside and get rid of any standing water. God knows what other guests are doing but I don't think they will be taking new ones in for some time.

None of us has much to say as we start mopping. For all the mess in the hotel, it has to be ten times worse outside.

All the while, I still have the nagging feeling that Marcos, desperate for his money, will try to get hold of Sophia. This could get very dangerous.

Chapter 36

We've done as much as we can in two hours to clear the debris inside the foyer. The water in the basement needs a pump. Given there's still running water in the street either from broken pipes or overflowing rivers, it seems pointless to do much more in the short term.

The owner comes round to speak to us.

'There are some volunteer groups organising in the town. If you want to help further, you can go to them. It seems that the storm wasn't as bad as predicted. Still bad but we missed the worst of it.'

I look at Sophia and Mia who both look at each other. With no cell phone signal there doesn't seem to be a better plan. We can't stand by and do nothing. I have never been much of community person but this is something else. The sounds of people hurt and crying against the howling wind will stay with me for a lifetime.

'Don't take anything with you of value. And don't stay out after dark. It will not be safe. Come back here.'

Given we don't have much of value with us except the cell phones and laptops it doesn't seem a problem. I don't think a black opal counts for much in this situation.

'Cell's not working anyway,' I say.

'Hopefully the power is back later today. Let's see,' the owner adds.

The owner loans us some boots which are ill fitting but better than my rather exhausted sneakers. It's warm outside with a hot sun beating down showing little sign of what happened last night. The storm has done its business and moved on rapidly south to forge more destruction.

The running water in the street is now limited to overflowing gutters but debris is everywhere; garbage, plastic and rubble. Our pickup has a pile of ceramic roof tiles on the hood. The windshield is smashed. It's not going anywhere soon. Other cars are on their sides or have similar debris on top of them. The houses around all look to be in one piece but there are a lot of people clearing up outside. It's a depressing sight, but as a normal residential street, I suspect this is the best I'll see today. I can't imagine what the poor areas will look like.

We head towards the central area of the city towards the Municipal Square. Sophia keeps trying to use her cell phone but with no signal it feels pointless trying.

'Maybe your friend will be around the centre?' I really hope so - whether kidnapped kids is the most important conversation, I don't know. As a foreigner I get the feeling I might not be welcome. We probably can't hang around too long being a burden on anyone.

'Gus. He will be out here somewhere. He was never a man to miss a chance to be a hero. He is the bold type, not easy to miss in a crowd.'

'Not like me then?' I say.

Mia laughs.

'Do I need to answer that?' Sophia says.

I laugh as well. Though for all my mocking myself, I'm here. Something even only a few days ago, I never thought possible. Not that I've lost my worry about what happens next, there is little else left for me other than to see it through. Going back feels almost as impossible as it was getting here.

My eyes survey every building, every person for signs of danger. The atmosphere is tense and whilst people are going about their business, that awareness of risk seems to keep us all quiet and focussed.

As we progress, the buildings become random in size and form, the external damage worse. Looking down back alleys I see mud and water covering streets. I'm not sure how much debris was there before but what is there now is coated in mud. Roofs are blown off and trees have fallen.

Street lights are bent and twisted or lie across buildings. More cars are at odd angles lifted off the street and displaced. Even with the equivalent of the National Guard and military, this will take months to clean up.

The smell of sewers gets worse. I daren't look down to see what I'm walking in. I'm grateful for the boots.

Ahead I see a gathering. Getting closer, there is more noise and people arguing. I wouldn't be approaching a crowd at the best of times but a city with this kind of reputation worries me more.

Sophia forges on ahead while I'm looking along side streets for escape routes. How fast can I run?

'Maras,' Mia says, pointing out so what looks like a street gang ahead. 'We need to get away from here.'

I look ahead and see people being pushed around. It all looks more random to me but I guess I have no idea.

Sophia pauses and takes in the same options as I do. She points down a side street that looks clearer.

'Let's go that way.'

I'm happy to go away from trouble but it feels inevitable that at some point we are going to come across these groups and we have to find a way to deal with them. It might be the next street or the next time we are here but they will be there. It's inevitable and I need to get my head around it.

We move quickly down the next street for a few hundred metres and find a parallel road to the centre which isn't blocked. It will do for now.

Will the Maras find us? Being an American, I'll be an easy victim and I wonder how I can deflect them. 'Take me to your leader, and also do you know where Opal Seles is being held?' Hardly going to respond with, 'come this way, sir.'

An image springs to mind of a large knife slicing through my throat and blood spurting in all directions. An unpleasant end. Would I feel pain or be dead before I'm even aware of it?

I push the image away. Creating new demons isn't going to me any favours. Stay in the moment.

This place is a mess, the situation is a mess, and I'm a mess. Walking closer to the centre feels like more trouble. I despair. The closer I get to the centre, the more my fear grows, all the same doubts spiralling. I have to discard them. I'm here. Deal with it Donnie. Grow a pair.

I search for a positive comparison. Playing my worst gig, out of tune guitar, hostile crowd in some cowboy bar that's smells of horse shit and stale urine. I've been there. Feels like crowd are one beer from turning the place over and smashing up the whole set including me and Rose. Yeah, I've played them, somehow found my way through to the end. We would clear out those joints in literally seconds once our set was done. No encores, no CD sales, just the get the hell out of there. Stop long enough to get paid and run.

Probably feared for my life, probably only time before this shit-show. Now seems fear is so much part of my daily routine, I don't even question it. Only question I have is how it ends, or even if it ends.

Got no answer to that one.

The town square is something out of a war movie. Army trucks and uniforms everywhere. People gather around in high-vis jackets and white hard hats.

'Let's go there,' Sophia says.

'We've come this far, I guess.'

We hurry towards the first group. Two soldiers with automatic rifles are ready to fire at the group and those approaching. As usual with military or even armed police they don't catch your eye so it's hard to feel safe with them or feel they are on your side. Is that deliberate, to avoid engaging empathically with someone you could easily be blasting a hole in their heads?

No point dwelling on that for the moment as we try to gauge what's going on.

There is a lady at the front, older, speaking quickly and loudly in Spanish. I can't make it out so look to Sophia to translate.

'There are looking for volunteers to help clear the roads into the city. There are trees down and they need to get vital supplies in and out.'

'That's too much for us isn't it? We are not exactly bodybuilders. Plus we don't want to be stuck out of the city.'

'Good point.'

We move to another group.

'These are asking for volunteers to take food parcels out, but we need a vehicle and we haven't got one.'

'Jesus, this is hard.'

We move onto another.

'There is an orphanage on the south side. The kids are trapped in a basement of a collapsed building and they need help to get them out.'

'We can do that, right?' Though what it practically involves I'm not sure. Sorting through rubble and pulling out kids seems to fit the description. We don't have any gear but if there are trapped kids I'm prepared to get my hands dirty.

The three of us look at each other and nod. I take a deep breath as I look round the square. The business of the people, the genuine wish to work together and save lives. This is far from the place we heard about. As we've already seen trouble isn't far away but for the moment this feels powerful. Inspiring.

After some more conversations with the organisers, we are given our own high visibility jackets, gloves and asked to climb into the back of truck. We follow dutifully, careful to keep Mia close to us. Is this the best place for a teenage kid, sorting rubble and rescuing people? Perhaps she should stay behind and help with the food distribution and coordination - but then we don't want to get split up. Neither of us are exactly made for this work, so who am I to say what she can and can't do? This is a girl who could stab a brutish adult twice her size in the leg without flinching.

Mia will call me a patronising shit if I say something, or some other smart insult. And she'd be right. She has far more fight in her than I do.

The truck has no seats, just a tarpaulin to cover us. The floor is rusty metal with lots of wood dust and debris - must have been from one of the forestry operations in the mountains. We huddle into a corner and find something to grab onto. I count ten people who have joined us in the back, a mixture of young and old, women and men. All of them look a bit rough with tired eyes, mud on their hands and faces as well as clothes that are stained. No judgement from me - who knows what they have been through in the last few days.

A girl, a similar age to me stares at me a little longer than is comfortable. I look away, nervous about speaking to anyone. Her hair is tied back, a red bruise across her forehead is sore and prominent on her rounded face. She's been crying and I feel her pain. Catching her eye, she smiles.

'Americano?' I read her lips rather than hear her.

'Si.'

I nod in acknowledgement. Is it that obvious that I don't belong here?

Dressed in jeans and a check shirt, she curls her legs up close and wraps her arms around almost in a ball. The smile remains even as she turns away. I wish I could read what she's thinking. The sound of the engine revving disturbs the moment. As the truck readies to leave, an army officer with the biggest automatic weapon I've ever seen slung over his shoulder jumps on board. A colleague joins him with a more familiar rifle. The larger weapon is set upon a tripod. The camouflage uniform is a darker shade than American army, I suppose designed for jungle battles rather than desert. They don't say much as they settle into position, more concerned with what's going on in the street than with us.

The way those army dudes look attentive carrying that serious weaponry makes me feel this excursion could be about far more than rescuing kids. I'm glad they are on my side.

I check the girl again but she's no longer looking at me. The moment passed already.

Out the side of the tarpaulin, I can just about see the road through the gap, though it's hard to get a decent perspective with the angle and constant movement. The truck engine roars and I stop looking out at the street. I feel sick with the half view of any movement.

Mia is sat up with her back to the front of cab, her eyes are closed, her crossed legs underneath her to stop herself falling with the movement of the truck. Sophia is in conversation with others but I can't understand and give up trying to listen. It's too noisy against the backdrop of engine noise.

The truck stops with a screech of brakes. We all fall forward. Given Mia and I are closest to the front that means that we end up in a crush. One army dude speaking loudly into his radio, puts an arm out indicating we should stay calm. Calm is the last thing I feel as I try to unpick the pile of strangers from on top of me. The girl from before, looks towards me as she disconnects herself from the pile. It's nothing… but something. I think of Rose and feel my face flush. Turning away, I focus on what's going on around me. Now really is not the moment.

A gun shot is fired and I peer through the gap. A soldier jumps to the ground facing to the front.

More voices.

'It's the Maras again,' Sophia says. 'They won't let the truck through. Say they will fire if we don't go back.'

'Seriously, who are these people?' I say. 'Those kids will die if we don't get there.' I realise my statement sounds over-dramatic given we are not exactly a fully equipped rescue service. In the circumstances, though, it seems crazy not to let us try to help. I can't hardly believe these people want to use dying kids as bargaining tools. But here we are.

I look through the gap and see several hooded men with rifles. The soldiers are outnumbered. They jump back on board and the truck reverses quickly. A few shots are fired in the air and some cheers.

'What bastards,' I say to Sophia.

'Welcome to our new world.'

The truck heads back along the road and turns again. The engine seems to struggle with stopping and starting and rounding obstacles in the street. I assume he is going a convoluted route round the back streets.

Shouts persist but I give up trying to scan the road. I can't grasp what's going on and just want to feel safe.

The truck stops once more and the soldiers get out. They encourage us to follow. As I step down to the ground, I see the problem.

A concrete building has collapsed on one side and half of it has fallen. The entrance is blocked completely. Iron barred windows can be seen at street level and faces peer out. Water is sitting across the drains and must be in the building below. The kids will be wading in sewage flowing from the street and I wonder if they have any food or water. The bars in the windows are wide enough to push bottles of water through - perhaps that's been done already.

Barred windows: great for keeping people in but also terrible for escaping in an emergency.

The group leader, a tall, bulky man, shouts loudly.

Sophia runs towards him and hugs him. I can only assume, random and lucky as it is, that this is Gus, the guy she wanted to meet. He is most definitely big and strong, and given he is organising this rescue, heroic seems a fair description.

Looking round at all the devastation, it feels more like a war zone that a natural disaster.

The soldiers from the wagon join the greeting before arranging themselves for protection. The enormous automatic weapon is taken from the wagon and set up. I think they are going to point this at any threatening gang but actually they line it up at the building entrance.

Seriously; one of those rockets could bring the whole thing down. The building would collapse completely.

It could also create a hole to get them out.

I stare at the group as they debate what to do. Everyone looking to each other but no-one seems to be making the decision. I seek my friend from before, hoping for some reassurance but I can't see her now.

The gun holder is set ready to fire.

Surely they are not going to take the shot.

Chapter 37

'Parada!' Gus shouts.

Another debate starts and the gunman relaxes and joins in.

'Gus told them to stop,' Sophia says to me.

'Thank God for that,' I reply.

Yeah - the big gun might help, but first they should be sure it's going to work.

Gus and the other helpers gather round the entrance to find a way in. The doorway is blocked with concrete debris and steel struts jutting out. It's hard to see if they have fallen into place or are squeezed out from the collapsed floors above. Unless we secure the structure above, the risk of moving any debris will bring the building down on us and the kids in the basement. Doesn't feel like the rocket is a good move.

The bigger problem, as we organise, is that we have no actual machinery. We have some ropes, crow bars and spades but nothing like earth moving equipment. We could do with metal cutters or at least something to bend or twist the metal bars. They are not wide enough to get an adult through but maybe they could squeeze a child out.

We start in the doorway.

Three men in hard hats dig away at the loose concrete to see if they can make a hole big enough to enter. As each bucket of stone is filled it is passed along a line and we dump it by the side of the road on an empty piece of land. Then Mia and some other young ones take the empty buckets back to the doorway. It's slow work and the sun is getting hotter. Every bucket feels heavier than the last. After thirty minutes there is a shout for a break.

Water is passed around and the whole bottle disappears in two gulps. As I turn round to survey the scene, I freeze.

Two big pickup trucks have arrived full of gang members with guns. The Maras point their AR-15s at our group as the trucks move in front of us. The soldiers we have are hopelessly outnumbered. Each of the gang are of varying shapes and sizes and covered in tattoos and odd piercings. They look as bad as those in El Paso. They don't look they came here for a negotiation.

The soldiers raise their rifles. It's a scary standoff.

Three of the men calmly jump down from the truck and approach the first soldier. The leader is wearing a cowboy hat and smokes a cigar. He has a scar down the side of his face, I assume an old knife wound. His henchmen are bulkier.

Gus speaks to the gang leader but I can't hear what they are saying. I look at Sophia but she shrugs so presumably she can't hear either. The obvious explanation is that he is pleading to leave us alone. The voices are raised as the first henchman pushes Gus out of the way. One of the soldiers steps in and is immediately pushed to the floor. All weapons now either point at the gang leader or the soldier on the ground. This feels like a confrontation that is only going to end up with bodies in the street.

The whole point of being here is to save lives, not take them.

I look back into the orphanage, unable to believe what they are doing. I'm tired, frustrated and fed up of being impotent with these violent gangs.

I tense up, blood pumping and rage takes over.

I drop the bucket and run towards the men screaming in English: 'Let us get on with the job! Kids are dying in there!'

'No,' Sophia shouts and tries to grab me.

The cowboy hat leader steps forward and launches the butt of his rifle into my face. The wood smashes like a hammer into my jaw and the pain ricochets through my head. I feel teeth dislodge. I fall to the ground. He follows up with a kick to my gut. I'm winded, struggling to breathe as he kicks again. This time my hip takes the brunt of the pain.

'Gringo, Americano,' he says and spits on me.

Sophia steps towards me shouting in Spanish. Gus steps in before the cowboy hat leader does the same again with her. Rifles are raised again. A scream from the crowd follows and the girl from before rushes out to me.

She screeches in Spanish to the gang leader. He laughs and he turns to the crowd, ignoring her.

'You ok?' She whispers.

I nod, crawling hoping to avoid being kicked again. She comforts me and helps me to my feet.

'Thanks,' I say. Seems another woman feels the need to look out for me. Could be embarrassing if it wasn't the fact that we were all as scared as each other, unsure what's coming next.

The gang leader speaks loudly.

Sophia translates for me.

'He says we owe money for entering their territory without permission. Fine is 10000 Lempira, about $400. We must all pay now or leave. If we do not leave they will start shooting.'

The cowboy hat leader mocks the soldiers, spitting in front of them. They know that if they start shooting, they will hit a few gang members but there are only three soldiers. Completely outnumbered and outgunned. Even the machine gun would have limited effect.

We look at each other. 'They must know they can't pay,' I say to Mia as quiet as I can between painful panicked breathing.

As a show of strength, all the gang get down from the truck and begin walking among the group. Mia stands close to me, the girl the other side. They walk towards the bucket line pushing the volunteers around. All the time, the standoff with the soldiers continues though they look defeated.

A bald-headed gang member with one of those piercings that stretches the earlobes, walks over to the big gun. Oh shit. What is he going to do? He checks out the firing mechanism and laughs. I think he's looking for encouragement from the leader.

One of the soldiers tries to stop him but a shot at his legs halts his defence. He squeals and crawls away for cover. The situation is awful. Is this guy really going to fire at the building?

He shouts, raises his fist and fires. The recoil from the gun knocks him over as the shell releases. Everyone covers their heads as the building explodes in dust and steel. Screams are heard from inside. What did the idiot just do?

When the dust settles even the leader looks uncomfortable.
I don't suppose blowing up a building with kids in was
something he set out to do.

'Pagaré,' Sophia shouts out that she will pay. 'Pagaré por
todos. Por todos.'

The leader approaches Sophia. He grabs her and rams her up
against the Pickup. I try to move to intervene but Mia stops me.
I wince with pain as she pushes me back. Gus tries the same but
he gets a gang member holding a gun to his head for his
endeavours. He steps back.

The group are all focussed on the confrontation, no longer
listening to shouts from inside the building.

I hear her mention dollars. Is she going to take them back to
the hotel? She hasn't got that number of bucks with her.

Gus tries again and he gets the attention of the leader. I'm
still feeling the pain in my side from the kicking and daren't
move. All I can hear is shouting and I don't know what's
happening. The leader lets Sophia go and grabs one of the
soldiers. Sophia comes back over to Mia and me.

'I need to go to the hotel with Gus. I've got thirty minutes to
get back otherwise they will start shooting us one by one. They
don't care about the kids. Typical of these monsters. I can take
the soldiers with me but if we can't come back with more they
will kill us all and the kids.'

'Shit, they're evil.' I say. Speaking is like chewing smashed
glass. I can taste blood and feel my lose teeth. My gums are
swelling as my face freezes up.

'Get used to it.'

'Can we carry on with the rescue?' I mumble.

'Yeah carry on. I've got half an hour. Don't speak to anyone.
Just keep your head down.'

I look towards the girl, but she doesn't catch my eye this
time. Probably better we both keep to ourselves.

Sophia leaves in the truck we came in and we return to
check out the hostel again. What we came here to do. Some of
the gang take off in one of the pickups. I guess to go find
another group to harass for money. Six remain watching us.

This is terrifying but it's best to concentrate on the task at hand. We still need to get inside the building.

The good thing about the blast is that it cleared the entrance. We can see inside but there is rubble everywhere. Despite our fear it didn't collapse.

We return to the chain gang moving buckets of rubble. I'm back in the line, one eye on the bucket the other monitoring the gang. I try to ignore my pain each time I pass a bucket along because I can't give up, not given what's at stake. I avoid speaking as instructed and, even if I could, I'm not sure what to say. Everyone is quiet. It's hardly the time for small talk.

A shout comes from the front and we all stop. The girl from before clambers over the rubble, her slight figure stretching as she slithers her way down into the basement. She crawls further inside. I am even more tense watching now I feel some connection with her.

The big guy at the front restarts the rubble collection. It looks like it's working. We shift more debris. Stone by stone, the opening gets bigger.

The girl appears at the gap and shouts. She is covered in dust, wipes her face, the earlier bruise revealed again. A couple of guys gather around to help.

She lifts a young child, also covered in dust through the gap. A cheer grows around the crowd. It's happening.

I want to leap and scream but we need to keep going. Plus the bruise seems to be growing where the gang kid kicked me.

Looking over at them, I can see them talking, lifting their guns once more, checking each other's stance. They are getting agitated with all the cheering. I'm worried they will intervene again. Though everyone else is ignoring them and getting on with the job.

My attention returns to building as the girl inside lifts the next child through the gap. Another one of the group climbs inside and soon there is a trail of kids appearing at the front. Each one climbs through and are organised into the corner.

As the kids escape is completed, a woman appears covered in blood and dust and struggles through the gap.

Eventually there are fifteen children aged between two and ten years old. Mia takes water over to them and helps them to drink. I feel elated and exhausted. Watching them drink clean water as if it was some kind of magic potion is heart-warming. I feel the pressure slip for a moment and wipe a small tear from my eye.

This is a rough tough place but the feeling of relief at seeing the kids survive is as good a feeling as I've known. The group are chatting again and more relaxed. The gang members stand back, their weapons pointed but the threat is not there.

As we clear the way and get the kids ready to go back in the truck, Sophia returns. She throws a bag at the gang. They check the contents and say nothing as they get back in the vehicles to leave. The clown who fired the gun is jubilant and taking the adoration of his friends. I've never felt hate before, never like this. Anger yes. But hate. I could shoot him, kill him and I wouldn't look back. The feeling scares me, but days like this are here to remind us who we are. I'm learning who I am, minute by minute, hour by hour.

Once they are gone, we clear the street and get the kids into the truck. The girl who got the kids out is the centre of attention and whatever importance I had to her has been superseded. Probably for the best, I think, taking one look back at the scene.

We head back to the centre, this time unhindered. We paid our dues for today. Who knows what the expectation will be tomorrow.

Back at the municipal square there are now food tents set up. I am starving, eating nothing since the last of the snacks this morning.

There is a grill on the go and some tortilla wraps. I can smell the meat cooking which is a making me nauseous. Mia and Sophia go ahead, grabbing the bread and rolling in some grilled chicken with some sauce. I look for something vegetarian but there is nothing.

Mia looks over.

'Just eat the bread.'

'You just eat the fucking bread.'

The words come out like daggers as my stomach ties in knots. I need to eat and I need something decent.

'Leave her alone,' Sophia says.

I search around, grabbing a piece of bread at the same time. I see some chorizo and tinned meats on the side with some pickle but that's it. Not even soup.

'Sorry,' I say, 'I didn't mean to shout. Just want to eat.'

'No place for a veggie,' she says, filling her face with tortilla wrap.

'I can help.'

I turn and the bruised girl from before is there. Covered in dust but she's managed to clean her face where the bruise is still the prominent feature.

'Hi,' I say.

'I got some good bean soup. Well mama made a big pot to keep us for days, just in case. Come with me, only five minutes from here.'

'Sweet. I mean thanks. Cool.'

'Donnie, you can't fuck off now. It's dark soon,' Sophia says.

'Few minutes only,' the girl says and then adds something in Spanish to Sophia.

Sophia stares at me. After all this time she can still make me feel like the bad guy even when all I want is something to eat. Not even want. I need something or I'm going to fall over.

'Fine,' she says, 'Five-thirty. We're going back. Thirty minutes from now. You're not back, you better hope your girlfriend's going to keep you safe tonight because we're done.'

I look at the girl as she waves me along.

'I'll be back,' I say, unsure where my confidence is coming from. I'm just following the girl.

Chapter 38

'I'm Donnie,' I say, holding my hand towards her.

'Maria,' she replies.

'Thanks for this. You don't know how hard it is trying to find anything that isn't boring to eat when you're veggie in this place.'

'It's ok,' she says.

We walk fast, past the main street away from the crowds. I look up trying to see where I am, checking back where I just came from. Conscious I need to find my way back.

'You were brave before, getting those kids out.' Her shirt and jeans are barely discernible under the dust but it's hardly important given the situation.

'It's nothing. I was right size to do it. So I did.'

She keeps walking fast and I feel my bruises ache as I try to keep up the pace.

The street is wide, like a boulevard, lined with large buildings three or four storeys, probably apartments or offices. Nothing much stands out. As with all the other streets we have seen today, much is boarded up and debris is strewn everywhere. It is going to take months of work to clean this city up again.

After one block we turn to the left. I see a street sign 'Calle 7' and note it as reference point for coming back to the square.

Another few buildings and we turn down a narrow alley, wide enough for a car but not much else. We approach what looks like an abandoned town house with steps up to a doorway. A doorway with no door except a few wooden battens across it. I climb through the gap in the wooden battens and walk into the hall. There is debris on the floor, boxes, clothes, shoes. We clamber over metal lamps, bits of furniture, tools and into a room at the back. It's some kind of squat with makeshift beds and blankets around. There is a big pot on top of a gas stove. A large older woman stands behind the pot stirring. It's dirty, smelly but this is probably what counts as home for these people.

Maria exchanges words with her as she empties a ladle of food into a bowl with a tortilla.

'Gracias,' I say.

She guides me to one of the beds and I sit down.

'The soup/stew, bit difficult to determine in the dark light, is very stodgy looking but I dip my bread in. Plenty of chilli heat and the veg is soft but I'm beyond caring. As long as it isn't meat I'm fine.

'This is great,' I say, as she takes a bowl herself. It's not great but I will not complain.

'Why you here Donnie? It's no place for American. It's dangerous.'

'I know, it's a long story, but not important just now.'

I eat a few more mouthfuls conscious I can't hang around.

'Your friends, they came with you.'

'Yes, that's right. I should go back in a moment. I said I would be back.'

'Sure,' she says.

She looks at her mother and puts her plate down. I hear a noise at the entrance and sense somethings wrong.

Through the door, a bare-chested young guy appears.

'Gringo.'

He grabs me, throws the bowl away and punches me in the face.

Burning with pain around the eye, I try to stand to defend myself, looking towards the exit.

'Stop.' Maria shouts.

'This is my brother,' she says to me. 'He wants to know why you're here. He wants money.'

With my hands covering my head for protection I try to speak.

'I got nothing, nada. Check my pockets, everything. I'm empty.'

He moves to hit me again, but Maria gets in front of him. He pushes her aside firmly and I realise where she got her bruises from. I look at her and wonder if she knew he would come when I came here. Was this a set up and I fell for it.

'Dollars,' he shouts.

It's dark in the room so it's hard to see his face but I can hear him slathering around the mouth. He's either drugged up or mad, it's hard to tell but I can't do a thing.

'Hotel tell him. I have money at the hotel.'

She explains whilst I think what I'm going to tell Sophia or even how I'm going to find my way there.

'You have to show him.'

He drags me up and pushes me through to the passageway. At the doorway he pushes me against the remaining wood battens across the door. They break as I hit them hard. I squeal again as the pain is fierce. Despite the pain I'm glad I'm out of the place again into the street. But then I see what's waiting.

Three men from a gang, no doubt Sula 7 from the number patterns tattooed on various body parts. The tallest in the middle is holding a black cloth bag. Doesn't take a genius to work out what is about to happen.

Maria's brother pushes me forward from behind. They surround me and I lift my hands to resist attempts to cover my head. A punch to the gut ends my resistance as I fall forward.

'Hey, hey. Grencho.'

I hear the voices laughing. I try to keep my balance as they grab my arms tightly. Rough hands, burning and twisting my skin. A cloth is tied tight round them, though I'm relieved they tie my hands at the front and not the back. I am pushed along the road. I try to adjust my eyes to see light through the thin material but it's impossible to get any frame of reference.

I hear a car door open and I am pushed into the doorway. My knee crashes into metal as I try to adjust myself into an imaginary space. They let go of my arms so I can navigate better. As I clamber in a little more, a push forces me to speed up. The car door slams and I hear the others get in.

We race out of the narrow street and judging by my weight falling to the left I assume we have turned right, back towards the boulevard and the street corner where I saw the 'Calle 7' street sign.

Calle 7. The home of Sula 7. I should have known.

Maria led me into a trap. With me cribbing about something to eat she must have taken her chance. Get some money from the stupid American. It's the way the world works here.

As the car speeds off, I have completely lost any bearings for where I am or where I am going. I begin to shake, nausea rising from my stomach. My worst fears in coming to this place are now realised. I should have listened. I should have stayed home. But I didn't. I'm here, shaking with fear and all I can think about is how this will end.

****

Not long, maybe fifteen, twenty minutes the car stops. Impossible to keep a track of time.

The conversation has involved a lot of laughter and excitement but none of them has attempted to converse with me. They probably can't speak any English but it makes no difference. I don't need to hear what they are saying to be guessing what options there are for me.

I think the straightforward option of killing me isn't likely because I assume they want to use me for getting more money. If they wanted me dead, I would be dead already, so I reckon I'm here for the purpose of bringing cash.

Guessing that they want money, am I going to be up for ransom or am I expected to raise the money myself. If it's a ransom who they going to get to pay for me? How much they going to pay?

I'm pulled out of the car and I sense into a smelly building. Wet plaster mixed with sewage brings the nausea back and wonder if this is going to be a permanent stench for the foreseeable future.

Pushed further forward I stumble but I'm kept on my feet by someone grabbing at me. The cloth bag is removed and my hands untied. As my eyes flicker with recognition of the dark room, I'm pushed from behind again. I fall forward onto a bed that I didn't even know was there. The door slams behind me and I'm left alone.

I scramble myself to sit up and get my bearings. I'm in a small bedroom, single bed. No light as what was once a window up high near the ceiling is now a board, with the fading day light visible slightly via uneven edges. The smell from outside is still filtering through. Placing my feet on the floor it is dry at least in here and the smell is outside not inside. The door frame is illuminated as light sneaks round the edges but that's the only light. In the corner, next to the door, I make out a metal bucket. No balloons for guessing what that's for.

I sit back on the bed, trying to keep calm preparing for a long wait. Reckoning now, that given they've locked me up with no cell phone and no means of communication that I'm up for ransom.

I curl up in a ball, my hands seeking out various bruises and injuries and attempting to soothe them. I close my eyes in the hope that sleep will come and when I wake up this nightmare will be over.

Chapter 39

I wake up with the room in complete darkness. Got to be late night as there no light on the edges of the window board or the doorframe.

No sound in the building so possibly they are out doing what gangs do at night, threaten people, sell drugs and generally cause mayhem.

I think back to Nashville. What I'd normally be doing on the strip right now, playing a gig, drinking with the guys, out with Rose. The atmosphere would be cool and friendly. Normal

Yet here I am, thousands of miles away kidnapped in some back street slum by gangs who would slice me open without a second thought.

A world away.

How did this happen? How did this happen to me? Yet here I am, at the centre of it. It's like a card game, one card falls and the rest fall collapse with it. That's my life never the same again. Going back to Nashville, assuming I ever do get out of this place alive, will be like coming home after some wild adventure. Returning hero or returning fool, humiliated after getting almost everything wrong.

Kidnapped. Even worse kidnapped because I am a vegetarian. Singled out and made myself a target. Hugh and Gary would spill their beer laughing at that one.

Put either of them here in my stead, what would they do? Yeah, they might have taken some putting down, especially Hugh with the frame of fighting bull. Still, they wouldn't get far here with these gangs that don't take no reasoning with. Gary is as racist as they come but even he would struggle to know what to do. He's right about one thing though; you can't be soft with the attitude of these gangs who are happy to kill children to make a buck. Kill first, don't even bother to ask questions.

Yet I don't feel ready to face that yet. Not even Rose and her A-Star judgement. Talking shit on stuff she has no idea about. But I've been here now, I've seen good people and I've seen bad. Reckon, none of them going to tell me what's right and wrong about these folk.

The door opens.

A torch light shines in and I cover my eyes from the glare.

'Danny, are you ok?'

It's Maria's voice.

'Donnie, not Danny.' Irritates the hell out of me when someone gets my name wrong. In the circumstances, the least of my worries but still it bites.

'Sorry, Donnie. I didn't mean this to happen.'

'Go fuck yourself Maria, you knew exactly what your brother would do.'

'They saw me speak to you, help you. Remember. They told me I had to get you alone. I didn't know, this is what they would do.'

Her broken English is pleading, probably correct, but I don't care. Niceties are over. I just want out of here.

'Fuck you, Maria, you could have warned me. Done anything but tell them where I was.'

The light continues to shine in my face and decide it's pointless arguing. Assume she came here for something.

'Here is your cell phone, you need to enter pin. Network is back working. You have money at hotel. They want it. Call your friend here. Do it and they let you go.'

Now I know what's coming, I'm happy to do something active. God knows what Sophia will do but first will be getting a line of communication open.

I enter the pin and navigate to the last number called. There are no contacts in the phone as it was a burner phone due for dumping. The phone has a signal so I assume everything is back up and running tonight.

She throws me some water and a banana. Takes the phone and I'm back in darkness again.

What price my head? I'm about to find out.

***

I fall asleep again because I'm exhausted. As soon as Maria has gone, the fight leaves me. Counting the numerous bruises on my body and face might help bring sleep but I dont even need that. And there is nothing to do in this black smelly hole except think about stuff, reviewing every step that led me to this place and questioning if I could have made better choices.

What choice should I have made that would result in a different outcome? Every choice, but then faced with what I knew and what I saw... who knows. It's pointless anyway. I'm here and I need a way to get out.

Mia and Sophia will be going crazy. At least I hope they are. They are both tough and bad asses at times but they are loyal. I've seen that. Gotta to believe they won't just leave me here and all this time taken is because a deal is being done.

In theory, the American government on hearing a US citizen has been taken by a local gang should be all over this with a crack squad of SEALs to come get me.

I laugh at the thought of the likes of John Henry in Nashville watching the TV as they screen my rescue. Would he be clapping and applauding the helicopter landing, shooting up the locals? Or would be hoping they bring me out in a box instead?

Delusional or mad. I've only been here a few hours, I've heard about people spending years couped up. Iraq or Syria or something like that. Suppose if Maria is going to be the one feeding me, at least she's pretty. I know I swore at her but I don't get the feeling she's a bad person. She just did what she had to do to survive which includes doing what her brother tells her and he's probably trying to survive in a gang. If I was here with Bernadette, would I be doing the same thing and using her to get money from rich Americans? Would I be the same as him, killing and murdering people for money?

No answer to that. We all do what we have to.

I turn over again. Bored of my self-indulgent misery. Waiting for what happens next.

The next time I open my eyes, light has crept through the frame of the small window above. A shot fires outside and there is a lot of shouting. All in Spanish, so I've no way to interpret it. It settles down and the noise merges with the traffic in the distance.

I sit back, nothingness continues but I don't want to sleep anymore. Time to be ready for whatever comes next. It will be today because Sophia and Mia won't let it go on.

Then I wonder.

Enough Donnie.

I am sick of waiting for something to happen.

Standing up on the bed I can reach the board above. I reckon it was put up there just to cover up from the hurricane so if I can push it with any force, it will give way. Is it big enough for me to crawl through and can I climb up there with all the various aches and bruises. Time to find out. If I really can do something for myself.

I stretch my arms out against the board. There is no glass or bars blocking the way, so it's easy to get pressure on the surface. I start to push.

Nothing. Not an inch moved.

The board is secure.

I try again. Pushing every ounce I can muster into my arms. A pain runs through my gut as I stretch and I have to let go. There is some give in it though. I can feel it. I need to lever it.

I search the half-light in the room for something.

The only thing I can see that has some kind of lever is the handle of the piss bucket. My stomach churns with handling it even if the contents are mine from last night.

Darn it. No time for squeamish.

I pick it up and turn it over, the rancid liquid filling my nostrils as it runs over the floor. Reckon, I ain't the one going to have to deal with it anyway.

Once the bucket is empty, I fiddle with the handle until it loops off the hook. A bit of force is needed to twist it but eventually I have a metal handle to use to lever the board.

Back in the window frame I force the handle into a small gap and use my hands to lever it down. The gap widens. Clear air appears. I press it again forcing it further pushing harder on the handle.

The gap widens.

I push again more confident now. It's working space for my hand to get through.

The handle slips and I curse as it flies out through the gap. I hear the metallic clang as it hits the floor below.

'Darn it.'

I should have been more careful.

I survey the gap. Wide enough to really push now. Reckon I've done enough. I grab the edge of the board, pushing and twisting with all my weight. My gut is sore but I'm not stopping. I will get out of here.

It gives, a squeaking noise as the board bends. It snaps and falls to the floor.

I did it. I fucking did it.

I pull myself up to the frame and scramble up. The pain as I stretch through the window frame is unbearable. I can see out, hanging half in and half out.

The drop below is ten feet. No-one is out there. But I have to turn my body some to avoid landing head first. I didn't think this through. There is no way to do this feet first either. There is a tarpaulin to the left covering a garbage area. Seems after the hurricane people have swept the debris to one side.

Maybe.

The edge of the frame is now too much. I can't hang here any longer. Either go back or go forward.

I've come this far.

I force my weight forward and try to use my hands to flip my body towards the tarpaulin. I curse the gym classes I missed. I am flying, not feet first but more like a sack of beets. I hit the tarpaulin which gives way completely but cushions me as I land on the smelly garbage.

I roll over onto my feet, bruises announcing themselves in new locations. I can feel grazes and scarring on my arms but I am able to stand. I look back to the building and the window I just came down from. Amazing.

Down on the ground, I have no bearings as to where I am. It's a narrow alley, which apart from the debris I landed in and sludge of the flood waters of two days ago has little to differentiate from the alley where I found Daniella dying. That feels like a lifetime ago from now. I'm pleased to find no-one around, despite the likely noise of my fall.

A stench of decay and rot permeates my nostrils and looking down at the filth and dirt of the last twenty-four hours on my clothes I'm not sure how much I'm contributing to it.

I brush myself down and limp forward, trying to run but resort to fast walking as the better option. One leg is not moving well. No time to investigate as I rush along the alley. No idea where I am or where I am going.

A dog barks and I turn to see where it's coming from. Off balance, my foot hits something and I fall forward. Catching my fall on my aching arms brings an instinctive grunt, lessened by the site of what I have fallen over.

A body. A small, tattooed man wearing just a pair of shorts, lay lifeless against the wall. His trailing leg is the cause of my fall. His belly is pierced open and red with dried blood, a serious stab wound. I stare for a moment into his lifeless eyes and wonder what happened to him. A deal gone wrong. A betrayal. Who knew in these streets?

'Danny!'

A shout. Maria, who still can't remember my damn name.

'Stop.'

Not stopping, no way I am waiting again. I don't even look back to where she is shouting from. I rush forward, forcing my bad leg to move more quickly.

The shouts bring more attention and as I approach the end of the alley faces appear.

'Stop Danny.' The voice is more desperate and realising my chances of escape are lessening, I slow down turning to see Maria rushing towards me in a yellow vest top and casual shorts.

'Come back, they will kill you.'

Looking back to the top of the street, faces stare down at me. Too far away to make out expressions, I decide I don't really want to find out if they are friend or foe. My instincts tell me everyone is the enemy.

Emotion overwhelms me, I feel my legs weaken as the realisation that my efforts at escape are doomed.

Maria grabs me and stops me from falling completely. I hold onto her because I fear if I fall, I won't get back up again this time.

***

Inside the building, she doesn't return me to my prison from last night but into a communal area like where I was trapped last night. There are beds and a battered sofa. In the corner there is a pot of food.

She points me towards a chair.

'Food. Vegetarian, don't worry. Not sure if it taste good or not but it's something.'

I nod, unable to speak or feel anything. Not even hunger. I'm just lost. I could cry or just close my eyes and wish I was anywhere but here. My bravado and energy of a few minutes ago are sunk.

'You must stay here. Today they will come for you and you go home. Get out of this city Danny. It's not safe for American.'

I don't correct her on the name this time. What's the point.

'When will they come?'

My eyes are nearly closed as the sentence finishes, feeling tired just speaking words. I didn't realise how failure could weigh so heavy.

'This morning. They pay some money. I don't know what it was. I never ask these questions.'

'I can't leave the city, Maria. You can help. I need to find a young girl. It's why we came.' I breathe heavily talking but need to at least try this one thing.

'What girl? I don't know any girls.'

She turns to the cooking pot as she heats it. I don't know if she is lying or worried or genuinely doesn't know.

'She was kidnapped here, she was connected to an Opal mine. Do you know where they hide these girls?'

'No,' she says, quickly. 'Don't ask me these questions, we will both be killed. They never tell and the price of telling is death. You know this.'

'I reckon.'

And with that there is silence. What more is there to say. I think she probably has an idea about it but given the obvious threat of her brother and his gang she is not going to put herself in harm's way. Hence why I am here and not with Sophia and Mia.

A few minutes later she passes me a bowl of beans in a tomato sauce. I lap it up and feel better immediately. Maybe my body needed something to keep it going.

With the food finished, Maria lights up a cigarette. My eyes light up the same way as she offers one to me.

Taking in a good gulp of smoke, I almost choke on the strength of the tobacco. Not a brand I'm used to.

We smoke in silence, reckon the mood is relaxed which feels odd given the situation. I suppose she doesn't want to make me a prisoner and I have lost the energy to run.

Her phone rings and immediately I sit forward.

She looks at me as she talks. Once she's finished, she reaches into a rucksack on the bed and brings out a black cloth bag.

'It's time,' she says.

I place the bag over my own head this time, at least retaining some dignity.

'Please do everything they say this time. Don't try to run. Promise me.'

'Sure,' I say, not really knowing what I will do. What more is there to say.

She makes another call and I try not to listen in. I'm more focussed on my own welfare and what comes next.

'Danny.'

There is a pause, under the hood I can't sense what she is thinking.

'What's wrong?' I ask.

Another pause and a murmur.

'There is a place in the hills. I heard about it.' She speaks quickly, reckon she wants to tell me quickly or not at all. 'I don't know the girl you talk of but everyone here know the Maras took the daughter of a rich American. It was a big laugh to them. They keep hostages in the old mine out of the way and easy to defend from soldiers. Maybe you go there.'

'It's dangerous.' She sniffles and I sense she wants to say more but I know she's already probably said too much.

'Maria, why you are telling me now?'

I hear a crashing a sound. A door. I don't need to be able to see to know that they are coming for me.

No time for the answer, she grabs my hand and then quickly lets' go before they come into the room.

Deep breath.

My legs feel like jelly as I am pulled to my feet. I pray it goes well but all my instincts tell me that everything could go wrong, will. A thousand miles from home in the hands of a merciless street gang with bag over my head. Bruised and battered scared for my life.

But for the first time in the last few days, I feel hope. Reckon I'm going crazy out here.

***

The same routine as the day before, forced into the back of a car, hands tied and completely blind from the bag over my head. The same excited sounds as they talk about what's coming. As they chatter, I wonder how this will play out.

Stand off in the square with me in the middle of the road, guns pointed at me, the bag of cash beside me as we swap places. Then everyone turns and runs their own way. Feels too neat, feels unreal and I'm sure if I was Sophia or Mia, I wouldn't trust these gangs at all. Gosh, remember Crazy Cruz and that hand over of cash. It didn't end well for him either. Feels like a lifetime since then as well. What has happened to me in just a few days.

I think about Maria's hand in mine just moments before her brother arrived with his mob. It meant something. It meant that she cared about what happened to me. It's a relief but also pointless. She's not here now and I reckon she's not stopping what happens next. Don't reckon I'll be seeing her again in this lifetime. Though feels like in this city, my lifetime is getting shorter and shorter, maybe hers too.

A loud bang. The engine roars as the car swerves. Another bang. I'm getting way too familiar with the sound of gunshot. The windshield shatters and there is a squeal of pain. The car veers to the side and slams into something solid. I'm thrown forward into the seat in front which collapses underneath me. There is a sound of more breaking glass and distress. I can't see but I think whoever was in the front seat flew through the windshield. The air has gone from my lungs. I try to get my bearings as I listen to moans from the guy lay over the hood. It doesn't sound good. There is a panicked movement beside me and shouts follow but still I can't see or move much.

Ambush.

It must be.

Winded from the collision, I try to calm my breathing and move back in my seat into a more comfortable position.

The door window is smashed and a gun is fired from the car. The chatter beside me is excited.

Then I feel hands on me as the focus changes. The door beside me is open as they push me out. I'm then grabbed roughly and I can feel the guy breathing heavily behind me as he holds the gun over my shoulder. I'm a human shield. Another shot smashes into the car door. I try to struggle, panicked, scared for my life but the guy smacks me with the gun instead. I yelp.

'Stay gringo, or I kill you.'

Reckon I'm already dead soon either way.

Another blast from a gun and the guy lets go. He slips down beside me. I reckon whoever fired that shot took a good aim.

I fall beside him, unable to move, exhausted, defeated and empty again.

The bag is removed roughly and I see Mia's face.

'Hey Donnie.'

She's smiling as she grabs me. I could cry. I am crying. Sophia comes round and between them I'm able to stand. They undo the ties on my hands and I shake myself free.

I see Sophia's friend Gus and soldiers fussing around the car.

'How did you know I would be…?' Of course, I know. Maria. She screwed her own brother.

'Donnie Knight, don't you ever pull that vegetarian shit with me again. I'll force feed you chicken if you ever go off like that.'

I don't even argue. I got nothing to say as they help me towards a pickup truck.

I'm still thinking about Maria and what might happen to her now. She saved me but doubt I'll ever be able to thank her.

***

Back to the hotel, I lay on my bed. Exhausted, battered and my mind ebbing and flowing like I'm in a wave machine. Or I've drunk a bottle of tequila. Definitely not that, I couldn't even lift my hand to take a swig. I've got nothing.

'What happened there?'

'I don't know, I guess I was set up.'

I can speak but it sounds like I'm talking through a muffler. It's so painful. Hope Sophia still has a stash of meds.

'You liked her,' Mia says.

'Your girlfriend going to have a lot to say about that Maria. I saw you, Donnie, you went off with her quicker than a dog on heat. And she saved your ass, so you two going to be getting it on real quick.

250

'I was hungry, that was all. And yes it was stupid. He just wanted money. They were scamming me.'

'Saw you coming,' Sophia says, 'I did tell you. Though half thought until she rang that you had taken up the bed with her and you wasn't planning on coming back.'

I lift my arm to acknowledge them. I can't argue y'all.

'Did she call you?' I ask, 'how much did they want for me?'

'Oh they ask for $10,000 dollars. A good price. But then I got a message straight after they arranged the drop. It had a location pin. All I needed to know where you were.'

'Took your time.'

There is a laugh from across the room.

'I'll pretend I didn't hear that.'

'How's your friend Gus, tell him thanks when you see him.'

'You'll see him tomorrow. Though wasn't much help finding you, we did that all on our own. He just brought the manpower. Most of the time he was ranting about the gangs and local politics. Saying that they had no chance. Not enough organisers and soldiers to protect them. You saw how impotent they are in small numbers. He was complaining how the city was a mess and living in San Pedro Sula is like a death sentence. It's only a matter of time before you get shot. He loved getting you out of that place, though. Nothing happier when shooting these gangs.'

I think about Hugh and Gary, they'd be saying exactly the same.

'They are seriously scary people,' I say. 'Though, obviously some are very nice people as well.'

'See, you are learning. Girls like your friend Maria, they're worth fighting for.' She takes another mouthful of rice.

'Oh Maria told me, about the gang. Where they take kidnap victims. Up in the mines outside the city and in the hills. They are well protected. It's a good a place as any to start.'

'Gus said something about that. Said that he had heard they use remote places in the hills, hard to find and heavily armed. It's almost a factory operation, especially if the families have money.'

'Brilliant,' Mia says.

'But that doesn't tell us anything more specific other than a general place. Maybe you can call Gus and ask him.'

'You such a fool Donnie,' she says, 'told you, already you will see him tomorrow. We already planned it. He says he will take us up in the hills so we can check a few places out.

'Yeah, sounds good.' It is good but I also can't even imagine getting out of bed in the morning, never mind going hunting kids in some random place in the mountains. My ambition is dwindling along with my physical capacity.

'I was thinking though,' Sophia says. 'I wonder if the hurricane apart wherever they are. There's a chance they've abandoned it. There are mudslides and flooding up in the hills. Anything could have happened.'

'Will they abandon the hostages?' I know the answer before I end the question. They will do whatever suits them. 'Suppose only way we'll know is to go up there.'

I turn over unable to think more about it.

Whatever I will find a way tomorrow. I must. Getting free today was my chance, an omen. So close, I can't fail at this last hurdle. But not tonight, now I just need sleep.

Chapter 40

Morning comes with a ringing cell phone.

'It's him?' I ask, barely awake.

She nods and puts it on speaker.

I sit up in the bed, stiff and sore everywhere.

Sophia grabs a drink from the remnants of last night's indulgence and takes a sip.

'Sorry Marcos, I was out of signal all day,' she says.

'Bitch, I know exactly where you are. I'm not the fool you think I am. Remember I have people everywhere. You're in Honduras playing the hero. Rescuing kids. Trust me, they are searching San Pedro Sula and when they find you and the gringo…'

'Marcos, listen,' she says and then curses in Spanish.

'Won't be long before they find where you are,' he continues. 'I look forward to the video of them slicing you up.'

'How did he track us here?' I whisper but she ignores me focussing on the call. I suppose after yesterday's kidnapping, Sophia's or my face must be all over the gang networks. Going all the way back to the US.

'Be careful, Marcos, I told you. Kill me or my friends and the money will disappear. You need to be nice to me. It would be very expensive exercise in letting your anger get the better of you. Call off Sula 7 or you know how it is. You won't survive long with no cash to pay your crew.'

He curses.

'I lived my life many times over girls. And better people than you told me I was going die soon - and they are the ones rotting in desert graves where no-one will ever find them.'

'Think of it is as a business opportunity, Marcos,' she says.

One thing about Sophia is she never backs down from a fight or a confrontation. I wish I could do that.

'I told you, you will get some good interest on the money, better than the bank,' she continues bluffing. 'As a good will gesture, there is two hundred thousand back in your account. Let me know when you need more and remember to ask nicely.'

He curses again and I wonder if he is ready to back down yet. How long does two hundred last? Is that enough for him to not need us?

'If you doubt me Marcos, I can set up a demonstration for you. I can show you how easily every cent of your drug money will be distributed in twenty-four hours to charities throughout the world - every one of them very happy to receive your money.'

The cell clicks off and there is nothing more to say. She turns it off and returns to the bed. Seems early morning none of us racing to get started on the day.

'How long can he survive off that cash?' I ask, yawning.

'With all the people he has to pay, depends on any shipments he has to pay for up front, how much he's got in storage. Maybe he'll last one to two weeks. The money has to be moving constantly for it to work. Anything sat in a bank account or stored in cash for a length of time becomes a risk or uneconomic. He's a businessman as well as a gang leader. Money is what keeps him alive and he knows it.'

'It all comes down to money,' I say, not really sure what I mean. As I lie back on the bed staring at the ceiling fan spinning round, I reflect on the day before; fighting battles with gangs, getting battered, the elation of rescuing those kids and then the terror of kidnap. Thoughts about money and cash seem so far away. Seems the conversation in this city is more about survival.

Chapter 41

A few hours later, we are back in the same square. Gus is waiting. Sophia hugs him tightly and it's the first time I notice a glance or a warmth between them. I can see where that's going to end. And she was quick to comment on Maria and me; not that there was anything to comment on. It was just circumstance. Anyway Sophia, deserves someone good, and Gus is good, I think. Certainly, a better man than I am to fix Sophia. I think of Rose in the same breath. When and where will I next hug her? Soon, I hope.

Not sure how I got out of bed, but I did. I've never ached so much in my life. My face, jaw, teeth. My back, my hands and arms from squeezing through that window and the fall. I normally have dead skin in my fingers from constant guitar playing but even that tough layer is torn and split. I took a pile of meds from Sophia's bag. They are keeping the pain at bay for now but not sure how long they will last.

Now after walking to the city centre, I've loosened up and I've put everything else to the back of my mind. It's such a big day.

The square is busy again, more rescue missions and aid coordination. There are more soldiers with guns as well, probably shipped from Western regions of the country. Pallets of water and grain are stacked high and being loaded onto trucks. It's more organised today.

'Gus will get us a wagon and some soldiers to help us,' Sophia says.

I shrug, happy to have some progress though I feel like a spare part breaking into conversations in Spanish with my out of place English, so I can find out what's happening.

A soldier comes back with Gus. He is introduced as Joachim. Joachim is everything you expect of a soldier, tall and bulky in shape, but next to Gus he looks a little small. Next to me they are both giants, but I won't dwell on that.

We talk more about the gangs and their history whilst we wait for the truck, though I think Gus and Joachim seem to like the macho chat on the details. Gary and Hugh would have been all over this, different knives, guns, torture techniques. I take it in on one level because they are speaking in English for my benefit, but do I really want to or need to know the various ways in which I might get murdered and the different preferences of certain gangs?

The machete, the garrotte, chicken wire. If you're a woman add in more horrific violence. How do people get to be this sick? I suppose I needed to go to college to understand that one. Not really getting me in the mood for the day.

Joachim gets a call on his radio and waves us on. Seems we are ready to go.

Reaching down to my jeans pocket, I check the opal is there. I've brought it as a good luck charm. Something like that. When I was checking in my bag this morning, it came to me. If I do somehow get to find Opal today, then it's there, isn't it? My work will be done.

I look round nervously at the people in the square. This place feels a lot safer than where I'm going. Yet after yesterday I think everywhere is just as bad.

Gus explains as we walk.

'There are some old mine works and farms up in the hills. Intelligence has always known where these gangs are hiding people but either because of bribes or political convenience, they are not always followed up on. They move around as well just in case a score needs settling. This area is the last place we have listed.' He points to a disused mine.

I don't reply - what can I say? I'm pleased to have somewhere to go, to find out. This is what Ryan Carter should be doing, not me. I'm looking for his daughter, taking risks that he wasn't willing to take. If and when I get out of this place, I'll make a point of reminding him what a coward he is.

Joachim has secured some weapons for us.

'She's famous now,' Gus says as he hands them out. 'Local hero. No-one stands up to gangs and gets away with it. Not only did she speak up, she paid money for everyone. If there was an election tomorrow, she would be the winner.'

Sophia frowns and Mia prods her, teasing her.

'Does that make you a target?' I ask, remembering the conversation from last night. She doesn't reply and I don't blame her. If I'm thinking it, so is she.

Though she seems to have more faith in Marcos playing ball than I do. She says he will see to it that she's not to be touched. He will want something at some point. Men like him don't concede so easily. Plus these street gangs are competitive and a major scalp might be strategically useful in a battleground like San Pedro Sula.

Gus and Joachim take the cab in front as we sit in the back like yesterday. It's a logging truck again. No comfort in the back but then it wasn't really intended to carry people.

The truck rattles noisily out of the square and the journey begins.

I hold the automatic rifle. A gun again. Will I do better this time than before? After yesterday would I still hesitate? No Gary or Hugh to dig me out this time. Gus and Joachim are decent replacements, but I don't know much or anything about them. Will they look out for me just the same?

Here I'm all Rambo like in jeans and t-shirt heading up a mountain road, potentially to shoot some bad guys and be the hero. I laugh to myself to keep from shaking with fear.

The roads are clearer today. Much of the debris pushed to the side so vehicles can get through. The back streets are still a mess of mud and standing water. Police and army patrols are everywhere, checking vehicles and people as they move around. Hopefully they will have pushed some of the gangs back into their hiding places. They will be biding their time, I'm sure.

We get waved through the checkpoints and there are none of the confrontations of yesterday.

Watching people sweep up and repair their houses seems therapeutic. A city recovering. Seeing the mass effort and volunteering shows that these gangs do not define this place. It's a city like any other, with good people all around. They sadly have to live with the curse of corrupt and evil politicians who let gangs rule. The more I think about it, the more I question why, with all these soldiers around, they don't just march through the city and clear them out? It's not like no-one knows who they are. They could decimate the gangs here and in the capital Tegus, couldn't they? It sounds simple to me, but obviously the government doesn't agree. Pointless me worrying about it either way, as I'm not going to be the one to solve the problem.

Outside the town, the road becomes steep and water is running freely towards us. Mud and tree debris is all around and the truck has to veer between various obstructions. I turn away when seeing the casualties including cattle, goats and dogs. Round the next bend a tree completely blocks the road.

We stop and a rope winch is attached to the front of the truck. Reversing slowly the tree is eventually pulled to one side. Another few hundred metres and the same again, though this time, smaller and lighter, a chain saw gets through it and we can move on.

This could be a long trip if this is how the roads going to be.

It takes two hours before we round a plateau and enter open farmland. Surviving cattle appear as normal in the fields. Apart from those less fortunate I wonder how they manage. Do they go hide behind a wall or just sit it out in dumb ignorance of what's occurring?

A few miles through the green valley we pull up down a small track and park up.

'We walk from here,' Sophia tells me.

The area is open valley, occasional trees with broken trunks or broken branches. It looks like typical green farmland though the plants are more of a tropical nature with the humid temperature. It feels anonymous. It's a farm, no doubt with people scraping a living off their cattle and other animals, selling them in the market down in the city. Unremarkable, except we're here are for a reason. Like too many things in this country, the gang leaders organise and get what they want.

The group clamber out the back of the wagon, I rather fall out, legs and body stiff and sore. We gather round Gus as he explains in his broken English what happens next.

'We are walking there, no talk.' He points towards a small rise in the land. He explains something in Spanish to Sophia who translates for me.

'The mine is behind that hill - we will approach quietly and see how things look.'

'Ok,' I nod, not sure what else to do. I have questions but then I don't think anyone has answers so pointless to do anything other than proceed. I pick up my gun, a bottle of water and start up the track.

Mia tags alongside me as before. Taking a child into an environment like this doesn't seem right, but as Mia has proved all along, she's far from a child and braver than all of us. I have also grown to think of her like a sister. I think of Bernadette back home and her laziness. I shouldn't compare the two but inevitably I have to. Bernadette will sort herself out one day, hopefully soon, but for now Mia is hundred times Bernadette. I guess it's the difference between experiences as a child and not having a mother. Mia is also smart and funny when she's in the mood. I know she takes the piss out of me and I'm sure I deserve it. I'm terrible at this cool stuff, but I'm still here and I'm learning. I give as good as I get from both of them. Arguments and squabbling are normal as well, being cooped up together.

Do the three of us count as our own family now? We've come this far. Mia has no-one else and neither does Sophia. How we go forward I don't know, but Mia has to be looked after. The same is true of Opal, if we find her. I can't abandon these kids. I feel it now more than ever on this trip.

Walking is slow but my stiffness from earlier is gone. I can live with the bruising and the aches; anything is better than the last few days.

I'm sweating heavily by the time we reach the hilltop and look down on the mine below. We lie low and creep slowly to the edge. None of us are prepared for what appears before us.

Surrounded by rugged farmland and trees is an industrial yard. It was fenced off but the fence is in name only now, with just the metal posts left in the ground. An old mine building is at the centre, which is now a shell of bent girders and half walls. It's completely collapsed. The roof has gone and looks like a century old relic. The enormous winch used to pull the gear out of the mine looks bare and rusty without the building surrounding the base. The storage building, presumably for machinery, is collapsed and the corrugated panels strewn about. Given the machinery, it might also be where they mill the rocks and get the ore out but it is such a mess it's hard to tell what is what.

Smoke comes from behind the buildings. Is that from a fire caused by the hurricane or is someone there?

There are some cattle grazing in the fields below the mine.

To the side of the yard, there is a pile of corrugated metal sheets and a shell framework, which looks like a decimated office building. A pile of mattresses and linen indicates there were some sleeping quarters smashed in the storm. It's like a dump site with all the debris strewn around.

On the hillside, there is a pile of boards with some writing on the front. I'm assuming that's the old entrance closed up. Given the overgrown trees around the entrance, it has been closed for years

That's the good bits.

All around, I can see bodies like a battlefield. Some quite clearly are children but a few adults as well. It's horrific. The storm had little mercy here. I choke with sadness, especially for the kids. And then for Opal. We came all this way to rescue her and it's possible she's lying in the field, battered and killed by the storm.

I can't see anyone walking about. I feel wrong being here. Especially with a gun, with all that death. Whoever these people are, shouldn't they be out clearing the bodies? Doing the decent thing? Maybe there is no-one left. I don't know. I feel sick. It's hard to comprehend the horror. Sophia pats me on the back. Mia is crying. Sophia shields her from the view.

'I know it's difficult,' she says to us both, speaking in a whisper, 'but we have to do this now. We have got to be strong. Those people are dead and we will have to deal with that. Now we have to see who is still alive and get them out.' She looks at me. 'I hope one of them is Opal, for you, for all of us. We came this far and we must finish it. You ok?'

I nod.

Mia lifts her head and wipes her eyes. 'I'm ok,' she says.

Joachim and Gus discuss a strategy and then explain it to Sophia.

'They are going to approach. Once it's safe they will call us.'

Feeling like the lightweight once more, especially my weak reaction to what we just saw, I let them go. They are more experienced with this kind of thing. I satisfy myself that I'm here and a key part of what's going on. If I hadn't started this journey none of us would be here at all. I'm the instigator, rightly or wrongly and whatever we find here might not have happened if it wasn't for me. I just pray some of the kids are alive.

The two follow the line of the fence. They try to keep low but I get the feeling that if someone is watching they can be seen.

A shot rings out from the yard. My suspicions confirmed. Joachim and Gus dive to the ground out of sight. Another shot.

And I hoped this was going to be straightforward.

Sophia lines up her AR-15 at the house and fires a round. Even knowing she was going to do it, the noise panics me. As she fires, shots come back but Gus uses the covering fire to move forward. I pick up the gun ready to do the same. My heart is beating fast as I look through the sight towards the mine building. I can see a body leaning round the half-collapsed wall. I fire my rifle which, jumps in my hand as I pull the trigger. I grab it more firmly. Both Sophia and I fire in unison. Joachim and Gus are at the equipment yard getting closer. They must be able to see the shooter.

But then all is quiet. No more gunfire. Did we hit him? Is he the only one? Or is it now a trap we are walking into?

Sophia pats me on the arm. I feel a little patronised but I'm not going to argue. It felt good to finally get a shot off. I'm not suddenly into killing people but I'm getting into protecting us and those kids. I avoid the sight of the bodies already strewn around and yes they were killed by the storm but they would have been safe with their families if it wasn't for these bastards. Every shot I fire is for those kids. I hold the gun tighter feeling surer of what I'm doing.

Tentatively, I can see Joachim crawl forward. Gus stays back.

I look at Sophia. 'I don't feel good about this,' I say.

'Nor do I. I'll go to the other side. Cover me.'

She picks up her rifle and rushes off to the side before I can say no. Just myself and Mia now. Playing commandos - only this time it's life and death.

I give the covering fire pointing as close as I can to the wall. Joachim and Gus move forward again, as does Sophia on the far side of the mine building. From nowhere a girl appears from under one of the panels and runs into the field. Immediately, I stop firing, scared I'll hit her. The girl is Mia's size and frame. She is black with mud. She runs for her life. Distracted for a moment, no-one sees two men, rifles pointed directly at Gus and Joachim. Unprepared, they hold their hands up. I can see them, I can shoot, but I can't be sure of hitting them.

'Shoot them,' Mia says.

'What if I miss?'

I fire, feeling that not doing so is pointless with them clear in my sight. I hit one of them and he falls to the ground. He's hurt but not dead. He rights himself, gets his gun in position and fires back towards me. The other remains still, pointing his gun at Gus and Joachim. Eventually the hurt man gets to his feet, holding his arm. I daren't shoot again with Gus and Joachim likely to get hurt.

The child is still running off to the side. Mia goes after her while I concentrate on the scene below.

Shit, we're all spread out now. I don't know what to do. Stay put, shoot. Go down there. Sophia is now at the mine building, her rifle pointing towards the two men. She will have a better shot than me. Do they know she's there? She edges closer, round the two standing walls at the far corner.

What to do? If they see her, anything could happen. I can't just wait for it to happen. But if I shoot, then chaos will kick in. One of us might get killed.

Mia returns with the girl round the hidden side of the hill. The girl looks terrible. Thin, dirty, clothes that seem burned into her rather than worn.

'This is Claudia,' Mia says. 'There are five more girls in a basement in the mill. Those are the only two men left outside but there are three more keeping the girls. She ran when she heard us coming. They panicked.'

I look back at the house and Sophia is now directly behind one of them. She could shoot but if she does, the other will get a shot out. It's bad either way.

The men turn quickly and the back edging towards the wall. She must have spoken. Now it's a stand-off. Time to move. I need to get closer.

'Keep Claudia safe,' I say to Mia. 'Stay here.'

I take the same route as Sophia down the side of the field, along the fence to the opposite side of the mine building. Running quickly, no-one takes any notice. They are too focussed on each other. A minute later I'm at the side of the house. They are talking, negotiating but I can't hear them properly or understand.

The two men have their backs to a wall as they discuss with Sophia to one side and Gus and Joachim, unarmed to the other. The men can't see me. Can I be the element of surprise?

Gus sees me. His eyes flicker my way. He doesn't react but seems to stand a little taller, like he's poised to move. Inside the wreck of the building there is broken and smashed furniture and machinery. A wooden table leg looks like an easy weapon. The gun doesn't seem to help me given I don't trust myself to fire straight in this situation but being able to swing the table leg will give me a small element of surprise.

I move closer.

The weight of the table leg has given me something to supress my shaking hands. The gun was the opposite.

I'm now two metres behind where the men are stood. The conversation still going on. Heated. Tense. Guns raised.

The man I shot in the arm is nearest me to me. He has a fat belly. His jeans, full of mud, barely able to stay up. The crack of his ass shows between the top of his jean and that bottom of his t-shirt. The other man is hidden from view. I move to the right so I can swing to the left. I lift the leg, ready to swing.

Gus shouts.

'Now!'

I swing and hit the fat man square across the head. The table leg drops from my hands with the impact. He lets go of his gun as he falls. Sophia fires the gun at the other man before he can react. Gus leaps onto the fat man using his size to overpower him. Joachim follows up. In a few seconds the fat man is being held to the ground, the other one lying in a pool of blood.

'There are five kids in a basement under the mill,' I say, dashing in that direction. 'There are three more armed men.

Sophia follows me into the remains of the building.

A man appears from a big hole in the floor, a hidden basement, pointing a gun at the head of a young girl. She is slight, tiny in fact, in a tatty, threadbare dress. Too young to be Opal. She's probably not even ten years old. How scared must she be with a rifle pointing at her head? She stands dead still.

The gang member is skinny, his jeans are black with grease and oil, a bluish vest top over his undeveloped dark body. As with the others, tattoos cover every part of his skin, indistinguishable from the grease and dirt. He's young, possibly not even twenty, but his youth does not hide the sinister hold he has on the gun. The cold lines on his face, the dark eyes barely visible with the dark skin tone offer little scope for conversation.

This is not going to end well.

We stop moving, placing our weapons to the ground.

The building is destroyed but the metal panels are lying twisted on the ground. There are buggy type vehicles with iron trailers, which I assume are for getting ore out of the ground. There is a bent and twisted belt with a breaking machine at the end. This is where they broke up all the rocks they got from inside the mine.

So many weapons to use, but we can't do a thing whilst he's threatening the kid.

Sophia speaks in Spanish and he laughs.

'I'm trying to tell him to give it up,' she says, 'he's got no chance of getting away.'

She speaks again and a reply comes. 'The girl dies if we don't clear out and then he'll shoot the others.'

'I'll ask him how much he wants to go free,' Sophia says to me. 'We can promise him some of the cash we got for bribes.'

'We haven't got enough.'

'Something, isn't it?'

She shouts her request over. It's clear the proposal is rejected but the discussion goes on longer.

'He says cash isn't worth anything to him when there are thousands of dollars of opals in the vault. Unless we can magic this open, they are not going anywhere.'

I remember the opal in my pocket. There could also be more here. Who does it belong to? Does Ryan Carter still own this place?

'Vault, stones? How come they have kept all those stones here?' I ask. 'And they can't get in it?'

'I guess if it went to a bank other people would have known about it,' she says.

'Tell him we can get help if that's the case. For the price of the girls we can get the rocket launcher.'

There is another exchange. I look behind me checking on Gus and Joachim. They have disappeared which is good. We don't need them getting caught up with another standoff.

The guy lets go of the girl and points with his gun to the basement.

'He wants us to look at it. I think we can join the girls in the basement.'

'Ok, is that a good idea?' I ask.

'I don't know,' she replies, 'but I feel useless out here and we can see what we are dealing with.'

We walk closer and see wooden steps down to an open concrete chamber. Perfect for hiding people I would imagine except when a hurricane wipes the place out. Against the wall are four girls huddled together. All are crying and scared, dirty and undernourished. God knows what they have been through. From their faces I can't see if one of them is Opal, they are all in such a state. Matted hair, torn clothes, filthy skin. Poor girls.

Including the man who escorted us in, there are three gang members. The other two are moustached, similar tattoos with piercings and bolt earrings, one older with patches of grey in his hair. They all look like they came out of a 19th century Midwest traveling circus. Our escort points us along the wall to a heavy metal door. The bar on the door is solid but with markings all over where they have tried to break it. The base has scaring from being torched and given the damage to the concrete around it looks like they tried to explode it. A smashed electric panel is on the wall to the side of the door.

Drill markings, dents from axes, it's clear they have tried everything to get into the room. I almost admire their determination.

Sophia speaks again and I await the explanation.

'It's sealed with a digital combination. They can't break the code. They are asking if we know the code.'

'How long they been trying to break in?'

'They found this place six months ago. They think there are stones in here which will make them rich.'

'Well that answers everything, Sophia. They sent Daniela to Ryan Carter to get the combination but they failed. She was supposed to call them back with the details. The girls were leverage. They must have known who Carter was and his relationship to the girl. Only they didn't factor in that he was a heartless bastard who wouldn't do anything.'

'Could be true, I don't know. Whatever you say,' Sophia replies. 'Doesn't change anything, does it? What do we do now? Any ideas? Because I've got many talents but code breaking isn't one of them.'

'I guess now's the time to make a call and ask the bastard straight. Can we get a signal on our cell here?'

She asks the gunman.

'Apparently there was a cell mast on the hill which provided satellite internet. It's screwed with the hurricane.'

'Didn't Joachim have a satellite phone, something that we could use?'

She explains again to which I assume he agrees. He's got nothing to lose whilst he has the girls. He knows we're not going to shoot him.'

I go and sit with the girls.

'Opal? Opal Seles?' I ask.

A taller girl in a red top puts up her hand. I can see it now.

'Tu madre es Daniela?' I ask in my best Spanish.

'Si, Si,' she says and then carries on speaking in Spanish and I realise the extent of my Spanish has failed. I also don't really want to throw in the word 'morte.' This is not the moment to tell her about her mother. Instead I smile and nod satisfied that I've found Opal. It feels like an achievement just doing that.

'Do you know mi mama?' The English is broken but clear.

'Si,' I reply, really wishing I hadn't started this conversation.

'¿Y mi papá?'

My heart melts. Maybe she knew some English from her father. But I still can't tell her more, I can't make any promises.

The gang men talk between themselves. I assume they are working out the next move, same as we are. Getting the stones out will not necessarily buy our lives, it does buy us time though. Time for something to happen.

Sophia returns with a military style phone. Definitely not like a typical cell phone.

'Joachim's called reinforcements,' she whispers to me. They are unlikely to speak English but they might recognise certain words. 'They'll be here in less than hour. We need to keep them busy until then.'

The men wait for me to make the call. Sophia gives me instructions on how to use it and then I dial Rose first.

'Don't say anything,' I say.

'Donnie, where the fuck are you?' she shouts.

'I'll explain later. Just get me the phone number of the DA's office. Do it now. I promise I'll call later and explain more.'

'Where are you? Tell me. This is still about that damn girl isn't it?'

'I can explain everything.' It's strange hearing her voice but I can't think about that now. 'Just get me the number. It's life or death for all of us.'

'OK,' she says and then is silent. She repeats the number to me and I say it out loud so I don't have to be the only one remembering it.

'Thanks, I'll call you later.' I cut the call, feeling guilty I don't say more.

I get connected to the office and it's only repeatedly telling his assistant that this an emergency about his daughter than she finally concedes and puts me through.

'Donnie Knight. I thought I told you we had nothing to say to each other.'

'I'm here with Opal now,' I say, no reason not to get to the point. 'Here I let you speak to her.'

I place the phone at her ear.

'Papá,' she says.

She continues in Spanish for a few seconds and then gives me the phone back. She is crying now.

'What you doing with her, Knight? I swear if she's hurt, then I'll come after you. I've got the whole of this Police Department on your tail and the FBI if it needs be.'

'Even they can't get me in Honduras, Carter. Listen, I'm here to save your daughter's life, so cut the crap.'

'Where are you?'

'I'm outside the strong room of one your mines. There are men here trying to break it down and get in it. Do you have the codes?'

'I told Daniela when she came asking me. It's a two stage thing. I have to put in a code remotely and then a code had to be input on the panel. I needed to protect the room from being cracked like this.'

I look over at door. There is a keypad but it's damaged. I'm not sure it will work anymore.

'How come you didn't set up the release when Daniela was there?'

'Because I knew as soon as I gave them the code they would kill Opal. She only has value as long as she is alive.'

'But they kept her here for weeks. You could have come here and done what I've been doing.'

'Don't preach to me, Knight. You have no idea what I've been doing. And you've no idea what's behind that door.'

'Convince me.' This bastard has wound me up.

'Leave it,' Sophia says. 'We haven't got time.'

'You need to release the door now,' I shout at him, then more firmly. 'Look, I can't control what these gunmen will do. Even if it's going to take some time, I need to start the ball rolling.

'You're playing with fire,' he says.

I ignore him. 'If I don't open that door, we are all dead, including your daughter. We need to keep this moving.'

'You better be right,' he says and then there is a pause. 'There's no internet is there?'

'The mast is down, so I'm assuming not.'

'Then you will have to rig up the satellite phone. Once you've set it up, call me back on this line.'

He reads a number out to me which I repeat out loud. Sophia taps it into her cell to store it.

The connection dies and I look at Sophia. How do set up a hotspot on a satellite phone? I look at the gunmen. They are looking at us wondering what we are discussing.

'If the army are coming soon then we start the process. By the time we've got this started they should be here. We've got a chance of getting out of this then.'

Sophia explains in Spanish what's happening. The men look excited. I seriously hope this works but no time to worry about it. They open the broken keypad. The shell around the keypad is broken but it seems it's not completely smashed. One of them must have realised that breaking the keypad might be terminal for the hopes of getting the door open or perhaps for their lives when they have to explain how much they fucked up when talking to whoever sent them here.

After a few attempts they manage to connect the door signal to the cell hotspot. We are close. I look at my watch. Ten more minutes have passed. We need another half hour in case the army doesn't get here in time.

I sit back on the bench with the girls and try calling Nashville again. I deliberately call the wrong number.

'Hello,' I say. Giving my same introduction as before, I pretend I'm being put on hold, then cut the call. I repeat the same again buying a few minutes.

One of them shouts at me and I decide I better do the real call this time. Won't take too much of time for them to realise I'm bluffing.

Two mins later I'm connected to the saintly Mr Carter.

'OK we are ready,' I say.

'I'm going to tap in a code here. Once I do a green light will appear on the door pad. After that I'll give you a code to type in on the keypad. That will release the door.'

'Got it,' I say.

'Look I'm warning you. When that door opens, they're going to be pissed. Massively pissed. No time to explain why but you need to be ready to run. Whatever it is, get Opal out of there as soon as that door opens.'

'Ok,' I say. I whisper an explanation to Sophia. She gathers the girls with her, though how to get them up the stairs without being shot I don't know.

'I'm ready,' I say.

Standing by the keyboard I wait for the green light to appear.

'I've sent it.'

The green light comes on. I feel a gun pointing at the back of my head. Vest man is holding it. I'm shaking with nerves. One wrong move and the bastard will kill me.

'Type in the following code' He recites a six digit pin.

I type it in.

A mechanical noise sounds. The lock releasing.

'We're in,' I say.

'Now run,' he says and the call is cut.

A loud click sounds and the door opens slightly. The gun is still on my head as the other two pull it back. Behind me I hear Sophia encourage the girls up the stairs. The men don't take any notice, the girls no longer of interest to them. I'm still stood facing the keypad unable to move. Glancing to my right I can see the open door. It's dark inside, then one of the men steps inside. A light triggers and the room is lit up.

I move my head slightly to peer inside. It's empty as far as I can see, except there is a bag in the corner, the men step inside to inspect it. Was this some kind of decoy? What's in that bag?

Empty room other than a covered bag. There's some kind of device in that bag. First thing anyone coming in here is going to do is look inside it.

Shit.

It was a decoy for whatever reason and is why Carter couldn't give Daniela the code. They would all have been killed, including Opal. We need to get out of here before they open that bag.

The second man follows the first one in, I can see they are trying to unzip it. I'm left with the one holding the gun to my head. I feel the pressure of the gun release as they start a conversation about what to do. I've got one chance to get away before they decide to start on me.

Deep breath, Donnie.

I ram my elbow back into his gut, turn quickly and push him to the ground. As he falls, I grab his gun but he is too strong and pushes me back against the open door. Slamming into the door closes it, trapping the other two inside the room. There are shouts from inside.

This guy is lightweight but feels strong against me. The gun a barrier between us as we each try to take control. I can't give him an inch.

His face is in mine, smelly breath and sweat. Horrible greasy man up close. He's crushing me against the door. I'm clinging onto the gun but I don't know how long I can hold on for.

He releases a hand and punches me in the gut. The same place I got kicked yesterday and I collapse in pain. I try to get control back but he's already pulled the gun from my grasp. He lines it up to shoot at me flat against the strong room door. This is it. I've no answer to this.

I hear a shot and the gunman drops. Another shot and he is dead in front of me.

Looking to the top of the steps I see Sophia with Joachim. He races down as I escape. Three soldiers follow behind.

'Leave them,' I say, 'Tell them, Sophia - I think there is trap in there. Carter warned me to get out of here.'

She shouts in Spanish and the soldiers turn back. As we reach the top stairs we run away fast past the mine building. I hear shouts inside as they come out looking for us. I look round to see them at the top of the steps guns raised seeking us out.

The mill building explodes. The noise is deafening. I feel a force of air throwing us forward. Concrete and steel shower down from the sky. The two men undoubtedly dead will have had no chance. I stumble at first and then get up. I turn and hug Sophia.

'We did it,' she says.

We hold each other for a moment. Over her shoulder I see a full army unit covering the field and for the first time in two weeks, I feel relief.

Chapter 42

'I have an idea,' Sophia says.

'What kind of idea?''

'About the girls and the other orphans.'

The truck winds its way down the valley, the girls huddled together in the corner.

'I thought about it ever since we passed that house at Puerto Cortes by the coast. You remember?'

'Yeah, the ruin.'

'I've been thinking. I can't go back to the US. At least not yet. And then there's Mia. And these girls might not be able to go home. I can apply for asylum for them in the US, but it could take forever. Given the current climate it might not even get approved. They need somewhere to live, somewhere they can be safe from the gangs. Somewhere they can get an education.'

'That place was a bit of shell. Is it fit to live in? Anyway, who owns it?'

'I asked Gus about it. He doesn't know, but he said he can find out. I can buy it with the money we have, do it up. You saw the gates. We can make it safe and secure, armed guards.'

'That's Marcos' money, not yours. You will have to give it to him at some point. Also – you'd be like a politician, with armed guards all the time.'

'I can find ways to use the money to make some money.'

'Not if you spend it all on a mansion.'

'Something tells me I can pick it up cheaply. I think it's owned by someone in the government, or rich family who've long since left Honduras. They are probably happy to have someone take it off their hands. It's probably worthless due to the cost of repairs. But that's ok. I have much better plans for it with my new army of friends here.'

'Gus going to help you?'

She blushes a little.

'Of course, he is,' I say.

'So now you have found Opal, what you going to do?'

I have been waiting for that question to come. I wish I knew the answer.

Winding down the road back to the city, I keep my eye on the girls. They huddle together for comfort, unsure probably what will happen to them. No-one can answer that at the moment but we have to hope it's better than what we've just come from. How scary must it be for a child being held at gunpoint, constantly threatened with no-one caring for them? Add in the poor conditions, the humidity at the mine, it must be awful.

The road straightens out and I feel safer thinking about the city square, the troops and city volunteers working together.

The wagon stops. I peer round to see what's going on. My heart sinks.

Gang again, guns lined up at the wagon. Waiting for us. Here we go again.

I look to Sophia. She looks exhausted, her eyes dark and hair straggly with the sweat of the earlier battle. She probably needs another fix, but I wonder if all this tension has distracted her from the dependency. What do I know?

She shrugs and stays quiet. I guess she is reluctant to show her face unless she has to.

I listen to the talk at the front. The conversation is tense but I'm unable to translate other than the odd word. Do they know what we've just done or who is in the back? If they discover us, we could be massacred and that would be that. Is it related to what happened yesterday when I was freed?

As if to confirm my worst fears, two gang members circle round and point their guns at us. Each of us is ordered out and we are lined up at the roadside. This time there seems no defence. They are different from the previous groups but carry the same characteristics. Shaved heads, ugly tattoos and piercings. I look into the eyes of the bandits. As usual their eyes give no indication of regret. They joke with each other and snigger. How can they enjoy murdering innocent kids? What kind of men sees that as a way to get their kicks? Only in a gang world.

Sophia speaks up as she always does. I feel so helpless at this point but even if was able to properly speak Spanish I would always be the enemy here. My accent would give me away in seconds.

She speaks loudly and pulls her cell from her pocket. I recognise Marcos' voice. Is this our getaway call? I hope so. Relying on a drug dealer for a rescue package doesn't feel like the soundest basis for starting off our relationship.

The gang member takes the cell and converses out of earshot. Who knows what deal is being done. I look along the line. The girls are dishevelled and distraught, holding hands. Opal on the end. Tears form rivers on her face as it mixes with the dirt. How did it come to this?

The leader returns the cell and comes up close to Sophia. He leans closer and spits directly in her face. She instinctively goes to punch him but he hits her in the gut. She keels over and falls to her knees. With her injury from last week, that's got to hurt badly.

I step forward to help but get a rifle butt across my head. My head explodes with pain and I join Sophia on the floor. All the guns are lined up again and once again I'm wondering if all of this is for nothing.

They hold their ground for a moment then look at each other. They laugh and turn back towards their trucks.

I breathe again as I stand up. Blood on my hands from the wound. I don't need to ask Sophia what she said. But it's proof, if proof is needed, that Marcos wants his money back, and that means whilst we can get him on the cell, we're safe. It still feels temporary, but if it gets us out of this place, I'm fine with it.

We return to the wagon as I before. The truck rattles on into the city and I'm relieved to get back to Principality Square unhindered.

The rice and beans at the square taste as good as any meal I've ever had. Sophia and Gus are talking together. The girls have been herded off to a medical tent to be checked up.

I'm surprised but then not very surprised when Gus hugs Sophia close. They share a brief kiss. Mia looks at me and smiles. Good luck to them.

Sophia lets him go and walks towards us.

'Romance?' I ask.

'Forget it,' she says. She can't hide her blushing.

'What's happening?'

'I've made a decision about the house in Puerto Cortes. I'll get it. Gus's going to help me. The girls can come with me when they are ready. They can't go back to their families, even if they know where they are. The local gangs will get them again once I'm not with them. They won't be protected. Someone's got to look after them. Mia as well.'

'Me?' Mia asks.

'Yes. You. We should never have brought you here but then you can't go back to US safely at the moment. Stay with me, Mia.' She hugs her. 'We got to stick together now, right?'

'Yes,' Mia says, surprised but also not disagreeing.

'So what you going to do?' I ask

'Gus has checked it out and it's an old palace owned by a dead minister. The family have gone to the US and are unlikely to ever come back otherwise they will find themselves getting unwelcome attention. Given what we've done here, he will talk to the governor and let me use it for a small fee. We can sort ownership out at some point when it becomes clear. I can't go back home, Donnie. I don't want to go anywhere near Marcos and The Sula 7 anymore. I don't really have anywhere I can call home these days. I've always wanted a place by the sea. I have the money to live. Why don't I give these girls a home?'

'I can't argue with you. Can I come visit?'

'That assumes they'll let you back into the US.'

'Yeah, I know, but it's clear now,' I say. 'Opal is safe, and that's what I came here to do. I have to go back and deal with business. And I have to see Rose. I have to go home.'

'Hey, Donnie.'

Turning I see Opal has come over. She looks much better, even in her white protective suit, and her face is clean. Her long brunette hair is tied back, revealing her fresh teenage looks. With the sharp cheekbones and greenish brown eyes, she reminds me so much of Daniela.

'Thank you for rescuing me,' she says in staggered English. I give her a quick hug and don't say anything. If I speak I know I'll cry. I'm already emotional. Reaching in my pocket, I take the opal out.

'You know I met your mother,' I say, speaking as clearly as I can so she understands.

'Did she die?' Opal asks.

'Yes, she was with me.'

She cries and hugs me again. I wipe my eyes and let her go again.

I hold out my hand with the black opal.

'She wanted me to give you this.'

She looks at the shimmering colourful stone. She is reluctant to take it.

'My Papá gave it to me when he left. He said he had to go to America because there were some men who wanted to kill him. He gave me this as a promise that one day he would come back for me.'

I nod along saying nothing. New information which is all useful. Not that it changes anything for me - but perhaps Carter is a better person than I give him credit for.

Why did Daniela have it and not Opal? I guess for safe keeping. A young girl is hardly going to be walking around with something valuable as that.

'You can keep it for me until I need it,' she says.

'Sure.' I put it back in my pocket.

'Will you see Papá?'

'Definitely,' I say. Nothing will stop me seeing him when I get back. If nothing else I need the truth, and he also needs to get the cops off my back.

She thinks for a moment to ask me something about him, but then the words don't come. I guess a lot is happening in a very short time.

'Shall we go get some food?' Sophia says. Opal follows her and I wave goodbye.

I wipe my eyes again. It's time for me to go home. I never thought I would ever feel like this about going back to Nashville. I can't wait to get back and sort this mess out. Consequences or no consequences.

Looking round the square, I find myself wondering if Maria is around. She got me kidnapped but then she also got me out. No sign of her so no way to say goodbye.

I sigh.

There really is nothing left for me to do other than go home.

Chapter 43

Nashville, Tennessee

Arriving back in Nashville feels like returning from another century. A two-day trip adds to the sense of distance, navigating the roads out of Honduras and getting to Belize. From there a flight to Mexico City and then onto Atlanta. With the horrendous transfer queues at Atlanta, I am so relieved to get on the final connection to Nashville.

My return is no doubt showing up on every police radar in the county, so as I walk out into the arrivals hall it's no surprise to see uniforms all around.

Rose appears in front of them and runs forward to hug me. She drags me to the side before the cops get to me.

The hug is a warm blanket. The familiar feel of her hands on my back, her fingers slotting into the right places. Her perfume rich and sweet. They say, you don't know what you've lost until it's gone. I already worked out what I lost running away the last weeks but that's not the same as coming home to it. Whilst I wrap my arms tight around Rose, it feels different. I am different. Will she be too?

'Thank God you're back,' she says. 'I'm going to slap you so hard when you get home, Donnie Knight. You're never damn leaving the neighbourhood without me ever again, ya hear me? Now don't tell them anything. We'll get you out, we got it covered already.'

'Don't worry - I think I've got a plan as well. Just need to get in front of the right people.'

We hold hands as we move forwards. The cops gather round me and I let go of Rose to place my hands at my back, ready to be handcuffed.

Despite the inconvenience of the arrest and no doubt a day of being harassed by law enforcement, I'm surprisingly relaxed. After facing ruthless gangs with no mercy, bent cops, border guards and a horrendous hurricane, a spell in the cells at Nashville P.D. feels like a trip to a luxury spa.

***

I wish.

Sitting in the holding cage in the centre of the police department processing room I realise how exposed I'm.

Across the room are two Latinos. The tattoos and piercings are the same as I've become familiar with over the last few weeks. One is bald, a cross detailed on his forehead. No eyebrows or facial hair, he stares directly at me, whites of his eyes bold against the blue ink of the facial markings. He wants to scare me and it works. I try not to look at him but then I need to protect myself, keeping an eye on what they do. The other has thick black hair and a moustache, a gym body not unlike Hugh's. He wears a black skull and crossbones t-shirt with sleeves stretched over bulging biceps. He laughs when I catch his eye.

The rest of the cage has two white drunks sleeping in the corner. A young black man is crying in the corner.

I look to the officers in the room. None interested in what's going on in the cage. Until their man is processed, I guess they're happy to leave us sweating in here.

There is a clock on the wall. Two hours have passed. I take turns to walk around my six feet of space and then return to sitting on the floor. Each time I glance at the Latinos I get the same stare back. They are loving it. They know I'm nervous and inexperienced.

I don't know what's coming but they do.

I look again at the bald one. He drags his finger across his neck. The big man laughs again. He then opens his hand and I see a blade open in his palm.

Fuck.

Seriously. How did he get that in here?

Both men step closer. I look to the officers. I rattle the cage but no-one turns my way.

They planned this. They knew they'd get a chance at me.

The two men are stood before me now, the blade now visible in his open hand. They watch me without moving, staring at me. My eyes switch between the two of them. My back against the cage.

'Help,' I shout, 'they're going to kill me in here.'

The big man does his now customary laugh.

'You're going die, gringo.'

I glance to the right to the room. No-one cares. No-one is looking.

The bald men pushes me back against the cage, the big man grabs at me and tries to get his enormous arm around me. I manage to slip under it and fall to the floor. Wriggling on the floor I dodge their kicks, screaming out loud. The big man reaches down to grab me, he picks me up, knee on my back then takes my right hand, flattens it out on the floor and slams his foot hard on it.

I scream in pain.

'Play the guitar now,' he says, laughing.

He then pulls me up again and grabs firmly hold of me. The blade now across my throat. He presses it against my skin but doesn't push it in. I'm shaking with fear and can't move. My hand is swelling and throbbing and can't move to defend myself.

'You going to die, guitar boy,' he says, 'and we going to watch you. You won't know when, but we will get you.'

The cage opens and a parade of officers pile in. The two gang men let go of me as if they expected this to happen. They are both pinned to the ground and cuffed. The big man drops the blade and kicks it out of view. I'm pulled out of the cage as they are forced into the corner.

Unbelievable. The big man is still laughing as he is cuffed against the cage wall.

***

Detective John Henry arrives in the interview room like a man who's been on an alcohol-free diet for weeks and just got his first beer. He's trying to hide his smile. I get the impression he would hug me if there weren't formalities to be observed.

'How's the hand?' he asks.

'Painful,' I reply, ignoring his smug smile. They have put a bandage around it. It's not broken but stings like hell. It'll be a few days before I'm playing guitar again, that's for sure.

I've been assigned a public attorney. I don't go for a paid lawyer yet. Sophia has given me some names, but I need to nail this first meeting, and then if it goes south I'll work out a new strategy. I'm hoping it won't take too long. My attorney is a legal intern with a smart suit. He's barely written my name down, hardly understood anything about the case.

'Donnie Knight,' the detective says, 'how the fuck did you get in so deep? Of course, I apologise for the welcome just now but then you play with fire, some say, one day you are going to get burnt. You get that don't you?'

I don't reply. What's the point?

'I got everything here. Murder 1st, 2nd and 3rd degree, arson, drugs, leaving the scene of a crime, false ID, fake passports, Assault, abduction of a minor, harassing a government official. You going for the biggest charge sheet of my career.'

'Hey dude, glad you are excited about it,' I say. 'Just remember, I'm the victim. I never asked for any of this.'

'Jesus, Donnie, you got a high opinion of yourself. You think you're some kind of special? Laws don't apply to you? Your hand not hurt enough? Those bruises not enough, you want to end up dead? When I told you to keep your nose out and let the police do their job, you weren't going to accept that. You decided to ask your own questions, get people shot and then somehow you decided to enter the world of street gangs. You actively engaged with these mad fuckers and you expect me to talk to you like a victim.'

'I know it sounds bad,' I say. This sounds stupid even as I speak the words and wonder if there is any point bothering. 'I didn't do half the things you listed, and the rest there was a reason for.'

'Oh God - you are aware the tape's running free and we're recording all this shit. Even half the offences on that list will get you banged up for a long spell. You going to struggle with that prison food with your vegetarian preferences - and you can forget thinking of yourself as 21st century Johnny Cash. Your guitar's going be firewood. These people will be queuing up for their piece of your famous ass. You hear me?'

I nod. Reckon, I need this to get to the point, though I do feel the weight on my shoulders again. I never did ask for this, and whilst I prepared my script, it all depends on whether people want to hear it. Could be that they throw away the key and I'm going to have to find that expensive lawyer to dig me out. New boy Chuck beside me will be useless. I know this already - just need to get on with it.

John Henry sits back, staring with a half-smile. He is enjoying this too much.

'Now why don't you start singing like one of your tunes? Isn't there a song you like called Guilty or something like that. It's a fine place to start. Hell, I reckon this is going to be a long old tune and I'm expecting to be crying by the end.'

'First,' I say, 'I need to see the DA. Once I talk to him, I'll explain everything.'

He looks at me down his nose.

'You don't get to make requests, Donnie boy. You are the criminal, the suspect and soon to be convicted felon. The only request you get to make is which of your prison buddies gets to scrub your back in the shower.'

'I need to speak to the DA or the whole story will be leaked to the press. And as you just said, it's a long one. And it won't matter one jot whether it's fiction or not, it's not going to be pretty. And before you ask, I have the evidence and the girl and a simple glance at her beautiful face will remove any doubts you have. Paternity can also be established if he wants to play awkward over this.'

'You got it all planned out, haven't you?'

'Reckon, I got what I got. You got what you've got.'

John Henry stands up and stares hard at me. My attorney looks bemused with the whole thing. He then leaves the room.

Chapter 44

It's sometime later when I'm joined in the interview room.

Ryan Carter sits opposite. I'm cuffed to the table and I notice all recording devices are off.

He's wearing a blue suit and red tie. The same arrogance I met in his office, but his scouting of my face gives me a sense that he has no idea what I've got. I wonder how much strategizing he's done before coming in here. Is he going to shoot me down or is ready to listen? By the very fact he actually came in means that he's wants to know what I know.

'I hear they smashed your hand earlier,' he says, looking at my bandage.

'Yup,' I reply.

'Sorry that happened.'

He doesn't sound sincere, but I take his apology at face value. It's not important in the scheme of things.

'What do you want?' he asks.

'I don't want anything. This ain't about me or money. It's about you and your daughter. That poor woman who came to see you to ask for help, and you abandoned her, didn't protect her, so she ended up getting shot.'

His forehead creases and a pink tone flushes in his cheeks.

'Don't make accusations you can't back up. Just so you know I already instructed lawyers about your last media stunt. You need to be careful what you say.'

'Oh, you want to go public with a defamation trial? I'm all for it.' I laugh.

Carter looks back to the door and I wonder if I'm just winding him up rather than moving this forward.

'No cameras, no recordings running here. The tape is off. Just you and I talking. We can sort this out I'm sure.' I can't believe I'm saying all this with so much bravado. But the last few weeks of watching Sophia has taught me not to let guys like

Carter intimidate. They hide behind titles and money but they're likely as weak and cowardly as everyone else.

'Doesn't matter what I think of you Mr Carter, does it? I'm not interested in going public with any of this which is why I asked to talk to you here. Seriously though, if you put it in the public domain people can make their own mind up. You're the politician, you can judge better than me how that will work for you.'

'Go on,' he says.

He looks round the room nervously, checking again if any of the machines are recording. I wonder if anyone is watching from behind the screen or he's cleared them out as well.

I place the black opal on the table.

'I'm not denying anything about Opal. She's my daughter and there's nothing smutty about it to fit your gossip story.'

'Come on. You know how the media will read it. They are not interested in nuance or subtlety. They will tear you apart.'

He looks away, unable to catch my eye.

'I won't be blackmailed,' he replies.

'I'm not blackmailing you, don't you see. I haven't proposed anything, demanded you do anything.'

'But you're threatening to go to the press. You literally did that.'

'We're here talking, Mr Carter. The moves are yours to make. You can't blame me for trying to protect myself and I know you are uncomfortable with how this might play out to your family. But as I keep saying. You get to decide all of this. I'm just asking you to take some responsibility for what's happened to your dead girlfriend and your daughter.'

'Don't get smart mouthed. I don't have to listen to this. Do your worst, but it's a long hard time behind bars.'

God this guy is hard work. Damn politicians never want to admit to anything.

'Now who's making threats,' I reply. 'Look, Mr Carter. I'm being as polite and courteous as I can. No smart mouth. I rescued Opal. You didn't tell me there was a bomb in that room. Why did you do that? I could have been killed. Opal could have been.'

He takes his time to reply, his anger slipping away.

'I warned you to get out. If I told you there was a bomb you would have panicked. It worked out ok in the end.'

I shake my head. It's not worth arguing. I did get out and it did work out ok, so we move on.

'I had to leave Honduras,' he says. 'We had a number of mines. The growing gang culture was out of control. Drug money was taking over industries like minerals and logging. We had few options left as more and more politicians were either paid off by the cartels or killed, so I had to leave. Taking Daniela and Opal wasn't possible - they weren't American citizens. We weren't married. I was going to, but once I was back in the States other things took over. I tried to protect them the best I could, but I guess eventually they caught up with me.'

'Why was the mine rigged like that?'

'I didn't want to release the minerals over to the bank; with mass corruption they would have landed in the hands of the gangs eventually. They would have sold them for cash and made a fortune on the back of my jewels. I couldn't let that happen, so I stored them in various locations around the mountains. In order to confuse anyone getting any ideas about robbing me, I set up some dummy sites with a surprise for anyone attempting to steal from me.' He shrugs his shoulders, pleased with his work.

'So, throughout Honduras there are more of these vaults with hidden gems in them. Or dummy ones with bombs in?'

He nods. 'Exciting, isn't it?'

'Not exciting for your daughter and your girlfriend,' I say, cutting through his arrogance.

'Let's get this straight. If I knew this would happen, I never would have done it this way. It seemed a good idea at the time.'

'Must be millions of dollars in those vaults,' I say. 'You could do so much good in Honduras with that money.'

'Sadly scarcity is value. Releasing all those stones on the market would kill the price. And would you pump any money into the country now? Not a cent would end up with good causes. You know that, so do I.'

I shake my head, he's so sure of himself.

'Who do you think killed Daniela?' I ask

He shrugs his shoulders again.

'I couldn't do anything when she came here. I tried to call people in Tegus to get the army out there, but no-one would risk stepping in. I told Daniela to go home and I would help her. Her death was nothing to do with me. The same gun fired at Detective Stephens killed Daniela. Impossible to say it was the same guy, given he's on the slab in the morgue, but got to assume he was taking care of a failed liability. I assume whoever paid to get her into the country decided they didn't want the burden of getting her back home again. So they disposed of her.'

Convenient explanation and I don't have a better one. I still think he could have done more for her and that can only be to protect his reputation. Nothing more to be said on that now. Interesting that John Henry was still trying to pin that murder on me when he knew full well that the weapon used had nothing to do with me. Still, he enjoyed his windup.

I let him stew for a while until he speaks again.

'And I suppose you want me to wipe out the charge sheet as some kind of thank you for rescuing Opal. Assume that's where we are going with this meeting.'

I shrug.

'I can't tell you what to do, Mr Carter. After the last few days, honestly, I'm exhausted. I told you what I know. If you tell me you'll make provision for Opal, maybe get her an education somehow, get her a passport, I don't really know what's in your power to do. Then it will be the end of the matter. And yes, I want to go home, but only you can decide that.'

'I'll see what I can do,' he says, without catching my eye. He then stands and leaves the room without looking back. I rest my head on the table hoping what I said has worked. I think so but who knows.

I'm really am so tired of this.

A few moment later and the door opens again.

A familiar face struggles with the door, limping in with a stick. She collapses into the seat Carter has just vacated. She has a broad smile on her face.

'Detective Stephens,' I say.

'Good to have you back in the country,' she says. 'I hear you've been a little busy.'

'I had no choice,' I say. 'I had to do it. For her, for the girl.'

'It's going to be ok,' she says. 'I don't how we're going to sort it out but we will. I just listened to that exchange.'

'How can you listen? There was supposed to be no recordings.'

She puts her finger to her lips. 'We left the mic on,' she says. 'No secrets in this place.'

I smile. I'm not the one with anything to hide.

'What you did was unbelievable. I can't even describe how brave that was. You shamed Ryan Carter - you *shamed* him. I know it and he knows it. If he doesn't do anything for that little girl he's got no business being the DA.'

She unlocks the chain holding my hands. 'He's at the front desk now, explaining to the desk officer how you are going to be released with no bail conditions.'

'I'm free?' I ask.

'There are some statements to write and paperwork to do - but yes, you are free to go.'

I stand up and hug her, half a hug as my right arm is too painful to move. She falters at first and then reciprocates, placing one arm around me, the other leaning on her stick.

Chapter 45

A week later, Country Rose is back on stage.

Rose is singing better than I ever heard her, which is good because I'm terrible. Plectrum drops, strings break, bum notes, sore fingers. So out of practice. I get the side stares but it's ok. Old times are back.

A few yeeh-hahs and stage bows and it's all over.

I take my seat back over at the bar with a beer.

Hugh and Gary come over.

'You made up with Rose yet?' Hugh asks.

'It'll take some time or it won't,' I reply. 'We got a few things to work out. I've got a few things to work out. How's the leg?'

'I'll survive,' he says.

'I'm sorry I quit on you guys. I had to run. I figured soon as the cops turned up, I was going to get banged up.'

'No worries,' he says, 'we cleared out before the cops arrived. For a while we thought you might be lying in a ditch somewhere, but given the victim was a Sula 7, no-one gives a holy shit who killed him.'

I think of Mia. She would have a different view of that. Mia was also not stupid; she knew the fate her father was due. It was only a matter of time.

'Hear you got handy with shooting up illegals and even blowing a few into the next life. Who knew Donnie Knight would kill more of the scum than I ever did? You moralising to me and Hughie and you were just itching to take them all out yourself.'

'Gary, they weren't illegals in Honduras - just gangbangers.'

'All the same to me,' Gary says. 'Every one of them dead is just fine. You did good. Proud of you.'

We clink glasses. Somethings never change. And he's right to a certain extent. I can't say I enjoyed killing those dudes, but I also never thought I did the wrong thing. No regrets. But I am never going to be Gary with his attitude and for a while I feared I was weaker than him because of it. But I wasn't weaker and now I understand a lot more about what I am capable of. I also know these vermin he talks about, are people just like us all. Some bad, some good and most in an impossible situation. Reckon we'd all be better people if we spent a bit of time thinking about that. Not that Gary ever will. No point me thinking otherwise.

Rose comes over and puts her arm around me.

'That's your last beer. Tomorrow, you going to be practicing like you got your first guitar boy. You played that guitar like you play with your dick. How the fuck?'

Gary and Hugh snort and chink bottles again. I'm not going to live this down.

'I know, I know. I'll be on it tomorrow.'

I reach over and kiss her on her cheek. It softens the moment but I feel it's a token one. Work to do, I guess.

The last few days have been a rollercoaster of emotions, despite it being good to be home. Even seeing Mom and Bernie back at the house. Mom has been driving me crazy with lectures on the devil, and wants me to talk to her Pastor. It's her way. She's glad to have me back. I know that.

Last night, I had a long call with Sophia and Mia. Never thought I would miss them so much. I guess we can't go through all of that together and not have some bond going on. They're busy working on that house to make it into a home. Gus has got a few guys and they already are getting it straight for her. Sophia's still dealing with her habit and handling a furious Marcos, who is plotting numerous ways to kill her and get his money back.

I wonder should I be helping them. Soon, I guess.

The black opal is back in my drawer at home. If nothing else, I need to give the stone back. For all its value, there is only one person it belongs to.

My phone pings and a message appears. An unregistered number.

I got your number from your friends. You have to come back now. They want money or they going to kill me. Please help. Maria

There it is. Right there. I look back at Rose and the others. Two paths in front of me. Two women needing me. One safe and sure, the other impossible to know what might happen. I'm not the same person who ran away from Nashville.

I read the message again.

Do I go back, do I play the hero again? Am I walking back into a trap once more? Decisions, coming a lot sooner than I ever thought. Honduras doesn't want to let me go just yet

I take another swig of beer and smile at Rose. What happens next, reckon I got no clue about that.

THE END.

9 781838 262419